An Alchemy of Masques and Mirrors

CURTIS CRADDOCK

TOR

A TOM DOHERTY ASSOCIATES BOOK • NEW YORK

AN ALCHEMY OF MASQUES AND MIRRORS

Copyright © 2017 by Curtis Craddock

A Tor Book
Published by Tom Doherty Associates
175 Fifth Avenue
New York, NY 10010

www.tor-forge.com

Tor® is a registered trademark of Macmillan Publishing Group, LLC.

The Library of Congress Cataloging-in-Publication Data is available upon request.

ISBN 978-0-7653-8959-6 (hardcover)
ISBN 978-0-7653-8961-9 (ebook)

Our books may be purchased in bulk for promotional, educational, or business use. Please contact your local bookseller or the Macmillan Corporate and Premium Sales Department at 1-800-221-7945, extension 5442, or by email at MacmillanSpecialMarkets@macmillan.com.

First Edition: August 2017

Printed in the United States of America

0 9 8 7 6 5 4 3 2 1

SAN AUGUSTUS

ROYAL CITADEL

EL VIÑEDO SUPERIOR

NAVAL ORRERY

ROYAL
AMPHITHEATER

THE GREAT HARBOR

HAMMER

ANVIL

EL ANTIGUO BARRIO

THE VORTEX MASSIF

Acknowledgments

My sincerest thanks go out to Carol Berg, Susan Smith, Courtney Schafer, Brian Tobias, and Saytchyn Maddux-Creech, without whose endless patience and good advice this book would not have become half of what it is. Special thanks go to Jedeane Macdonald for holding the door open. Thanks also to my editor, Moshe Feder, for giving me this chance. Thanks to Caitlin Blasdell for taking me on. Also a very special thanks to Donna Hume for everything else.

CHAPTER

One

Jean-Claude clung to the *St. Marie*'s guardrail with one hand and to his tether with the other. He wanted a word with Captain Jerome, who stood on the quarterdeck, an impossible distance away. Unfortunately, doing the impossible was a sworn part of Jean-Claude's duty, so he slide-stepped awkwardly toward the skyship's stern as the vessel climbed a tall ridge of turbulence. The whistling wind made jib sails of his tabard's loose sleeve flaps, tugging him toward the rail and the emptiness beyond.

All around him, deckhands scurried about, tugging on lines, adjusting sails in a madman's dance choreographed to the boatswain's cry. Jean-Claude reached the curling stair to the quarterdeck and climbed, stumbling as his leather riding boots slipped on cloud-slicked steps. He achieved the top of the stair just as the *St. Marie* crested the pressure ridge.

The masts creaked, and the vast spiderweb of rigging hummed with tension as the ship's enormous stresses shifted. For a moment, Jean-Claude hung weightless, floating free as a smoke puff on the wind. His toes strained to reach the deck beneath his feet but succeeded only in propelling him away from it. The skyship banked, bumping and tilting him halfway over the rail. Beyond that flimsy frontier and far below the turvy sails thrusting down beneath the hull awaited the Gloom, a fathomless abyss of lightning-shot clouds. Those clouds beckoned him like the pillowed embrace of a familiar paramour. Against all good sense, he yearned toward the abyss. His grip on the rail slipped.

Then his own weight landed on him hard. He hit the deck with a knee-popping thump. His boots slipped and he tumbled to his backside. His heart rattled around his ribs like a die in a cup. Carefully, he eased away from the edge of the ship.

He hated skyships. How many men before him had been claimed by the fatal impulse to let go? How many had felt the sick urge to fall forever, down to where the clouds never parted, the rain never ceased, and the wind ripped ships and men to pieces? Every time Jean-Claude saw it, it called to him.

I should have stayed a farmer. If only he had been an obedient lad, dutifully following a plow through rocky fields, he would never have sneaked away from his chores to watch the Duc d'Orange's forces bring battle to the raiding Mark of Oberholz. Then he would never have chanced upon the wounded duc or hidden him from the mark's search parties. He would never have earned the duc's gratitude or been shoehorned into l'École Royale des Spécialistes. He would never have been attached as liaison to the Comte des Zephyrs, and he never would have been ordered to get on one of these hundred-times-damned flying boats.

From the forward rail of the quarterdeck, Captain Jerome watched Jean-Claude's progress with evident amusement.

"Six weeks aloft and you still haven't got your sky legs," Jerome said with an aloof, aristocratic delight that suggested he'd expected no better. A landless, penniless seventh son of minor clayborn gentry, Jerome treasured the singular noble privilege to which he was entitled: disdain for the lowborn. His sole redeeming feature, in Jean-Claude's eyes, was that he was good at his job, an asset rather than an impediment to his crew, a circumstance all too rare in the gentry-swollen navy.

Jean-Claude scrambled to his feet and tried to recover poise as well as balance as the skyship accelerated into the next aerial trough.

"You said we were about to make land!" His own privilege, as King's Own Musketeer, was deferring to no one outside his own very short chain of command. Of course, keeping that privilege meant completing his missions without falter or fail, no matter the distance or danger. Orders like "Deliver this message from my lips to the comtesse's ears ere the baby is born" did not account for time spent evading pirates or allow for being blown a week off course by an unanticipated aetherstorm.

Jerome stood on the rolling deck as if nailed to it, not a hair of his white powdered wig out of place. He jerked his chin toward the bow and said, "We're coming in widdershins on the trailing edge," as if that clarified the matter. "If we don't undershoot and ram the light tower, we should make harbor within the hour."

Jean-Claude turned. With the *St. Marie* on a decline, l'Île des Zephyrs rose into view. There was the afternoon glitter of Lac Rond tucked in amongst the rolling hills. Nearer at hand, the green blanket of the forest crept out of the wrinkled uplands and took a peek at oblivion over the scalloped edge of the sky cliff. Thin plumes of smoke, the telltale signs of human endeavor, curled from behind a ridge to the left. There, on a promontory of rock overhanging the endless fall, was des Zephyrs's light tower, its reflector flashing rhythmically.

"Aren't we coming in a little high?" Jean-Claude asked. Skyships could not fly over land—his academy instructors had said aetherkeels needed a certain amount of air to support them, and flying over rock robbed them of buoyancy—and the *St. Marie* seemed to be aimed at a hillside.

Captain Jerome gave a long-suffering sigh. "You can't steer a skyship to where her destination is. You have to steer her where that destination is going to be. Helmsman, make ready to slip. Steer to port on my mark. Reef the main sails and level the beam screw."

"Aye. Steer to port. Reef the mains. Level beam screw. Aye!" replied the helmsman. Farther down, the boatswain picked up the cry, bellowing a series of orders that must have made sense to the crew, for they scampered about as if the Breaker herself were nipping at their heels. Lines and canvas shifted. The ship shuddered as if in anticipation.

"Steering a skyship requires forethought, strategy, calculation," Jerome said. "Helmsman, now!"

The helmsman leaned into the wheel, and the huge fantail rudder flagged to the left.

"You might want to hang on to something," Jerome said mildly.

Jean-Claude grabbed a piece of railing that no one else seemed to be using and swallowed hard. The ship nosed to the left, turning away from land, then rolled over some invisible frontier and began to tilt and slide to the right, until Jean-Claude swore it was going to flip over and throw them all to their deaths. He clung to the rail as the ship tried to fall out from under him. Wind buffets sent his feet sliding. Blood flowed from his mouth where he had bitten his tongue.

The *St. Marie* veered to a course nearly parallel to the sky cliff, angling steadily downward, picking up speed . . . gliding. The turbulence dissipated. It felt like the ship was tobogganing down a smooth, icy hillside with only the occasional rippling bump. With effort, Jean-Claude unclenched his white-knuckled fingers. "What happened?"

Jerome cupped one hand and twirled his finger over it. "Large masses like skylands produce an aetheric vortex, and the vortex has grooves in it. Poke a hole in the bottom of a bowl full of water and you'll see what I mean. We're riding one of those grooves down and toward the center. This one should take us right under des Zephyrs's light tower. Then we deploy braking sails and pop up like a cork in the harbor. Of course . . . timing is everything."

"You are a madman," Jean-Claude said, and Jerome tipped his tricorn, taking it for the compliment it was.

The *St. Marie* drew level with the cliff wall, a pockmarked scarp a hundred feet high. Then they passed below the rim where the sinking Solar illuminated the belly of the skyland, a vast downward-pointing cone of rock bristling with an upside-down forest of salt-encrusted, aether-emitting cloud-coral stalactites that kept the skyland aloft.

The last leg of the voyage progressed as safely and quickly as Jerome had promised, but not nearly fast enough for Jean-Claude. Six weeks he had spent on this cursed vessel, racing to the capital and back, to plead with His Majesty on behalf of the wicked, wretched Comtesse des Zephyrs. He would just as soon have pushed the vile woman and her villainous relations off a sky cliff. Alas, what duties le roi commanded, his most loyal, most junior musketeer must perform, and he had said des Zephyrs's bloodline must not fail.

In truth, Jean-Claude suspected that le roi's position atop the house of cards that was the Célestial nobility was not nearly as stable as his public demeanor suggested. His most recent war had not been a success, and by its undue protraction it had seriously depleted the empire's ability to compete for land in the unexpectedly profitable new continent, Craton Riqueza. The kingdom of Aragoth had found a way to traverse the Sargassian Still, that great belt of dead air between the northern and southern sky that had so vexed the navigators of the last century, and they had come back with wondrous tales of a new land, backed up with chests of gold and sacred quondam artifacts. As Aragoth's fortunes rose, so did l'Empire Céleste's fall, at least by comparison. Thus, Grand Leon was busy appeasing his nobles, including the execrable des Zephyrs, while he gathered his strength for some new far-reaching scheme. Grand it would be, of that there was no doubt. Le roi had no interest in any prize smaller than a craton.

From his cabin, Jean-Claude collected a large painting of His Imperial Majesty, le Roi de Tonnerre, Leon XIV. The painted face glowered dyspeptically at him, as if to chastise him for his rude handling. Jean-Claude covered it with a sheet and secured it at all points by wrapping both arms around it. Damned ridiculous thing.

When he scrambled from the shore boat onto the solid stone landing at the quay, his legs wobbled from sheer relief. It didn't matter in the least that skyships were held aloft by precisely the same incomprehensible forces that held up skylands; the skyland didn't feel like it was going to fall out from under him. He would have dropped to his knees and kissed the stable ground if he hadn't been met by Pierre, the comte's chamberlain, a diffident man with a rabbitlike twitch to his lip.

"Jean-Claude, Jean-Claude. Thank the Builder and Savior you've come," Pierre cried, breathless and flushed. "It is the comtesse. It is her time. Even now she awaits only her roi's blessing."

"So soon?" Jean-Claude felt as if someone had slugged him in the gut. Even with all his delays in getting here, he ought to be well forward of the mark; the physicians had told him the Comtesse des Zephyrs was not supposed to deliver for another week at least. This was ill news . . . at least for des Zephyrs.

"She is in considerable distress. Her wails were quite piteous."

"Haste then. Haste!" The strength of duty surged within Jean-Claude. Clutching the painting, he dashed up the cobbled street and leapt aboard the comte's carriage, displacing the whip man toward the center of the bench. "Drive, man. Ply that scourge!"

With a snap of his wrist, the whip man sent the coach horses racing. Pierre, not quick enough, chased after them for a few strides, then bent over, coughing in the dust. Jean-Claude's heart thundered in time to the horses' hooves. If only his honor would allow him to fail his sworn mission, this could be the end of des Zephyrs's line. Le roi's long-standing decree that Sanguinaire ladies must personally attend him at the hour of their delivery or else have their whelps denied names and decreed bastards was just another link in the endless chain by which he bound the nobility to his will. Normally, gravid dames were forced to travel to his palace to give birth, an inconvenience that kept most ladies of childbearing years from ever leaving Rocher Royale and required their husbands to visit them often.

Ah, but the Comtesse des Zephyrs had already miscarried so many times, and this pregnancy had been so terribly complicated . . . and so Jean-Claude had been dispatched to plead the comtesse's case to le roi. Would he deign to spare his dear aunt's bloodline, or would des Zephyrs be allowed to perish? Alas for Jean-Claude's eloquent tongue and His Majesty's good sense, for he had sent his portrait as surrogate, his idea of a compromise, so the vile family might linger into another generation . . . if Jean-Claude was on time.

Scattering peasants, townsfolk, goats, and chickens, the carriage raced through the town of Windfall and thundered out the hinterland gate, past the queue of carts waiting for nightfall to bring their goods inside the walls.

Ahead, des Zephyrs's estate stood atop a massive acropolis. At its foot stood the Pit of Stains, a half-round theater in the ancient Aetegian style, carved out of solid rock. Jean-Claude's heart tightened as the coach approached that venue. In other cities, amphitheaters were full of life, used to enact plays and celebrate festivals, but the Pit of Stains was desolate, barren save for a pattern of reddish discolorations scattered about like fallen maple leaves, the lingering traces of the Comte and Comtesse des Zephyrs's cruelty.

Once a month, the comte's white-liveried guards paraded ten condemned men, women, and children to that stage. Some of the victims were actual criminals, but most were rounded up for the spectacle on false pretense or none at all. Witnesses, the families of the damned, were herded into the theater seats, and everybody waited until the comte and comtesse arrived, at high noon, to perform the execution.

The prisoners were unshackled and then the comte and comtesse released their sorcery. Des Zephyrs were saintborn, direct descendants of the Risen Saints. As such, they carried la Marque Sanguinaire, the mark of one of the ancient sorceries, in their veins. Their shadows were not gray like those of normal folk, but crimson, and they stretched away from the aristocrats' feet like great elastic ribbons of blood. These bloodshadows flowed onto the stage, surrounded the prisoners, and slowly constricted.

There were rules to this game. Only the first two prisoners to be touched by the shadows were killed. Nobody wanted to be amongst that count, so as sanguine shadows filled the amphitheater floor, the condemned huddled together on a shrinking island of light, scrambling to be as far from the creeping doom as possible, pushing one another out of the way, begging for a mercy that would not come.

All too quickly, the victims turned on one another, the stronger thrusting the weaker into the oncoming flood. Sometimes, a brave soul would sacrifice himself or herself to save the others, but as a single selfless act was not enough to turn the tide, it rarely prevented a brawl to avoid the fate of being the second victim.

Jean-Claude had borne witness to the ritual once and still shuddered at the memory. The comte had not smiled—he never smiled—but his eyes gleamed in delight as his bloodshadow devoured a man not much younger than the musketeer. The sorcerous stain entered the boy through his shadow. His flesh turned transparent and melted, his body losing shape and coherence as the red tide absorbed him, destroying him down to the very soul.

Terrified and horrified, Jean-Claude had done nothing to stop the murder. Legally there was nothing he could do. By most ancient and sacred law, the Sanguinaire were owed their due. Shadow feeding did not have to be fatal or even greatly hurtful. Other Sanguinaire nobles took their due from their subjects without recourse to murder. Many nobles paid quite well for the service and afforded their donors places of honor that had folk vying for the privilege. Not the des Zephyrs.

"Only a full feeding gives full benefits," the comte proclaimed. "Only fear satisfies the shadow. Only death sates it."

When the bloodshadows withdrew, nothing was left of the boy but a soul smudge, a patch of russet that seemed to writhe just beneath the surface of the stone, squirming in the sunlight. The remaining prisoners had been pardoned. They returned to the relief of their families, and, all too often, the reproach of the kin of the slain. "You killed my son." "You pushed my sister in." "You should have died."

And that was the elegant mechanism of the spectacle of slaughter. It kept the downtrodden divided, almost as resentful of one another as of the so-called nobles who commanded and performed the murders.

The coach sped by the killing ground, and it seemed to Jean-Claude that he could hear the ghosts of long-ago screams. *And this is the bloodline I must preserve.* If the comtesse's child lived and thrived, it would join its parents on that platform, and there would be three fresh smudges on that platform every month. That thought filled Jean-Claude with revulsion, but le roi's desire had been specific. Three clayborn peasants a month to keep the des Zephyrs happy were but the crumbs wiped from a silver plate from Grand Leon's perspective.

Jean-Claude prayed the comtesse would die in childbirth . . . of course that would allow the comte to remarry, perhaps to a more fertile wife . . . Not desirable. Let her live, then, but crippled, and let the child be stillborn. Better for everyone that way, even the child; no child of the des Zephyrs would have a chance of escaping their corruption.

Atop the acropolis's plateau sprawled the Château des Zephyrs, sweeping arms of pale marble reclining indolently on a rolling, grassy sward. As daylight faded, alchemical lamps flickered to life in every window, as was the custom in Sanguinaire houses. For there can be no shadow without light.

Jean-Claude leapt from the carriage before it stopped, alighted on the landing, adjusted the portrait, and burst through the silver-trimmed double doors even before the doorman could throw them wide.

"The master bedroom, monsieur," the doorman called after Jean-Claude's retreating back, but Jean-Claude had already mounted the stairs and made the turn. From the wide-flung doors at the end of the corridor came a piteous grating wail. The comtesse had a voice like shattering glass at the best of times. Her distress in labor sounded like a cat fight in a porcelain shop.

Jean-Claude slid to a stop just outside the threshold, straightened his rumpled tabard, and marched in. "Your Excellencies," he said, for the comte stood, powdered and dressed in his finest whites, sipping a chalice of red wine and looking more bored than dutiful, at his wife's bedpost. The air swam with a nauseating swirl of blood stench, wine fume, and sweat.

Comtesse Vedetta lay in bed, breathing shallowly, her upper half absurdly dressed for a party, white wig askew, her lower half obscured by a privacy screen. When Jean-Claude had left on his errand, her thin face had been drawn and haggard. Six weeks on, she looked skeletal, an appearance exaggerated by the sweat-streaked white face powder and the black smudges of mascara around her eyes. Only the flint in her gaze gave notice of a jealously hoarded reserve of strength and malice. By the foot of the bed stood a worried-looking midwife and a man in clerical robes.

The Temple man was short and squat and carried a heavy satchel slung over one shoulder. His cassock had a black trim, and he wore a black mantle embroidered with interlocking gears, screws, and pistons, the Ultimum Machina, sigil of an artifex. Where his left eye should have been was a bulging orb of quondam metal, the color of bronze with a purple patina, set with a large red gem. Such prostheses were common amongst the Temple's highest ranks, marking their dedication to the Builder's perfection. As far as Jean-Claude was concerned, anyone who thought plucking out their own eye was a good idea probably wouldn't recognize perfection if it walked by naked waving a flag.

But what in the darkness of Oblivion was such a potentate doing here? There were only seven artifexes in all the Risen Kingdoms, one for each of the remaining saintblood lineages. Only the Omnifex in Om stood closer to the Builder, and he only because he had a taller hat. Jean-Claude had to wonder what strings the comte had pulled to ensure the man's attendance on his offspring's birth.

The artifex glowered down at the comtesse like a judge at a trial. The glow from his artificial eye cast her in a bloody crimson hue. With aspergillum in hand, he sprinkled her with blessed water while delivering the ritual litany of admonishment given to all women on their birth bed. "Remember that this is your duty, your penance for Iav's great sin. She thought to steal the secret of life from the Builder, and so must new life be torn from your flesh."

"Silence, wretched cur!" the comtesse snapped, her mouth as foam flecked as a rabid dog's.

The artifex paid her no heed but continued in a gravelly voice, "This pain is your due. This trial is your judgment. Succeed and you may be forgiven, your soul restored when the Savior comes. Fail and you shall fall into the pit from which there is no salvation."

"Jean-Claude," said the comte blandly, "how good of you to join us. I trust your mission is accomplished." Only a slight tightening of his stance hinted at how desperate he was that his statement be confirmed; if le roi had rejected his petition, then these last nine months had been a waste, along with all the resources he had dedicated to shoring up his leaky dam.

"You . . . servants' . . . entrance," the comtesse spat at Jean-Claude, her normally eloquent venom reduced to breathless grunts.

Jean-Claude bowed to her. *Vile harridan.* "Your Excellency, forgive me, but I did not think you wished to insult le roi by bringing him through the chicken yard. By his decree, I present His Imperial Majesty le Roi de Tonnerre, Leon XIV." He unveiled the portrait with a flourish.

The comte made a leg for the painting, "Your Majesty." The midwife curtsied. The artifex made a sign of respect. Even the comtesse managed to bob her head at it.

Jean-Claude settled the painting on a long-backed chair. "His Majesty instructs me to inform you, from his lips to your ears, that as this portrait is his presence, so am I his eyes and ears in this matter." He presented a letter affixed with the royal seal.

The comte looked vaguely ill, which put him more on par with his wife, but accepted the letter. The thought of a lesser man judging the fitness of his offspring would no doubt disrupt his humors for days.

The comtesse's body convulsed weakly, and she groaned. The midwife ducked behind the privacy curtain. "One more push, Excellency."

The comtesse gnashed her teeth and curled her clawlike fingers into the sweat-stained silk sheets. "Wretched . . . sow!" she spat between contractions.

So temperamental was her womb that the comtesse had been restricted to a peasant's diet of boiled oats, beans, eggs, and garden vegetables for the whole duration of her gravidity. For the last few months she had been forbidden the slightest exercise. The physicians had even gone so far as to forbid her the use of her sorcery for fear of upsetting her delicate humors. Over the months, while her belly bloated, her limbs had withered. Now her carmine shadow looked thin and gray, almost ordinary.

Please let the bloodshadow wither and die. There was no greater terror for the Sanguinaire than to be blighted and lose their sacred sorcery. Such unfortunates were called unhallowed and were deprived of much of their status.

"One more push," pleaded the midwife.

"I'll . . . show you . . . push!" The comtesse groaned, bearing down on the bulge in her belly.

Jean-Claude assumed a parade rest and watched the comtesse's struggle with as much outward dispassion as he could muster, even as he willed disaster and despair on her efforts.

"It's coming!" the midwife cried.

The comtesse screamed and squeezed with a demonic strength.

"I have its head, Excellency, just one more push."

"Curse your . . . damned pushes!" She grunt-pushed once more and then gasped, her flinty eyes open wide.

"It's out. I've got it."

The comte's eyes lit up. "Is it a boy? A son?"

The midwife examined the child. Her face fell.

"What is the matter, you stupid cow?" the comtesse snapped. "Is it whole?"

The midwife's voice was very small. "It . . . it is stillborn, Excellency."

The comte's expression hurried through a range of emotion from dismay to frustration. The comtesse sagged back in her pillow, limp and almost lifeless without the energy of her anger.

Jean-Claude's antagonism proved bitter, for his heart twinged painfully at the announcement of the stillbirth. Rationally, logically, this was probably the best outcome for everyone. Even so, it seemed unjust that the comte's and comtesse's heartbreak and despair could only come at the cost of an innocent life. The child was not to blame for its parents.

The artifex produced a cloth sack from his satchel and stepped forward to take the child from the midwife. He rumbled, "Comte, Comtesse, you have my condolences. I will perform the rite of kind passing."

As the midwife made to shroud the baby's face, a thin brief mewl cut through the silence. The comte's head snapped up. "What was that?"

"Nothing, Excellency," said the midwife without looking up. "Just the death rattle."

The comte subsided, but Jean-Claude lunged to the screen and peered over. The baby shouldn't have had any breath to be its last. As a farmhand, he had witnessed the births of many animals, but never of a fellow person. This was definitely more alarming. Cows and sows didn't have to distend like that. The midwife cradled the child in one arm and firmly pressed a cloth to its face with the other.

"Witch!" Jean-Claude darted around the blood-soaked end of the bed.

"No, monsieur!" the midwife cried.

Jean-Claude tore the newborn from the midwife's grasp and planted his boot in the woman's belly, sending her sprawling to the floor.

"Musketeer—!" the artifex bellowed, but Jean-Claude whipped the cloth from the little one's face. It began to wail.

Alive after all, the newest des Zephyrs was clearly a girl, and there was nothing wrong with her lungs. This was not as good for the des Zephyrs as a son, but certainly no cause for despair. She'd be worth a lot in the marriage market. So why had the midwife tried to murder her? Had she been paid, or was this to have been revenge for some past injustice, or . . .

It took him a moment to see what the midwife's trained eye must have noticed immediately. Under the ragged, slimy veils of birth, the child's left hand was a pudgy fist, but her right wrist tapered off to a stunted hand with only one twisted finger. *Poor thing.*

Jean-Claude's heart sagged in its rigging. The Almighty Builder's devout followers believed deformities such as this marked unclean souls, abominations, the Breaker's get. Just as Jean-Claude would have slit the throat of a two-headed calf, the pious midwife meant to dispatch this child, deny her a name and consign her to the sky. Jean-Claude could not imagine the des Zephyrs would do any different once they saw the facts for themselves. They would not want their name sullied with rumors of impurity. They would kill the girl and bemoan the loss of their chance at dynasty and then carry on as before, but with extra self-pity.

"By the Builder," the artifex said, his posture and tone horror-struck. "Witch!"

The midwife's face went pale. She looked back and forth between the cleric and the comte. "No! Master, you—"

"Silence!" roared the artifex.

"You tried to kill my child," growled the comte. His crimson shadow stretched and slid, an oily ribbon, across the white marble floor.

"No, please!" the midwife pleaded, but the comte's bloodshadow seized her shadow by its neck and shook her like a terrier with a rat.

With a flick of his wrist, the comte flung the woman across the birthing chamber and onto the balcony. She struck a pillar with a resounding crack and then lay still.

Too late, Jean-Claude said, "Excellency, stop! Ah, we should have questioned her, found out if she was working with others."

"Time enough for questions later," the comte said. "Have I a son?"

"A daughter," Jean-Claude said. At least until they discovered her peculiarity, and then they would be thanking the dead midwife for her initiative and discretion. Perhaps they would affix a memorial plaque to the pillar where the comte had smashed her.

The artifex reached for the child. "Allow me to inspect—"

"Let me see her," snapped the comtesse, "I must claim her."

"Of course," Jean-Claude said automatically, even while shielding the girl from the artifex with his body, delaying the inevitable. These folk would give this poor helpless scrap to the sky, and there was nothing Jean-Claude could do to defend her.

And then the squalling stopped with a hiccough. The babe opened her eyes. Blue eyes. Blue as the crystal cold sky of the uppermost heights, pale, translucent, and deep as the heavens.

Her pudgy left hand reached up and touched Jean-Claude on the nose. There was a rushing in his ear and he felt as if he were falling, as if he'd finally managed to fling himself off a tilting skyship.

"Hand her over." The comte's voice seemed to come from a very long way off, but it was no less menacing for that. He would murder the child.

Over my cooling corpse.

But Jean-Claude had no authority in this. The girl needed a greater champion.

But the only man who could effectively lay his hand in protection over his smallest subject was Grand Leon, and he was not here, at least not in person. Jean-Claude's gaze strayed to le roi's picture on the chair. It was not a current likeness. It showed Leon XIV in the prime of his life, with broad shoulders and a head of dark ringlets that hung past his shoulders, not heavy jowled with hog fat around the middle as Jean-Claude had last seen him.

But Jean-Claude was le roi's eyes and ears. Why not his mouth and tongue? Except, he hadn't been given permission to speak in Grand Leon's name . . . or had he? "Do not let des Zephyrs's line perish from the world," seemed to authorize nearly any action to protect this child.

Yet, if Jean-Claude dared invoke le roi's name, he would be called to account, and he knew damned well Grand Leon cared only for this child's value as a political pawn. Le roi would not be pleased to have an abomination so close to the royal blood . . . unless Jean-Claude phrased his explanation very carefully. The Comtesse des Zephyrs was le roi's maternal cousin, and her mother had helped lever le roi onto the Célestial throne against the wishes of the Omnifex. *I feared your dear aunt's blood should fade entirely . . . a favor to her that she should be eager to repay . . .* Yes, that had the right ring to it. *I was only thinking of you, Majesty.*

What are you thinking, boy? You can't lie to Grand Leon!

Well, not a lie as such. He would leave certain things out of his report, edit it for brevity. There had been an entire class at, l'École dedicated to herding aristocrats. It had been deceptively titled Proper Obeisance. As it was listed as an elective, the academy's noble scions had ignored it like a bad smell. Jean-Claude had found it . . . instructive.

You are the Breaker's own get, mongrel, and you are going to get yourself killed.

"Give her here, you idiot," the comtesse demanded.

A wicked humor twisted Jean-Claude's cheeks into a smile. Perhaps he would rue this day, but if so, it would be for defending a child, not for abandoning her.

"Of course, Your Excellency," he said. "But first, her name. As the duly appointed representative of His Imperial Majesty, le Roi de Tonnerre, Leon XIV, I present you with"—the name had better be a good one. Le roi's beloved mother perhaps? Yes. May she rest in peace—"Princess Isabelle."

CHAPTER

Two

"Hurry up!" Isabelle called over her shoulder as she skipped and slid down the steep, narrow alleyway between the hostelry and the warehouse. She leapt over piles of garbage washed up from the last rain and squelched through slippery slicks of some nameless slime. Her house slippers were not meant for this sort of use, but when she slipped away from the nannies, handmaidens, and other handlers in the manor house in order to have an adventure, she took the shoes she had on. In the future, she would make sure to stow some outdoor shoes with her other secret treasures in the old millhouse.

"Slow down!" Marie protested, picking her way down the treacherous slope behind Isabelle. She had gathered her skirt so as not to muddy its hem and was trying to walk on pointe like a ballerina so as not to muddy her slippers.

Of all the noble girls her father surrounded her with—"As befits a princess," he'd said—Marie was the only one to have earned the title of friend. She liked horses, didn't cry at skinned knees, didn't get all green at the sight of Isabelle's wormfinger, and didn't ever snitch.

Marie asked, "Why are we going this way? Why can't we take the road?"

"This way is shorter," Isabelle said. The road was made for horses and carts and meandered ever so gently from the docks, up a series of switchbacks, to the bluffs above the town. Taking the road took forever. "There's a race-built frigate in the harbor. It's supposed to be amazing." This was entirely true, if not the entire truth.

"Oh," Marie said, slowing down still further. "You've been reading mathematics again, haven't you?"

"What makes you say that?" Isabelle asked, surprised and a little alarmed at her friend's insight.

"You're never in this much of a hurry unless you want to try something philosophical, and that means you've been doing math. Besides, if you'd just wanted to see the ship, you could have just asked, and we could have taken a coach."

Isabelle clutched her shoulder bag to her side with her right arm. Her wormfinger twitched in response to her agitation. After several false starts, she thought she'd managed to distill some aether from the air and capture it in an aetherglass phial, but she wouldn't know for sure until she tossed the phial off a sky cliff to see if it fell or floated.

Isabelle didn't want to fight with Marie over this, but she didn't want to lie to her either, so she said, "So what? Math's fun."

Her little brother, Guillaume, said math was hard and that's why girls weren't allowed to do it.

"It'll melt your brain," he'd said.

That was what made Isabelle interested in the first place, and she'd stolen her brother's math primer and read it by moonlight. Maybe it was the moonlight that did it, but it was as if she'd wandered into a secret treasure cave. The numbers opened up to her, and they talked to her, and they said the most amazing things.

Marie came to a halt on a dryish patch of ground. "You're not supposed to do math or philosophy."

"You're not supposed to steal cookies, or climb trees, or ride straddlewise, either," Isabelle said. "If you think about it, if you don't do anything you're not supposed to, there's hardly anything left. You might as well just sleep all day."

"The Temple doesn't care about cookies, but they do care about math. It's against the Builder."

Isabelle sniffed her contempt at the theological argument. "The Temple already thinks I'm Breaker marked because of my wormfinger and because I'm unhallowed. I don't see how doing math is going to make it any worse."

"Maybe not for you," Marie said.

"You can go back if you want, but you won't get to see what I'm going to do. Besides, if you quit now, you'll just have to climb up the way you came, and you're already more than halfway down. Going down and then taking the road back up is much easier."

Then Isabelle bounded away.

"Hey!" cried Marie. "No fair. Wait for me!"

By the time Marie caught up to Isabelle at the bottom of the alley run, her shoes were sodden and her hem was muddy, and since she couldn't do anything about it now, she apparently decided it didn't matter. "Race you to the point," Marie said.

Isabelle almost darted away, but she heard a familiar adult voice singing, loudly and without musical merit, ". . . but a woman's shift and apron they were no use to meeee . . ."

Isabelle grabbed Marie by the back of the shirt with her good hand and pulled her behind a mucky rain barrel just as the musketeer Jean-Claude staggered by, a quart mug in one hand and a wine sack in the other. He fetched up against the rain-dampened corner of the warehouse and stood nose-to-brick with the building, as if challenging it for the right of way.

Isabelle wrinkled her nose and whispered, "He's drunk."

Marie said, "He's always drunk, my mother says, a disgrace to the uniform, doesn't know why your father keeps him around."

"He has to; le roi makes him," Isabelle said. "I don't know why." Or at least she didn't believe the story she'd been told, that the king had foisted Jean-Claude on her parents as a punishment for having Isabelle. Who exactly was it supposed to be punishment for? Whatever the case, she could not remember a time when the beer-stained musketeer hadn't been around, staggering into and out of her path, mostly oblivious to her presence, mostly at inopportune moments like this one.

Unfortunately, Jean-Claude was just the sort of adult who could take Isabelle by the ear and drag her back to the manor house without fear of repercussion, and if he didn't shove off soon, Isabelle was going to miss her chance to try out her experiment, and she might not get another chance for weeks and weeks. She was just about to climb back up the slope and come down a different way when Jean-Claude heaved off the wall and lurched down the street at an angle that suggested a skyship at odds with the prevailing wind.

Isabelle traded glances with Marie. Marie looked ready to scamper back the way they'd come, but Isabelle gestured for her to follow and sneaked to the mouth of the alley. She peeked around the corner in the direction Jean-Claude had gone just in time to see him disappear into the next alley down the street.

Isabelle hesitated; the next alley was a dead end. There wasn't any place for Jean-Claude to go except the butcher's hanging closet. Should she and Marie try to sneak past before he came out, or should they wait? As like as not, he'd gone in there to make water and would be facing the other way . . . maybe.

Isabelle screwed up her courage, gestured for Marie to follow, and scurried past the mouth of the alley. The quick glance she risked showed what looked like the musketeer wrestling with his trousers and losing.

She didn't slow down until she'd reached the next intersection and slipped around the corner. Marie joined her. They held their breath, listening for pursuit, then locked eyes with each other and broke into giggles.

They hurried down to the wharfs, past the net makers and the lumberyard and the warehouses that would soon be full of fine spring wool from the skyland's famous Lande Glacée sheep. They climbed up on a bale of sailcloth to stare up at the race-built ship, a two-masted schooner of the newer, flat-bottomed style, long and lean like a reef pike with the turvy masts slightly longer than the tops, the bowsprit horizontal like a fencer's thrust. It was clearly a merchant's ship, brightly painted with a sprawling mural of great colorful birds carrying long silk banners. Isabelle itched with the desire to sneak aboard and get a look at the aetherkeel, to see, just once in person, how the great machines were put together.

Marie got bored with the ship before Isabelle and said, "Come on, let's go see this secret philosophy thing of yours. People are staring."

Isabelle spotted a cluster of ragged-looking men loitering by the schooner's gangway. Their faces, tattooed with sigils of the saints, marked them as Iconates. They believed something about the Risen Saints being ghosts that got involved in people lives, which seemed like an awful lot of bother for a bunch of dead people.

Marie was right, though; several of the men were bestowing them dolorous looks. Isabelle slid off the back of the bale. She and Marie looped around a warehouse to get out of sight and then hurried to the far end of the quay, which was usually abandoned at this time of day. Isabelle looked back along the docks. The Iconates were still huddled like suppliants at the foot of the schooner.

Satisfied that they hadn't been followed, Isabelle crouched amongst the piles and unlimbered her shoulder bag. She withdrew two glass phials, one with a cork painted red, the other green. She held up the green one proudly. "Distilled aether."

Marie eyed her accomplishment dubiously. "Looks empty to me."

Isabelle considered trying to explain how she'd contrived a galvanic compressor to pump the sublimating infinitesimal proto-gas into the phial, but Marie didn't stay up nights worrying about things like that.

Instead Isabelle said, "Only one way to find out. The red one really is empty; if it falls faster than the green one, we know the green one had aether in it." *Otherwise it's back to the books.*

She stepped up to the very edge of the docks and peered down. The cloud tide was low today. A vague greenish tint along the top of the clouds indicated a rising Miasma, hopefully one that the sun would bake away before it reached the level of the town and sickened those who could not reach higher ground.

Marie eased up beside her, getting down on her knees and clinging to a bollard in order to peek over the edge. She winced as a sudden updraft caught her hair. The wind lifted Isabelle's skirt and whipped it around her calves.

"I wish you'd at least hang on to something," Marie said.

"I've only got one hand and I need it for this." Isabelle waited for the gust to subside and, holding her breath, dropped the phials into empty air. The bottles tumbled and fell, like glittering jewels. *Yes, yes, yes!* The green bottle drifted downward fluttering like a leaf on the wind while its twin dove straight for the crushing depths.

Isabelle squealed in delight. "It worked. It worked!" Not that she'd ever had any doubts. Not many. A few. She hopped up and down, much to Marie's consternation.

"Saints, Izzy," she gasped. "You're going to fall off!"

Isabelle skipped back from the edge and reached down to pull Marie to her feet. "Did you see that? It worked!"

"Yes," Marie said, looking more relieved to be away from the precipice than excited for Isabelle's achievement.

Isabelle babbled on, lifted by the force of her own ebullience. "That means the lodestones in the flux oscillator don't have to be continuous as long as they're balanced."

Marie gave her an exasperated look that was much older than her thirteen years. "Which means what?"

"It means I can build a bigger distiller."

"I mean, what are you going to do with it, build a ship?"

Isabelle stopped hopping about, her attention arrested. "Maybe I could." And wouldn't it be wonderful if she could just sail away, escape forever her wicked father and brother?

"You're mad!" Marie protested, though the spark of adventure rekindled in her eyes.

"Maybe," Isabelle said faintly, retreating to that inner dark place where she could concentrate and the good thoughts happened. She knew how aetherkeels worked, but that wasn't the same as being able to build one.

"Witch!" bellowed a ragged masculine voice. "Breaker's get."

Isabelle snapped out of her reverie to see three of the Iconates stalking down the pier toward her, hatred etched into their faces. The one in front was a gaunt man with hollow eyes. When he spoke, ropes of yellow spittle, thick as phlegm, dangled from his lips, a sure sign of the galfesters. Indeed, his voice sounded as if his tongue were made of mud. "Caught you in the act, didn't I? Throwing potions in the air, calling sickness up from the depths. Breaker take you back!" He shambled toward her.

Fear drained thought from Isabelle's mind. She stepped back but realized she had nowhere farther to go.

"Stay back!" she shrieked. This was just the sort of thing her governess was always threatening would happen to her if she stepped out of bounds. *The wicked men will get you, barbarians and heretics.*

"Leave us alone," Marie said, stepping forward. "My father is Lord du Bois and she is the comte's own daughter."

Galfesters laughed, spitting up bubbles of slime. "Think I don't know that, little witch? Great lord's daughter had the mark of corruption. Now the sheep die on the hillside. Now the nets bring up no aerofish. Now good, faithful people die while the corrupt thrive. You think we don't know why? You think we don't know where the curse comes from, Breakerspawn? You murdered my wife! You killed my son!"

Shock and disbelief overcame Isabelle's fear. "I did not," she protested, but there was no arguing with the madness in those eyes. People had been accusing her of being the Breaker's get all her life. Even the household servants whispered it when they thought she couldn't hear.

"Pit worm," Galfesters muttered, shambling straight for Isabelle. She scampered left but his friends spread out to block her escape. Two more steps, and he'd be on her. There was no place to run. Marie whipped out her maidenblade.

"Marie, don't!" Isabelle cried. The short blade was supposed to be a girl's last defense against dishonor, meant for her to cut her own throat rather than allow herself to be ruined by a rapist. Isabelle's governess had spent many hours drilling Isabelle on exactly how to make the cut, always with the breathless suggestion, "Think of the great honor you will do your family."

But Marie aimed the knife at Galfesters, a kitten hissing at a mad dog.

Galfesters rounded on Marie. "Cursed b—"

There was a loud ceramic crack and an explosion of pottery shards around Galfesters's head. Someone had hurled a crock at him. He toppled in a spray of baked clay and landed hard on the edge of the pier. Isabelle skipped aside. His club flew end over end out into empty space. His cronies blinked at him, then whirled to see what had felled him.

Jean-Claude, rushing from the alley, bellowing like bull, was on the first one before he could react. The musketeer threw an elbow at his head. The Iconate spun halfway around in a shower of blood and teeth and sprawled on the ground. The last one thrust a boat hook at Jean-Claude but hit only air as the musketeer glided to one side, seized the haft, and yanked his assailant off balance. A swift kick and a thudding blow to the neck laid him out like a rug.

Galfesters groaned and pushed himself to his elbows.

Marie, still livid, stepped forward and gave him a sturdy kick in the ribs. "That's what you get!"

The Iconate waved an ineffectual hand at his attacker. "Pit spawn."

Jean-Claude stepped in, planted his knee in Galfesters's back, grabbed a fistful of hair, and yanked his head back. "If Isabelle is the Breaker's get, then I am her hellhound. Now, who ordered this attack?"

Galfesters's wild stare fixed on Isabelle. "Pit spawn! Cursebringer! Your fault—"

He lunged against Jean-Claude's hold, ripping out clumps of his own hair in his frenzy.

Isabelle extended a trembling finger down the quay. "He was standing by the schooner."

With a grunting effort, Jean-Claude wrapped an arm around Galfesters's throat. Isabelle circled away from him. Her heart was pounding, and a wild urge to flee kept clawing at her mind.

Jean-Claude glanced Isabelle's way. One glinting blue eye caught her wide-eyed stare.

"Stay put," said the musketeer in a tone of such steel conviction that Isabelle's normally restless soles felt nailed to the ground. Jean-Claude squeezed until Galfesters stopped twitching, then let him go with a plop. There must have still been some life in him because he coughed, and phlegm drizzled from his mouth. Jean-Claude searched through his clothes. The musketeer muttered imprecations under his breath and moved on to the next man.

Isabelle's thoughts slowly came unstuck, and she assembled all she had seen. People had been calling her names as long as she could remember—worm child, Breaker's get—but no one had ever tried to kill her before. Her skin felt cold and she was shaking like a leaf. Marie was breathing heavily and her grip on her knife was so white knuckled that Isabelle thought her fingers might fuse like that.

Jean-Claude finished his search of the downed men, then faced Isabelle and Marie. A somber look darkened his face, but there was no sign of the drunkard about him. "I think I should get you two home."

"Are we in trouble?" Marie asked shakily, as if the fire that had sustained her had now burned out.

"I should think not," Jean-Claude said. "At least, not if you get changed into clean clothes and put yourself back where you are supposed to be before a general alarm goes up."

Stunned and subdued, the girls followed Jean-Claude up the long, winding cart road toward the manor, but even the brisk pace he set could not entirely quell Isabelle's curiosity. "Who were those men?" she asked after she got used to his rolling rhythm. "Iconates?"

Jean-Claude did not answer immediately, and his face was screwed up like Isabelle's brother's whenever he was dealing with a tricky bit of arithmetic or grammar. Finally Jean-Claude said, "The man who attacked you is named Tallie. He used to be a fisherman until he took his boat too deep into the Miasma, brought up a catch of the galfesters, and passed it around to his family. That broke his mind and drove him into the embrace of the Iconates."

"Oh," Isabelle said, flustered by the humanity of her erstwhile assailant. "But you said someone ordered them to attack us."

"It's one of the possibilities I'm investigating," he said. "I doubt those three were part of an organized plan, but someone may have put a worm in their ear."

"But . . . why?" She knew people thought she was a witch, but she couldn't get her mind around Galfesters's hatred. It had been spilling off him like heat from the Solar.

"Because the world is full of men who think that Her Highness Princess Isabelle des Zephyrs, cousin once removed to Grand Leon, should have more fingers and less intelligence. They think she should be beautiful, brainless, beatific—"

"Boring," Isabelle supplied. "Barmy."

Jean-Claude smiled down at her fondly. "And a bounty of other brevities beginning with 'B.' Yes. Fortunately for you, I find their arguments unconvincing."

Isabelle forged into new territory. "You said you were my hellhound."

"Perhaps an unfortunate choice of words. Say rather that I am His Majesty's sheepdog. I wander around distant fields, stick my nose in other people's privates, and growl at curs."

Emboldened by Jean-Claude's frankness, Marie said, "My mother says you're a disgraced uniform."

"Only on Templedays. The rest of the week I am a sot, a drunkard, a reprobate, a clown, a fool, a dolt, and a dullard. Except, of course, on Feastdays, when I take upon myself the duties and responsibilities of chief glutton, and on Fastdays, when I indulge in inestimable digestible, comestible heresy."

Isabelle untangled Jean-Claude's meaning from his sideways words. He was playing with her, an adult game of everything-means-something-else, but he wasn't playing it in the same way her father did, with words full of cutting traps. This was more like a puzzle she was meant to solve.

"So you're just pretending," Isabelle said. "Why?"

"Because no one is afraid of the village idiot."

Isabelle's mind was still swimming from these revelations when Jean-Claude guided them into a narrow lane between the pickers' tenement and the bluffs below the manor yard. He took them straight to the old millrace that provided Isabelle's and Marie's usual method of secret egress from the manor grounds . . . or maybe not so secret after all, since Jean-Claude apparently knew exactly where it was.

Jean-Claude shooed them toward the steep, narrow channel. "You two should stay away from town for a few days. This is a dangerous time, and I need you to be alert for anything strange or unusual. If you do that for me, I'll let you know when it's safe to sneak out again. Do we have a bargain?"

Isabelle was surprised. A bargain? No adult had ever made a deal with her before. They just told her what to do and then mostly pretended she wasn't there. But would he keep his end of the bargain? Adults were always failing to keep promises, but Jean-Claude had apparently been aware of their excursions for . . . how long? And he had done nothing to stop them thus far. And she had a great many questions for him, just as soon as she could figure out how to put them into words.

She put on her best princess voice, which was rusty from disuse, and said, "We have a bargain, monsieur."

Marie held out her hand palm up. "Builder keep you."

"Until the Savior comes," Jean-Claude replied, completing the traditional farewell. He doffed his hat to her and swept a low bow. He waited until she and Marie squirmed through the curtain of vines overhanging the millrace before turning and sauntering away. By the time they'd climbed ten feet, they could hear him singing a bawdy drinking song. They did not understand all the words, but it made them blush anyway.

The long, familiar ascent of the millrace gave Isabelle time to think of other things, such as how brave Marie had been. How had she done that? Isabelle's whole mind had gone blank, white with fear. Even now, she didn't feel normal. It was like she was running on a bog. As long as she kept going she'd stay on top, but the minute she stopped, she'd sink and be drowned.

The girls scrambled out of the hole in the roof of the old millhouse at the corner of the edgeward cow pasture and had just about reached the stile leading to the paddock behind the stables when a shrill voice caught them by the scruffs of their necks.

"Isabelle!" shouted the head governess. "Where have you been? And you!" She jabbed a knobby finger at Marie. "You'll be lucky if I don't have you whipped to the bone."

Isabelle and Marie cringed. The governess was not so foolish as to disfigure them, but there were punishments that didn't leave a mark.

"Come here," the governess said, even while storming toward them. "I have been looking for you two for an hour! The comte has summoned you both, and look at you. You're filthy! I'd strip you down and send you in there naked if I thought you had any sense of shame, but you'd enjoy humiliating your father in front of his guests. Builder do us all a favor and turn you into a pig. You'd be cleaner."

She grabbed Isabelle by the ear, much too hard, and dragged her back to the manor house. "Stop mewling. You will learn to behave as a proper lady, or I will break you."

The berating went on through the entire process of being stripped out of layers of clothing, scrubbed like a dirty pot, scraped dry, and stuffed into her most formal gown, rose pink with a spray of white lace at the throat. The double knot in the silver cincture around her waist announced her maiden status to anyone who cared.

None of this rough handling distracted her from her more pressing question. Why had her father summoned her? She prayed to whatever powers would listen that he had not come up with yet another scheme to try to force her to manifest a bloodshadow.

Father had never been able to accept that, saintblooded though she was, descended in a direct line from the Risen Saints themselves, she was unhallowed and had no sorcery. He kept trying to drag magic out of her soul using his own bloodshadow as block and tackle. How many times had he racked her with his own power, ripping away at her very soul in the effort to provoke some latent power to rise and defend itself? Year after year, that had been her fate, until her brother, Guillaume, had manifested his bloodshadow.

At last, Father had a viable heir, undamaged, ensorcelled, and of the correct gender. Ever since, Father had done everything short of exiling her to pretend Isabelle didn't exist, a dearth of attention for which she was profoundly grateful. *Please don't let him start in again.*

Isabelle's heart fluttered with dread, and her skin was cold. A squadron of governesses herded her toward the audience chamber. She reached the glass promenade, a long, tall hallway with an entire wall of windows that looked out over rolling pastureland to the rocky Oreamnos Hills, which clung like barnacles to the skyland's rim.

Marie was already waiting there, looking very pretty, and very nervous, in her best ball gown, pale blue. Her cincture had only one knot, signifying a maiden betrothed. Some lord from the Craton Massif had picked her for his son as soon as she'd become eligible. She was to be delivered in two years, when she'd ripened to fifteen.

Which reminded Isabelle of the second reason Father ever called her: to parade her in front of old men who were searching for brides for either themselves or their sons. Had the merchant ship in the harbor brought her a suitor? She could imagine herself married to an aeronaut, soaring on one of the great ships . . . but usually suitors got one look at Isabelle's worm-finger, learned about her magical blight, and made their good-byes. Even the fact that Isabelle was le roi's cousin did not impress them.

Her lack of marital prospects was not a good thing. She was twelve; the bloom was very nearly off her rose, and she had been made to understand that the world had no use for princesses who could not manage to get married.

Yet if some new suitor had come, why summon Marie? She could only make Isabelle look homely by comparison. Half a girl wide and a girl and a half tall, with a long face, Isabelle was well on her way to being horsey.

Marie fell in beside Isabelle and whispered, "What's going on?"

"I have no idea," Isabelle said.

"Is this because we ran off?"

"No. They were looking for us before they knew we'd run off, remember?"

"Hush, you two," said the governess.

Marie stiffened up. The doorway to the audience hall loomed before them.

In the silence that congealed while everyone marshaled themselves to stand before the comte, voices drifted through the door, muffled almost below the level of hearing.

An unfamiliar voice that sounded like it had been hammered out of copper said, ". . . royal blood cannot be diluted or corrupted."

"I do not care about your pet theory," her father replied, dry and disdainful. "In the meantime, this charade grows wearisome."

"Have you also grown weary of your prize, or shall I take that from you as well?"

Isabelle's curiosity flared and she strained to hear more of the conversation. Who would dare speak to her father like that in his own house? And what prize were they talking about?"

Alas, the doors swung open and a short fanfare of trumpets announced her presence in the audience hall.

Isabelle pulled herself even straighter and did her gangly best to glide into her father's presence. The audience hall was built to classical proportions, like an Aetegian chapel, with height, width, and length as strict multiples of the golden mean, a fact that Isabelle was sure only she found interesting. Everything in the chamber was clad in polished white marble. A double colonnade of classical columns surrounded the main floor, with a two-step dais in the position traditionally occupied by an altar.

Two thronelike chairs sat upon the dais. The lesser chair was empty, as it had been for the ten years since Isabelle's mother had died giving birth to Guillaume.

The greater chair was made of loxodont ivory, the legs and arms carved from great curving tusks. Isabelle's father was ensconced therein. He was dressed in his court finest, white brocade doublet embroidered with thread of silver and festooned with pearls. One of Isabelle's secret books said ivory was a kind of tooth. With Father's bloodred shadow spilled out in front of him like a tongue, the whole arrangement gave the impression of a great mouth about to bite him in half, though that was too much to hope for.

Standing to one side of her father was a Temple hormougant. Isabelle had never seen one, but their vestments were unmistakable. Most Temple officers wore yellow, but the hormougant wore a white chasuble trimmed with black and silver interlocking gears over a black cassock. The panels of his long stole were embroidered with black winged daggers. His skinny body was bent over a distended gut that swayed like a kettle when he shifted his weight. Both his eyes were white as lumps of lard, but a single green gem glowed from a metal setting in the center of his forehead. In one hand he held a staff of quondam metal, an artifact left over from the Primus Mundi. She could tell because the metal was the color of brass with a purple patina. It was capped with a spiny ball, like an urchin.

But what was a hormougant doing here? They were the Temple's prophets, interpreters of ancient signs, judges of Enlightenment who decided which new discoveries comported with the Template of Creation and which were heresy. Was he here for Isabelle? Did he know she'd been studying math?

Curiosity had been Saint Iav's great sin. Her striving to understand the secret of life had unleashed the Breaker and shattered the world. The penalty for a woman prying into forbidden secrets was to have her eyes plucked out. Isabelle's thoughts fled to the cache of books hidden in a gap behind the molding of her bedroom's wainscoting. Had they brought Marie here to witness against her?

Isabelle's heart squeezed so tight she thought it would implode. She and Marie made their way at a stately pace down the white carpet that bisected the glossy white floor, designed to show off bloodshadows. They curtsied at the foot of the dais.

Her father scowled at Isabelle and said in a sepulchral tone, "Princess Isabelle des Zephyrs, have you claimed your sorcery?"

"No, Father," Isabelle said evenly, even as she cringed inside; it was going to be one of those audiences, another attempt to wake the nascent blood-shadow Father was convinced she had to possess. This hormougant was only the latest petitioner to have some plan for her sorcery's miraculous vivification. What would it be this time? Would it be another potion, a diet, a strange regimen of exercises, or would he resurrect old favorites like attacking her with his bloodshadow and trying to provoke hers into a response?

"The time has come to determine once and for all, in the eyes of the Temple, if you are truly unhallowed or merely obstinate and spiteful. Only a hormougant can make that decision."

Despite her father's nasty tone and the warning Jean-Claude had put in her ear, a hope flickered in Isabelle's chest. Could this truly be the last time she had to endure trial by ordeal?

She regarded the hormougant with increasing interest. "Enlightened, I . . . Can you certify that I am unhallowed?" No more tests. No more torture.

"Indeed," he said.

Her father snarled. "Are you so eager to reject your birthright, then? Do you think it is not good enough for you?"

Isabelle winced. "No. Of course not, but, Father—"

"No one who rejects their saintly blood is any child of mine."

Tears stood in Isabelle's eyes, and she felt as if she'd been kicked in the chest. It was stupid to talk to him, stupid to think he'd ever care about her, but she couldn't stop trying. "I don't reject it. I just don't have it." Having a bloodshadow would make her a true Sanguinaire, a proud link in an endless chain stretching back to the Risen Saints. Not having a bloodshadow was a defect even worse than a wormfinger. Without sorcery, no one would ever want her.

"Your denial is insincere," her father said. His bloodshadow rippled at his feet like a restless snake.

The hormougant said, "Do you consent to the test?"

Isabelle summoned all her courage. If Marie could be brave in front of all those Iconates, then Isabelle could be brave here. She cast a glance at Marie for strength. "Yes."

The hormougant nodded to the comte. The comte fixed his gaze on Isabelle's friend and said, "Lady Marie du Bois."

Marie popped up like a startled doe. "Excellency!"

Isabelle's breath caught; what was her father doing?

"You are my daughter's handmaiden sworn to her service, bound to her need, subject to her command, and protected by her mighty hand. Yes?"

"Yes, Excellency."

"Then it is her duty to protect you."

The comte's shadow darted across the floor toward Marie. Marie hopped away, but des Zephyrs's sorcery grabbed her gray shadow by its ankle and jerked her to a halt.

"Father, no!" Isabelle bolted toward Marie, but adult hands snared and held her fast.

The bloodshadow pierced the boundary of Marie's shadow and began filling it up, the red stain spreading through the gray silhouette like ink spreading in water.

Marie screamed and tried to pull away, but the sanguine rot spread to her shadow's legs and arms, making her movements dull and sluggish.

"Stop!" Marie screamed, even as the color drained from her skin. "Please!"

"No!" Isabelle surged against her captors. She knew what it felt like to be mauled by a bloodshadow, the icy razors of pain, the mind-sucking soul numbness.

"You can stop it, Isabelle," her father said. "Your bloodshadow can fight mine. Stop denying your birthright."

Isabelle reached within herself, searching inside for something, anything, but there was no answering will echoing up from the depths of her soul, no tincture in her inner darkness.

"Please! Mercy," Marie begged. In the middle of the marble floor, she looked like a fish mired in mud, her body slowly writhing, useless limbs flopping, mouth agape, and eyes staring.

"Stop!" Isabelle wailed. *Not Marie. No!*

Isabelle wrenched free of her handlers and sprinted toward Marie. The color drained from Marie's features. Her hair turned white. Her flesh became translucent. Isabelle tried to cover her, to somehow get in the way, but a strand of her father's bloodshadow whipped out and pinned her shadow by its neck. Suddenly, she couldn't move at all. Her body might as well have been made of wood. There was nothing she could do. About anything. Nothing!

"Fight like a sorcerer!" her father spat.

"I can't!" She had tried. She had searched. There was no magic in her.

"You are weak," her father said. "Worthless."

Marie's whole body arched. She loosed a horrible haunted wail. Isabelle could see all the way through her skin and flesh, all the way to her bones.

Tears flooded Isabelle's cheeks and she thought her chest would explode with helpless horror. "Stop. Please!"

The comte said, "The weak cannot protect their own. They deserve no mercy."

Marie's wail became a deathly keening, a threadbare sound, unraveling into nothing.

"Are you satisfied, Sleith?" Father asked the hormougant.

"Yes. Isabelle is unhallowed."

The bloodshadow withdrew from Marie, gorged and sated, its color thick, rich, like the finest wine. The bloodshadow's grip on Isabelle's body released as if cut. She stumbled forward and hugged Marie around the shoulders, but her friend's skin was ice cold, her expression slack, her transparent eyes unfocused as a doll's.

"Marie!" she shrieked. "Come back!" She rounded on her father. "Bring her back!"

"She will not return," her father said. "She is a bloodhollow now, but do not worry; she will serve you as she always has, only a bit more . . . docilely."

Isabelle squeezed Marie tight, as if that could force heat and life back into her numb flesh, even as she cursed her father. "I hate you! I hope you die!"

Marie shrugged Isabelle's grip off, and Isabelle stepped back, but the hope that bloomed in her mind died when Marie's ghostly features warped and her father's visage emerged from within. "But if I die, so does your friend. I am the only thing keeping her alive. As a bloodhollow, she is an extension of me, my eyes and ears and hands and voice, and she will keep watch on you . . . always."

Many sets of hands took Isabelle by the arms and tugged her, sobbing, from the room. Bloodhollow Marie trailed behind.

CHAPTER

Three

Crepuscular light angled in the wide window of the single modest room Isabelle occupied at one end of the servants' wing of the Château des Zephyrs. In one corner stood a small printing press Jean-Claude had somehow acquired for her. Most of the rest of the room was filled with books and art supplies, like the back room of a museum without all the dust.

Isabelle sat on the low couch that served as her bed and had Marie lift her feet, one at a time, and spread her toes so Isabelle could check them for bruises. Her transparent flesh made such insults difficult to see, but even minor wounds could fester and spread.

Satisfied that the bloodhollow was undamaged, Isabelle said quietly, "Dress yourself. Gather my paints."

Marie moved off to do as she was told. For twelve years, nearly half the span of her life, Marie had padded silently after Isabelle, fetched and carried and performed other small tasks. It was not her fault that she also acted as a lens through which Father could spy on Isabelle. In return, Isabelle attended all of Marie's needs, examining her from crown to toe every morning and evening, keeping her fed, watered, cleaned, and clothed.

It was a strange sort of symbiosis they had, each one tending the other, spending energy in a downward, inward, self-negating spiral. Effort that should have been spent exploring the world and unlocking the secrets of the universe, or tending an estate, or raising a family, was instead spent tilling dust on barren ground.

Yet Isabelle could not quit. An untended bloodhollow would not care for itself. Without Isabelle's attention, the revenant that had been her friend would collect wounds, rot, and fall apart, if she didn't starve to death first. Even if Isabelle could have borne the thought of such a fatal indignity heaped upon Marie, the notion of being trailed around by a putrefying near-corpse held no appeal. Nor could she put Marie out of her misery, for fear that her father would murder some other innocent soul to replace her.

Not that he had any obvious targets. After news of what he had done to Marie got around, Isabelle had become social poison. No one would allow their daughter to associate with her for fear of being next. Even the servants preferred to leave her meals outside her door, knock once, and run away.

This suited Isabelle well enough. Talking to people was risky. You never knew what they really meant with their words. Even if they weren't lying, even if they'd learned to speak precisely, you could never tell who they were going to talk to next. The bookbinder you confided in today might need a favor from your father tomorrow; best not to talk to him, lest some unguarded word slip and be carried off like an uncrewed skyship to disaster and ruin.

As time went on, she'd grown more comfortable with silence and solitude. She frequently went months without talking to anyone save Marie, who hardly counted, and Jean-Claude. Ever since the day her father hollowed out Marie, Jean-Claude had made it his habit to cross Isabelle's path at least twice a day. He was father and friend to her, bringing her gossip of the town and news of the world. He kept her from going mad, or at least any madder than she already was.

She hardly missed other people at all. Hardly. Most days.

Today, however, she meant to receive a guest, a mathematician from Brathon. Fortunately, she wouldn't have to speak much, just "Hello and thanks for coming," polite formalities devoid of significance or dangerous connotation. Then she could sit and listen to his lecture.

Isabelle pulled the cover off her mirror and took stock of her appearance. She didn't have the resources to waste on finery, so the best she could say about her clothing was that it was well preserved. There were no stains on her somewhat dowdy bodice nor rips in her pleated sleeves. She'd long since clipped her hair short for convenience and comfort, but her long, curly white wig was full of bounce and devoid of lice.

She pinned on a thin demi-veil, just long enough to shade her eyes, as a nod to her noble status. A deep-throated glove fitted with adjustable wooden fingers disguised her wormfinger. Alas, there was not much she could do with her face. It was too long and lean for the current fashion and sported a nose like a rudder. At least she didn't have boils.

As soon as Marie had gathered her things, Isabelle pulled herself up, hefted her tripod easel over one shoulder, and faced the exit. By Temple order, the certificate declaring her officially unhallowed, signed by Hormougant Sleith and stamped with his seal, hung by the door for all to see. It was something on the order of an anti-diploma, a formal declaration of complete unworthiness and abject failure. She tried not to let it disturb her, but it was always there, an indelible mark of shame. It put her in mind of a sailor receiving his hundredth lash. What did his tormentor imagine the last blow would teach him that the first ninety-nine had not?

She took a deep breath for courage and pushed out into the world. The morning had dawned fine and clear, not too cold for the month of Thawing, with a brilliant blue-white sky. It almost made her wish she could hit the footpath, turn right, and head for the Oreamnos Hills to paint skyscapes or dig into the collection of books on empirical philosophy, history, and mathematics she had cached in an old mine shaft.

Instead, she turned left and descended into Windfall. She walked swiftly and without stopping, long legs striding out. Marie almost had to trot to keep up. Townsfolk saw her coming and paused in their business to point and whisper in each other's ears. Isabelle had no desire whatever to know what lies they were telling about her. She'd given that up after being apprised of the widely held belief that she'd asked for Marie to be hollowed out as a favor, so she could have a bloodhollow servant like a proper Sanguinaire.

That lie had shattered Isabelle in part because it lay so close to the truth. Isabelle had chosen for her friend to be destroyed. Or at least she had said yes, even if she hadn't known what she was assenting to, even if the result would have surely been the same if she said no.

Isabelle plowed through that bitter memory and mounted the steps to the town forum, a colonnaded square topped by a tiled roof. There a small group of well-dressed men had gathered, but neither Jean-Claude nor her esteemed guest was amongst them.

She turned her back on the gathering and erected her easel facing the distant harbor.

"Set up here," she said to Marie, who proceeded to assemble the rest of her kit before retreating to the shadow of one grooved column to stare into the middle distance.

Isabelle adjusted a spyglass to focus on the harbor, looking to frame a painting.

There were three Célestial warships in the harbor today, and not the first set she'd seen lately. Jean-Claude had told her war was on the horizon, and the Imperial Navy was taking on supplies at every port, even one so remote as this. So thoroughly had the navy looted the town that the mayor had dared petition the comte to open his private warehouses to relieve the famine.

The comte, of course, had refused. "If your ranks have grown so great that you cannot feed them, then a culling is in order. Begin first with the sick and the old, and then with the very young. Give to the sky those who do not carry their own measure, and you will find there is plenty for those who remain."

The mere thought of her father made Isabelle sick. Cruelty was his only delight. Isabelle turned her spyglass away from the warships, looking for a more cheerful subject.

She settled on a colorful Gyrine clan balloon that was tethered to the harbor's farthest promontory. Onto her canvas, Isabelle brushed in the distant sky, bright blue above, passing through a pale ocher horizon to a deep green-blue below. She scraped on a few cream and white clouds with her palette knife and began shaping the giant patchwork gas bag, catching the mounting morning light in shades of cream and amber.

With quick, sure strokes, she captured the wood-and-fabric gondola the size of a three-story tower that dangled beneath it. Water barrels, cargo nets, ballast bags, and even cages of small fowl hung from spars that quartered each of the rickety-looking structure's levels. The Gyrine were not particular about their breeding. Men, women, and children of all skin hues, clad in colorful clan motley, busied themselves about the hanging nest, clambering around the outside like squirrels on a tree, apparently oblivious to the fatal drop below. The balloon's outlandish colors and patterns teased her imagination with wonder as to where all the bits had come from. What strange and wondrous places had these people seen? What must it be like to live untethered to a spot of land, unbound by law or tradition?

"Your Highness!" boomed a great, round, impudently familiar voice. Jean-Claude ambled toward her, his solid frame weaving slightly as he tacked into a wind of faux inebriation. In one hand, he held a sack of some awful liquor, and with the other he guided a portly gentleman with a brown mustache and spectacles. This had to be Professor Isaac Henswort, the guest she'd been awaiting.

She wondered why Henswort's black wig was festooned with milk-colored ribbons. That must have been the latest fashion in Brathon . . . unless Jean-Claude's sense of humor had got the better of him again, like the time he convinced a visiting silk merchant that a codpiece in the shape of a pistol would be appropriate to wear to an audience with the comte. She prayed he would not do that to *her* guest.

Isabelle tried to put on a smile, but her imagination boiled up a hundred things that could go wrong. What if she offended him? What if she said something that betrayed her heretical pursuit of empirical knowledge and he ended up relaying it to her father? Henswort was of the right social class to be invited to dinner. Should she ask him not to mention to anyone that she had invited him here, or would that simply make him suspicious?

Her expression stiffened into a pained grimace.

"Highness," Jean-Claude called again, waving his white-plumed hat as if to hail a far-off ship. Ever since that fateful day when he had saved Isabelle and Marie from one horror and unwittingly delivered them into another, he had never quite removed his drunkard's mask—burying his own shame, she suspected—though he made his deception transparent enough for Isabelle that she could see through it. He staggered up the forum steps, leading the slightly embarrassed-looking Professor Henswort between the two clockwork sphinx statues that overlooked the plaza.

Isabelle was supposed to say something to Jean-Claude, to acknowledge him in a princessly way, but her mouth was dry and her voice didn't want to work. What if her father was listening in through Marie? Isabelle had cost Marie her humanity with one ill-chosen word. How much more damage might she cause with another?

After a difficult moment, Isabelle muttered, "Musketeer," which wasn't so much a greeting as an unsupported noun.

Jean-Claude favored her with a brief worried look, then folded it back into his usual insouciant mask. He swept his hat to present his guest to Isabelle. "Your Highness, allow me to present Professor Isaac Henswort of the Brathonian Fraternal Society of Empirical Philosophy, here at the request of your mutual friend, Lord Martin DuJournal."

"Professor," Isabelle managed. "I'm glad you're here. DuJournal will be pleased." There was ever so much more she wanted to say, but even those few words made her voice shake. *He's going to think I'm an idiot, or mad, or both.* Talking was like trying to force a wedge under a door; the harder she pushed, the more stuck she got.

Professor Isaac smiled and bowed and started talking before he came all the way up again. "Is he here? Lord DuJournal, that is? I want to congratulate him on his solution to Grocephalous's conjecture." He craned his neck as if trying to see around her, as if Lord DuJournal were hiding behind her skirts.

Which, in a sense, he was. Lord Martin DuJournal was Isabelle's nom de plume, her key into the back door of the forbidden world of empirical philosophy. Three years ago she had made herself the patron of the fictional lord and published several mathematical treatises in his name, including *The Epistles of a Mathelogician*, in which she imagined him as a swashbuckling sleuth of numbers.

DuJournal's work had been very well received by the intelligentsia on Craton Massif, both for its literary content and for the fact that it resolved two outstanding problems in aethermechanical computation. Much to her delight, his works had even been reprinted by the major universities. That in turn brought in enough money to allow Isabelle to invite Professor Henswort to present his proposed solution to Agimestes's Final Theorem, a fiendishly difficult problem of multiple symmetries.

Still tongue-tied, Isabelle made a helpless gesture, but Jean-Claude broke in smoothly. "Strewth! I forgot to tell you. I saw DuJournal getting on a ship, I did. Said something about the war. Said he was hunting the Great Alagor—Algae—"

"Algorithm." The word popped out past the blockade in Isabelle's throat.

"Thassit," Jean-Claude said. "Don't know how he'll bag it, though. Didn't take any guns."

Henswort gave Jean-Claude such a stymied look that Isabelle feared the musketeer had overshot his joke.

She lined up five words and pushed them out the hatch before they could protest. "DuJournal begs you carry on."

Henswort looked mildly crestfallen. "Ah. Of course." Then he recalled his social duties. "My thanks to you, Princess, for agreeing to publish my proof."

"My pleasure," she said, and that much was absolutely true.

Unfortunately, Isaac did not seem to consider his obligations faithfully discharged, because he went on, "And give my regards to your family. I trust your father is doing well."

"Dying," Isabelle said. "Red consumption." It was a malady unique to the Sanguinaire, a prolonged and excruciating death. *And good riddance to him* . . . except it would also be the end of Marie. And would that not be best all round? There was no cure for being a bloodhollow—Isabelle had scoured every source she could obtain on that topic—and if there was no cure, wasn't Isabelle keeping her alive only because all the alternatives were worse?

And because she is my friend. And so she tended an animate corpse in the hope that somehow all her research was wrong. Was this what Marie would have wanted her to do?

"Oh." Isaac was nonplussed. "I am sorry. I did not know. But I do hear there is good news. Your brother is getting married, to Lady Arnette, daughter of le Duc du Troisville, isn't it? A very rich man. Good for your fortunes."

Isabelle winced, for she was sure her good fortunes were the last thing on anyone's mind. As like as not, the Duc du Troisville saw the marriage as a lever by which to wrest control of the des Zephyrs's domain for himself on the occasion of her father's death. Jean-Claude seemed to think Guillaume would be an easy mark; he had all of Father's vices without any of his cunning.

She only realized she had failed to respond to Henswort's cue when Jean-Claude broke in, "Oh yes, rich as butter, her father. She's no eyesore, either, but jus' between you 'n me"—he leaned in conspiratorially—"she's mean as a snake but not half so smart."

Henswort backed off quickly, waving a handkerchief to disperse Jean-Claude's cultivated fume. "That's no way to talk about a lady, or in front of a lady."

Isabelle put her left hand on Jean-Claude's shoulder to warn him off. To Henswort she curtsied and said, "Your lecture." She gestured him into the forum with her gloved right hand.

Professor Isaac looked moderately flustered. He glanced into the forum, where the intellectuals were mingling, then made two quick bows to Isabelle and mumbled, "Princess. Builder keep," before disappearing between the columns.

"Savior come," she replied to his retreating back, her tone as hollow as the custom. Someday the Savior would come and rescue the Risen Kingdoms from corruption, or so the Temple claimed, but she had never found someday on any calendar.

Jean-Claude leaned against a column with the indolence of a cat in a sunbeam. He was apparently in no hurry to depart. Isabelle sent Marie to fetch fresh bread from a bakery at the base of the acropolis; there was no telling when her father might decide to take an interest in Isabelle's business and peek out through his bloodhollow's eyes. Even in his crumbling state, he still vexed her.

After Marie had passed out of sight, Jean-Claude levered himself off the column and said, "Is everything well? You seemed uncomfortable."

Without Henswort's presence, the knot in Isabelle throat unwound, but she couldn't have Jean-Claude thinking she was an idiot, so she said, "You were rude to my guest."

He shrugged unrepentantly. "I was distracting him from the fact that you looked like you were about to vomit very vexing volumes—"

"Of vitriol," Isabelle said, unable to suppress a smile; they'd been playing the alliteration game so long it had become a private ritual. "And various voided victuals vouchsafed by the letter 'V.' I'm well enough, just distracted. I fear what will happen to me when Father dies." It was hard to imagine a more wicked person than her father, but he'd mostly let her be since she had proved unhallowed. "Guillaume hates me, and he'll be in charge of me, with Arnette egging him on."

Jean-Claude allowed himself to be diverted. "I have some thoughts on that. We might be able to get you out of here."

Isabelle's hand went to her throat. "How?" Could Jean-Claude really procure her freedom? She hardly dared hope.

"It occurs to me that there is a man of our mutual acquaintance, a mathematician of some renown, who might offer to marry you. Lord Martin DuJournal."

Isabelle snorted into her sleeve. "Are you mad? You want me to send a marriage proposal to myself?"

"Certainly not. I suggest Lord Martin DuJournal write a letter to your father requesting your hand, suggesting a bride price, even. I'll have some friends of mine vouch for DuJournal's bona fides. Your father will stuff you on the first skyship to Rocher Royale."

Isabelle shook her head in disbelief. "It's completely daft. No one will believe it."

"People believe what suits their desires. No more, no less. Besides, would you rather have Guillaume ruling your life?"

Put that way . . . "What if I'm caught?"

"What if you aren't? You'd be technically married to a man who is always off having adventures. No one would expect him to be around. You'd be profiting by 'his' works and free to do as you please."

"I'd spend the rest of my days living a lie."

Jean-Claude gestured up toward the château on the acropolis. "The strangled life you lead cooped up in that miserable room is a lie. You should be free to fly."

"I don't know," Isabelle said. It sounded amazing, and terrifying.

"At least think about it," Jean-Claude said. "You've got time. I have to consult with Grand Leon before I do anything."

Isabelle raised her eyebrows. "Why would le roi care what happens to me?" She'd never so much as corresponded with her imperial cousin once removed.

"He sent me, didn't he? Not that he could have pried me away with a pitchfork."

Isabelle glowed with daughterly affection, which was more than she'd ever had for her real father. "You always told me His Imperial Majesty's exact words were, 'If you seek to foist my mother's name on this deformed wretch, you can watch her yourself. Now get out!'"

Jean-Claude said, chuffed, "His Imperial Majesty is wise in his pique. I would trust the job to no one else. Speaking of which . . ." He mimed a draw at his endless sack and slurred back into character. "Good thing I went t'docks to retrieve Professor Henpecked. Poor sod might have been trampled, or pressed, or worse. Soldiers everywhere, sailors and officers. You could tell the officers 'cause their pants were too small and their hats were too big. Comes from having big heads and small wassnames." He made a point of adjusting his codpiece. "Stands to reason."

Isabelle shook her head and gave this blatant innuendo the bare eye-roll it warranted.

Jean-Claude carried on, "Thing is, there was a bit of news I weren't expecting, a bit that needs looking into all careful-like."

"What sort of news?" Isabelle asked.

"Henwarts mentioned that he'd been traveling with a royal emissary from Aragoth. Unfortunately, the emissary neglected to divulge the nature of his mission, and apparently the professor wasn't interested enough to give it much thought."

"Should he have?" Isabelle asked. Jean-Claude found all sorts of intrigue . . . intriguing. He solved politics like she solved math problems. It was a domain she let him have all to himself. She'd never found anything but pain down that road.

"It's been my experience that nobody who wasn't born here ends up on l'Île des Zephyrs by accident. It's too far out of the way. And seeing that l'Empire may soon be at war with Aragoth, I find the unexpected presence of an Aragothic emissary disturbing."

"Are you going to the château? If he's here to see my father, that's where he'll be."

Jean-Claude staggered backward theatrically. "Me, Your Highness? Alas, a lowly soldier such as I is not worthy to step foot upon such privileged ground. Besides, it's such a horrible long walk, all uphill. Wine flows better downhill, methinks, into taverns, streets, and gutters. Builder prevail that I shall not find myself awash in sewage come the morn."

"I see," said Isabelle. He would spend the night with all the sailors and soldiers and other passengers who had accompanied the emissary hither and who had no doubt seen or heard something that would give a clue to his purpose that Jean-Claude could cross-check. She wished . . . she almost wished she could join him on one of these dockside tavern tours, if only to verify his tales. They always sounded so . . . alive. So spontaneous.

She was no good at spontaneous, though. She barely got by with careful planning.

She changed the topic. "One more thing before you go. Those ribbons in Professor Isaac's hair . . ." She made fluttering motions near her hair with her fingers.

Jean-Claude's grin nearly dislodged his mustache. "I'm afraid he did that to himself."

Jean-Claude made a graceless bow—he'd had lots of practice getting it wrong—and wandered off, singing in a key only normally obtainable by braying donkeys.

Isabelle turned her attention to the forum. Beyond the colonnade, Professor Henswort was just beginning his lecture. The Temple's prohibition against female scholarship did not, as far as she had ever been told, preclude sitting on a porch painting harbor scenes while a lecture took place behind her. The presumption seemed to be that even if she overheard the forbidden subject, she could not possibly understand it.

Professor Isaac said, "The proof of Agimestes's Final Theorem begins with a discussion of limits . . ."

Isabelle tuned her ear to the lecture, wiped her brushes clean, and dipped her finest point in paint thinned enough to flow like ink. She didn't want to smear anything he said.

She bent her mind to Isaac's math and her brush to the canvas, sketching in dense mathematical symbols around the equator of the balloon. Only someone versed in Isabelle's personal shorthand would recognize it as anything other than a fancy belt of stitching.

Her pulse skittered and her face flushed as the proof built upon itself, tantalizing her mind with greater truths. Agimestes's Final Theorem had remained unproven mathematically for over two hundred years. If it could finally be nailed down, it would revolutionize aetheric navigation and so many other things. Sweat broke out on her brow and ran down her nose as the logic web approached its moment of maximum complexity, a dozen threads of reason pulled tight as harp strings. Brilliant . . .

But wait. Her brush faltered as one of the deductions struck a sour note. She double-checked her notation, hoping she was wrong . . . *Damn.*

The proof was flawed, the intricate weave of reason snarled on a simple fallacy, easy to overlook in the deeper context of the proof. All that work for nothing. Well, not nothing exactly. She'd at least learned one more way the theorem wasn't solved. She noted the snarl in his reasoning with hash marks in a trail of stitching up the side of the balloon.

Unfortunately, being a woman, she couldn't just march into the library and point out Professor Isaac's mistake. That would be a job for Martin DuJournal in his next missive.

———

Jean-Claude ambled along the dilapidated docks of Windfall's small harbor, pausing to take dry swigs from his magic sack. In the middle of the day, with the catch boats out, most of the people on the docks were sailors and marines from the warships.

Every skyship to make port in Windfall in the last six months had carried a plague of rumors of war. King Carlemmo, the Glasswalker king of Aragoth, was dying, and there were competing claims to the succession. That meant a civil war was brewing in l'Empire Céleste's nearest, largest, and most prosperous rival. If that actually came to pass, every one of Aragoth's neighbors would likely become involved in the struggle. The uneasy peace the Craton Massif had enjoyed for the past decade or so was about to be shattered.

The Célestial warships in the harbor now were likely part of a raiding force meant to strike at Aragoth's colonies on Craton Riqueza. The new land was the source of that formerly minor kingdom's great wealth and rise to power.

The Célestial navy had tried to prize Aragoth's iron grip from the new craton two decades ago but had been thoroughly rebuffed. At the time, common wisdom predicted that defeat would be the end of Grand Leon's rule in l'Empire. As usual, le roi had proven his enemies wrong. It was true he'd never attacked Aragoth's holdings directly again, preferring to undermine them indirectly, but during a succession debate, the Aragothic Armada might be divided, and Grand Leon must have imagined military conquest possible.

The three warships in port today were the fifth group to land in Windfall over the last two months, and they'd descended on the town like locusts, stripping the town bare of provender. The warehouses had been left with doors open, their interiors picked clean. Only the locals with the most urgent or unavoidable business dared traverse the docks. They went about in carefully organized groups to deter press-gangs. Most families had made the grim calculation of sending their men, including boys as young as eight, into the hills, leaving the women to mind what was left of the shops and a few old codgers to crew the catch boats. The women might suffer, but at least they would not be carried away to feed the rapidly swelling Imperial Navy.

Jean-Claude did as much as he could to combat this pillaging. There wasn't much he could do about the plundering of stores, but more than one would-be rapist had found himself on the receiving end of Jean-Claude's boot—any one of those girls could have been Isabelle—and he let every ship's boatswain know exactly whose balls would end up being fed to pigs if he got wind of any misconduct. He'd only had to carry through on that threat once before word got around. When the castrated man's captain had complained, he'd ended up in the market for a new set of teeth. Jean-Claude didn't often call on his authority as King's Own Musketeer, but when he did, it left a mark.

Jean-Claude made his way in due course to one of the few businesses still in operation, a drinking den called the Bosun's Ballast. It was a long, low, dingy building with narrow slits for windows. A noticeable tilt in the floor tended to concentrate most of the serious drinkers and their effluvia in one corner. There was a pile of them there now. The one on the bottom was moaning and making feeble gestures for help. None of the other patrons paid him any heed.

Jean-Claude made the ascent to the bar and thunked his elbows down like pitons to keep himself from sliding away. "What ho, demoiselle?" he slurred. "A pint and a pie for your best customer."

The tapster, Demoiselle Planchette, was about ninety years old and might have been knotted together from old hawsers and sailcloth. She made a churlish snort and said, "I'll let him know when he come in, belike. Now, what'll you be having? Ain't got no meat. Ain't got no pies, neither."

"A pint then, y'auld witch. And none of that piss you're selling the sailors."

"Ask for the moons while yer at it. Me special reserve got requisitioned two shiploads ago. Right now I'm making do on floor rushes and turnip peelings. This time tomorrow, it'll be turpentine." She slapped down a mug of something that was, he suspected, technically alcohol, but only because it had a good lawyer.

"What news of the ships?" he asked. "There's naught left for any crew to pillage, unless they be termites to gnaw on the wood."

"Doesn't stop 'em from trying," Planchette said. "Last I heard they were sending parties up t'hills to look for hidden caves full of food. Won't find nothing but sheep camps."

Jean-Claude shook his head. "I hope they don't find those, either." Any sheep a provender party found up there would end up as mutton, yet another blow to the poor folk here.

"If I was you, I'd be worried about your own job," Planchette said.

"What do you mean?" Jean-Claude asked, lacquering his tone with worry. The more unnerved he sounded, the more Planchette was likely to tell him, after she'd had her fun with him, of course.

She gave a one-toothed grin. "Weren't it you got sent here to watch the worm princess?"

Jean-Claude didn't have to feign puzzlement or alarm. "Aye. Why?"

Planchette's misty eyes gleamed with mischief, like candles in the fog.

"Guess." She had no malice in her, aside from the petty grudges all humans carried, but she could string out a tale until her customers died of thirst.

Jean-Claude's pulse quickened, but he pulled his hat down to obscure his eyes and asked the saints for patience and calm. She hadn't actually said Isabelle was in danger. She hadn't mentioned the emissary. He would gain nothing, and more importantly Isabelle would be no safer, if he bolted out of here and ran to check on her.

"I've no idea, demoiselle. How should I?"

"From what I gather, 'twas an Aragothic courtier debarked this morning, all fancy-like in red robes lined with vermin."

"As far as I'm concerned, all nobs are vermin," Jean-Claude said.

"And here I thought you worked for le roi."

"That doesn't mean I like him," Jean-Claude said. Respect was not the same thing as like; neither was admiration. How could one like a man who had ordered the burning of cities and commanded the assassination of entire families, even if he had been compelled by inescapable logic to do so? Even the inestimable Duchess Sireen, who loved le roi with the dedication of a martyr, called him a heartless cur.

"Any road," he said. "What about this nob?"

"Yeah. He was one of them Glasswalkers with the silver eyes."

Jean-Claude's eyebrows lifted in surprise. As l'Empire Céleste's high nobility were Sanguinaire, so Aragoth's were Glasswalkers, descendants of a different saint line. They were capable of casting their reflections—they called them espejismos—from mirror to mirror and manifesting at the other end. He'd only seen it once, in the Célestial capital at Rocher Royale. An espejismo had stepped from a full-length mirror like he was coming through a door. It had been unnerving to watch, the glass rippling like water before settling back into a smooth plane.

"What was a Glasswalker doing on a skyship?" Jean-Claude asked. If one of that ilk wanted to visit l'Île des Zephyrs, all he had to do was step through a mirror.

Planchette said, "Come here to see about your princess I think. Least that's what the coxswain said, though maybe he was trying to lift my skirt up."

"What would an Aragoth want with Isabelle?"

"Didn't tell me, but what does any man want with a woman her age?"

Jean-Claude scoffed. "That's impossible. He's a Glasswalker. She's Sanguinaire, at least by blood. Bloodlines don't mix."

"Aye, but she's got no sorcery, does she?"

"Doesn't matter," Jean-Claude said. "Not if her family had been unhallowed for six generations would the Temple permit a cross." So why didn't his argument sound convincing even to his own ears?

"Temple's not what it was," Planchette said.

"I suppose I should go talk to this Glasswalker then," Jean-Claude said as casually as possible. Coming here had been a mistake. He should have hunted the emissary down straightaway. "Do you know where he is?"

"I imagine he went up to the château with that other fellow."

Jean-Claude paused. "What other fellow?"

Planchette's smile grew even wider and more empty of teeth. "The other fellow is the one who brought the Glasswalker here."

—

It was not until Marie had returned and packed up all of Isabelle's paints that Isabelle's mind spun down from the vertiginous heights of nonharmonic, countercyclical perturbations to the ordinary world of rude flesh and social morass. It was very hard to get up that mental mountain, but coming down was always a disappointment. Would that her body had no needs to attend and she could stay atop that peak forever, a being of pure mind and crystalline focus, grappling with a deeper and more beautiful reality.

She gathered up her new canvas. The color and proportion were good. She could come back in later with some glazes to enhance the depth and increase the luminosity. A glance toward the forum showed that Henswort was in good hands amongst his admirers, so she shoved off.

She wondered if Jean-Claude had made any progress on discovering the emissary's purpose. She looked forward to hearing what he found out, though no doubt it was some business of her father's.

She was more interested in Jean-Claude's idea to have her fake a marriage to Lord DuJournal. It seemed like a mad plan, but why not? She had very little to lose.

Absorbed in thought, she ascended to the château and pushed open her door.

"Welcome, Highness," came a flat, metallic voice from within.

Isabelle shrieked and nearly jumped out of her skin. Her tripod clattered to the ground. She wanted to bolt, but fear nailed her feet to the pavers.

"My apologies, I did not mean to startle you," said the intruder, stepping toward her and into the light. He moved with a mechanical clank, a hiss, and a gurgling sound like boiling mud. His back was rounded with a large hump. His right hand was made of clockwork mechanisms, gears and screws and pistons that emitted oily clicks whenever he moved. His right leg, too, sounded mechanical, and seemed slightly longer than his left one. A deep cowl shadowed his entire face, but a bright pinprick of emerald light gleamed out from beneath. More terrible than this was the staff he carried in his metallic hand. It was the same purple-tinged, spine-tipped implement that Hormougant Sleith had carried on the day her father had destroyed Marie.

Yet this was no hormougant. This was an artifex. There was no mistaking the divine-eye symbol of his office or his quondam-metal limbs. He was one of the Seven Great Guides, each of whom the Temple made responsible for maintaining the purity of an entire sorcerous bloodline. They were subordinate only to the Omnifex himself.

His vestments were of the most elaborate and ostentatious type. His cope was a tapestry depicting the awakening of the saints in the Vault of Ages after the breaking of the Primus Mundi. It showed their rise through the underworld and the founding of the Risen City of Rüul. His chasuble continued the tale with the anointment of the children of the saints, the Firstborn Kings, and of the clayborn women they took to wife. Those were the Blessed Queens, who gave birth in turn to the Secondborn Kings, who were, in turn, the direct ancestors of all living sorcerers . . . and unhallowed culls like Isabelle.

Isabelle shied back one step. What terrible errand had brought an artifex here, to her very room? Her mouth moved, but she'd lost the ability to so much as squeak.

The artifex said, "As there is no one else to do so, allow me to introduce myself. I am Artifex Kantelvar, from the Collegia Aragoth." To her utter surprise, he took a knee before her like a supplicant. "And I have come to beg an audience."

CHAPTER

Four

Isabelle stood rigid, staring at Kantelvar. This was a trap. It had to be. No artifex would ever make obeisance to any woman, let alone her. But he remained down, waiting for her permission to rise.

And what choice did she have? She wanted to run away, but she imagined that would be seen as suspicious. For a long moment, she could not bring herself to speak, but Kantelvar seemed determined to outwait her.

"Greetings," she muttered at last. Surely that could not be offensive, unless he took offense at her not using his whole elaborate title. "Exalted One," she added for good measure. Only a very few clergy received the honor of melding with the Builder's divine machines.

Kantelvar rose, using the spine-headed staff as a crutch. "You are afraid of me." His voice was like hammered copper. "May I ask why?"

Isabelle fidgeted, trying to craft an answer that could not be used against her. If an innocent woman had nothing to fear, then a fearful woman must not be innocent.

"Your staff," she whispered. "Where did you get it?"

Kantelvar turned to look at his staff as if noticing it for the first time.

"The last person to hold this staff was a Temple hormougant. When he died, it was given to me as part of my Exaltation."

Isabelle took the tiniest measure of satisfaction in learning Sleith was dead, but she said nothing. She would not invite reproach, but why in the world was Kantelvar here?

"Is this important?" asked Kantelvar, rolling the staff in his hand. His expression was shadowed, his body language impossible to read, but the question itself implied no censure.

"Because that hormougant caused my friend to be murdered." Isabelle gestured to Marie.

Kantelvar's attention shifted to the bloodhollow, and he was silent for a moment before saying, "That would have been over a decade ago."

"Yes," Isabelle said.

"And this is the same bloodhollow?"

His toneless voice somehow made his sentence worse. "Yes," Isabelle said, her throat tightening.

"Extraordinary," he said. "Most bloodhollows don't last five years, much less ten, and in such good condition."

Impotent fury and despair filled Isabelle's lungs. This heartless clockwork was talking about her friend as if she were some sort of antique vase. But good sense reasserted itself before she could say something for which he would be compelled to punish her. Better to get this conversation over with.

"How may I serve you?" she asked. Whatever misfortune he had come to deliver would not be mitigated by delay.

"That is a matter best discussed inside." Creaking and sloshing, he ushered her toward the door.

Isabelle steeled herself and stepped inside to find out what malicious surprise he had in store. A quick survey of the room gave her no clues. Everything was as she had left it. Marie trailed her in and automatically began putting art supplies away. Isabelle centered herself in the room and faced the artifex.

Kantelvar shut the door and made a circuit of the room, examining her artwork as he went. This had to be for show, as he'd been lurking in the room when she arrived. He paused and waved his gloved hand over a painting she'd done two weeks ago while thinking about celestial mechanics. It was a scene of two of the three moons, Kore and Bruma, rising over the hills at twilight. The skin of the paint was not yet firmed up enough to stack the canvas.

He said, "These are very good. You have an eye for detail and a soft touch with light." His coppery voice clicked on the sharp edges of syllables. "These streaks of illumination are an interesting touch."

Dread wrapped a fist around Isabelle's chest and squeezed; the streaks of light she'd painted chasing the moons were precise ratios of the arc length traversed by the moons against the backdrop of the celestial sphere over a fixed period of weeks. The difference in the length of the streaks clearly demonstrated elliptical orbital paths.

"Yes," she said, praying he took his observation no further. There were too many secrets in her artwork, things that could get her eyes plucked out and her ears staved in. She glanced aside at the printing press and tried desperately to remember if she'd left the acid etching of complex number multiplications loaded on the printing plate. That would be hard to explain.

Kantelvar leaned on his wicked staff, tilting his head to the side and turning it to stare up at her, as might a man with a very stiff neck. There was another painful pause as he took some measure of her. Was it too much to ask that he think her a harmless lackwit and leave her be?

"How much do you know about the kingdom of Aragoth?" he asked.

If there was a question Isabelle had been expecting less than that one, she could not name it.

"Practically nothing," she said, though in fact Jean-Claude kept her up on what gossip wafted in from that fascinating kingdom. "Nothing," was always a good answer even when it wasn't strictly true. Nothing was what people wanted her to know.

"Hmm. To put it plainly, His Majesty el Rey de los Espejos, Carlemmo II, is dying and there is a choice of heirs. His elder son, Príncipe Alejandro, is married, but his wife has proven barren. Carlemmo has petitioned him to divorce and remarry, so his line may have issue, but the wife's family is very powerful and will not stand to have its grip prized from the crown.

"Some of the Sacred Hundred—that is the advisory council of high nobles in el rey's court—have begun pressuring Carlemmo to declare his younger son, Príncipe Julio, to be his rightful heir so that the line of succession will remain direct and unbroken. Alas, Julio is unmarried."

Isabelle couldn't imagine that problem would be hard to solve. Every Glasswalker sorceress in Aragoth must have been eager for the chance.

Kantelvar waited for her to respond. When she didn't, he made a weary noise, like the last air being let out of a bagpipe. "Unfortunately, there are very few female Glasswalkers. For nearly two hundred years Aragoth was under Skaladin rule. During the occupation, the heathens made a point of hunting down and murdering every sorceress they could find to appease their false god. Without saintblooded women to have saintblooded children, the Glasswalkers dwindled almost to extinction. The reason the Sacred Hundred bears that name is that by the time the Skaladin were evicted, there were only a hundred or so Glasswalkers left. In the centuries since, their numbers have climbed, but the population has become rather . . . closely bred. Once one removes Julio's first and second cousins from consideration, along with women who are already married or betrothed, the pool of potential applicants dries up to a puddle of infants, crones, and mental defectives."

Isabelle stood mutely, her skin going slowly cold, for she could see which way the wind of this conversation was blowing, and it made no sense at all.

Kantelvar said, "As there are no candidates left inside Aragoth, we must therefore look outside. That, at last, brings me to you."

Isabelle was stunned despite having guessed this was coming. "Impossible. It's forbidden." She shouldn't have had to tell that to an artifex. The care and breeding of sorcerers in preparation for the coming of the Savior was the Temple's raison d'être. Canon law stretching back to the Dominion of Rüul forbade the dilution or intermixing of those bloodlines. Such unions brought forth abominations, the Breaker's get. It was a rule even Grand Leon, famous for his contempt of the Temple, assiduously observed in the many marriages that bound his empire together.

Was this the trap she was meant to fall into, to be tempted by this offer and thereby prove herself morally corrupt? But surely such a scheme would not require an artifex, and why else would an Aragothic ambassador come to l'Île des Zephyrs?

"Why should it be impossible?" Kantelvar asked.

"I'm Sanguinaire," Isabelle said. "By birth if not ability."

"Demonstrably not." Kantelvar pointed with his staff to the certificate of unhallowedness by her door. "But though you lack sorcery, you are provably saintblooded."

"An inheritance without property. A broken cup," she protested, even while her pulse raced and her imagination conjured dreams of sitting on a throne in that strange far-off land, her wise and kind husband lowering a crown onto her head. What would it be like to command deference from her peers instead of being subject to their scorn? And what resources she would have, money and influence to spare!

But no. Such dreams were too dangerous to entertain. No one in all the Risen Kingdoms would permit her such a place in the world, much less offer it to her; more likely she'd be thrown to a mob and torn to pieces.

Kantelvar's expression was still hidden and his voice was flat, but he straightened his spine and opened his hand like a hidden king rising up to bestow alms on the downtrodden. "Say rather your womb is a fallow field waiting for the right season and the right seed."

Isabelle said nothing. If she was going to be damned, it would not be by any slip of her tongue.

Undeterred, Kantelvar continued, "Such cross-marriage has the most famous of precedents. During the Dominion of Rüul, the Firstborn Kings faced a similar problem to what Aragoth faces today. There were not enough female saints to ensure the continuation of the saintblooded, so the First-born Kings took clayborn women to wife. These Blessed Mothers were not only noble of mind but deemed worthy vessels for divine seed. And lo, they brought forth the Secondborn Kings, whose descendants are still with us today.

"But sorcery is not the only birthright. Sometimes the gift is that sacred fertility, that ability to blend dynasties without corruption. That is the prize that has been handed to you."

Isabelle boggled. Kantelvar was suggesting that everything wrong with her was right. *Almost everything.* Her wormfinger twitched in her glove like a caterpillar in its cocoon.

Isabelle shook her head. As little as she wanted to speak, she must not let herself be drawn into Kantelvar's trap. She would not rebel against society's judgment. "I was imperfectly formed." She was flawed. Broken. To aspire to anything else would get her punished.

Kantelvar's emerald lens focused briefly on her right hand, her wormfinger encased in its glove, before returning to focus on her face. "Your deformity is a mere accident of the womb, not a reflection of your worthiness as a vessel for . . . for Aragoth's seed."

Isabelle wished she had someplace to retreat to, but this was her sanctum. She had nowhere else to go except to fold up inside herself, and there was no more room in there.

Kantelvar continued unopposed, "Princess Isabelle des Zephyrs de l'Empire Céleste, greatest-granddaughter of the saints, will you marry Príncipe Julio de Aragoth and become a Blessed Queen?"

Isabelle licked her lips, trying to come up with some answer that made sense. More than anything, she wanted out of here, away from her father's grip . . .

"My father will never allow it," she realized aloud.

Marie stepped from the corner where she'd been lurking. Her face distorted like thin fabric as her father's visage pressed through the veil of her flesh. Even occupying Marie's body, his face was wasted and frail, and his voice was grating as a saw blade.

"In fact," he said, "an agreement in principle has already been reached. The sale of breeding stock, as it were."

Dismay filled Isabelle's heart and she shrank away from the horrific visage, turning her back on both of them. She berated herself for even imagining hope. Of two things in this confusion she was certain: If her father was party to it, she wanted no part in it. And just as surely, she would be given no choice.

Father said, "If you are done inspecting your broodmare, come and let us discuss payment."

"And what precisely do you imagine you are owed?" Kantelvar asked.

"You bargained for a rump princess, but what you are getting is a Blessed Queen. That is surely worth—"

"You were given more than you deserve," Kantelvar retorted, "and you will be happy with it, or I shall see to it you are left with nothing, which is what you actually deserve."

Part of Isabelle's mind scurried to keep on top of the conversation, but part of it fell back in time. She'd heard this exchange before, or a very similar one, the day Marie had been destroyed. Isabelle had been listening through the door when Hormougant Sleith threatened to withdraw some boon from her father. But that couldn't be the same boon as this, could it? Twelve years ago, Rey Carlemmo hadn't been sick, and if she recalled correctly, Príncipe Alejandro hadn't even been married, much less to a barren woman. There would have been no reason, then, to posit the need for a Blessed Queen.

"Under the circumstances," Father said, "I imagine that losing your prize would grieve you more than me losing mine."

Before Kantelvar could respond, Father's visage disappeared from Marie's face. He might still have been present beneath the surface, silently listening, or he might have gone away completely. Better to assume the former.

Kantelvar stared at the bloodhollow for a moment, apparently thinking. Then he raised his staff and pointed the spiny end of it at Marie. Tiny arcs of lightning danced between the spines. "No more spies," he muttered, his voice barely a buzz.

"No!" Isabelle lurched between Kantelvar and Marie, hugging the bloodhollow to her. She had no idea how Kantelvar had bound lightning to his staff, but she'd read enough to know that even the thinnest thread of galvanic fluid could be deadly.

Kantelvar withdrew his staff with a jerk. "Saint Céleste—Princess, stand aside."

"No," Isabelle repeated. "Don't destroy her, please."

"She's your father's spy." He somehow extruded incredulity through his mouth grille.

Isabelle shook her head. "She's my friend. Was my friend." The rest was beyond her ability to explain. What stranger could understand twelve years of torturous, painstaking caretaking? Preserving Marie had become a purpose in itself.

Kantelvar tapped his staff on the ground in a slow rhythm. After a moment, he said, "Walk with me. Leave her."

He lurched out the door, clockworks clinking. Isabelle released Marie, whose blank stare recognized neither threat nor salvation.

"Stay here," she instructed Marie. She departed and shut the door between them.

She caught up with the artifex on his way along the garden path toward the central wing of the château and asked, "What did Father get in exchange for me?"

"That will remain a secret unless he decides to break his bargain."

Isabelle seethed with frustration. She wasn't even allowed to know what she was worth in terms of the price she'd commanded.

"What about my bargain? If I am to give myself to this as you request, what do I receive?" she asked, imagining she would regret her impetuousness. Words had consequences, and an artifex had the power to make those consequences hurt.

"And what would you like, in exchange for yourself?" Kantelvar asked evenly, as if this was not an unreasonable question.

Isabelle hesitated. For more than a decade now she'd gotten along by staying silent and out of sight. Yet she had found a way to make herself heard in the world. She had her printing press and her math, and she was *good* at it. It was a small life, perhaps, but it was her own, and she clung to it like lichen to a rock. She did not want to be dragged out into the sunlight again, to be stripped bare of all protection and mocked for her flaws.

"What are you offering?" she asked.

"Aside from the chance to become a queen, rescue a kingdom from inevitable civil war, and save a sorcerous bloodline from extinction?"

Isabelle hardly knew what to say. Yes, those goals were noble and worthy, and anyone would be proud to achieve them. *Am I greedy for wanting more?* Yet she had not been selected for this role because of anything she had done, not for any new idea or act of will. She was just the right-shaped cog for the hole.

"Why me?" she asked. "Surely there are unhallowed Glasswalkers."

"None to speak of. If a Glasswalker family has a child who fails to manifest sorcery the child is given to the Builder, which is to say they are disowned, declared dead, and handed over to the Temple. It is not the sort of legal proceeding that would be easily undone, even if the Sacred Hundred would tolerate someone with such close ties to the Temple."

Isabelle dearly wanted to withdraw from this conversation. Clearly, Kantelvar and her father were going to do with her just as they pleased. Her opinion was as irrelevant as if she were complaining about the weather, but if she was going to be sent off to new masters she needed to know more about them. "I thought the Aragoths were devout."

"Compared to Célestials, yes. Especially the Aragothic peasants. Their nobility, however, are the ones governed by the Temple purity doctrine. As such, they are happy to acknowledge the Omnifex's authority, but they prefer that he stay in Om."

"But still—"

Kantelvar held up a hand to cut her off. "I did not say that persuading the various sects and crowned heads to support you was easy, only that the other options were even more difficult. Do you not want this chance?"

"What I want doesn't matter," Isabelle said. It was one assertion Kantelvar could not possibly disagree with.

Kantelvar fell silent. Isabelle used the moment to catch her breath and try to stop the world from spinning. The messier this deal got, the more she believed it. It wasn't clean or fantastical but rooted in ruthless and cynical politics.

At last Kantelvar said, "I will offer you something, personally. A bride gift, if you will."

Isabelle eyed him warily. "What, or is it a secret?"

"It is a secret you should keep, at least for the time being. I will revivify your friend, free her from your father's grip, and restore her mind."

Isabelle stopped as short as if she'd slammed into a wall. In the barest whisper she asked, "You can do that?" She'd spent years searching for any hint of a cure and found nothing but myths and baseless rumors.

Kantelvar leaned on his staff. "It is an arcane process, difficult and uncertain. I have attempted it twice. I succeeded once. Neither bloodhollow was in as good condition as yours."

"How?" she asked, the dry husk of a word fluttering from her lips only after she had stripped it of all desperate pleading.

Kantelvar faced her, or at least turned his cowl in her direction. "I make no guarantees, but the vital spark cannot be completely gone or you friend would not have grown. Only living things can mature."

Isabelle felt dizzy. He could cure Marie. Maybe. It was foolish to put any faith in this. She had endured false hope many times, only to have her heart shattered. But what if . . . what if . . . ? After all this time her work might be redeemed, her mistake absolved, her obsession justified. What if Marie might come back?

"Let me see your face," she said, a mad impulse, but she had to know. Had to make absolutely sure this was not the same man who had condemned Marie all those years ago.

Kantelvar recoiled. "That is not a good idea. My visage is more than repulsive. I go hooded to *prevent* people from being afraid."

Isabelle found this strangely heartening. Her left hand covered her right. She knew what it was like to generate revulsion in others. All she had to do was show her wormfinger to send some squeamish people into fits.

"I insist," she said, though it was utter madness to demand anything from an artifex.

Kantelvar shifted from foot to foot as if wrestling with himself. At last he stilled and slowly peeled back his cowl.

Isabelle's eyes widened in amazement. He was not Sleith, that much was certain. The right half of Kantelvar's head was mechanical, or at least encased in mechanisms of quondam metal. How deep they went beneath his skull was impossible to tell. A telescoping tube with a glowing green lens bulged from his right eye socket. A clump of wires and hoses emerged from the back of his head, gathered in a queue, and snaked under his vestments.

The left half of his face was as scarred and pitted as a fortress after a siege, the skin pale and waxy. His left eye, bloodshot with an iris gray as dishwater, seemed to wander without reference to what the rest of him was attending. His mouth . . . by the Builder, his mouth had been sewn up around a circular grille that gave him the look of a permanent howl of anguish.

Isabelle's amazement overwhelmed her disgust. How was he even still alive? Even the Temple, which claimed proprietorship of all quondam artifacts, didn't really know how the mechanisms worked. The saints had passed on knowledge of how to use some of the leftover bits from the Primus Mundi, knowledge that was amongst the Temple's most closely guarded secrets, but the fundamental principles underlying their function remained completely opaque.

A thousand questions fizzed in Isabelle's brain, but none of them made it as far as her mouth. She could not show too much curiosity, nor speak any word that might suggest she possessed even a smattering of empirical philosophy.

"How do you eat?" Isabelle managed at last. Everyone had to eat.

"I ingest what sustenance I need through this tube." He opened the lid on a tube that had been inserted in the hollow of his throat. A brief whiff of bilious stink wafted from the opening.

"Did it hurt?" She gestured at all of him.

"I felt no pain," he said.

—

Isabelle's skin crawled as she entered her father's audience chamber, the white marble vault where so much of her life's pain had been concentrated. Memories revisited themselves upon her mind: the razor-sharp sting of a bloodshadow attack, the helpless paralysis, the horrifying numbness of her mind draining away, the absolute horror of Marie's hollowing.

She forced herself through the memories, like a foot soldier fording a deep, swift-running stream. Her past had been ruined here, her friend worse than murdered. She would not let her future be ruined here, too.

Kantelvar strode up the strip of white carpet that marked the aisle to the foot of the dais atop which her father sat. Comte Narcisse des Zephyrs had been poured into a white doublet that was much too big for his withering frame and propped up in his chair, his rheumy eyes half closed, in the center of his bloodshadow. The sorcerous manifestation was thicker and darker than ever, and it flowed over him, like a great tongue constantly probing a rotting tooth. The sorcery he cherished was consuming him from within, ravaging him like a cancer, growing stronger the more he fed it, feeding on him if he refused to give it other prey.

On the first step of the dais stood her brother, Guillaume, as tall and fit as their father was shriveled and weak, a direct contrast to their respective intellects. His white riding boot rested on the second step; he could not wait to climb into his father's chair. Isabelle feared for anyone under his authority when at last all restrictions on his appetites were released. She might escape into this Aragothic marriage, but the people of Windfall would not.

Guillaume bestowed on Artifex Kantelvar a look of deep suspicion that turned into pure unmasked loathing when he gazed at Isabelle. His bloodshadow wriggled like a carpet of snakes at his feet.

"Ah, the traitress dares to show herself," he said. "I might have seen her giving herself up to a dog, but I never dreamed she would stoop to be a Glasswalker's whore."

Isabelle returned his loathing but refused to rise to the lure. Father usually brought Guillaume when he wanted to taunt Isabelle to tears or bait her into foolish anger.

Beneath Guillaume on the step stood Lady Arnette, plump and healthy. Her round face might have been pretty were it not for eyes like chips of flint. "I don't know about that, love. If the object is to weaken the Aragothic royalty, I can think of no better way than giving them Isabelle. I only wonder if the poor príncipe knows he's getting damaged goods."

Across from them stood an enormously fat man in a deep-red doublet with slashed sleeves showing cloth of gold beneath. His craggy face was brown as saddle leather, and his graying hair was brushed straight back and gathered in a queue. His eyes were orbs of pure silver.

He fluttered delicate fingers on hands that seemed much too small for a man of his girth. In a thick accent full of rounded vowels he said, "Comte, please, control your offspring."

The comte replied, "Don Divelo, my apologies, but Célestial tradition requires that everyone be allowed to speak their mind in open court," but he was looking at Kantelvar when he said it.

Liar, Isabelle wanted to say. Father was letting Guillaume carry on in the hopes of offending the ambassador enough to threaten the marriage contract and force Kantelvar to renegotiate whatever deal they had.

Kantelvar took no knee before her father, showing him less respect than he had shown Isabelle. "Pay them no heed," he said to Divelo. "If dogs bark it is because their master allows them. These two curs are as toothless as their master is powerless."

Arnette shot back, "Wolves howl when they hunt, when they come upon prey that is old, weak, and stupid." Her bloodshadow flowed down the steps toward Kantelvar, a slow but inexorable flood.

Isabelle stepped back from the spreading crimson stain. She knew she couldn't outrun a bloodshadow—they could snap out with the speed of thought—but that in no way reduced the urge to try.

Kantelvar raised his staff and slammed the heel down on Arnette's encroaching stain. Sparks of green lightning shot through the bloodshadow, bright light scattering it in all directions. Arnette shrieked and toppled. Guillaume was too slow to catch her. She hit the marble with a thud and lay there twitching.

Isabelle gasped in amazement. She hadn't known there was anything that could hurt a sorcerer through their bloodshadow.

Guillaume rounded on Kantelvar. "You bastard!" His bloodshadow flowed forward but came up short when he found himself staring at the cage of glittering sparks that danced around the hedgehog tip of Kantelvar's staff.

Kantelvar said, "In point of fact, my parentage is of no consequence to my position, but if you want a discussion of bastardy, let us begin with the wretched sow drooling on your father's floor. The thing that calls itself Lady Arnette was not sired by the Duc du Troisville. This would be of no great consequence if her mother had found another Sanguinaire with whom to dabble, but instead she lowered herself to rut with a mere cook."

Arnette, still quaking, sputtered, "You lie!"

"Evidence can be provided, sworn testimony and physical proofs. The political complications would be messy and expensive for everyone involved. Now, does anyone want me to continue?"

Silence welled up, thick as tar, until Father wheezed, "Guillaume. Take your wife. Go."

Guillaume whirled on his father. "You cannot let this stand!"

"Get out," rasped the comte. "Try to sire some piglets on that great sow of yours, or get a swineherd to show you how."

Isabelle's heart fired with vindictive glee as Guillaume's face darkened to the color of a turnip. True, his humiliation did not aid her at all, but even had she been waiting her turn on the gallows she would have grinned as her brother tried to help his bride out the door without actually touching her.

"Now to the matter of concessions," the comte said to Kantelvar. "You lied to me when you bargained for Isabelle. You said your plans for her were of little consequence, and now I find she is to be a Blessed Queen. You have bargained in bad faith, and a bargain in bad faith is no bargain at all."

"I said," Kantelvar enunciated, "my plans for Princess Isabelle were of little consequence *to you*."

"I am about to be related to el rey de Aragoth, a matter of great consequence."

"This is the man to whom you referred as, I quote, 'a lack-witted, spineless scrap of lady's ribbon whose sole contribution to history will be the remarkable ignominy and brevity of his rule.'"

"Do not spin word webs at me, you old spider," Father snarled, leaning forward with such force that he nearly fell out of his chair. "Let me make myself plain. You will not have Isabelle unless I have satisfaction. She belongs to me!"

"What is it you want?" Isabelle asked, since nobody else seemed about to.

"Shriving," Father said, not even bothering to level a curse at her. To Kantelvar he said, "Rid me of this!" With obvious effort he lifted his hand and let it fall on the arm of his chair and the bloodshadow draped there. "I know it can be done."

Isabelle followed the comte's calculation. Losing the bloodshadow would cost him much, but not so much as his life.

"The bloodshadow is a gift from the Builder," Kantelvar said flatly. "Even if I could separate it from you without killing you, which I cannot, to destroy it would be heresy of the greatest order."

The comte snorted. "Compared to the obscenity you are planning, I think not."

"Regardless, it cannot be done," Kantelvar said.

"Then I shall keep my daughter," Father said. "Let Aragoth burn."

Don Divelo said, "Your Excellency, be reasonable. You ask the impossible."

Isabelle was not quite so sure of that. If Kantelvar could revivify Marie, why not remove a Sanguinaire's bloodshadow? Of course, the ability to perform one miracle did not imply the ability to perform another.

Kantelvar made a mollifying gesture. "Pay him no heed, Don Divelo. As I said, he is powerless." From somewhere in his voluminous robe he produced a large scroll stamped with the Great Seal of l'Empire Céleste. "Comte Narcisse des Zephyrs, your lord and master, His Imperial Majesty le Roi de Tonnerre, Leon XIV, hereby grants his permission for Princess Isabelle des Zephyrs de l'Empire Céleste to marry Príncipe Julio de Aragoth and commands you to give her all aid and support . . . should *she* accept this mission."

Then he turned to Isabelle. "Highness, do you accept?"

Isabelle felt dizzy; she hadn't anticipated Grand Leon, but of course her imperial cousin must have been party to this contract. She took a deep breath—for time, for courage—and sought for clues. There were many ways Grand Leon could have phrased this proclamation. He could have ordered her to go on pain of death. He could have taken her away from her father and made her his own ward. Instead he gave her permission. True, an imperial permission was just one eyelash short of a command. It was not expected to be refused . . . but it could be. And he'd called it a mission, an adventure with purpose, sanctioned by the crown.

In a strange sort of way, across time and distance, a man she'd never met seemed to be asking, "Are you brave enough? Do you dare?"

Answers had consequences.

"Yes," she breathed. "Yes, I do."

CHAPTER

Five

Isabelle stood beside one of the cushioned wing chairs next to the big bay windows in the hub-ward sitting room that had become her de facto audience chamber. For two days she'd received a constant stream of . . . she wanted to call them petitioners, but none of them were actually asking her for favors. Well-wishers, she supposed. They were mostly her father's subordinate lords, guild leaders, and military officers, none of whom would have attended her funeral if she'd died before her betrothal.

Now every last one of them insisted on performing some minor service for her in the hopes that she would remember them as she ascended to the lofty social altitude of an Aragothic princesa, or possibly, hopefully, queen. There was no guarantee that King Carlemmo would actually appoint Príncipe Julio his heir once he married, or that the succession would not be the subject of armed debate. Yet even if she ended up as a reserve princesa with no real authority, she would have unfettered access to those who did, an advantage even the loftiest ambassador could not match.

So now everybody wanted a share of her. It was a bitter irony that she'd only become someone worth knowing at home when she was on the verge of being shipped away forever. Still, she gained nothing by spurning her various supplicants. A noblewoman's primary function, aside from bearing heirs for her noble husband, was being connected to other nobles, and the contacts she cultivated here would serve as her currency for investment in the Aragothic court.

Isabelle smiled up at her current supplicant, a stout nobleman with a vein-webbed nose and watery eyes. He had just given her a an exquisite jewelry box of polished blackthorn wood.

Isabelle inspected it dutifully. "Thank you, Lord Antionne. I'm afraid I don't have any jewelry to go in it."

Lord Antionne's expression grew a bit wooden, and Isabelle realized he must have thought she was asking him to cough up a trinket on the spot.

He said, "That was imported all the way from l'Île de Noire." It was supposed to be a reminder of his successful trading ventures. His contacts on Craton Riqueza made him a useful man for a princesa of Aragoth to know.

"I will treasure it." She propped up an awkward smile, an expression that fooled no one, she feared, but sometimes all one could do was move past the current awkwardness to the next awkwardness.

Marie, who hovered always at Isabelle's side like an unquiet ghost, took the box and placed it on a table with Isabelle's other presents. It was starting to look like a pile of bier gifts.

The business of the audience finished, Lord Antionne let himself out, and not before time. Never had she talked so much, said so little, or felt quite so lonely. As useful as all her newly affirmed acquaintances might have been, none of them were really interested in her for her own sake. They didn't know her, and the one person who did remained conspicuously absent.

Jean-Claude had been missing since they parted on the steps of the library at the hour of Professor Isaac's lecture. Could something have happened to him? The thought gave her jitters.

The only mention of him had come when her father had introduced her to a thin, pointy man whose doublet was festooned with dueling ribbons and whose face was marked with scars. "This is Captain Vincent. He will be the head of your new honor guard, a troop of reliable men, loyal to the family, and we will finally be rid of that damned musketeer."

Isabelle's stomach soured at the thought of being surrounded by a dozen of the comte's spies at all times, extending his control of her far across the deep sky.

Her father must have seen the dismay on her face, for his lips compressed into a thin but satisfied smile. "Jean-Claude's much vaunted, much flaunted authority does not apply in Aragoth, and I cannot imagine His Majesty would wish to sully l'Empire's reputation by sending the sot to a foreign capital any more than I would wish to tarnish your appearance by including him in your entourage."

"Fear not," said Vincent in a voice of smoothed grit, like oiled steel. "I am sworn unto my death to protect you, and I have never failed in any charge."

Isabelle wanted no more to speak to Vincent than to her father, so she merely nodded without enthusiasm. Somehow, she had never imagined her world without her fey but faithful musketeer ambling through it. The comte's revelation only made it more urgent that she speak with him.

She finally reached a lull in her flood of petitioners. Her head ached and her energy was depleted down to the bone. She had tried to offer only small talk and social platitudes, but saints only knew what ammunition she had inadvertently given them all to hurl at her . . . and this was only a very small sample of what she would experience in a royal court.

Anticipating dinner, Isabelle sent Marie to fetch the right-hand prosthesis she used to feed herself, then sat in the wing chair and basked in the rippling golden rays of the late afternoon sun. The sunbeams diffracted through the beveled edges of the windows, forming tiny rainbows, an obvious demonstration of the principle of diversity in aetheric density. *What does it tell us about the nature of light that it can be subdivided? What does that tell us about the nature of the Builder?*

If at all possible, one of her first projects as princesa or queen would be to build her own university. That would give her much opportunity to rub up against the world's brightest minds. She would have to dedicate at least one laboratory of her future university to the study of light. It seemed far too fundamental a thing to be left unexplored.

"Your Highness." Jean-Claude's jovial voice boomed from the glass-paneled double doors on the far side of the room, as if finding her here were a delightful surprise rather than a deliberate act.

She bounced from her seat and smiled at him in melting relief. "Monsieur musketeer, welcome. I trust you have heard my most excellent news." She prayed it was excellent, because it was certainly forever.

He was dressed in a drab brown coat over his fine linen blouse. He doffed his white-plumed hat and made a leg for her, pointing the toe of his scuffed and dingy boots. Refusing to dress up when he entered the château was one way he tweaked her father's nose.

He strolled across the room, his hound-dog eyes and drooping mustache looking genuinely puzzled. "News, Highness? I'm afraid nothing of any importance ever finds its way into these hairy ears."

Isabelle laughed. "You are incorrigible. I know you've heard of my betrothal. You'd have to be considerably more deaf than a post not to have, but that's not the whole of it. The artifex, Kantelvar, has promised to bring back Marie!"

Jean-Claude's bushy eyebrows rose in true surprise. "Truly? That is wondrous indeed, but I have always been given to understand that such a thing is impossible."

"He says he has done it before. He himself."

Jean-Claude's expression became thoughtful. "Did you ask him when, and why you, who have scoured every mountaintop and rabbit hole for news of just such a miracle, have never heard of it?"

With more than a little effort, Isabelle simmered her roiling enthusiasm down. "I didn't think of it at the time, and I haven't seen him since my audience with the comte." And, if she was to be brutally honest, this was one assertion she didn't want to challenge.

She asked, "But where have you been?"

He ran a hand through his thinning, graying hair and leaned against a white pillar. "I have been in my cups, of course, listening to a constant babble and gabble of rumor. Apparently there's been an incredible transformation. A woman once feared as a witch has transformed into a beautiful princess, and she's sailing off to become a good and noble queen of a distant land."

Isabelle puffed a disbelieving breath. "Am I supposed to be flattered by this change of heart?"

Jean-Claude shrugged. "Their praise is offered with the same passion and sincerity as their slander, and should be taken just as seriously."

Isabelle blinked, slightly stunned, but of course he was perfectly right. She'd have to think on that later. "But surely such gossip wouldn't take you three days to collect."

"True. Mostly what I have been concerned with were the rumors of your predecessor's death and how mysterious it was."

Isabelle's mouth opened to respond before she fully grasped what Jean-Claude had said. She found herself spluttering. "Predecessor? Explain."

"I found out from Mademoiselle Odette the dyer that Príncipe Julio was betrothed before. Captain Kyle of the *Sunflower,* a merchantman, informed me that the príncipe's bride-who-was-not-to-be was one Lady Sonya de Zapetta from El Sangre Aragothia on Craton Riqueza. Unfortunately, she took ill en route to San Augustus. She was diagnosed with the gray pest, so the story goes, and chose to fling herself overboard rather than risk infecting the crew."

Isabelle blanched at this horrific tale and made a warding sign against the pest. "How . . . noble of her."

"Yes," Jean-Claude said acidly, "it's not at all likely that a pack of cowardly sailors seized a terrified young woman from her sickbed and threw her screaming into the abyss. In the end, the crew was let off on a quarantine skyland, and the ship was burned down to the aetherkeel, but by the Builder's grace, no one else got sick. It's a miracle to be sure; the pest strikes like a hurricane, not like an assassin's knife."

Isabelle quieted her voice. "You believe Lady Sonya was murdered."

"A metaphor only," Jean-Claude insisted, but he belied his assertion when he added, "Cântator'dok, the Gyrine Windcaller, just arrived from San Cristobal, where the plague-ship crew was eventually landed. He spoke to some of that crew. The disease they describe is inconsistent with the progression of the pest. Monsieur Clovis, the vintner, has received a recent letter from his brother in El Sangre Aragothia. He mentioned an excess of fire beetles, and an ongoing drought, but no gray pest. 'Plague' is not a word I would choose to describe just one death. We shall have to be on our guard."

Isabelle marveled at Jean-Claude's clairvoyance. Who else could spend three days carousing and return to present her with some very suggestive intelligence from half a world away? Someone she did not want to lose.

"We have another problem," she said. "My father intends to prevent you from accompanying me to Aragoth."

Jean-Claude contrived a pained expression, but his eyes twinkled. "Pshaw! I am a King's Own Musketeer. Your father can bellow like the boor he is but cannot stop me from going where I choose. The only one who might prevent me from accompanying you would be the ambassador the Aragoths have sent to escort you. Once I announce my intention to go, the comte will certainly ask him to forbid me setting foot on Aragothic soil."

"Then I will tell Don Divelo that you are to be my personal guest. Once he has given his word to me, he will not be able to retract it."

Jean-Claude swept his hat almost to the floor. "I am most honored."

A soft tread in the hallway opposite Jean-Claude announced Marie's return with Isabelle's prosthesis. The bloodhollow opened the door, padded to Isabelle's side, and stopped. Father's face manifested through her ghostly visage.

"To whom were you speaking just then?" he asked.

Isabelle looked up, but Jean-Claude had silently taken himself out.

"My ladies," she said. "Now, if you don't mind, I need Marie to help me with this glove."

—

Isabelle stood on the balcony overlooking the spinward fields, a canvas before her and paints to hand. She didn't normally paint pastoral scenes, but there was a soft quality to the evening light, like golden honey drizzled across the land, that she wanted to capture. *And I'm never going to see this place again.* That realization wrenched her heart in spite of all her enthusiasm for escape. She knew every fold of this land, every glade and rill, every street and shop of the town. It was the only place she'd ever known, and its colors had bled into her soul. *Who will I be somewhere else?*

"Your Highness." Kantelvar's greasy clicking voice drew Isabelle's attention back to the here and now. She turned to watch the artifex hiss, clank, and gurgle up the stairs behind her. He'd forgone his cote today in favor of long purple tippets emblazoned with the silver sigil of Saint Céleste, a four-armed woman bearing a gearwheel, an escapement, a spiral spring, and a ratchet.

"Your Exaltedness," she said. "Thank you for attending me." After a third day of being drowned in petitioners, Isabelle had discovered the joy of minions: ladies-in-waiting to accept gifts and supplications on her behalf, and runners to fetch people she actually wanted to talk to. Jean-Claude had referred a few ladies of exceptional competence and Isabelle filled out the roster with people who had at least been polite to her and who had shown wit and kindness to others. Most of them were from lesser families, none of them had a drizzle of sorcery, and all were grateful for the secondhand status her elevation afforded them.

Kantelvar bowed deeply to her, which unnerved her. He need not have shown such deference even to a queen, so why to her? "How may I serve Your Highness?"

Isabelle needed to talk to Kantelvar about Lady Sonya—she had rehearsed the conversation with Jean-Claude—but her throat locked up at the moment of commitment. Politics and assassinations were too dangerous a subject.

Isabelle took inspiration from his garb. "You are devoted to Saint Céleste. It seems an odd choice for an Aragothic artifex." It was always easier to talk to other people about themselves, erasing herself as a subject as much as possible.

"I was not always assigned to Aragoth," Kantelvar said. "It is more of a historical oddity that l'Empire Céleste was named for her, given that she was l'Étincelle rather than Sanguinaire."

"But she was married to Saint Guyot le Sanguinaire," Isabelle said. "He named his kingdom after her, or at least that was the story I heard." It was one of the great vexations of history that most knowledge of the saints, and most of the wisdom they had brought with them from the Primus Mundi, had been lost with the city of Rüul. What was left over mostly had the weight of old cloth, threadbare fabric many times patched and embroidered.

"That is a lie told by the Sanguinaire to try to claim her as one of their own," Kantelvar said, his voice ringing like a hammer on an anvil. It was the most emotion she'd heard from him, genuine anger, but it dissipated as quickly as it flared. "It is true that Saint Céleste had a child by Saint Guyot, your Grand Leon's direct ancestor, or so he claims, but those were desperate times. Unfortunately Saint Céleste was the only one of her kind, and her sorcery did not manifest in her children. 'Ghostbred' is the term of art for that outcome."

"What was l'Étincelle, or does anybody know?" Isabelle had never even heard the term before, not that saint lore was near the center of her interests.

Kantelvar did not answer immediately but tapped the foot of his staff on the flagstones, something he seemed to do when making up his mind.

When he spoke, it was in a low buzz. "When a great forest burns, the rising heat will carry away some leaves unscorched. So it was with the annihilation of Rüul. The city itself and all its marvels are utterly gone, but some scraps have been found, scattered to the edges of the world. The Temple considers collecting them a sacred duty second only to preserving the bloodlines in preparation for the Savior. We call this collection the Hoard of Ashes. Of course, all of what we have recovered is fragmentary, and the meaning of most of it remains opaque, but there are hints and clues. If those suggestions are to be believed, Saint Céleste could give an animate force, l'Étincelle, to nonliving matter, stone and metal."

Isabelle's curiosity fizzed with excitement. Now, that would be an amazing power to possess. Just imagine all the mechanisms she could make, the instruments. Imagine a lens that could flex to adjust its focal length, or a cogwheel that could turn itself.

"But you did not summon me to discuss ancient history," Kantelvar prodded.

"No," Isabelle said, forcing her mind onto the topics she'd been avoiding. Rehearsed or not, she could not escape the dread sensation that speaking would only cause her trouble; it was impossible to ask a question without giving the listener a club to hit her with.

At last she said, "If it pleases you, there are aspects of my betrothal that confound me."

"It pleases me to ease your confusion," he said. His head swiveled beneath his cowl. "I note your bloodhollow is absent."

"She is helping pack my things," Isabelle said. The comte was already furious that she had managed to get Jean-Claude a berth on the skyship and an invitation to her wedding ceremony. She didn't want Father spying on her now, either.

She said, "When you explained how you selected a bride for Príncipe Julio, you didn't mention Lady Sonya."

Kantelvar actually stiffened in surprise, his emerald eye gleaming from under his hood. "She was not relevant to your qualifications."

"Only because she was murdered."

Kantelvar might have denied it or asked how she knew. Instead he said, "That is very astute of you."

He seemed disinclined to go on, and Isabelle nearly lost her nerve, but if she was going to be queen she'd need to handle harder questions than this. "Was the killer apprehended?"

"No," Kantelvar said. "But the actual murderer is of little concern. Likely he did not even know who he was working for."

Isabelle fired off another well-rehearsed question: "And who was he working for?"

Kantelvar shook his head noncommittally. "The pool of suspects with both desire and ability to perform such an insidious murder is small. It is almost certainly one of the more politically ambitious members of the Sacred Hundred. Rey Carlemmo has people investigating the matter as aggressively as possible, as do I. Rest assured, the traitor will be discovered."

"And you mentioned none of this to me?"

"I did tell your bodyguard. Protecting you is his duty."

Isabelle wanted to say, *My true bodyguard figured it out on his own, and he always tells me that I must know enough to take care for my own safety. "If you're going to do something foolish, at least be smart about it."*

Kantelvar continued. "You have other concerns to attend than the rude business of murder. I assume you have been studying the makeup of the Sacred Hundred."

Isabelle squirmed at being put on the spot. What would happen if she answered wrong? "Don Divelo has been lecturing me."

"Hmmm . . . He is one of the queen's partisans. I will lend you a more evenhanded book on the history of the Hundred and another on Aragoth's great families. You must exert yourself to ingratiate yourself with them."

Isabelle felt a chill that had nothing to do with the evening air. There was nothing quite as futile as trying to ingratiate herself to someone who was determined to despise her; she could never lower herself far enough to slide under the blade of their contempt.

"And what about Príncipe Julio?" she asked. Her impending husband had been remarkably absent from their discussions. "Do you know him?"

"He came to me for training. He has the potential to be the greatest Glasswalker Aragoth has seen since the days of the Secondborn Kings."

"But I mean do you know him personally. Was he . . . were he and Lady Sonya beloved of each other?"

"They had never met," Kantelvar said.

"Does he have a lover?" Isabelle asked. *Am I going to come to him as a horrible disappointment?*

Kantelvar hesitated and then said, "He does not want for female companionship, but he has no special attachments."

Isabelle's emotional strength flagged—Julio's experience would find her incompetent—but she pushed on. "And how does he treat his paramours?"

"None of them have confided details to me, Highness, but neither have they complained, nor spread vicious rumors about him."

Isabelle got the feeling she was asking these questions to the wrong person. She ought to talk to one of Julio's servants. Jean-Claude always said that one of the best ways to judge a man was by how he treated his inferiors.

Kantelvar went on, "He is handsome, intelligent, well respected, puissant at arms. A worthy husband."

But will he find me a worthy wife?

"When will I meet him? Will he come here?" she asked. Most mirrors in l'Empire Céleste were deeply scored with a grid of fine lines to break up the espejismo of any Glasswalkers trying to manifest through them, but Château des Zephyrs had a special room for receiving Aragothic nobles bearing news or doing business. She always found their silver eyes fascinating.

"I'm afraid not," Kantelvar said. "Protocol forbids such a meeting before the wedding."

Isabelle shook her head. Why did tradition always insist that ignorance was the optimum state for important transactions involving women?

"Did the príncipe take any part in choosing me?" Isabelle asked, trying not to sound too plaintive. Was he even interested? Certainly she would have preferred having more than a yes-or-no say in her own matrimonial prospects, but then how would she have chosen? Her circle of acquaintances was small enough to be graphed as a point.

"The electors decided to shield him from the decision-making process so as to frame the marriage as practical rather than personal. It makes it easier to justify politically."

Isabelle shook her head in dismay. "You are setting up a relationship that is supposed to be so tightly bound that two people are living inside each other's skin, and you don't imagine it will be personal? Who were these electors?"

"Carlemmo, the old Omnifex, and me," Kantelvar said. "And intimacy will come later. Two people who are thrust together by outside forces are more likely to find common cause than two people who merely drift together on a gust of feckless, transitory passion."

Isabelle had no basis to argue that assertion, but another fact caught her attention. "You said the Omnifex, but he's been dead for nine months." The College of Artifexes's inability to select a new Omnifex was a scandal that had found its way even to l'Île des Zephyrs.

"Signing the decree that permits this cross-marriage was very nearly the last thing he did before he died."

"But that was before Lady Sonya was killed. My name should never have come up."

"There were politics involved," Kantelvar said, lightly rapping his staff on the floor. "We electors decided that it would be better to name two potential brides in the treaty. Lady Sonya, being Aragothic, was the least controversial choice, so she was named first. To be perfectly blunt, one of the reasons your name was included was that it was supposed to provide some protection for Lady Sonya. I'm sure you can see why."

The bitter logic left Isabelle numb. "Because if anybody killed her, they would be stuck with me." She'd not been chosen because of her virtues but because of her faults. Once again she was the Breaker's get, the fate so terrible that anything else looked good by comparison. "I'd be as well received as a gut wound."

"Which is why we are going to make absolutely sure you arrive safely for your wedding at the royal citadel in San Augustus."

"How can you be sure?"

"No expense is being spared on your personal security," Kantelvar said, "but more importantly we are hunting the assassin's master, which will make it harder for him to move against us without attracting attention to himself. Capturing him will likewise discourage imitators."

Isabelle was not soothed. Kantelvar seemed to have a great deal of confidence in things for which there was no certainty. She dipped her paintbrushes in solvent and began scraping off her palette. She'd lost the light and her enthusiasm for the painting before her.

"Are there any other questions I can answer for you, Highness?" Kantelvar asked.

Isabelle wanted to point out that he hadn't really answered the ones she'd already asked.

"No . . . wait. Yes, there is one. I almost forgot. You said you revivified one other bloodhollow; how is it no word of that ever came to my ear?"

"Because I am discreet. There was a minor noble family, every bit as delightful as yours, deep in the Forest of Sorrows. I was called there by a Sanguinaire widow. Her unhallowed son could not inherit his father's domain, and so she tried to draw his sorcery out of him, using her own bloodshadow, with results you can anticipate."

Isabelle winced in sympathy for the poor boy. "She went too far and turned him into a bloodhollow."

"Yes, so she called me in and I reconstituted him."

"And what happened after that? What was his state of mind?"

"I didn't know him before he was a bloodhollow, so I have no basis for comparison, but he seemed compos mentis to me. His mother requested that I never speak of the incident to anyone. Apparently she never did, either."

Two of Vincent's guards braced to attention as Isabelle approached her room. They were stern men in infantry uniforms, white tabards with the des Zephyrs blue triskelion crest over leather jerkins and gray shirts. One of them opened the door and took a quick look inside, presumably to make sure no assassins had taken up residence in her absence. Inspection completed, he bowed her in. Isabelle muttered shy thanks to him, slipped inside, bolted the door, and leaned against it.

Her mind boiled with revelations about politics, assassins, and betrothals. It was all excited steam, too hot to touch, much less organize. She needed rest and routine and time to let things settle down enough that she could make sense of them.

Isabelle placed her painting of the landscape next to other recent paintings of the harbor, the millhouse, the townsfolk about their daily business. It was not the detailed and meticulous style favored by portraitists, but a looser, more vibrant expression of light and shadow. They were her memories, and they were heartbreaking, but her heart kept thumping just the same.

Marie stood against the wall like a caryatid, not even waiting, just being, like a statue.

Not for long. The promise of getting Marie back, of finally divesting herself of this desperate burden, sang to her more clearly than anything else she'd been promised. She knew nothing about being a wife, or of fulfilling her duties as the bearer of children, or of being a queen. Those were just words, merely dreams, but she had been living in the ruins of Marie's destruction for nearly as long as she could remember, far longer than she had been the girl's friend.

She put Marie through a series of stretching and strengthening exercises, then had her strip down for her evening inspection. Might this twice-daily indignity at last be bearing fruit? Kantelvar had said Marie was in better condition than either of the other bloodhollows he'd treated.

Isabelle sat back on her haunches and frowned, for that wasn't all Kantelvar had said. He'd said, "Only living things can mature." But how had Kantelvar known she had matured? He hadn't been here when she was hollowed out. Of course he must have known Isabelle and Marie had been children at the time she had been changed, and Marie had grown up a little, though she looked sixteen instead of twenty-five, much as some plants deprived of sufficient water grow more slowly than those fully nourished.

Isabelle shook off her unease. This upending of her life was making her crazy. If Isabelle was going to call herself an empirical philosopher, even if only in the privacy of her own head, she must be mindful not to entertain the phantasms of anxiety and fear. Right now she had only a feeling that something was . . . off, and even that was shapeless.

—

Dawn drizzled the Oreamnos Hills with a glaze of amber as Isabelle and Jean-Claude strolled the curving lane of the Château des Zephyrs's plum orchard on the morning of her scheduled departure. The buds on the trees were just beginning to swell, like they had every year of her life. She wouldn't get to see them bloom. That thought clung to her like a cobweb. Indeed, she was so hung about with gossamer memories she felt like the ghost in a haunted house, all but gone.

And she had to become so much more. A queen. Would that truly be allowed?

Footsteps on the gravel behind reminded her of Vincent's men, set to guard her against assassins, apparently on the presumption that they might reach her even here, in this mote on a sunbeam that was l'Île des Zephyrs. They were also set to spy on her. In this new life, even her protectors served her enemies. All except Jean-Claude.

While Isabelle and Jean-Claude steadily increased their pace to put meters of separation between themselves and their pursuers, Jean-Claude had been waking up the gardens with boastful recounting of his latest small victories: "You should have seen the look on Guillaume's face when I pointed out I had an invitation to a royal wedding and he did not. He puckered like he'd had a shaved lemon stuffed up his arse."

When Isabelle judged they had enough of a lead not to be easily overheard, she said, "What else have you discovered about this marriage treaty?"

"Nothing to speak of," he said at a much lower volume. "'Twould seem the negotiations were rather closely held. Unfortunately, my friend the shepherd has been too busy avoiding conscription to have received any news from his brother in Rocher Royale, so I haven't heard any rumors from that direction. How did your conversation with Kantelvar go? Did you ask him the questions I suggested?"

"Yes," she said, giving him a précis of the conversation. "I was chosen as Lady Sonya's second as a sort of guarantee. Who would murder her knowing they would get stuck with me as alternative?" It had been a blow to her pride to know that she had been a booby prize, but pride was coin she could afford to spend.

Jean-Claude listened intently and replied, "If you were meant to be a terrible warning, we should have heard about your candidacy long before now. It should have been heralded to the widest possible audience to gin up more support for Lady Sonya as the preferable choice."

Isabelle tried to look at the problem mathematically. "Surely there are a limited number of people who stood to gain from Sonya's death, other people who might have a candidate to put forward. They were the only ones who needed to be told, and they could be counted upon to be paying attention, couldn't they?"

Jean-Claude made a tsking noise. "In my experience it is just as unwise to overestimate your opponents as to underestimate them. What else did you learn from Kantelvar?"

She shook her head. "I have the feeling I missed more than I caught from what he said. I'm just not very good at this sort of thing. Have you learned anything interesting about him?"

"I don't have as many friends of friends in Aragoth as I'd like," Jean-Claude said. "But I get the impression Kantelvar was a recluse. He had a large estate outside of San Augustus, preferred to make people come to him for favors and let his ambassadors do his traveling for him. That is, until just about a year ago, when the old Omnifex recalled him to Om, presumably to work on this treaty for your marriage."

"He bothers me," she said, clasping and unclasping her hand as she groped for specifics. "He quoted my father as saying that Carlemmo's reign would be notable only for its brevity, but Carlemmo has been on the throne for twenty years. That's only short when you compare it to Grand Leon. So when did my father say that to him? I don't think he's ever been on l'Île des Zephyrs before."

Jean-Claude scratched the edge of his beard. "He wouldn't have to be. Your father keeps a bloodhollow in Rocher Royale so he can do business at court without ever leaving his demesne. He might have one in Aragoth as well . . . but, come to remember it, there was an artifex here once, on the occasion of your birth."

Isabelle's eyebrows lifted in surprise. Jean-Claude had told her the true story of her birth, how the midwife had tried to smother her, to fortify her against the rumors and lies that had sprung up around the event. "You never mentioned that before."

Jean-Claude shrugged. "Truthfully, I'd forgotten him. He was administering the admonishment of Iav to your mother in her labor. I didn't ask his name. That's the problem with clerics. You see the yellow robe and you think Temple. Well, sometimes you think, *Oh look, the bugger's gone and pissed himself,* but usually you give them the benefit of the doubt. It's pretty thick whitewash."

"You don't find it odd that one of the Seven came all the way out here just to attend a birth?"

"At the time, I thought your father might have summoned him to provide some extra theological oomph to your mother's delivery. That was before I realized your father has almost as little use for the Temple as I do." He grunted as if begrudging this similarity of thought.

"After that, I whisked you to Rocher Royale and presented you to Grand Leon. I delivered my report, you received his official blessing, and then he banished me back here. By the time we returned, the artifex was gone, and I had no cause to think of him again."

"And yet here comes another artifex to whisk me away," Isabelle said. "Or is he the same one?"

"No," Jean-Claude said. "Not even if you add on all the clinks and clanks the current one is wearing."

"Ah, so you don't think the two events are related?"

"It's a good question that needs looking into. In the meantime keep your eyes open and your wits about you, and I'll talk to some people who might know more about that first artifex."

The winding path left the orchard and climbed up a stone stair leading to an overlook of the deep sky. Today l'Île des Zephyrs stirred a layered soup of low-hanging clouds. The thin green film of the Miasma overlaid crisscrossing yellow tendrils of the Upper Veil. Beneath them roiled the lightning-shot Galvanosphere. Streaks of lightning chased each other through the indigo murk, igniting tingles along Isabelle's spine and all the way down to her fingertips. Even her wormfinger felt more alive in the presence of the storm. If only she had a long enough cable to fish up a bottle of that lightning, what might she learn from it?

Isabelle waited until Jean-Claude had recovered from the climb before asking, "Do you think there is any chance of me becoming queen, happy ending and all?" she asked. *Or am I going to end up dead?*

"Alas, there are no happy endings, only interesting middles," Jean-Claude said. "As for your marriage, the Aragoths made you a promise. I intend to see that they keep it."

CHAPTER

Six

The Aragothic royal courier, the *Santa Anna*, was a week out from Wind-fall, bumping along through turbulent skies. Captain Santiago directed the ship's operations from the quarterdeck. Jean-Claude clung, one-handed, to one of the stanchions holding up the captain's sunshade. He strove for non-chalance even as his stomach lurched in a rhythm exactly contrary to the skyship's undulations. It had been more than twenty years since he had set foot on one of these flying death traps. He had almost forgotten how much he hated sailing. The wind tugged his greatcoat, threatening to whisk him from the deck like a tuft of thistledown and send him tumbling into the Gloom.

He shut his eyes against the ship's damnable lift-and-drop and fanta-sized about stable land. Maybe someday, when Isabelle didn't need him any-more, he would return to the hinterland of his birth, la Valeé du Vin Rubis, where the sky had an actual horizon, not just a hazy guess, a place where he could tip over in any direction without fear of plunging to his death. Maybe he would take his severance and start a little farm, or better yet, an inn, someplace unlikely to fall off the face of the world . . . once he let go of Isabelle.

When she was married, it would be her husband's job to protect her, and no doubt the husband would find Jean-Claude about as welcome as an infestation of lice.

Dolt, you knew you would have to give her up when you started this.

Yes, but twenty-four years ago, he had barely known her. She was just a handful of newborn, a set of healthy lungs, a pair of bright blue eyes, and a way to tweak her parents' upturned noses. How was he to know she would turn into the most delightful—he hardly dared think the word "daughter," not with its suggestion of bastardy—but the most wonderful ward any man could want? In the face of a world that hated everything about her, she remained curious and compassionate.

As her warden, encouraging her to take the next step was part of the job. She had to leave him behind, like a newborn chick leaving its cracked and empty shell.

Isabelle shrieked. Jean-Claude's eyes flew open. But it was a squeal of delight, not fear. Isabelle leaned over the ship's rail, pointing with her proxy hand and laughing. "Look, leviathans!"

Vincent, by her side, wore a bored, supercilious smile, as if he were indulging a child. "Indeed they are, Princess."

Jean-Claude's hand clenched so tightly on the stanchion that his glove picked up splinters. What was that fool doing, letting her get so close to the edge? What if she tipped over? She was tethered, but the rail could give way or the line could break.

"Isabelle," he croaked, but she was too involved with her adventure to heed him. She had taken to the skyship as if she was born to it, and would have been scrambling up the rigging if protocol and petticoats had permitted.

"Isabelle!" Jean-Claude forced himself to let go of the upright and stagger to her side, clipping his own tether to the rope—like the rail, far too flimsy a precaution.

The ship rocked. Jean-Claude pitched forward, and only his mad bulldog grip on the rail prevented him tipping headfirst off the ship.

Isabelle gesticulated emphatically at the leviathans, enormous, glittering, aether-filled bodies, easily as long as the *Santa Anna* and her escort ships. They undulated slowly through the sky, propelled by translucent membranous fins that ran the length of their bodies. Their mouths, which opened like parasols on four long, slender jawbones, were filled not with teeth but with something that looked like pink feather down. Even as Jean-Claude recovered his balance, the great beasts turned their tails up and dove slowly into the Miasma.

"Jean-Claude, did you see them?" Isabelle asked. "It looked like they were feeding, but what is there in the Miasma to eat? Perhaps they consume the vapors, but why doesn't it make them sick?"

Down past the inverted forest of turvy masts sprouting from the bottom of the ship, past the leviathans, waited the nether skies: the Miasma, the Galvanosphere, and the Gloom. Isabelle had told him that empirical philosophers had calculated the depth to the heart of the world as more than ten thousand kilometers. Jean-Claude had not asked how long it would take to fall that far. The immense dark depth enticed him, shrinking his world around the edges.

He yanked his gaze from the seductive abyss and fixed it on Isabelle. His voice was a rasp. "Come away from the edge, please. It isn't safe." Builder knew he'd spent most of his life keeping her safe from assassins, kidnappers, and lesser enemies. It would be inexcusable to lose her en route to her wedding.

"Don't be so fussy," she said. "I'm perfectly safe. I'm double tethered. Even if the ship capsizes, I'll just hang here, like a spider from a thread, until somebody pulls me up."

Jean-Claude eyed the ship warily and muttered, "Don't give it any ideas." His toes clenched in his boots, trying to grab the deck and take root in case the ship suddenly flipped.

Vincent laid a well-manicured hand on Jean-Claude's shoulder. "Monsieur musketeer does not look well. Mademoiselle, if you will permit me to escort your guest below?"

"I do not need your help." Jean-Claude tried to shake the younger man off, but it was hard to do with almost every muscle in his body locked.

Isabelle's brows beetled in worry. "You do look a bit green. Why don't you go inside and have a cup of tea?"

Jean-Claude suffered himself to be towed away. Like a doddering old man. It was either that or cause a public scene. Vincent directed him belowdecks, into the undercastle, a gun deck beneath the hold, currently unoccupied. No doubt he thought it would be the perfect place for a private manly chat. At least belowdecks, the sky didn't insist on rocking around so much, but, damn it, Jean-Claude couldn't watch Isabelle from here, not that there was much to guard her from on a skyship.

Of course, that isolation came with problems of its own. All the gossip he'd gathered about Aragoth was months old, and he had no way of freshening his store until he arrived in San Augustus. It would take precious time to make enough contacts to get a worthwhile finger on the pulse of Isabelle's new city. If the sampling he'd gotten from the *Santa Anna*'s crew was any indication, it would be rough going. The sailors made signs against evil behind her back, and muttered about witchcraft and abominations. "To each his own kingdom," as the teaching went; ten kingdoms for ten sorceries, seven now that two bloodlines were extinct and a third banished.

"Monsieur, a word," Vincent said.

Jean-Claude looked up into Vincent's cold gray eyes. "Just one? Certainly." Jean-Claude didn't like the man; he was too much le Comte des Zephyrs's creature. Isabelle had, in her father's eyes, suddenly gone from being an embarrassing liability to a very valuable asset, so he'd bought the best sellsword he could obtain, a man loyal only to coin.

Vincent fixed a disproving look on Jean-Claude. "In a word then, desist. In slightly more words, I bid you to recall that you are Princess Isabelle's guest, not her guardian. Now that the need of *serious* guarding has arisen, His Excellency le Comte des Zephyrs has selected a serious guard. Your continued assistance will not be required . . . or tolerated."

Jean-Claude sagged theatrically. "Too true. In all these years, never has my mettle been truly tested in Her Highness's service. Alas, my orders come from le roi." He reached under his tunic for the pouch containing his carefully preserved orders—they hadn't been renewed in twenty-four years—but Vincent flung up a warding hand.

"You have no authority outside l'Empire Céleste. You no longer possess even the delusion of being the princess's protector. Because Her Highness values your sagging hide, I will tolerate your presence, but only so long as you do not interfere with my duties. If you become an impediment, or persist in being an embarrassment, I will remove you."

Jean-Claude considered Vincent's hands—finely muscled, callused, and scarred—and his high collar bedecked with dueling trophies, jeweled pins in the shape of crossed swords. Le roi had made dueling illegal for Sanguinaire—saintborn blood was sacred—but it remained a popular method of suicide amongst clayborn nobles and military officers. This created a small but lucrative market for men like Vincent, who were good at dispatching easily provoked young men at the behest of older, wealthier ones.

Jean-Claude was not proud to admit that he had once been one of those young hotheads, nor was he fool enough to deny it. Even now he was tempted to taunt Vincent into violence—teach the whelp a lesson—but serving Isabelle required temperance. Even so, Jean-Claude could not bring himself to cultivate the man's goodwill.

Jean-Claude rubbed his face and worked his jaw. "Your proposition is noted. Now, if you will kindly lend me your boot, I need something in which to vomit."

"Drunken sot."

"Better than being des Zephyrs's lickspittle. Or was it his cock you sucked to get this post?"

"Cur!" Vincent whipped the white glove from his belt and slapped Jean-Claude across the face.

Jean-Claude reeled, stung more in pride than in flesh. His anger flared up, and it felt good. Oh how he yearned to take this runt to pieces! Only the weight of experience held him in check, not the ache of old knees, surely. Never play the other man's game. Vincent was good, and Jean-Claude had never been much of a fencer. A fighter, yes—give him a tavern full of crockery or a pigsty knee-deep in mud and he'd teach this pup new ways to bleed—but he was no duelist, to be hemmed in by rules or honor.

Jean-Claude spat on the deck. The gobbet was pink with blood from his split lip. "I am sure that you will stand fast if one of Isabelle's enemies is polite enough to challenge her to a duel."

Vincent curled his lip in contempt, and he dropped the glove at Jean-Claude's feet. "Coward. Until you have the balls to pick that up, stay away from the princess. She is my first priority, and I will brook no meddling from you." He turned and climbed through the hatch.

Jean-Claude let him go. *Isabelle is my* only *priority*. He walked in circles a few times to shed the gut-churning energy of constrained anger. He plucked the gage from the deck between thumb and forefinger. He considered using it to wipe his arse next time he went to the head and then flinging it at Vincent's feet, but that would likely be an insult too far. He couldn't get rid of Vincent, so he'd have to use him instead. That would be much more satisfying. He squeezed between the cannons and threw the glove out a gun port. It whisked away in the wind.

And yet there was something about what Vincent had said, not what he was talking about, but his actual words. *She is my first priority.*

And *that* was what was wrong with this whole cursed scenario. Priorities. If Jean-Claude had been an evil bastard attempting to abrogate Príncipe Julio's marriage and faced with a bride and a spare, he would have killed the lightly guarded spare first. It would have been less work that way. Presumably the threat against Sonya had been anticipated from the beginning, and she had been guarded, however ineffectively, but it was not until after her death that all this extra attention had fallen on Isabelle. If the evil bastard had done things the other way around, Jean-Claude might have been blindsided. There would have been no second line of defense.

That thought made Jean-Claude even queasier than the skyship's heaving. But for his notable failure to protect her friend Marie, Jean-Claude had always managed to keep Isabelle one step ahead of intrigue and danger, but this betrothal had hit him like a broadside from the fog. No one had even whispered of it on the l'Île des Zephyrs before Kantelvar arrived.

He commanded his rubbery legs to obey and half-dragged himself up the ladder with a mind toward having a word or three with the boatswain—if the man was any good at his job, he'd hear every rumor and muttering aboard ship—but he had to divert into the ship's hold to avoid being plowed under by a bounding gang of sailors en route to the turvy sails. Their simian acrobatics made him dizzy, so he slumped down on a crate—one of Isabelle's two meager trunks, actually—and covered his eyes to make the world stop spinning.

When he opened them again, he saw his face staring back at him, gray and pasty, from the surface of a full-length mirror. The cloth that had been tied over its face had been pushed to the side, bunched up in the ropes that held it in place. He grabbed the edge to pull it back into place so he wouldn't have to look at himself, but it had been jammed between the rope and the frame with force and would not be casually dislodged.

Grumbling, he leaned in to make a better go of straightening the cloth. Who was down here undressing the cargo in the first place? Not the Aragothic sailors, that was certain. They were very cautious about mirrors and the constant threat of sorcerous meddling they represented.

At last, Jean-Claude's conscious awareness caught up with what his back brain was trying to tell him. This mirror had no scores or cracks. He did not recognize its frame. And the cover had been pushed aside . . .

Jean-Claude's legs arrived at the frightful conclusion an instant before his brain. He bolted into the ladder well. The mirror had been planted in Isabelle's luggage and a Glasswalker had come through it, and there was only one possible reason for that: Príncipe Julio's last bride had been assassinated, and now a killer had come for Isabelle.

Jean-Claude launched himself up the ladder, scattering a troop of off-duty marines crowding his path. "Make way. Make way!" He erupted onto the main deck and dashed to the quarterdeck, but Isabelle was gone. Jean-Claude's heart rattled as if kicked by a frantic rabbit, but he kept a tight hold on its scruff.

He seized a young crewman by the shirt. "¿Dónde está la princesa?"

The young man pointed down. Jean-Claude dropped through the nearest hatch, but that led to a gun deck. She wasn't in the hold. She couldn't just vanish! The sound of female voices caught his ear. He followed the sound through a narrow doorway into the keel run, a cramped tunnel of a room that extended most of the length of the ship. The already tight space was very nearly filled by the cylindrical steel-clad shaft of the aetherkeel. Flickers of sickly light, like green lightning, flashed behind glassed-in portholes in the barrel of the beast, and the whole thing throbbed from one end to the other with a buzz like a swarm of locusts trying to find a way out.

Captain Santiago, Keel Master Ordo, Vincent, Isabelle, and two of her ladies, Valérie and Darcy, were crammed into the wedge of space alongside the aetherkeel. Jean-Claude's heart started beating again at the sight of her.

Santiago curled his mustaches, smiling beatifically, while his keel master held forth on the device itself. ". . . without it, the ship could do nothing but float helplessly downwind. We would have nothing to push against; we could not tack into the wind."

"I see." Isabelle raised her voice to be heard over the machine's insectlike razz. "It's very impressive. I . . . uh. Would it be possible . . ." Judging by Isabelle's pasted-on smile, she was having trouble with her tongue again. No time for that now.

"Mon capitaine!" Jean-Claude shouldered past the ladies. "Forgive my intrusion, Highness. Captain Santiago, you have an intruder on board."

"Intruder?" the captain asked. "A stowaway, you mean?"

"I mean an intruder. There is a mirror in the hold with its cover torn away from the inside. There is, or was, an uninvited Glasswalker somewhere aboard this ship."

Isabelle frowned. "All of my mirrors are scored, which is a crime in Aragoth, so I didn't bring them."

Captain Santiago scowled. "The ship will be searched." He bobbed his head at Isabelle as he shouldered by. "Highness, excuse me."

Isabelle turned to Jean-Claude. "Did you smash the mirror?"

Jean-Claude stiffened, mortified by this oversight. "I didn't think of it."

Vincent said, "Highness, we must get you to a launch."

As much as Jean-Claude hated to admit it, that was a good idea—get her off the ship.

"Come!" Vincent said. He took Isabelle by the arm. The whole flock scurried out of the keel run and down the stairs. They bunched up on the lower gun deck, where two crewmen flung open trapdoors to reveal the launch cradled under the ship.

A dreadful bell rang somewhere above. Ordo's head snapped up. "¡Fuego!" He charged from the room, toppling handmaids like so many squealing ninepins.

Fire! It was a skyship's deadliest enemy.

"Load up!" Jean-Claude bellowed.

"Marie!" Isabelle cried, looking around frantically for the bloodhollow.

"I'll find her," Jean-Claude said. "Go!" Jean-Claude seized Vincent by his bejeweled collar. "Get her off the ship! Make sure she stays there!"

"I don't take orders—" Vincent shouted, but Jean-Claude had already scrambled to the ladder well. From the hatch above came a blast of white heat and the crackle of flames.

Sailors screamed. Over the roar of the fire, Santiago bellowed, "¡A su vez a estribor! ¡Salto! ¡Salto!"

The ship shuddered and groaned, like a beast in pain, and began to roll, nosing down. Flaming splinters rained through the hatch. Jean-Claude climbed—floated—through the hatch above, just in time to see an unfamiliar figure dart into the hold where the mirror was. The Glasswalker, trying to escape!

Jean-Claude caromed off a wall, just managed to hook the doorframe, and swung himself into the hold. Thin smoke filled the space and alchemical lanterns bobbed crazily at the ends of their chains.

Gravity came back redoubled. Jean-Claude slammed into the sloping deck and slid down it along the cramped corridor between the stacks of Isabelle's luggage. There was the mirror with its flapping cover and a dim figure stepping slowly into it, as if pressing through a doorway filled with mud.

"Halt!" Jean-Claude pushed himself to his feet and rushed the figure, drawing his main gauche as he went.

The saboteur's head turned. He had a lean face and a high-bridged nose. A long red scar ran down the right side of his face, leaping from brow to cheek. His eyes, orbs of pure silver, flashed in alarm. His mustache and goatee were ragged, his teeth white, and he was dressed in a monkish habit singed down one side. He slithered into the mirror, his face and torso sinking into its silvery surface. Only his right arm remained in the real world, gripping the frame for leverage, and the silver of the mirror flowed toward his hand like oil up a wick.

Mon dieu! Jean-Claude grabbed the trailing hand and jabbed his main gauche through the espejismo's wrist. The man behind the mirror thrashed, his mouth open in a silent scream.

Jean-Claude hauled on the arm and snarled, "Come back here." The Glasswalker inched toward Jean-Claude—it was like trying to haul an ox out of a mud pit—but the silvery sheen continued to creep up the saboteur's arm.

The ship tilted backward and all the stowage groaned against the ropes.

A plume of smoke, a jet of fire, and a deafening bang erupted behind Jean-Claude. Hot sparks sizzled into his cheek, and the mirror shattered into a thousand pieces. The espejismo's hand dissolved into a silvery mist, and Jean-Claude stumbled backward into a tightly lashed stack of crates.

Vincent stepped through the cloud of gun smoke, slowly lowering his pistol.

"Breaker's hell," Jean-Claude shouted so he could hear himself over the ringing in his ears. "You idiot. I told you to guard Isabelle!"

"I don't take orders from you!" Vincent replied, shouting just as loudly. "My men have her on the launch, and I knew you would be no match for a sorcerer."

Jean-Claude gestured to the shattered mirror. "I had him in hand. We needed to question him! And you shot him."

"He was slipping away. He would have dissolved from your grasp or dragged you in with him."

The ship lurched. Jean-Claude's weight went from normal to double as the ship began to rise, crushing him to the deck.

—

Isabelle's heart had stopped hammering, but her face was still cold and damp when she returned from the launch to the *Santa Anna*. The main deck resembled a forest in the fog. Shards of shattered glass and blackened splinters covered the deck. The crew swarmed hither and thither, scuttling shadows amongst singed ropes and scorched sails. Thanks to Captain Santiago's inspired dive through a rain cloud, the fire had been extinguished, but how badly had the ship been damaged?

Jean-Claude appeared out of the smoke and she rushed to him, throwing both arms around him in a hug. "Saints be praised!" Then she pushed off. "Did you find Marie?"

"Not yet," Jean-Claude said. "I ran into the Glasswalker; nearly captured him too, but Vincent cleverly stopped me."

"You had no chance," Vincent said, appearing beside him, red-faced with anger.

"Stop," Isabelle said. "Both of you. Please."

To her amazement, both of them went quiet.

Someone had tried to kill her, and they'd been willing to burn down the whole ship to do it. She had known there would be an attempt . . . or attempts, but the actual experience left a cold knot in her breast that evinced no sign of thawing. It brought her back to the day on the docks all those years ago when the Iconates had tried to kill her, but those were only madmen, deranged by grief. This was more like what Father did in the Pit of Stains, cruel and calculating.

Could she live with such threats lurking always at her back? Did she have a choice? Jean-Claude had proved an able watchdog today, her very own hellhound as always, but le roi would soon recall him to l'Empire Céleste, and then who would protect her? Vincent had the comte's interests at heart more than hers. As far as she could tell, Príncipe Julio considered her just one of any number n of potential brides, fully interchangeable, and where was the protection Kantelvar had promised?

For that matter, where was Kantelvar? And Marie? Both Jean-Claude and Vincent were at her side, but she'd seen no sign of her friend or the artifex. Before the fire, she'd sent Marie to fetch some wine, but Marie didn't do well when she encountered something unexpected. She'd keep trying to carry out her orders no matter how stupid they were in her new context.

Isabelle found the captain, still covered in soot and smelling of smoke, on the quarterdeck bellowing orders to his crew. He whirled and regarded her with a look that reminded her horribly of a powder keg with a lit fuse. "Princesa. I am pleased you are safe, but now is not a good time for you to be on deck. Return to the cabin, por favor."

His glare cowed Isabelle into silence and retreat, but Jean-Claude stepped forward. "Have you seen Artifex Kantelvar or Marie?"

"I don't give a damn where the tinker-man or the bloodhollow is." Santiago turned his back on them and resumed shouting at the crew. The four escort ships had formed up with the *Santa Anna*, and one of them was beginning the delicate negotiation of drawing alongside to offer aid.

Isabelle left the captain to work out his rage on other people and descended to the main deck. To Jean-Claude and Vincent, she asked, "Has the rest of the ship been searched for additional sabotage?"

Vincent said, "I have my men doing it now."

"But would they recognize it if they saw it?" Jean-Claude asked.

Vincent glowered at him, but Isabelle said, "It's a fair question. Your men aren't sailors." *Coldhearted killers, yes. Aeronauts, no.*

"I will press some sailors into service." Vincent tipped his hat to her and shoved off.

"You two need to learn to cooperate," Isabelle said.

Jean-Claude shrugged. "I like him just the way he is. He inspires me. Besides, the more your enemies are worried about getting around him, the less they will be worried about getting around me."

Isabelle frowned; she disliked social friction as much as Jean-Claude reveled in it, but that was not her primary concern at the moment. She had to find Marie. Had she run afoul of the saboteur? *Please let her be safe.*

She returned to her cabin. Jean-Claude stepped forward to open the door for her. A pain-filled groan came from within. She pushed quickly inside, fearing she would find someone dying. The room was a mess. The door to the chart room had been blown off the hinges, and everything that wasn't covered in soot was waterlogged from flying through the rain cloud. The door and a sky chest that had pulled loose from its moorings had slid into one corner, pinning Kantelvar there.

Jean-Claude hauled the crate and the door off him and helped him to his feet. His saffron robes were scorched and sodden, and what little exposed flesh he had was grayer than normal and goose pimpled.

"Are you injured?" Isabelle asked.

"What happened?" Jean-Claude added.

Kantelvar retrieved his staff and leaned heavily on it. His voice wheezed like a depressurized pipe organ. "I was attacked. I suffered a bruised forehead and injured pride. Both will recover. Was . . . did you capture him?"

"No," Jean-Claude said. "He was a Glasswalker. I caught him trying to leave through a mirror in the hold. I had him by the arm, but Vincent bravely shot the mirror."

"What happens when a mirror is destroyed while an espejismo is passing through it?" Isabelle asked. The Aragothic artifex ought to know how Glasswalker sorcery worked.

Kantelvar asked, "Was he in the mirror when it was shot?"

"Three-quarters of the way through," Jean-Claude said. "All but his arm."

Kantelvar swayed on his feet and his voice whined like an overtaxed axle. "It is very likely . . . he is most likely dead or lost between mirrors. Unless he has a strong anchor on the other side, he may not find his way out again, which is worse than dying, or so I am made to understand." He slumped down on a sky chest. Bruised pride indeed.

Isabelle said, "We can't assume he's dead. At worst, he is lost for how long?"

"It . . . depends on how organized his mind is."

"I left him with a dagger wound through his arm," Jean-Claude said helpfully.

"In that case, probably not very organized," Kantelvar allowed. "Assuming he is not dead, could you recognize him if you saw him again?"

"With that scar on his face he'd be hard to miss," Jean-Claude said. "Didn't you get a look at him?"

"Yes," Kantelvar said. "But there might have been more than one intruder."

"What exactly happened?" Isabelle asked.

"I went into the chart room to check our progress in the orrery, but someone had opened a valve in the simulacrasphere. The room was frigid, and there was frost on the walls. I rushed over to close the valve, but I heard someone behind me. I turned and saw his fist coming down. That is the last thing I remember." Kantelvar rubbed at his temple. "He must have ignited the aether, trying to burn the ship out from under us . . . that is, from under you, Highness."

Isabelle said, "A ship catching fire and falling into the Gloom doesn't leave any evidence that can point back to anyone, but thanks to a whole lot of very quick thinking, it didn't work, and now we know what the assassin looks like."

"Oh, better than that," Kantelvar said, "I know who he is . . . or was. He calls himself Thornscar: a nom de guerre, I'm sure. He's an anarchist, but he'll work for anyone who he thinks will help bring down the rightful king. I imagine he was the one who murdered Lady Sonya. I wouldn't count him dead until I saw the body. Perhaps not even then. Stubborn."

"I've never heard of him before," said Jean-Claude.

"He's a local problem," Kantelvar said. "His complaint is against Aragoth's royalty, and he is extremely persistent and unpredictable. If he lives, he will try again, unless I stop him." He lurched up and stumped to the exit.

"Where are you going?" Isabelle asked.

"I must go . . . I will take one of the escort ships and precede you to San Augustus. If he's not dead, he's wounded. It's an opportunity. I need to find him before he recovers."

Isabelle only just refrained from putting a hand on his shoulder. She almost asked if he was fit to travel, but they were already traveling, and he would be moving from a damaged ship to an undamaged one, a move Isabelle herself would consider once an assessment of the injury to the *Santa Anna* was complete.

"You'll be breaking up the fleet," Jean-Claude pointed out. "The next attack may be more direct."

Kantelvar said, "If he was going to meet us in the deep sky, first he'd have to know where we are."

"He found us before," Jean-Claude pointed out.

"He found the *mirror*," Kantelvar said. "Distances and directions in the Argentwash, the space between mirrors, are not analogous to those in the mundane world. And even if our enemy knew where we were, he would have to have a fleet capable of reliably confronting the royal navy's most elite squadron. Anything they don't outgun they can outrun."

"Be careful," Isabelle said. "You still have a promise to keep to me."

Kantelvar bowed to her. "Of course, Highness. Builder keep you."

"Until the Savior comes," Isabelle replied.

After Kantelvar shuffled off to harangue the captain into giving him a launch, Isabelle dragooned her ladies and Jean-Claude to look for Marie. They found her belowdecks in the kitchen store, tangled in netting. Isabelle's heart was in her throat as she ordered Marie cut loose. Like a fish caught in a net, she would have kept squirming, trying to complete her last directive, until she died of exhaustion.

Isabelle took her back to her cabin and kicked everyone else out while she did an inventory of Marie's wounds. She had a dozen ligature marks from being tangled in the net and bruises from being bounced around. Those would have to be carefully monitored. She would not have Marie developing abscesses or gangrene, not when she was so close to being saved.

When that was finished, she let her ladies back in and suffered herself to be soaped, scrubbed, patted dry, corseted, gowned, powdered, painted, manicured, coiffed, gloved, and perfumed. Her handmaids exerted themselves to make it appear as if she had never been near a sabotaged skyship on fire, as if they could make the whole event unhappen. It was a perfect waste of an hour that could have become several hours had not an invitation arrived for Isabelle to join the fleet captains in conference.

Isabelle brushed her skirt as if to smooth out her dread of being trapped in a room with so many strangers all used to getting their own way. She was happy to have been invited—it showed they did not discount her completely—but she prayed she wouldn't be asked to contribute. No matter how many times she reminded herself this was not her father's house, she could not shake the conviction that any point she made would instantly become the one everyone condemned.

The junior officers' cabin had been fitted with a table, which, being inadequate to the purpose of seating all present, only made the place more stuffy and crowded. She joined Captain Santiago at the head of the table. Don Divelo took up most of one wall by himself, owing to his alarming girth. Vincent and Jean-Claude had flattened into the corners behind Isabelle. The captains of the three remaining escorts and a few of Santiago's officers were arranged around the other two sides of the table.

Santiago concluded his report, ". . . no structural damage. *Santa Anna*'s skyworthiness was not compromised. I see no reason to transfer Princesa Isabelle to another ship."

"Because the enemy knows she is on this one," Don Divelo said. "Clearly your precautions were inadequate."

Santiago's swarthy face grew red at this insult to his competence, but before his temper got the better of his tongue, Jean-Claude interjected, "To say that Isabelle's security was inadequate underestimates the resourcefulness and determination of our enemies."

"The musketeer is most wise," Santiago said.

Perhaps offended by Jean-Claude's defense of the captain, Don Divelo drew himself up as if about to deliver a lecture, but Jean-Claude spoke first. "What I want to know is how that mirror got aboard this ship. It's not one of Isabelle's."

Santiago shouted for the boatswain, who stepped in smartly and looked rather puzzled when the question was repeated to him.

He said, "It showed up at the docks with the rest of la princesa's things. The manifest said 'paraphernalia.' It was not specific to each item, so we loaded it."

"So the enemy has an agent in Windfall," Jean-Claude said.

"There's nothing we can do about that now," Vincent said. "The mirror is smashed. The plot is foiled. We must turn our attention to threats in front of us."

"Because whoever is behind us is just going to give up," Jean-Claude said dryly.

Captain Santiago broke in, "On my life I swear no one else will board this ship, nor will any of my men betray la princesa. They are all known to me."

Vincent said, "What do you imagine the enemy will do now their sabotage has failed? Howl into the wind?"

"We won't know unless we ask," Jean-Claude said. "Don Divelo, I understand you are a sorcerer of great refinement."

The ambassador's silver eyes gleamed at this compliment, and he settled slightly. His feathers were still ruffled, but he no longer seemed inclined to squawk. "I am no Cerberus Cortez, but my skills are adequate."

Jean-Claude said, "I have heard that you can walk through the glass as if it were an open doorway and you have guided many important people safely through the Argentwash."

Divelo made a dismissive gesture with his fingers, but his voice was clearly pleased. "I have only done my duty."

Jean-Claude said, "It so happens that I have need of a great sorcerer."

Divelo's expression grew wary. "To what purpose?"

"I need you to take me to l'Île des Zephyrs, so I may track down whoever put that mirror aboard this ship."

Don Divelo sniffed. "What you ask is accounted a high honor amongst Aragoth's most faithful servants, not something to be handed out lightly to a clayborn Célestial."

Isabelle tugged at her veil, a nervous habit. She'd been hoping to avoid becoming involved in this conversation, but Jean-Claude's idea was a good one.

Steeling herself, she said, "I would ask it as a favor."

Divelo's whole expression brightened and he steepled his child-sized hands. "A favor for you, Highness, is an honor for me."

Isabelle kept smiling, though if history was any guide, repaying this favor would cost her dearly. She should have pointed out that helping her was a favor to Príncipe Julio, assuming she could speak for him. Should she try to renegotiate, or would that simply make her look more a fool?

She looked to Jean-Claude for reassurance. To her relief, he touched the brim of his hat in salute.

Vincent protested, "Your Highness, with all due respect, Jean-Claude is known to be . . . inconsistent. Perhaps I should go to l'Île des Zephyrs to make these inquiries."

Isabelle's chest was tight, but this needed to be her choice. "But I would feel much safer with you and your men here guarding me. Besides, Jean-Claude knows everyone in Windfall."

Vincent frowned at Jean-Claude but said, "You have a point."

In truth, Isabelle didn't like sending away the only person on board she truly trusted, but no one else was so well equipped to discover the traitor on l'Île des Zephyrs.

CHAPTER

Seven

Jean-Claude shifted from foot to foot and tried not to look nervous as Don Divelo produced a key from a ring under his sash and unlocked the iron grate that guarded the face of the full-length mirror in his cabin aboard the escort ship the *Lanza*. Any unwelcome Glasswalker trying to emerge would have to squeeze through that narrow grid to be able to manifest.

Jean-Claude glowered at his sallow reflection. Asking to be taken through the mirror had seemed like a good idea at the time, but as the heat of inspiration cooled, phrases like "lost between mirrors" and "died from the shock" leaked in. Mirrors were just things of glass and silver; one should not be able to step through them and end up somewhere else.

"Do not worry, señor; I will not drop you," Don Divelo said, replacing the key on its gold chain around his neck.

Vincent smiled. "If monsieur is too afraid to go, I can send a real man to take his place."

"An empty threat, monsieur," Jean-Claude growled.

Isabelle's face looked waxen but she said, "I have full confidence in Jean-Claude's courage and ability."

And for that alone, Jean-Claude would walk through fire . . . or mirrors. Or mirrors on fire, for that matter. "Let's get this over with. What happens next?"

Don Divelo raised himself to his most authoritative height, his bountiful midriff nearly cresting the sash around his waist. "It is said that Cerberus Cortez, the Secondborn King of Aragoth, could pass his true flesh through a mirror, split his reflected self in parts so as to be many places at once, and even pass through his reflection on water. Alas, but those arts are lost to us. Even so, what remains is still the most remarkable sorcery in all the world.

"I will take the reflection of your true essence to le Château des Zephyrs. Your corpus, the part of you that lives and breathes, that eats and shi—er, drinks, shall perforce remain behind. Your espejismo, the part of you that thinks and acts, will manifest on the other side, where it shall emerge from the mirror to walk about as if it was made of flesh and blood. Yet it will not be flesh and blood. To you, everything will appear to be backward. While you are there, you should refrain from eating or drinking, as the part of you that does the digesting is here, and you cannot bring back anything you did not take with you. This makes food problematic."

Vincent murmured, "But will anyone recognize him without a wine sack in his hand?"

Jean-Claude ignored Vincent's jibe; he'd worked hard to maintain his intoxicated reputation and was glad to know it was holding up. The journey ahead, though, filled him with trepidation and he fought the urge to hunch. "What must I do?" The less time he had to think about having his soul ripped out, the better.

"Take my hand, close your eyes, and allow yourself to be pulled. Do not hold your breath. Remember, the part of you that breathes is staying here." He held out his hand.

"Then how am I supposed to talk?" Jean-Claude said, stalling in spite of himself. Sometimes people didn't come back from these trips. Or they came back insane.

"Air will still go in and out; you just won't assimilate it." He took Jean-Claude's wavering hand, said, "Close your eyes," and touched the mirror. "And don't panic."

Jean-Claude closed his eyes, but not before he caught a glimpse of Don Divelo going very still while his corpulent reflection detached itself from the face of the mirror and drifted backward into some deeper space. It kept hold of Jean-Claude's reflection and tugged.

—

Two sailors caught Jean-Claude's body, preventing him from falling as his spirit departed. Isabelle stared in fascination as Don Divelo's espejismo towed Jean-Claude's out of the mirror frame, both drifting like a pair of windblown ghosts. She rushed to the mirror and peered into it as if it were a window but saw only the reflection of the room, sans the two travelers.

The sailors ensconced Jean-Claude and Don Divelo in chairs designed for the purpose of supporting Glasswalker sorcerers during their out-of-body wanderings. Jean-Claude's face, normally elastic and expressive, sagged like wet linen without the animating force of his personality. Leaning back in the chair, his eyes closed and his arms folded, he most greatly resembled a corpse. Isabelle touched his cheek to assure herself he still lived.

Noxious worry seeped into her mind. Had she sent him off to die in the strange and terrifying world between the mirrors, or to be murdered in some back alley in Windfall? What if he encountered Thornscar?

But Jean-Claude would be very offended if he knew how much she worried about him. He was a King's Own Musketeer, after all, and though he wrapped his pride in sackcloth and rolled it in the mud, it was still precious to him.

Yet even if he came back triumphant, with Thornscar's heart in a jar and all her enemies laid low, she was still going to lose him. By delivering her safely to her wedding, his tarnished honor would get a new shine, and noble marriages were always a good excuse for handing out medals and citations. She had no doubt le roi would recall Jean-Claude to his service and deploy him on some other important errand. She'd probably never see him again. The mere thought of that made her feel hollow as a dried-up well.

Yet maybe Jean-Claude would attend some other birth, rescue some other infant, succor some other child. Maybe somebody else needed him even more than she did. Isabelle closed her eyes and let go the stale breath of selfishness. When the time came, she would have to be brave enough to share.

—

Having his reflection torn from his body felt to Jean-Claude like being peeled out of his skin and dragged through cold, gritty, metallic butter. The stuff oozed into every orifice he owned and a few that he assumed had been invented for the purpose. Against the advice of his porter, he held his breath.

Jean-Claude wasn't sure how long the passage lasted, or if it lasted any time at all. Was there any distance between the mirrors, or did the concept of space even apply?

Then he encountered the barrier. It felt like having his face pressed against a frozen sheet of silk, cold and smooth. He dented it, and it tried to deform him.

"Press hard." Don Divelo's voice seeped into his awareness without passing his ears.

Jean-Claude pushed, though he had nothing to push against; he willed himself forward. The fabric enveloped him, squeezing him, oozing through him as he crossed through it.

Chill, dry air slapped his face. He had almost forgotten what air felt like. He gasped. Air passed his lips but felt dead in his lungs, though he did not feel he was suffocating.

"You can open your eyes now," Divelo said, patting him on the shoulder.

Jean-Claude cracked an eye and found himself in a weirdly familiar room. Familiar because it was the mirror-gate room at the Château des Zephyrs. Weird because everything was skewed in his vision, stretched on one side and compressed on the other.

"Now I know what vomit feels like," Jean-Claude said. "Why is everything lopsided?"

"A peculiar effect of perception, que? Your dominant eye has moved to the opposite side, so everything is distorted, and of course your perceptions of left and right are reversed."

Indeed the room's one barred window was on the opposite side from where Jean-Claude remembered it. Two comfortable wing chairs sat opposite the window, and a locked door—the hinges were on the wrong side—stood across from the mirror. Jean-Claude faced the mirror and saw that he, or rather his espejismo, had no reflection. The lack of it made him shudder. He turned to Don Divelo, but the man was not just distorted but distinctly taller and leaner. His gelatinous girth had been compacted into a solid column.

"You look . . . different," Jean-Claude ventured.

"As do you," said Don Divelo. "It's called soul distortion. Your free reflection is shaped not just by your physical body but by your inner nature."

Which implied Don Divelo's inner nature was strong and solid instead of flabby. Such a distortion could equally well represent vanity.

Jean-Claude asked, "What do I look like?"

Don Divelo buffed his palms against each other. "Hmmm . . . I would have to say, lupine."

Jean-Claude crossed his eyes trying to see if he had a wolflike snout, but it looked just like his nose to him.

"How much can you change?" he asked. "If you can change completely, you could pretend to be anybody."

The changes are mostly small and involuntary, though you can control them somewhat with practice. Most of us develop an ideal that we sculpt over time."

"I don't like it," Jean-Claude said. There were many things going on in his mind that he didn't want on his face.

"You will get used to it in time," Don Divelo said. "It's easier if you concentrate on something else, like finding your rival's agent."

Indeed, having a mission could help one overcome all sorts of distractions. Jean-Claude tried the door and found it locked, to prevent uninvited Glasswalkers from emerging into the château at will. There was a bellpull, presumably to summon a servant to identify an unexpected visitor before giving them access.

"I do not wish to be seen," Jean-Claude said.

Don Divelo's eyebrows lifted, making coinlike discs of his mirrored eyes. "Why not? Surely the Comte des Zephyrs ought to know his daughter's ship has been attacked."

Jean-Claude made an emphatic cutting gesture with his left, or rather, his right hand. "The person I am looking for is surely a member of des Zephyrs's court. Bringing this to the comte's attention will only alert the prey to his danger." Better by far if he could get out of the château without being detected. The trail he sought began in town at the docks, where a mirror had been added to Isabelle's luggage.

Don Divelo's eyebrows beetled. "How do you know he was a member of the court?"

"Several reasons, but mostly because he had an unscored, full-length mirror to hand for the purpose. Those things are rare and expensive here."

Don Divelo made a scornful noise. "In Aragoth, it is considered an honor for every household of any worth to keep and maintain a mirror for the use of their noble masters."

Jean-Claude bit his tongue on a tart retort about the honor of being forced to enable others to spy on oneself—he needed the fat bastard to carry him back to his body—and said, "Perhaps the Aragoth who is behind this did not realize how rare such mirrors are in l'Empire Céleste. It is certainly not a question that I can answer from in here."

"Very well. Stand away from the door." He approached the bellpull.

"Wait. What will you do while I am gone? And how will I find you again?"

"I will speak with Isabelle's father regarding the details of his family's attendance at his daughter's wedding. When you are ready to return—and you must return before your real body suffers from dehydration, exhaustion, or hunger—simply tap a mirror, any mirror, and I will know where you are and come fetch you back to the ship."

Jean-Claude pointed to the mirror from which they had emerged. "This is the only unscored mirror that I know of."

"Scoring works because it breaks up the reflection and fractures the speculum loci; there is no contiguous space big enough for a Glasswalker to manifest. But right now you have no reflection and I don't need to manifest to pull you through."

"Good to know. And, purely for academic interest, mind you, what happens if someone stabs this body in the back?" Whoever had placed the mirror aboard the ship likely had other swords at his disposal.

"Your body might live, for a time, but without the part that thinks."

Jean-Claude grunted understanding. He stood with his back to the wall next to the door. Don Divelo tugged the bellpull. Shortly, footsteps approached and a shadow darkened the lozenge-shaped window in the door.

"Ah, Don Divelo." Jean-Claude recognized the chamberlain's voice. Keys rattled in the lock, and the door glided open on well-oiled hinges. "Welcome to Château des Zephyrs. We were not expecting you."

Jean-Claude's thoughts thrilled with anticipation, but he could not feel his faraway heart racing or his blood thrumming. It was damnably disconcerting not to be able to feel excited.

Don Divelo stepped smoothly through the doorway. "I did not anticipate you would, but I thought the comte might like to discuss the details of his attendance at his daughter's wedding . . ."

The door eased shut again. Jean-Claude slid the blade of his main gauche between the strike plate and the bolt. The chamberlain turned his key in the lock and swore quietly when the bolt refused to slide home. Jean-Claude grabbed the door handle and leaned back, keeping the door pulled shut as the chamberlain gave it a tentative tug. *Go away!*

"Is something amiss?" Don Divelo asked.

The chamberlain gave the door another tug. "Ah, apparently not."

Jean-Claude sagged against the door and waited until the footfalls receded, then he peeked through the window, eased the door open, and slipped out.

Escaping the château, with its white marble halls, labyrinthine servants' corridors, tall rooms, and wide balconies, was not as easy as it should have been. More than once, Jean-Claude got himself turned around in a space that should have been familiar. Descending the acropolis and navigating the tangle of narrow, backward streets was even more awkward, but he forged on to the taproom of the Bosun's Ballast, or rather the "Bosun's Ballast" as the sign above the door insisted on proclaiming.

The place still smelled of spilled ale and stale straw, but it was leaning the opposite direction from how Jean-Claude remembered it. The number of drunk sailors passed out in the corner seemed to have swelled on a tide of incoming naval vessels.

"What ho, demoiselle," Jean-Claude said. "A pie and pint for His Majesty's finest."

Demoiselle Planchette turned and squinted at him with beady eyes. "His Majesty's finest are shoring up me foundations, but what are you doing here?"

Jean-Claude settled at the bar. There were few patrons at this time of day, and so he had the lady all to himself. "Ah, mademoiselle, it is a long story, and filled with shame, but the pain of its recollection would be much mitigated by a pint."

She poured, and he began with, "As far as anyone is to know . . ." Sloshing the beer around, but not drinking it, he spun a tale about a drunken binge, missing Isabelle's ship, and being left behind. ". . . And so I sit before you a defeated soul, doomed to the everlasting torment of my duty failed."

Planchette shook her head and spoke sotto voce. "What a load of chicken droppings."

Jean-Claude placed a hand across his breast and contrived to sound offended. "Madame, I have never dropped a chicken in my life."

Planchette waved this away. "Oh, don't worry. I'll cover your sorry arse with the threadbare blanket it wants, but I saw you get on that ship, all bright and blue as a robin's egg in your musketeer's uniform, and so did plenty of other people. And now you're back, and your sword's on the wrong hip, and the feather in your cap is on the wrong side. My grampa, he was Aragothic, so I know all about what Glasswalkers kin do. What's really going on?" A sudden look of concern crossed her face. "Nawt's happened to the princess, has it?"

Jean-Claude patted her hand. "Her Highness is fine, thanks to yours truly, and I want to keep it that way. To that end, I'm here to see a man about a mirror . . ."

—

Restless in Jean-Claude's absence and in no mood to be cooped up in her cabin, Isabelle poked her nose into the chart room, where the fire had started. A sudden sucking chill met her at the threshold, turning her breath to frost and bringing goose pimples to her skin. Rainwater and charred wood made a frigid slurry on the floor. At the very center of the room, an enormous cold had frozen the water into a lumpy sheet of gray ice entombing a scorched and twisted stump of bronze and brass that had once been the ship's orrery.

Even more than the aetherkeel, it was the invention of the alchemical orrery, with its simulacrasphere filled with denatured lumin gas and sympathy engine, that had enabled the exploration and colonization of the deep sky. Everything on the deep sky moved and whirled on currents of air, making traditional maps useless for navigation. Only an orrery loaded with properly calibrated chartstone shards could be certain of its position relative to its origin and destination.

Unfortunately, as this orrery's shattered sphere and cracked pedestal attested, hypervolatile lumin was extremely explosive. Presumably Thornscar had come into this room—had he looked for Isabelle in her cabin first?—then he had cracked the simulacrasphere; the lumin had sprayed into the room. He had set a light to it, mayhap while running out the door. There had been an explosion and a fireball, but Santiago's quick thinking had extinguished the fire before it could spread. The rain cloud had put out the fire, but the remaining gas expanding from the cracked reservoir had frozen the water solid. Fire and ice.

Carlos, the *Santa Anna*'s navigator, was circling the damaged orrery and pawing at broken pieces with a badgerlike determination. Isabelle resolved to disturb him as little as possible, but she wanted to get a good look at the shattered device. Something about the whole sequence of events felt unbalanced, like a complex equation missing an unobvious constant.

She had spent a great deal of time researching the alchemical properties of aether, and while she had no practical experience working with full-scale alchemical machinery, she had detonated quite enough of her small-scale experiments to become acquainted with its capricious nature. Or, as Jean-Claude would have said, "It's just not empirical philosophy unless something freezes, catches fire, throws sparks, dissolves into slime, or explodes."

And yet all those pyrotechnic failures had left her with a rather clear and well-defined idea of the damage explosive aether was capable of inflicting. Therefore, once panic had worn off and she'd turned her head to the numbers, this sabotage just hadn't summed up. The amount of aether in the simulacrasphere at the temperature and pressure at which it should have been operating would have caused a really impressive bang and a fireball, enough to blow doors open and ignite paper and cloth, as evidenced by the scorched sails, but it had clearly not been enough to blow the ship apart or set fire to the thick wooden structure. So had this been a failure of concept or execution?

Isabelle eased across the floor, dancing from dry spot to dry spot, to get a better look at the orrery's broken stem.

"Princesa!" Carlos yelped, popping up from his task of collecting shattered formulae glass. "Come away from there."

Isabelle froze in her tracks and looked around to see if she had missed any death traps. She saw none.

"Why?" she asked.

Carlos looked flummoxed by this question, as if the ship's figurehead had come to life and spoken. "It's not right. You . . . might get dirty."

Such were the excuses conjured up when she trespassed on a man's domain, no matter how feeble his claim to the territory. It was infuriating that the pressure of his disapproval actually backed her up a step.

She regained her balance. "I just want to have a look," she said, seeking a justification with legs. "I've always found clockworks so beautiful."

Carlos stood up and made a clumsy bow, making a sweeping gesture toward the door. "Princesa. Please . . . I am really very busy."

"I can see that," Isabelle said, stooping to pick up a section of the fractured viewing sphere. "Perhaps you would care to explain exactly what you are doing."

Carlos tugged at his collar, clearly unnerved to have her hovering over his work. "It's . . . complicated."

"Hmmmm . . ." Isabelle waved the formulae glass over the open throat of the orrery. It didn't glow, so there was no more aether escaping.

"Highness, what are you doing?" Carlos asked. He came toward her, perhaps with the thought of escorting her away, but he moved slower and slower the closer he got, the proverbial hare unable to catch the tortoise.

"It's complicated," Isabelle retorted. She peered down the device's neck, through a tangled mass of broken gears and fragmented complexity-matrix beads. It took her a moment to discern the reality of a device she had hitherto seen only in smuggled drawings by candlelight. There was the analogical multi-switch whirring away, and the cryodynamic manifold hissing softly. The actual algorithmic engine of the device seemed to be intact. All those delicate pieces; the explosion just hadn't been that powerful.

She muttered, "So the simulacrascope went off with a bang that cracked the aetherfeed, but judging by the amount of ice that was deposited, most of the gas escaped after the fire was extinguished?" The damage could have been worse if Thornscar had allowed more gas to escape before he ignited it. Had Kantelvar's interruption startled him into making a mistake, or had he just not known enough about simulacraspheres and aether? And how had he set it off without getting caught in the blast?

"That is . . . substantially correct," Carlos said. "But how does . . . do you know so much about aetherscopes?"

Isabelle was recalled to her social obligation of ignorance. "Oh, I don't know much, really, but when my family had naval officers in for dinner, I always did get stuck at the end of the table with the navigator and the keel master, and men do insist on talking about work." It was a sad but useful fact that all but the most suspicious or perspicacious of men could blot out any memory of her intelligence if only she gave them permission.

A rap on the door frame drew her attention, and she turned to find Vincent standing there. He produced the requisite bow and said, "Highness."

"Vincent," she said warily.

"May I have a word?" he said, leading her from the chart room onto the deck, where they could be easily observed without being easily overheard, thanks to the wind.

Isabelle checked her posture and fixed a neutral expression on her face, preparing to be berated for some failing. "Yes?"

He bobbed his head, a calculated fraction of a bow. "Highness, it occurs to me that, in addition to sending your, ah, minion to dash about the Île des Zephyrs in search of the saboteur's conspirator, there is another well of information from which we might draw."

"And what would that be?" she asked. She had no personal reason to dislike Vincent, but he was her father's man—dangerous to her autonomy even when he defended her person. She had to assume every word she spoke to him would be relayed back to her father.

Vincent held out a hand, palm up, as if offering a gift. "Your bloodhollow."

Isabelle was appalled. "Marie?"

Vincent nodded. "I am given to understand that bloodhollows see everything, hear everything, and remember what they witness with absolute clarity. They don't have personalities to get in the way."

A resentful frost formed around Isabelle's heart. "I am aware of that." The comte had often used Marie's eidetic memory as a bludgeon against Isabelle.

"If this Thornscar or one of his accomplices crossed your path any time between your betrothal and your embarkation, if they were doing any reconnaissance, as they should have been, the bloodhollow may have seen them. If we were to question her, or better yet have your father sift her memory—"

"No," Isabelle snapped.

"But she may have seen something without knowing it."

"She sees *everything* without knowing it," Isabelle said. Then she made a soothing gesture as if to soften the sharpness of her words. "I mean, you are right. She might have seen something. I will question her, but I will not involve the comte."

Vincent looked perplexed. "It would be more efficient. Your father—"

"The comte is a monster," Isabelle said. In her anger, words came more easily but were harder to control. "A murderer of children and a defiler of souls. Tell me if you can what crime a thirteen-year-old girl could possibly have committed to deserve being turned into a bloodhollow."

Vincent took a step back from her in alarm, and Isabelle forced herself to dismount her tower of rage. He was not necessarily an evil man, and he was certainly no fool. There was no point in alienating him; quite the opposite.

"I know you work for the comte, not me, but he is dying, Breaker take him. Yet when he is dust, you will still need an employer, and I will be, at the very least, a princesa of Aragoth." If she could winnow his loyalty away from her father, that would be an unprecedented victory.

"Do you not think that your husband will provide for your security?" Vincent asked.

Isabelle's mouth worked around some mumbles as she fought to articulate the idea blooming in her mind. "I am certain that he will, but a royal woman needs someone under her command who is not beholden to anyone else, even her husband." As much as she loathed the idea of setting someone else in Jean-Claude's place, she must plan for the contingency and be well out in front of it.

Poor Príncipe Julio; he was supposed to be the most important thing on her mind right now, but instead he seemed to be receding into the background of her unfolding crisis.

"You have a very keen mind," Vincent said. "It is too bad you were not born a man; you would make a wonderful officer."

Irritation rose in Isabelle's mind, but she stopped it from expressing itself anywhere but in a tightening around her eyes. Why was he baiting her? Was he really that much of a boor? No, he was feeling out a potential employer. She rallied her words again. "I am already malformed and unhallowed; being male is a handicap I can live without. Besides, I would much rather be in the business of appointing wonderful officers than be one."

Vincent settled back, his expression still closed, and said, "You put an interesting offer on the table, but I cannot pick it up while I am still under contract."

"It remains there for the time being," Isabelle said. "But now I must speak with Marie."

"I shall accompany you."

Isabelle held up her hand to forestall him. "I thank you for the offer, but no. Interrogating a bloodhollow is not like interrogating a normal person. Extra care must be taken so as not to damage them."

"But they have no feelings," Vincent said.

"Precisely. It is much easier to injure someone who cannot feel pain than someone who can. Rest assured, though, I have a great deal of practice at this. Her memories are just piled up, twelve years of unsifted experience in layers like silt. And if you go tromping around in it, all you get is clouds of mud."

"I still think I should—"

"No!" Isabelle railed against the automatic male assumption that anything she might do, they could do better, even if they had no experience with it whatsoever. Jean-Claude would never have doubted Isabelle's assessment.

She scraped Vincent off and entered her cabin. Marie had been put to bed, kept warm against the high-altitude chill. Isabelle roused her and performed the ritual bruise checks, attended the bodily waste functions, directed the consumption of food. Could Marie be brought back to herself, guided out of the dark pit into which she'd been condemned all these years? Kantelvar . . . hadn't promised success, but he claimed to have had success before, a greater miracle than anyone else had ever boasted.

Will she be sane? Will she thank me, or despise me for so enabling and prolonging her suffering? If so, at least she will hate me of her own free will.

Once she was satisfied of Marie's health, Isabelle drew heavy curtains across the portholes, stuffed bedding in the crack beneath the door, and snuffed the alchemical lanterns. Darkness filled the room. *And there can be no shadows without light.* The comte would not be able to interrupt.

The skip's rocking and the impenetrable dark combined to make Isabelle's gut a little queasy, but she schooled her voice to calm and soothing tones and said, "Marie, I'm going to ask you a few questions. If you do not know the answer, say, 'I don't know.'"

Carefully and gently she went, so as not to scatter and scramble whatever was left of Marie's consciousness. "I'm going to be asking you about things you have observed. I'm going to be asking you about people . . ."

—

Night was just wrapping her shawl across the shoulders of the hills behind the Château des Zephyrs when Lord—soon to be Comte—Guillaume and his companions cantered into the yard on fine coursing steeds. They laughed gaily amongst themselves, expounding upon, and grossly inflating, the events of the day's hunt.

Jean-Claude, sitting on a low stone wall before the front gate, could not help but notice they had only two grouse between the six of them. His dear departed mother would have clubbed him if he'd spent all day hunting and come back with such a paltry catch, but these men had never in their lives hunted to stave off hunger, or grubbed in the dirt, or chopped wood until their backs ached, nor did they care for those who did . . . but those were old complaints and not important to the task at hand.

A pack of stable boys appeared from behind the house and swarmed round the horses to help the riders dismount and take their steaming steeds away. Jean-Claude rose and ambled toward the approaching party. "Good evening, my lord."

It took Guillaume a moment to pick Jean-Claude out of the crowd of stable hands. When he did, his brow pinched in surprise and suspicion, but by the time Jean-Claude reached his side, he'd propped up a practiced smile, the sort one wore when preparing to dodge. "Good evening, my good musketeer. What are you . . . I thought you had taken ship with dizzy Izzy."

Jean-Claude smiled grimly even while evolving plans for making Guillaume pay for that slight. "I have returned, and I am on His Majesty's business."

"I . . . see. In that case, how may I serve His Majesty?"

"He would have a word with you, personally, on a matter of some delicacy. Walk with me." Jean-Claude tipped his hat at Guillaume's companions—"Gentlemen"—and then strode off across the field, leaving Guillaume to catch up, which he did in a huff of unaccustomed effort.

"What is this about?" Guillaume asked impatiently.

"It is a matter of grave importance that impacts the future of l'Île des Zephyrs and indeed the whole empire."

Guillaume scoffed. "As if His Majesty would entrust you with important business."

Despite his bravado, Guillaume had a tendency to twitch, and his bloodshadow rippled in agitation. Jean-Claude might have been the town drunk, but he remained a King's Own Musketeer, and interfering with a King's Own Musketeer in the discharge of his lawful duty was a capital offense.

Jean-Claude led Guillaume down a slope into an orchard along the very same path he had walked with Isabelle just days ago. The buds had burst and leaves yearned skyward. "My master is very interested in knowing from whom precisely you received instructions to place a mirror aboard Princess Isabelle's ship."

Guillaume looked genuinely surprised. "Eh? I don't know what you're talking about."

"Really? I have very reliable information that says the mirror was taken aboard at your direction." Planchette had told him about a longshoreman, who had told him about a linkboy, who had told him about Guillaume's attaché. "It was such a thoughtful gift that the sender deserves an appropriate thank-you in return."

Guillaume hesitated, as if struck by a thought, then shook his head. "You are mistaken, monsieur. Now, if you will excuse me—"

"I will not," Jean-Claude said, grabbing Guillaume by the scruff of his collar and impelling him deeper into the plum grove. "The mirror came from your household."

"Unhand me!" Guillaume twisted. Jean-Claude obliged him by shoving him into a pile of cut brush so that he tripped and landed on his backside.

Guillaume's face burned. "Cur!" His bloodshadow lunged for Jean-Claude but broke up, confused, when it encountered the interlaced shadows of the orchard's branches and leaves in the lengthening dark.

"I don't think your pet can find me in this tangle of darkness. Pity." After seeing his first execution in the Pit of Stains, Jean-Claude had dedicated countless hours to researching and devising ways to defeat bloodshadows. Obscuring one's shadow in a tangle of shadows worked unless the sorcerer had the presence of mind to sift and shift all the shadows apart. Le roi could do it, but Guillaume was not that dedicated to his craft.

Jean-Claude drew his rapier and set the tip against Guillaume's throat, just above the knot of his cravat. "Who told you to put that mirror aboard?"

Guillaume tried to crab-walk away. "I don't know what you're talking about!"

Jean-Claude forced him onto his back. "This is not a good time to cultivate ignorance. Its rewards tend to be empty. Bled dry, in fact."

"Breaker take you!" Guillaume squeaked. "I don't know."

"If not you . . . then it must have been your lovely wife."

"No!" Guillaume shouted, and the trees rattled as his sorcery thrashed at their shadows. A lucky swipe brushed the shadow of Jean-Claude's hat and sent it tumbling from his head. To Jean-Claude's surprise, the hat evaporated like a puff of fog before it hit the ground. So what would happen if he dropped his rapier, or fired a bullet?

He slapped those questions aside and pressed his advantage with Guillaume. "I see I have struck a nerve. How noble of you, trying to protect your lady. Or perhaps you are only trying to protect yourself; as her lord and master, you could be implicated in her treason."

"Treason? How is a mirror treason?"

"Aha! So you admit it."

"I do not! She is innocent."

"Which means you are guilty," Jean-Claude said. He doubted a creature like Guillaume was actually capable of love, and the malfeasant Arnette was not a woman to inspire devotion, but there was some loyalty in Guillaume's heart, and was that not a virtue? And was it not a sin to pervert a virtue into a weapon? Isabelle would not be proud of him for this, or for many other deeds. His only solace was that she need never know of the bones he had broken in her service.

Jean-Claude summoned his coolest demeanor. "Your wife is of du Troisville, and the Duc du Troisville has extensive trading interests in Aragoth. Someone in Aragoth asked her father to instruct her to put that mirror aboard ship. I believe I shall have to ask her who that was. I imagine le roi will not be pleased with the answer. Perhaps he will put her to the flame and attaint the whole line."

"Because of a mirror? Madness!"

"Not because of the mirror itself, but because of the Glasswalker assassin who came through it and tried to murder Isabelle."

Guillaume's face went waxy in the failing light. "No!" he said; defeat this time, not denial.

"Fortunately for you, you will probably be able to deny knowledge and escape fatal punishment, though it may cause le roi to reconsider the distribution of your father's estates upon his death. He wouldn't want them falling into the hands of a man who couldn't even prevent his wife from committing treason."

"It wasn't treason. It was supposed to be a gift. She didn't know!" Guillaume blurted. Three lies in a row, Jean-Claude suspected, and if finding out who Isabelle's Aragothic enemies were weren't so important, Jean-Claude would have nailed Guillaume to a wall for his part in the scheme. Alas, mortal justice was as imperfect as divine justice was ineffable.

"Then give me the name of the Aragoth who made this request. Speak truth and your wretched wife will never lay eyes on me. Lie to me and there is no place in the deep sky you will be able to run from me."

"But . . . How do I know you'll keep your word?"

Jean-Claude made a mirthless smile and bent the skin of Guillaume's throat with the tip of his rapier. "You'll just have to trust me."

CHAPTER

Eight

Isabelle stood in the *Santa Anna*'s hold, beneath a single swaying alchemical lantern that made her shadow weave drunkenly across the narrow space. Vincent, two guards, and one handmaid hovered in attendance while she examined Thornscar's empty mirror frame. The shattered glass had all been swept away and disposed of with elaborate ceremonies meant to ward off bad luck, but the empty frame had been left in place and secured with its original rope and canvas veil.

"So, except for the mirror being gone, that's what it looked like when Thornscar was passing through it?" she asked Vincent.

"Not precisely. The fabric was pushed aside."

Isabelle grabbed the fabric and tugged it to the side. This took effort because of the way the ropes crisscrossed the frame. She circled the frame and looked through it from the back.

"What is the significance of this inquiry?" Vincent asked.

Isabelle brought two fingers down on the rope with a chopping motion. "Why didn't he cut the rope? It would have been easier than fighting with the canvas."

"Perhaps he was only half emerged from the mirror and couldn't get at his blade," Vincent suggested.

"Did he have a blade?" Isabelle asked. "Did you see one? Marie did not." As it turned out Marie had seen the invader as he rushed up the stair. He'd shoved her into the storeroom and slammed the door on her. Very strange behavior for an assassin.

Vincent frowned. "He was already most of the way through the mirror when I got here, and the light was bad, worse than it is now."

"But you didn't see a blade?"

"No, I did not," he admitted grudgingly.

"And he clubbed Kantelvar rather than stabbing him."

"So it would seem, but why is this important?"

"Because I find it hard to imagine a man intent on murdering a well-defended woman on a ship full of well-armed marines would make his bid without so much as a knife. Even I have a knife." She tapped the maiden-blade on her belt. Isabelle despised the weapon's loathsome official purpose but kept the blade and used it to cut canvases for painting and to core apples.

Isabelle asked, "And after he squeezed out of the mirror, what did he do?"

"He went looking for you. He didn't find you in your cabin, so he went next door to the chart room and tried to set the ship on fire using the orrery, but Kantelvar interrupted him. He subdued Kantelvar, ignited the orrery, and came back down here, where he was cornered and hopefully killed."

Isabelle folded her arms and drummed her fingers against her upper arm. "Your analysis matches the facts."

"But you do not agree with it," Vincent surmised.

"Why did he go above looking for me?" She gestured to the hold around her. "Here we have wooden crates, bales of fine des Zephyrs wool, ingredients for a magnificent fire. Why not just step out of the mirror, set the hold on fire, and then step back out again? Much simpler, safer for him, and more likely to work."

"There are five ships in this fleet," Vincent said. "He probably wanted to ascertain for certain that you were on this one. If he just set the ship on fire, he'd have had no way of knowing if he'd actually gotten you, especially since the first thing anyone would do in case of a fire would be to get you on a launch. Or, perhaps, it was meant to be personal. He wanted to kill you himself as a proxy for the royal family. In either case, he couldn't find you, and his time grew short, so he improvised with the closest tool to hand."

Isabelle suppressed a shudder at this dire idea. If she were the type to take afternoon naps instead of badgering the captain to show her the inner marvels of his ship, she might have been in that room—

"Highness!" called a cabin boy from the far end of the hold. "Don Divelo and the musketeer have returned! They are safe. They're being ferried over from the *Lanza*."

A knot of tension eased from Isabelle's heart. Thank the Builder Jean-Claude was safe. She could never tell him how much she worried about him. To be afraid for a brave man was an insult to his abilities that could cripple his heart.

—

Isabelle, Vincent, Santiago's whole command crew, and the captains of the remaining escort ships crowded into the reserve officers' cabin to hear what Jean-Claude and Don Divelo had to report. The press of bodies warmed the room and woke the unwashed smells that clung to nearly everyone, but even that stink would not have prevented Isabelle from rushing up to hug Jean-Claude. Alas, the propriety of the audience forbade any physical reassurance of his well-being.

Jean-Claude doffed his plumed hat, eyed it speculatively, then bowed toward Isabelle and the head of the table. "Greetings, Highness, Captain. Please tell me you have some wine."

"I imagine you are quite parched," Santiago said, and a goblet of wine was delivered into Jean-Claude's hands.

Jean-Claude took a mouthful, then wiped his mouth on his sleeve. "Gah! Someone might have mentioned that mirror passage tastes like tomatoes boiled in ammonia."

"It takes different people in different ways," Don Divelo said, sounding anything but displeased. "Some believe that the experience reflects the traveler's character."

Isabelle asked Jean-Claude, "Are you well?"

Jean-Claude brushed at his arms as if dislodging spiders. "As well as any man may be after he's been turned inside out and dragged through cold, gritty mud. Now I know what a hide feels like when it is tanned, and I lost my hat." He held the hat up again and glowered at it suspiciously. "It disappeared beyond the mirror, but it was on my head when I got back."

Don Divelo said, "You lost your hat's reflection. When next you stand before a mirror with your hat on you will feel it on your head but not see it in your reflection."

Jean-Claude shuddered like a damp dog dislodging water and muttered imprecations about sorcery. Someone pushed a chair toward Isabelle, but she declined it. There was no way for everyone to sit down, and being the only one to sit would put her head at the level of other people's bellies.

Isabelle said, "Jean-Claude, pray tell us what you discovered."

Jean-Claude held out his cup for a refill and got it, but he refrained from further imbibing. He said, "Thanks to Don Divelo's excellent guidance, I was able to track down the person who placed the mirror aboard this ship. After much hard work and diligence, I extracted from this miscreant the name of the mastermind behind the plot to assassinate Princess Isabelle. His name is Duque Ramon de la Gallegos Diego."

A surprised murmur quickly rose to a buzz as everyone started talking at once. Isabelle was acquainted with Diego's name. He was King Carlemmo's cousin by some degree, but she knew almost nothing else about him.

"But that makes no sense," Don Divelo said, quieting the other Aragoths by dint of his noble status and courtly experience.

"Why not?" Isabelle asked.

Divelo said, "Duque Diego is a member of the queen's faction." At Isabelle's uncomprehending look, he added, "Alejandro, the elder prince, is the heir apparent, but he is not Queen Margareta's son. If he ascends the throne, she loses influence and so does everyone in her faction. The only way Diego wins is if Julio takes the throne, which he has no chance of doing if he is not married."

"Perhaps he does not object to the idea of marriage so much as the match that has been made," Vincent said.

"He has two daughters," Santiago said.

"But he does not want them married to Prince Julio," Divelo said. "Right now, the factions are about evenly balanced. If Diego married either of his daughters to Julio, that would bring him closer to Príncipe Julio, but it would add nothing to the weight of the faction. The ideal marriage must bring some extra weight to the queen's faction to tip the balance of power in her favor. Before Princess Isabelle's betrothal, it was assumed that Margareta would try to marry Julio to the daughter of one of her more powerful enemies and thus shift the balance of power. There were several of them just waiting for the right bribe to switch sides."

Isabelle's brows furrowed. "I was told that all the other candidates were unsuitable, too young, or too old, or too close in blood."

Divelo said, "In politics fault is where you find it. There were several women, second cousins, who might have been chosen, had they not been vetoed by the Temple."

"You mean Kantelvar?" Isabelle asked.

Divelo shrugged. "The bull came from the Omnifex. Whether Kantelvar wrested it out of him or not, I cannot say."

Jean-Claude said, "Seems to me, Isabelle brings the entire weight of l'Empire Céleste to the queen's faction."

Divelo raised one hand, palm up, and made a balancing gesture. "Perhaps, although I must say the choice . . . pardon me, Highness, but the choice of an outsider is still . . . controversial. If it played well, it might add weight, or it might cause the whole side to collapse."

"How does the king fit into all this?" Isabelle asked. "Whose side is he on?"

Don Divelo spent a moment rubbing his second chin before answering. "Until King Carlemmo fell ill, he seemed to favor Alejandro, or at least he tended to side with his elder son against his second wife on the occasions when their domestic disputes became political."

"And what about Príncipe Julio?" Isabelle asked. "Does he have a part, or is he merely a pawn to these greater players?"

Divelo shifted his great weight uneasily and said, "When Julio was first told of the arrangement of his marriage, he was . . ." Divelo groped for a sufficiently neutral term.

"Less than enthusiastic," Isabelle supplied; she was the only one in the room who politely could.

Divelo cleared his throat. "To be clear, he offered no disrespect to Your Highness, but he thought that the marital strategy his mother proposed was ill advised. He preferred a more conventional approach. Odd for a man who is so frequently unconventional, but he hasn't been the same since his accident, and he seems to have capitulated to his mother on that topic."

"What accident?" Isabelle asked, alarmed.

Divelo's eyebrows lifted. "His hunting accident, last Hoarwinter. Has nobody told you? He and his squire were out coursing red deer in the

Slatefinger mountains when they got separated from the hunting party and fell into a crevasse. The squire was killed and Julio was badly wounded, his leg smashed. By the time they got him out, he had the drowning lung. He lost part of his leg and much of his strength. It took him months to rise from bed, and the debility has made him more sullen and temperamental."

Isabelle was appalled. Was she the one being sold damaged goods? No, that was not fair. A missing leg did not make a man any less a man, any more than a wormfinger made her less a woman. Yet such an injury had to come as a great shock to a man's soul, especially for such a young man, two years her junior, who had not reached the natural apex of his physical prowess.

"I was told he was one of the greatest swordsmen in Aragoth," she said.

"Before the accident, perhaps," Divelo allowed. "Since then, he does not get about much. The leg, you see."

Isabelle shook her head, trying to rearrange her as yet unsubstantiated imaginings of her future husband. Why hadn't Kantelvar told her this? Sadly, the artifex was not here to be questioned.

"This is beside the point," Vincent said. "Assuming that the musketeer has not been misled, the question becomes how to deal with Duque Diego."

Divelo said, "Unless you have more proof than the testimony of this musketeer, I suggest diplomacy."

"We should warn Queen Margareta," Isabelle said. If the queen was Isabelle's chief advocate in Aragoth, she had to be apprised of this treachery within her own ranks. She addressed Don Divelo directly. "May I trouble you to carry this news to the queen for me?"

Divelo considered that for an extended moment. "My duty is to the king, but I think, in this, your desire and his would be congruous. I shall attend to it immediately." He made a bobble that passed for a bow in the crowded chamber and then backed out the door.

The gathering broke up. Isabelle made farewells to the captains as they departed for their ships and then took herself to the galleon's quarterdeck to clear her head. There was more intrigue in Aragoth than she had imagined, and she had imagined a great deal. She needed to get to the bottom of Duque Diego, but she didn't have enough information to work with. Also, she had just impulsively sent her best source of information to be decanted first by a woman who apparently had Isabelle's betrothed under her majestic thumb. Though perhaps that was not such a bad thing; when Divelo came back, Isabelle could ask him what questions Margareta had posed to him.

Isabelle clipped herself to a line and leaned against the railing. The sun had disappeared beyond the clouded horizon and a million stars danced overhead. A million million. All around her, the deep sky closed in, milky clouds coalescing from the abyss below and spreading out in a great blanket until it seemed the *Santa Anna* sailed on a great lake of mist. The wind had lessened and the ship seemed to stroll rather than bound across the pearlescent surface.

In spite of the fire and the fear of the day, or perhaps because of it, the vision struck a silver chord in her breast. She stared into the distance, trying to drink in the tableau, to absorb it and be absorbed by it. She had looked into the sky many times. Sometimes she had cast her dreams across it to strange and distant lands. Sometimes she pondered its elemental composition and the organization of its aetheric forms. But never had she stood within it and seen it for itself, austere and beautiful, without need for interpretation or understanding.

"I could live here," she murmured.

"Princess," Jean-Claude called, making his way heavily up the stairs behind her.

She turned to see him clamp himself to the quarterdeck's forward railing.

"A word with you, if you please," he said. "And could you not stand so close to the edge?"

"I'm perfectly safe," she said, or at least as safe as she was ever likely to be with disaffected nobles and a homicidal sorcerer trying to kill her. But Jean-Claude clearly had no ship legs—he kept trying to fight the motion of the ship, as if he could force it to stay level by applying counter-pressure to every wobble—so she unclipped herself and glided to him, attaching herself instead to the mizzenmast.

In a low voice, she asked, "What else do you have to report that you avoided telling the council of captains?"

Jean-Claude fumbled with his belt clip and finally got it to attach to the safety line, then he looked her in the face and said, "Only one thing. It was your brother who put that mirror on the ship."

Isabelle was aghast. Even from Guillaume, she could scarcely believe it. "But why? Even if he loathes me, he has nothing to gain and everything to lose."

"I believe he was trying to do a favor for his wife, and I believe that she did not know the nature of what was planned. After all, who would trust

Arnette with such information? They were more concerned with winning favors from Duque Diego than with dispatching you."

"What did you do to him?" she asked, morbidly curious and terrified of the answer.

Jean-Claude grinned through the pall of sky sickness that obscured his usual good humor. "The very worst thing I could think of. I bested him in battle and then let him go. If he has the slightest sense at all, he'll try to distance himself from the whole matter. He certainly can't tell your father about it."

"And if he hadn't been my brother?" Isabelle asked.

Jean-Claude shrugged and tried to look insouciant. "I think these plots are tangled enough without confusing them with further suppositions."

Isabelle's mouth twisted in a non-smile at this transparent evasion, but she let the matter drop. Jean-Claude defended her with extreme prejudice, but there was no point in forcing him to confess how extreme.

⏤

Isabelle and her ladies had retired to her cabin for the night, though the day's excitement lingered and nobody seemed inclined to sleep. Five out of six women, including Marie, had exchanged dresses for nightgowns. The sixth, Valérie, was out strolling the deck with Vincent, much to the delight of the other ladies, who had been running low on gossip. Isabelle wondered if she shouldn't put a stop to the liaison or try to use it to bend Vincent to her service, but she knew how much she hated being used that way. If you couldn't gain someone's loyalty without twisting their affections, then you couldn't get it at all.

The ladies embroidered and chattered, making small talk and wild conjectures, while Isabelle immersed herself in a thick book of Aragothic history, which sadly consisted mostly of a chronology of battles, as if the only debates that mattered were the armed kind. There was some mention of marriages with an eye toward their territorial value, but nothing of any philosophical interest. Still, she dedicated herself to committing as much of it to memory as possible, as any responsible would-be queen ought.

"Would-be queen." Those words were fraught with complications that she had not even begun to unravel, not the least of which was that Aragoth already had, in Margareta, a queen who was relatively young, healthy, and ambitious. Divelo's description had painted a picture of a formidable woman who seemed intent on keeping power for herself rather than handing it over to her son. Of course, that was only Isabelle's interpretation of one man's opinion delivered during a discussion of a different topic.

So what did Margareta think of Isabelle? It occurred to Isabelle that one more reason Margareta might have chosen Isabelle as her son's bride was because, as a foreigner, she would be isolated, out of place, and easier to dominate. Or it could just be that Isabelle's own filial experience had given her an incredibly jaded view of parental relationships.

She'd left a porthole cracked open, and a chill breeze played across her naked arms in a tingling counterpoint to the heat of the alchemical lanterns that burned and buzzed over the desk. She held the book open with her right arm. Her wormfinger, unbound from any glove, curled and uncurled of its own volition, forever like a separate animal trapped in her flesh and striving to escape.

Returning her attention to the history book, she made a note to herself to be very careful when dealing with the Aragothic border lords, for they had long been at odds with their Célestial counterparts. During the century of occupation by the Skaladin hordes, Célestial barons had wasted no opportunity to gobble up Aragothic lands on the pretext of keeping them out of the hands of the heretics. Most of those territories l'Empire still held, even a hundred years after the Skaladin had been driven out.

She tapped her finger on the name of a province, El Bosque de Dolores, and tried to remember where she'd heard it before. Perhaps if the hour were not so late and the surface of her mind not so turbulent, the information would have come to her. According to the text, it had been wrested from l'Empire before the Skaladin invasion and was rightly proud of never having yielded to the endless enemy. There was a précis of a decisive battle, the death of someone called the Silver Baron, and then nothing much else. On the next page was the start of another war. She combed the fingers of her good hand through her short shock of unbound hair and tried to be interested.

A rapping on the door intruded into her thoughts. Valérie's voice squeezed through the cracks: "Highness. Don Divelo has returned, and he has brought Queen Margareta."

—

Flanked by Jean-Claude and Vincent, Isabelle paused outside Don Divelo's cabin door to catch her breath. She smoothed her hastily donned skirts, nudged the combs that held her white wig in place, made sure her veil was fixed, and tried to keep panic from her heart. She had anticipated a swift response to her ill news about Duque Diego, but she had not expected a visit from the queen herself. She had planned to present herself to her future royal in-laws with grace, dignity, and all due ceremony in one of Aragoth's fabled mirrored halls, not rushed, crushed, and crammed into Divelo's cabin aboard a man-o-war.

A guard in Aragoth's royal livery stood before the door. His eyes were Glasswalker silver. He said, in poor la Langue, "Leave weapons."

Vincent bristled. "I am Princess Isabelle's guard."

"I am Queen Margareta's," the guard rumbled.

Jean-Claude shrugged, handed over his rapier, and thankfully refrained from saying anything sharp. Vincent reluctantly followed suit.

The guard opened the door and announced, "La Princesa Isabelle."

Isabelle glided in, though she had to duck under the low lintel to do so.

The queen had taken the captain's chair as her throne. She wore full skirts of royal purple silk and satin, a like-colored bodice, and a short velvet jacket of a style Isabelle had no word for. Somewhere under there, a leviathanbone corset struggled mightily to keep an obviously matronly figure squeezed into a maidenly shape. Perhaps that was why she looked so dyspeptic . . . or perhaps the straining corset was soul distortion. Representing what state of mind? A silver net veiled her dark hair and every inch of her costume was festooned with constellations of silver embroidery, stitched opals, and river pearls so that she looked like a goddess of night. She also wore her golden coronet, tilted aggressively forward, making this an official state audience.

At her flanks stood two more royal guards, fully armed and armored with polished cuirasses of alchemetal steel, astronomically expensive but bulletproof. Before her, in courtly attendance, were all the remaining ship captains, their officers, and Don Divelo. No pickles had ever been packed so tightly.

Space was cleared for Isabelle, who curtsied demurely, eyes downcast, to Queen Margareta. She did her best not to droop, or worse, drip, in the sweltering dark. She fought with the nervous thickness in her chest and breathed, "Your Majesty. I am honored by your visit."

Margareta's voice was dry. "Really? I should think you would be terrified. So much of your future depends upon my goodwill, after all."

The queen's observation struck deep and sharp, like a needle lancing a boil; Isabelle's greatest fear was falling under the sway of another tyrant like her father.

Isabelle gathered her wits and forced her unwilling mouth to move. "Honor is distinct from fear, Your Majesty, but not opposite to it."

"Kantelvar told me you were clever," Margareta said. "He did not mention silver-tongued. Rise, girl. Let me get a look at you."

Isabelle stood and took the opportunity of being examined to return the scrutiny. Margareta's skin was flawless, pale, and glowing. The queen's silver eyes were flat in this light, and though her words had been friendly, her expression was closed. There were more etchings of anger around her eyes than of laughter, and her mouth was set in an unbending line.

Margareta said, "In your own words, tell me of this assassin who affrighted you."

"I did not see him," Isabelle said, "but I am made to understand that he gained access to the ship through a mirror placed aboard by an agent of Duque Diego."

The queen's brow darkened. "And how do you come by that information? Begin at the beginning, leave nothing out."

In the stuffy, sweltering cabin, Isabelle told the story from the moment Jean-Claude had burst into her tour of the aetherkeel until his return from his mission to l'Île des Zephyrs.

"And who was Diego's Célestial agent?" Margareta asked when Isabelle failed to identify her brother.

Isabelle's pulse raced and she looked to Jean-Claude.

"His name is . . . or rather was Hugh le Petit. He was a merchant, down on his luck and deep in debt." Jean-Claude made a dismissive little wave as if that was all the explanation that was necessary.

"I take it he is now beyond the reach of questioning," Margareta said.

"He did not respond well to interrogation," Jean-Claude said.

Margareta's lips pursed and then she returned her attention to Isabelle. "It is a peculiar guest gift you have brought into our house, not at all customary. Most people bring poetry, or artwork, or quondam artifacts, but you, fair Princesa, lay at our feet a grave accusation against one of our great lords."

Isabelle did not miss Margareta's usurpation of the royal pronoun; this was not a woman who looked forward to ceding power. Isabelle kept that thought to herself and said, "My apologies if I have acted inappropriately. I only provided the information I received."

"And do you trust the source of this information?" She pointed to Jean-Claude with her nose.

Isabelle lifted her chin. "With my life."

"But is your life his *only* priority? He is a royal musketeer, his Célestial master's personal lackey, and what better way to discommode us than to cast doubt on one of our most trusted nobles?"

Jean-Claude's brows drew down in a scowl, but he kept his tongue.

Outrage on his behalf flared in Isabelle's heart, and she had to tamp down her tone of voice. Stick to logic. It was her only tool. "This marriage is meant to sweeten relations between our nations, not sour them."

"Ah, but that is the beauty of this ploy. It covers l'Empire Céleste in a blanket of virtue. It shows that I can better trust my new foreign allies than my own nobles."

Isabelle's heart twitched, but she understood Margareta's fear. And how could she say the queen was wrong? Carefully she laid out the simplest truth she could manage. "I cannot speak for His Majesty, but neither I nor Jean-Claude wishes to disrupt the very faction we are attempting to join. This union is not low-hanging fruit to be risked for some greater prize." At least she hoped it wasn't.

Margareta raised two fingers. "Peace, daughter-to-be. As it happens, we agree with your assessment. Diego opposes this marriage to the hilt, and the majority of our court agrees with him. Marrying our royal scion to the daughter of a different bloodline shatters all precedent, and that prospect terrifies them, especially in this time of uncertainty.

"As of this moment, the opposition is disorganized, but any public accusation against Diego without ironclad proof to reinforce it will provide them with a rallying cry. We cannot allow that." Her silver-eyed gaze bored into Isabelle's as if trying to read her soul. "All our hopes depend on the success of your marriage. I only pray that your womb is not as temperamental as your mother's."

Isabelle's eyebrows twitched upward in surprise, but of course Margareta would have been apprised of la Comtesse des Zephyrs's much maligned infertility; like mother like daughter, or so it was said. Still, that was a hypothesis that could only be tested experimentally . . . with a man she'd never met.

Isabelle wound her courage up like a spring. She did not dare ask a favor, but a question . . . would Margareta take offense? "Majesty, if I may be so bold, does Príncipe Julio know any of this?"

Margareta huffed. "Julio was present when Don Divelo presented his story to me. He agrees that we will deal with Diego . . . privately. It goes without saying that no one here will so much as breathe the name Diego to anyone in San Augustus, lest he be forewarned."

There was some shifting of weight amongst the captains but no protests, which was good because there wasn't enough room in here for an argument.

Emboldened, Isabelle aligned herself behind the wedge of her curiosity and gave a push. "May I make a request?" This didn't have to rise to the level of a favor, she hoped.

Margareta regarded her with the closed expression of a person who received thousands of petitions a day and said no to most of them. "What request is so small that you require it of me?"

"Only a message to Príncipe Julio, from my lips to his ears. I look forward to meeting him."

Margareta's expression relaxed. "Of course. You shall have your chance. In deference to your Célestial traditions, a great masquerade is being planned in honor of your arrival."

Surprise pulled a response from Isabelle's lips. "But Artifex Kantelvar said tradition forbade a meeting."

Margareta said, "Kantelvar is . . . old-fashioned, an appropriate temperament for a cleric."

At the thought of being able to meet Julio before the wedding, delight bloomed in Isabelle's breast, only to be blown away by a frigid wind of doubt. If Julio could meet her, why hadn't he bothered to try? Why wasn't he here? Kantelvar said he had opposed this marriage from the beginning. Perhaps he still did, and this indifference was his way of expressing it.

⸺

After the steaming closeness of the audience cabin, the chill night breeze slapped Isabelle's face with fingers of ice. High thin clouds threaded their way through the glittering maze of stars. Isabelle did not return to her cabin.

She was too keyed up to sleep and too tired to think. Instead, she made a circuit of the ship, climbing to the quarterdeck, crossing the stern, and then making her way forward. Her good hand absently occupied itself folding and unfolding the prosthetic digits covering her wormfinger. The closer she came to Aragoth, the more treacherous the path forward became. The queen's faction was fractured; the queen herself burned with the sort of ambition that scorched anyone who came close; Isabelle's betrothed was apparently a broken man who wanted nothing to do with her; and, oh, yes, people she had never met were trying to kill her.

She reached the forecastle and leaned out over the forward rail, a position that would likely have given poor Jean-Claude fits. Would that she could just fly away, go somewhere nobody cared that she was a princess and only cared that she was Isabelle. There were several problems with that notion, of course, the first and most obvious being that she was not in control of where this ship was going. Even if that were of no issue, escape was a null set. If she ran away, people would look for her. If she managed to escape them . . . well, she'd spend the rest of her life holding her breath waiting for that condition to end.

On her next circuit, she stopped before Captain Santiago and asked, "How long will it be until we reach San Augustus?"

He said, "Two weeks, if the winds do not betray us."

Isabelle made an unladylike grunt. While she was cooped up on this ship, her enemies had two weeks to plan her demise. Of course, Margareta had said she would deal with Duque Diego privately, though what that entailed, Isabelle could not guess; it could be anything from a knife in the back to an exceptionally stern talking-to. And Kantelvar had said he intended to lay a trap for Thornscar, if the man was still alive.

Isabelle resumed walking. There was so much going on, all out of reach. All being handled, or was there something she'd missed? She needed to sit down and sift it all. No, belay that. She needed to sleep, to let her mind rest and all the data settle. Then she needed to figure out what questions she should be asking.

—

The next morning, Isabelle sat on the *Santa Anna*'s quarterdeck, charcoal stick in her left hand and easel erected before her. The early sun warmed her back through half a dozen layers of clothing. The cool breeze caressed her face but found no loose strand of hair with which to cavort. Even her hair was a prisoner to fashion and tradition, a captive denied parole.

Marie stood beside her, speaking in ghostly whispers: "There was more shadow here. Stubble here."

For three careful hours, Isabelle had painstakingly toiled over a picture of Thornscar based on Marie's unimpeachable memory. This was a technique she'd practiced before, and she'd been able to produce sketches and paintings of people she'd never seen as if they had been seated before her.

"Anything else?" she asked in a calm, patient tone that was nearly a mantra of meditation.

"No," Marie said in her hollow voice.

Then she leaned back to take a better look at her creation. He was a lean-faced man with a high-bridged nose that put her in mind of a young centurion. His mustache hung down in points below his chin in the high-Aragothic style and his cheeks were covered in stubble. The long scar that puckered his flesh from brow to chin merely gave him character.

She turned to her bodyguards. "Is this our man?"

Vincent, who had been pacing the deck, came up behind Isabelle and said, "Incredible! It is him exactly. I would not have believed such a thing possible."

Jean-Claude, his face ashen with sky sickness, sat against the forward rail with his hat over his eyes. "If you do not believe in impossible things, you will have a hard time keeping up with Isabelle."

Vincent glowered at Jean-Claude and then said, "Are you aware that she has offered to hire me as her bodyguard once my current contract has expired?"

Jean-Claude lifted his hat and squinted at Isabelle, who flinched. She should have consulted with Jean-Claude first. Would he think she didn't trust him or meant to abandon him? Damn Vincent for bringing it up.

I'm sorry, Isabelle mouthed to Jean-Claude.

If he noticed her or not, she could not tell. Instead, Jean-Claude focused his attention on Vincent and said, "Were you wise enough to accept?"

Vincent, deprived of the reaction he was looking for, said, "I'm still considering it." He returned his gaze to the picture and said, "You do realize it's backward. If you ever see the man in the real world, the scar will be on the other side."

Isabelle said, "True, but he's more likely to come after me as an espejismo than as a real person; it makes his escape so much easier."

CHAPTER

Nine

Jean-Claude had been long at work by the time day broke. The Solar's disk, a reddish blob seen through the eastern haze, rose above what passed for the horizon. Isabelle had once tried to explain to him why the sky changed color like that, but she'd lost him after the bit with the aetherbottle and the prism. Jean-Claude was content with the fact that the Solar was far away and unlikely to attack.

The *Santa Anna* was only a few hours out from San Augustus. After Thornscar's failed assassination attempt, the trip had been tense but uneventful, so much so that everyone's nerves were stretched tight in painful anticipation. Being a guard was like being a racehorse left to stock up in its stall for days, only to be expected to run flat out at a moment's notice. That was one of the reasons Jean-Claude usually chose to actively hunt Isabelle's enemies rather than passively secure her person.

Artifex Kantelvar had preceded them to San Augustus by two days. Now one of the queen's Glasswalkers brought him back to the fleet via mirror to discuss Isabelle's security with Vincent.

Kantelvar's espejismo was the oddest case of soul distortion Jean-Claude had yet seen, though his experience with the phenomenon was limited. The priest's saffron robes had taken on a luminescent quality, as if they glowed with an inner light. Gone were his characteristic limp, his mechanical limbs, and the hump on his back. If not for the testimony of his Glasswalker porter, his knowledge of the flotilla's passphrases, and his detailed recounting of shared history, Jean-Claude would not have believed he was the same person. Was this what the man had looked like before receiving the honor of having his limbs hacked off and replaced with clockworks? Jean-Claude had to suppress an urge to snatch off the artifex's cowl and see if there was a real face behind it.

Instead Jean-Claude leaned against the chart room wall, paying heed but offering little comment while Vincent and Kantelvar hashed out the details of Isabelle's security along the parade route from the dock to the royal enclave at the citadel. The plan was quite elaborate but did not deviate terribly much from the one they had discussed before leaving l'Île des Zephyrs.

The problem with such a script was that the enemy was likely to read it. All a potential assassin had to do was change a line or two to take himself from a bit part to top billing.

Vincent, dressed in the padded gambeson that would serve as the underpinning for his alchemetal armor when the time came for him to debark, tapped his finger on a map of San Augustus and spoke to Kantelvar. "How, precisely, is Isabelle's coach armored?"

Kantelvar said, "The coach itself is made of ironwood, two inches thick and banded with steel. It would take a cannonball to penetrate it, and we have cleared the route of all artillery."

Jean-Claude snorted, "Just how much unsecured artillery does San Augustus have lying around?"

"Normally, very little," Kantelvar said, "but with so much trouble anticipated, the city's nobles have taken to supplementing their traditional guard with foreign mercenaries. Officially they are all kept out of the city, but many of the units have been there for months, and the borders tend to leak."

Jean-Claude's eyebrows lifted, but it was Vincent who asked the next question. "How many of these sell-swords are there?"

Kantelvar said, "At last estimate, around fifty thousand, with more scattered about the countryside within a few days' ride."

"And the king allows this?" Vincent sounded incredulous.

Kantelvar made a circling motion with his right—no, his left hand. "It is the traditional duty of the nobles to raise regiments in times of trouble. In fact, it is the traditional justification for their privileged status. They can hardly be prevented from assembling troops in anticipation of a crisis."

Jean-Claude said, "So, the war for Aragoth's succession, Builder forbid it should come to pass, may well be won by a foreign general who may then decide not to give up his prize."

"An unlikely outcome, but possible," Kantelvar allowed. "It therefore behooves us to ensure that there is no succession debate, and that means delivering Isabelle safely into her husband's arms and praying she gets quickly with child."

Jean-Claude bristled at politics that treated Isabelle like a broodmare, but there was no benefit in arguing about it. One might as well protest the necessity of rain in farming.

"So an ironwood coach," Vincent said, gathering the dropped threads of conversation. "What about the windows?"

Kantelvar said, "The windows in the front of the coach are false, just curtains over wood. Isabelle will sit there, facing backward. There will be a wedge-shaped mirror, warded to keep a Glasswalker from coming through, that will show her reflection out the rear windows so that the crowd can see her. To anyone outside, it will look as if she is sitting in the rear seat. You, Vincent, will sit behind the wedge mirror. In case of an attack, either you or Isabelle can slam the partition door shut, at which point it can only be opened from the inside or with a special key that is kept at the palace."

Vincent twisted his mustache and said, "That seems adequate." He turned to look at Jean-Claude and added, "You have been surprisingly quiet through all of this."

Jean-Claude shrugged one shoulder. "I would not presume to teach you your job. My question is to His Learnedness. What steps has he taken toward capturing Thornscar, which was the ostensible reason he left us in the first place?"

Kantelvar said, "I have reason to believe that Thornscar survived being stabbed in the arm. He is being pursued quietly, and he should be rounded up within the next few days. We cannot pounce too overtly for fear of alerting Duque Diego that his assassin had been identified, especially as we intend to use Thornscar's testimony as evidence against Diego later, after Julio is king. This is especially important because you managed to kill the only other known conspirator, this Hugo le Petit. If Diego knew Thornscar was identified, he would certainly cut the man's throat. He could even use the act to 'prove' his loyalty to Príncipe Julio's faction."

"Even so, shouldn't we wait until he is taken before we make landfall?"

Kantelvar's fist tightened on his spiny-headed staff and his voice did not quite conceal irritation at this question. "No. Even though Thornscar survived, his sorcery was certainly discommoded by the trauma you both inflicted, or so the Glasswalkers tell me. He will not be a threat, but the longer we wait, the more time Diego will have to procure an alternate assassin."

"If he has not done so already," Vincent said.

"Do you have any notion of who the next assassin might be?" Jean-Claude asked.

"The most likely suspects are being watched," Kantelvar said. "If you wish I will prepare a full briefing for you when you arrive."

Jean-Claude would have liked for such preparation to have already been done, but he allowed that Kantelvar hadn't had time for it, and having the information right now would not change Jean-Claude's plans for the cavalcade. Having seen all that he needed of Kantelvar and Vincent's designs, he excused himself to go to the head but instead made his way to the forecastle, where Isabelle had erected her easel and turned her attention to capturing the Craton Massif in paint.

The continent loomed off the starboard bow, filling up that entire quadrant without itself being fully revealed. The coastal precipice crinkled off to the left and right until it disappeared in the haze. Beyond the headlands, the level of the ground rose gradually, a patchwork of cultivated fields giving way to woodlands, foothills, and finally mountains, before being swallowed up by the distance. Towns and villages dotted the coastline. Jean-Claude could just make out the local temples, their brass-clad domes glittering in the morning light. People and animals were still too distant to perceive and their absence made the land look curiously abandoned and forlorn. Far ahead, at the very edge of vision, lay San Augustus. The sprawling crescent city, curled about its famous deep-sky harbor, was little more than a pale smudge at this distance.

Jean-Claude gripped the rail next to Isabelle and refrained from entreating her not to stand so close to the edge. He needed her attention on other things.

"Jean-Claude," she said. Her eyes twinkled, and she smiled delightedly. "Have you noticed how the Craton Massif disappears into the distance?

We're higher up than most of the mountains, so we ought to be able to see all the way across the surface of the disk to the far coast, but we can't."

"Yes," said Jean-Claude. "Doesn't the atmosphere get in the way or something similar? I thought you knew that." It was unlike her not to know facts of that nature.

"Correct," she said, "but I was sitting out here watching the stars fade and thinking how odd that was. I mean, how can we see the stars at all when we know they're much farther away than the other side of the craton? That implies there is more atmosphere between here and the other side of Craton Massif than between here and the stars. In principle, it means that using simple optics I should be able to gauge the upper limits of the sky."

The ship pitched and Jean-Claude's stomach heaved rebelliously. Jean-Claude glowered at the distant city. The sails were full, and the ship was pitching, rolling, and bobbing like a drunken dancer, but despite these obvious signs of motion, they seemed no closer to the harbor entrance than they had been this morning. He said, "I would settle for finding a solid place to land. Do you know how long until we make port?"

"Captain Santiago says it depends on the sky." She leaned forward on the rail, which nearly gave Jean-Claude a heart attack, and said, "The craton is rotating at roughly the same speed we are traveling along its edge, rather like a hand turning a wheel. The whole landmass makes one rotation every ninety-seven days or so. At this point on the edge, that translates into a little less than four knots. We could sail in closer to land and get picked up by the cratonic vortex, which would carry us along in parallel to the coastal rotation, and then we could just sail up the coast, but Santiago says the headlands farther ahead put off a tidal trough. It stretches off the point like a ribbon in the hand of a spinning child. When we hit that trough, we'll be able to glide down into the city in about an hour."

Jean-Claude shook his head in fascination. He understood not one word in ten of that aeronautical jibber-jabber, but Isabelle spoke as if she were ready to give lessons on the topic.

He sidled closer to her and whispered, "Fascinating, but remember to guard your philosophical tongue." Isabelle's foes would be looking for any excuse to discredit her. They would not hesitate to accuse her of heretical numeracy.

Isabelle winced as if he'd slapped her. "I'm sorry. I know I should be more careful. I'm not any good at this. You're the only one I can talk to." She stopped herself short, clearly not finished. Jean-Claude gave her time.

After a long hesitation she asked, "What if Grand Leon calls you away?" she said. "Once I'm in Aragoth. Once I'm married . . . and then I started thinking, what do you want? You've been stuck with me twenty-four years."

"And proud of every moment." Alas, it was ever so much easier to befuddle his enemies than comfort his friends. Frequently there was no comfort, only truth. "Time moves on. You sow, you tend, you harvest, and there must be a winter. Grand Leon may call me away, but if you can't survive without me, then I have truly failed you."

"I haven't been doing well so far."

"That's not true. You've made good moves and you're very reserved."

Isabelle huffed a laugh. "Is that what it looks like to you? I'm nothing but terrified most of the time."

Jean-Claude scratched his mustache and said, "Under the circumstances I would be utterly remiss to advise you to be less careful. Rather I would say, trust yourself more. Your father had a kind of power over you no one in Aragoth ever will. These people need your cooperation and you must demand recompense. They will try to bargain you down. Threats and intimidation are nothing but negotiating tactics. Recognize them as such and make it easier for them to give you what you want than to push you around."

"You make it sound so simple."

"For the most part it is simple, just not easy."

Isabelle did not look reassured. "If the task were simple, success and failure would be obvious."

"Failure is usually obvious, but since you're not dead, we must be succeeding." He looked around, but none of the bustling sailors were close enough to eavesdrop. "Speaking of which, we have just finished arranging for your security in the cavalcade from the dock to the palace, and I wanted to go over your part in it."

Isabelle sniffed. "You mean aside from sitting quietly in the center of the coach with Vincent and Marie across from me and burly men on either side," she said. "I'm surprised you didn't claim the right to ride in the coach as well."

"What good would I do anybody in there? Can't see anything from inside a coach. Besides, the coach is only a diversion. The procession from the docks to the citadel is a window of vulnerability. The route will be well guarded but it will also be packed with peasants, pedestrians, and, no doubt, assorted other persons beginning with the letter 'P.'"

"Pensioners, plumbers, philosophers," Isabelle added wryly. "Partygoers, pallbearers . . ."

"My point is, there will be too many people to watch. An assassin willing to sacrifice his life for his cause might get close enough to harm you. The only way to assure that does not happen is to make sure you aren't where he thinks you are. This afternoon, when you and your handmaids get dressed, I want you to switch clothes with one of them."

Isabelle's eyes grew wide. "Then I will ride unobtrusively in the handmaids' carriage while she rides in the coach with Vincent?"

Jean-Claude smiled at her astuteness, but he was still ahead of her. "Not exactly. The handmaid will take your place in the carriage. In your trunk, I've left a soldier's uniform that I took from the quartermaster's store. With a helmet for your head, cuirass for your figure, trousers, and boots, you'll make a strapping young officer. Then you will ride in the cavalcade. One uniform amongst many. It's the perfect camouflage."

"But won't any potential assassin have studied my face? My father did have pictures of me made when he was trying to marry me off."

"Possibly, but he will be looking for a woman. He will most assuredly not be staring into the faces of the guards. He does not want to be seen and he will not wish to draw their attention. You will be invisible."

"To the assassin perhaps, but don't all these soldiers know each other?"

"Not as much as you'd think. With as many nobles attending as befits the arrival of a princess, there will be private soldiers galore, so many different liveries that the result is anything but uniform."

"This would be a lot easier if we had a Goldentongue glamour charm," Isabelle said.

Of all the saintborn sorceries, the Brathonian Goldentongue illusionists were the only ones Jean-Claude had ever actually envied. So much of his own work involved changing people's minds—okay, shoveling horseshit by the cartload—that being able to alter his enemies' perceptions at will would be like owning his own feedlot.

He said, "That would be nice, but there are none to hand, and it would unnecessarily expand the circle of people who know what we are about."

Isabelle considered this. "Speaking of which, I will not require one of my ladies to take such a risk for me. If one of them volunteers for this duty, I will be grateful, but I will not dragoon anyone."

Jean-Claude bowed his head to her, glad she had accepted the general plan and was making it her own by taking control of the details. "A conscript would not serve to fill this post in any case; all she would have to do to spoil it is fail to act like you."

"And what happens if we aren't attacked and we reach the royal citadel peacefully and Príncipe Julio is waiting for us? Will he be introduced to the wrong woman?"

Jean-Claude hesitated; he hadn't thought in any depth about the *social* consequences of this charade. "He's not supposed to meet you until the ball tomorrow night."

"Ah, but could you resist the chance to get a peek at your future spouse? I keep thinking, if it were me, I couldn't wait. I'd find a way to get a glimpse." Romantic longings gleamed in her eyes. "I'd want to get to know him before the wedding, to find out what kind of person he is, to see his private face before his public one . . . unless he's not interested." She chewed her lower lip.

"He'd be mad not to adore you," Jean-Claude said soothingly, though, in truth, if the young buck hadn't made any effort to meet Isabelle so far, Jean-Claude doubted the laggard would bestir himself to greet the coach. More than ever, the idea of handing over his precious charge to some disinterested stranger churned Jean-Claude's gut. How could any ruffle-wearing, peeled-grape-eating, sedan-chair-lounging aristocrat be worthy of Isabelle?

Isabelle said, "I know so little about him, most of it contradictory. Kantelvar says he is a great man, but everyone else depicts him as bitter and broken. He has surely shown no interest in me, not a secret visit, not even a message of greeting."

Jean-Claude ached at Isabelle's uncertainty. "I'll find out what I can about him." He'd start by talking to the príncipe's servants. If you want the measure of a man, see how he treats his inferiors.

And what would he do if he found Príncipe Julio cruel or stupid? He could not toss Isabelle into a cesspit of a marriage . . . except that Grand Leon had signed the marriage contract. Was there any way, if worst came to worst, that he might convince le roi that this marriage was not in l' Empire Céleste's best interests? Not, he feared, without a considerably more politically compelling reason than Isabelle's marital happiness.

Isabelle leaned against the rail, staring into the middle distance, her painting forgotten. She said, "Part of me cannot help but wonder what it would be like if Príncipe Julio did meet the wrong woman, if he accepted her as his wife. I could disappear, go wandering, see the world unencumbered by everyone else's expectations."

Coming from Isabelle, this was idle speculation, the by-product of a mind that looked at any situation and saw a dozen possibilities and a thousand implications . . . but the idea had appeal. If Isabelle wanted to run away, Jean-Claude could go with her. Except . . . flight did not equal freedom. Even if chains of duty did not bind them to a narrower course, relentless pursuit surely would.

She continued, "Since I was very young, I have been faced with an impossible dilemma. It is my purpose to marry into an honorable Célestial bloodline, bear children, and be a good chatelaine for my husband's household. It is the only destiny for which one of my station is deemed fit, yet for most of my life, it has been patently obvious that those goals were unattainable. No one was ever going to want me, not even as a thing. It was frustrating, and yet, now that the world has turned . . . those failures offered a sort of freedom. No one expected anything of me, so I was free to expect things of myself.

"Now here I am, halfway across the deep sky, destined for marriage and children, but to a bloodline I could never have anticipated. When the impossible happens, the world shudders, for if one impossible thing can happen, why not another? I cannot help but wonder what other impossibilities are out there, waiting to be challenged."

Pride and terror flooded Jean-Claude, and he chose his words carefully. "Is that what you want? To run away?" And what would *he* do if she decided to bolt this dangerous and suspicious marriage? His obligation as le roi's musketeer was clear, but his duty to Isabelle was . . . compelling.

Isabelle shook her head. "I don't think 'want' is a big enough or subtle enough word on which to hang the future. Perhaps Príncipe Julio will be the best thing that ever happened to me. Or perhaps he will be worse than my father. I only wish I had some way of finding out before it is too late."

Jean-Claude nodded in acceptance of this ambiguity and swore to help bring her clarity. "I will do my best to provide you with what intelligence I can once we have you safely ensconced in the palace. Until then, secrecy is our watchword. Tell no one but your handmaids what you are doing, and don't come out of your cabin until it's time to debark. If you do come out, I'll take it as a signal that you could not find a volunteer. Other than that, there's no point in tempting fate."

Her lips thinned in a wry smile. "Because Vincent will see through the disguise, and you don't want him to know what we're about until it's too late to stop it."

Jean-Claude's face stiffened, which was itself a dead giveaway. He tried to relax his features, but he imagined that made him look exactly like a naughty child trying to look innocent with stolen pie smeared on his face. Isabelle was quick. He knew she was quick, and she still got ahead of him. She laughed at his stunned expression.

"How did you know?"

"Because this is . . . artful. Vincent prefers to test strength against strength. He doesn't trust art. He would never agree to it."

"But you will?" Jean-Claude asked, just to be sure.

"I trust your judgment and your subtlety. Besides, I want to see the city, and you can't see anything from inside a coach."

—

It was early afternoon when the predicted aetheric trough appeared. Santiago barked orders, and the crew swarmed into action. Jean-Claude bowed Isabelle into her cabin, then attached himself to Vincent with a mind to distract him from any interference he might chance to make in Isabelle's preparations.

The *Santa Anna* slid down the sloping wall of the craton's aetheric vortex—*Progress at last!*—until it was level with the equatorial rim. A long, loose caravan of ships—merchants, catch boats, leviathaners, and other sorts Jean-Claude didn't recognize—stretched out toward the Craton Massif like so many beads cut loose from a string. An equally long line trailed out behind them. Coastal corvettes plied the sky around them like so many cloud sharks, keeping order in the line.

Jean-Claude glowered at the ships in front of them, in between him and solid ground, then turned to Santiago and asked, "This is a royal ship of the line, isn't it? Shouldn't they make way for us?"

Santiago nodded. "The cutters will move us to the front of the line as soon as we are in position to turn for the harbor. Until then, have patience; even crowns must wait on the wind."

Jean-Claude made a disconsolate grunt and stared at their destination, so close and yet so out of reach. Flying, as they were, a hundred meters above the Craton Massif's coastline, he had what he supposed was a magnificent view of San Augustus.

A pair of massive fortified stone towers, known far and wide as the Hammer and the Anvil, guarded the vast harbor's entrance. The harbor itself was a wide, deep well of rock, open to the sky at top and bottom. As far as he understood the nature of such geography, the enclosure of the harbor created its own calm eddy of aether, a non-current in which skyships could safely tether without fear of being dashed against the rocks.

Beyond the harbor, the city of San Augustus climbed a series of steep, terraced hillsides forming a great bowl filled with a salad mixture of red-tiled roofs, verdant parks, coppery temple domes, and white marble buildings of state. It was at least thrice as big as the Célestial capital at Rocher Royale. Of course it was also many times older than Grand Leon's city.

Away from the harbor and atop the highest hill stood the royal citadel. Looking through Santiago's glass, he could just make out where the old walls from the age of chivalry had stood, before they had been replaced by a modern star-shaped fortress with sloping walls and cannon emplacements galore. Not for the first time on this trip, he lamented that skyships could not fly over land; it would make getting Isabelle to the citadel so much easier. *If wishes were fishes, urchins would dine.*

In the wide open center of the fortress, like a jewel in a gilded box, stood the royal palace, an enormous rambling structure that climbed over the hill like a vine. *And this is where we are taking Isabelle, a warren of stone and strangers.* Every unfamiliar face belonged to a potential assassin. Was it too late to turn around and take her away?

Probably much too late. For years, le roi had unofficially, discreetly backed the skyland kingdom of Brathon against Aragoth in their competition for a controlling interest in the savage but fabulously wealthy lands of the Craton Riqueza, the continent of riches, beyond the equator, a colonial competition l'Empire Céleste had entered very late with very little. Le roi was not in any position to win the game, but he was in a position to pick the winner, for the right price.

The question in Jean-Claude's mind was whether Isabelle's marriage to Príncipe Julio represented a full-scale change of alliance, or if the arrangement merely increased le roi's bargaining leverage with the Brathonians. As a King's Own Musketeer, this was a question Jean-Claude could reasonably ask of his master—*Which way do you want me to jump, sire?*—but what if le roi said Isabelle was to be a sacrificial pawn? It was not an answer he wanted to receive. Better to stick to the same orders he had been following all her life, the command Grand Leon had never bother to rescind: protect her.

The towering pillars of the Hammer and the Anvil loomed larger and larger until they filled the entire forward sky. The mouths of hundreds of massive gun emplacements yawned like wolves baring their fangs in warning. As the ship entered the channel between the towers, the shadows of the fortresses spread across the deck and seemed to swallow the wind. The sails grew limp, and the rigging thumped and banged with shifting tensions. Jean-Claude swore he could hear the muttering voices of the murderous guns embedded in the stone to either side of him. His skin prickled in gooseflesh despite the afternoon's warmth. What if the assassin had suborned a gunnery officer? He could blow the *Santa Anna* to flinders before they knew what hit them.

It seemed to take a very long time, but finally the *Santa Anna* emerged into the harbor proper. It was a veritable maze of long, thin piers, each supported by its own squadron of aetherballoons, stretching toward the center of the harbor, like a great spiderweb. Longshoremen and sailors scurried along those pathways like so many ants, to and from the hundreds of skyships, stacked three levels deep in places, that rocked at their moorings. Immense treadmill-driven wooden cranes lifted and lowered goods and supplies up and down the cliff face. Warehouses were built right into the stone sides of the shaft. The whole thing looked like a colony of gigantic cliff swallows. Colored lanterns hung in a variety of patterns at the ends of the piers, guiding the harbor pilot as he steered the *Santa Anna* to a berth reserved for royal ships.

—

Jean-Claude kept his face perfectly straight when a woman emerged from Isabelle's cabin wearing Isabelle's dress, her white wig, and a concealing veil. She was about the right height, but under so many layers, even Jean-Claude couldn't tell if she was an imposter or not. When Vincent, dressed in his finest uniform complete with a shiny new alchemetal helmet and cuirass, took her arm to guide her down the gangway, she was careful to fold her right hand with her left, just as Isabelle did with her prosthetic fingers. Had Isabelle been unable to find a volunteer for this charade? But no, this gowned figure did not have Isabelle's careless walk.

Jean-Claude straightened his own rarely worn dress uniform, a bright blue tabard with a golden thundercrown, a coronet made from jags of lightning, and sparkling silver trim, and took his place at the back of the column of debarking passengers, just in front of the first group of Aragothic officers and ahead of the two-score troops. Worry crept into his heart as he failed to lay eyes on Isabelle. Presumably she had donned her soldier's uniform and was waiting for an opportunity to join the throng. Had she, working with only one good hand, been able to put the unfamiliar clothing on? Of course, she would have had at least one lady to assist her. Had she already debarked the ship, or had she had some inspiration and run off to do some other mad thing? One could never *assume* with Isabelle, though one could *trust* her.

Surrounded by Vincent and his guards, the decoy, her handmaidens, and Marie debarked onto a graceful jetty that was built like half an arched bridge and supported in part by thick cables strung from pillars onshore. The mechanics of the arrangement entirely eluded Jean-Claude. The important thing, from his perspective, was that it wasn't moving.

Yet when Jean-Claude stepped onto the jetty, his knees buckled, and he slumped against the railing. He cursed his treacherous body; after nearly three weeks being sloshed about like the dregs of Templeday ale in that rickety wooden deathtrap, his legs had forgotten how to handle unyielding wood. Captain Santiago and his officers brushed by him, cool and confident, apparently unfazed by the transition from ship to shore.

"Need a hand up, good sir?"

Jean-Claude looked up at a slightly built young soldier with a waxed mustache, brown hair, and eyes like pools of summer sky. *Thank the Builder.*

Jean-Claude forced himself upright despite the fact that the world kept washing up and down. "No, thank you . . . Sergeant." Isabelle's uniform had acquired frogging since the last time he'd seen it. He impelled himself into the line of offloading marines. Isabelle formed up next to him so that they made their own rank.

Jean-Claude noted the stripes on her uniform sleeve. "I see you've been promoted."

"That was Darcy's idea; her father is military and she says sergeant is a very useful rank. High enough that nearly everyone listens when you bellow an order, low enough to avoid attracting much attention."

Jean-Claude touched the brim of his hat in acknowledgment of this point, but added, sotto voce, "You'd better walk like a sergeant then, a little march, a little swagger, and for the Builder's sake, don't fold your hands in front of you."

Sergeant Isabelle checked her hands and said, "This feels very . . . odd."

"It takes practice. For now, just keep your mouth shut and your eyes open."

At the foot of the pier, a group of dignitaries had gathered to greet the woman playing the part of Isabelle. There were several Aragothic nobles, and a trio of Temple sagaxes in lieu of an artifex. Kantelvar was not present. His espejismo had retreated to his body in the palace to direct security from that end.

"I hope I don't have to remember any of those people's names," Isabelle muttered as her handmaiden accepted formal greetings on her behalf.

"You can always have your doppelganger introduce you. Which lady is it, anyway?"

"Can't you guess?"

"Hmmm . . . a little shorter, just as slender, and has a sense of humor . . . Valérie."

"Very good," Isabelle said. "She also speaks Aragothic. I've caught her reading over my shoulder a few times. I think she might have some interest in learning."

Jean-Claude and Isabelle moved with the crowd of soldiers who were fanning out along the quayside. Another, larger group of royal soldiers in red-and-black uniforms, the processional guard, stood arrayed in a small but well-decorated plaza before them. The compressed size of the venue made the numbers look greater than they actually were. All the civilians who must ordinarily have given this place its function had been cleared out.

The greeting ceremony took remarkably little time for a royal event. Jean-Claude supposed there would be longer introductions later when a larger number of important people were present. Then the gathering rearranged itself, and the Aragothic dignitaries led Valérie toward the coach. Jean-Claude and Isabelle struck out toward an equestrian queue where horses were waiting for visiting riders.

On their way, they crossed paths with the sagaxes, talking in low voices amongst themselves.

". . . must not have children," one of them complained, "it's an abomination."

Jean-Claude shared a glance with Isabelle and they deflected their course to trail the clerics. Temple influence was much stronger in Aragoth than in l'Empire Céleste, and it would be useful to hear what the local clergy were thinking.

The second sagax said, "I don't know about that. Artifex Kantelvar says—"

"Kantelvar is mad," snapped the third. "Ever since his Exaltation. All that spewing of signs and portents."

"He used to be more concerned with his rents and debtors. Now it's all 'The Time of Reckoning is at hand, the Savior is coming.'"

"Peace abide, brother," said the first. "When the new Omnifex is elected, he will put a stop to Kantelvar's schemes."

The third said, "Even if Julio is king?"

"Even kings must bow their necks to the Builder's law," said the deep thinker. "A crippled king, a soul-blighted queen, and the chance of an abomination child will put the people on our side." Then, perhaps fearing to be overheard, he looked around and espied Jean-Claude and Isabelle. The conversation died.

Jean-Claude casually veered off toward the horses.

"That was . . . disturbing," Isabelle said.

"Something to question Kantelvar about, to be sure," Jean-Claude said. Isabelle had never been popular with the clergy, but the Temple artificers in Windfall had been content in the knowledge that her putative impurity was no threat to the Builder's design. Not so, here. She must have seemed a nightmare come to life for the devout.

"Do you think that's true?" Isabelle asked. "That he thinks the Reckoning is at hand, the Savior is arising, and the world is about to be remade?"

"He's never mentioned it in my hearing," Jean-Claude said. "I don't know enough about him to know what he believes. It's one of the things I intend to find out. I know some people in San Augustus"—he considered the scope of the sprawling city—"assuming I can find them. I'll make more friends from there."

"Do we have that much time?" Sergeant Isabelle asked. "They're pushing this marriage as fast as protocol allows."

"Do we have any choice?"

They acquired horses and mounted. Fortunately, Isabelle didn't need any help. Once young Isabelle had made it plain that she was going to ride horses, he'd arranged for her to learn it properly.

They formed up with the cavalcade. Jean-Claude's attention was drawn to the princess's heavily armored coach. Vincent was just helping Valérie into the coach when he paused and gripped her hand. Her *right* hand. He stepped back and looked around, a thunderous expression on his face.

"Damn, he's twigged to it," Jean-Claude said, but how much of a scene was the man willing to make?

Valérie tugged on his arm, and there was an angry whispered conversation before he reluctantly allowed himself to be dragged on board.

Jean-Claude let out a breath of relief. "I can't believe he didn't throw a fit."

"I can," Isabelle said. At Jean-Claude's inquisitive look she said, "He's been up Valérie's skirts six nights out of the last seven."

Jean-Claude snorted. "Damn, I didn't think he had it in him."

"Logistically, I believe he had it in her." Isabelle flushed at her own joke; she could never have made such a ribald comment to anyone else.

Jean-Claude nearly guffawed himself out of the saddle, and it took him a moment to restore what passed for a serious mien. "But do you trust him with your handmaid?"

Isabelle shot him a reproachful glance. "I trust her to make her own choices."

Jean-Claude conceded the point by changing the subject. "He's going to be in a foul humor when we get to the palace."

"Wouldn't you be," Isabelle said, "if I suddenly disappeared and all your elaborate preparations went to waste?"

"These preparations have not gone to waste; I could not have designed a better distraction if I'd had a month," Jean-Claude said. The thought of losing Isabelle, on the other hand, was too dreadful to contemplate. "Remember, your duty is to see to it that, no matter what else happens, the princess reaches the palace in one piece."

Her face stiffened slightly at his sober tone. "I will."

"The proper address is 'Yes, sir,' soldier."

"Yes, sir," she repeated enthusiastically, snapping off a wrong-handed salute.

The procession was suitably impressive, led by outriders, a troupe of musicians who announced their progress with a marching song. A color guard with the flags of Aragoth, l'Empire Céleste, and the house des Zephyrs came next, followed by a squad of royal cuirassiers, then a platoon of pikemen followed by the royal coach. The dignitaries and their escorts, including

Jean-Claude and Isabelle, rode next. Behind them came the handmaids' carriage and yet more guards bringing up the rear.

Outside the porte cochere awaited a mob of city folk, a throng of brightly dressed people hoping for a glimpse of their new princesa. Some waved ribbons and cheered. Others brandished icons of the Builder's gearwheel eye and shouted unwelcome. Jean-Claude kept a wary watch on these. Just how much effort would it take some clever assassin to work a group of believers into a killing frenzy, murder by mob?

Jean-Claude wished they could have dispensed with the street theater entirely, but it was important for the new princesa to be witnessed by the people of Aragoth. An enthusiastic populace could be a powerful impediment to courtly intrigues. Whoever plotted against a popular princesa became a villain in the eyes of the people, and wise nobles never forgot that the people were the foundation on which their towers rested. They did not want that soil shifting.

The cavalcade trotted along the city's main road, a serpentine path that meandered up the many-terraced slope to the citadel. Peasants and freemen filled the streets, parting only when the cuirassiers drew nigh upon them. Most of the buildings along this road were of dressed stone from the foundations to the first-floor windows and of pale stucco from there on up, often to a height of four stories. Despite the width of the street, Jean-Claude had to crane his neck to scan the rooftops, but he was pleased to see the silhouettes of royal crossbowmen standing watch at regular intervals, just as Kantelvar had promised. Muskets were a more fashionable weapon and better in a battle of massed ranks, but they were far too inaccurate for countersharpshooter work.

It was all the security anyone could have hoped for, but Isabelle's enemy was both crafty and bold. Jean-Claude rechecked his rapier and pistol, assuring himself for the thousandth time they were primed and ready. He sifted the onlookers with his gaze, playing a solitaire game of *If I were an assassin, where would I be?* In the crowd by the side of the road? *It's not the best angle. There are lots of people in the way, and how would I escape?* A rooftop, wearing a guard's stolen uniform? *Easy to escape, but how do I strike? I can't see my target from that angle.* In a dark window? *Do I want to be trapped in a building with hot-blooded pursuit on the way?* Of course, a Glasswalker assassin need not be trapped anywhere there was a mirror . . .

He was peering into a shadowed cleft on the right side of the road when the crack of gunfire erupted on his left, a thunderous bang that nearly stopped his heart.

A hundred things happened at once. Time turned thick and gelatinous. Jean-Claude's head swiveled, but even that simple movement was like swimming in molasses. Dark smoke and angry red sparks plumed from a second-story window. There was a gray flash of movement. Inside the coach, Valérie screamed. People in the crowd joined the chorus. The driver cracked his whip and the royal coach lurched forward, gathering speed. Half the mounted guard closed tightly around it as it hurtled up the street, a distraction that would draw off any further assassins.

Jean-Claude whirled farther around to find Isabelle staring in the direction of the window. Unhurt, thank the Builder.

"Go!" Jean-Claude shouted at Isabelle. "Remember your duty."

The mounted dignitaries urged their mounts into a gallop. Isabelle hurtled after them while the pikemen pressed the crowd back. Crossbowmen on the roof launched quarrels through the open window . . . but where were the other gunshots? Only a fool would rely on a single musket shot for an assassination attempt.

Jean-Claude goaded his horse in the flanks and charged the building from which the shot had come. Peasants scattered before him. Soldiers already poured in the ground-floor entrances, and crossbowmen had leapt onto the roof.

Jean-Claude stood up on the saddle—twenty years ago this would have been a lark—and pushed off, not quite a leap; grabbed the sill of the window from which the gunshot had come; and heaved himself up. Momentum was on his side. Gravity was not. He got his elbows up on the sill before his initial thrust ran out. The room was empty of life, though the burning stench of gunpowder lingered. There was a full-length mirror on the right-hand wall.

Damn! Jean-Claude struggled to drag himself into the room. His feet scrabbled on the stucco. If only he were twenty years slimmer . . . he squirmed through the window until his bulk passed the tipping point and he toppled inward. He hauled himself upright just a heartbeat before the opposite door burst open and two Aragothic guards charged in.

"Where?" barked the first guard, looking wildly around.

"Gone," Jean-Claude said, gesturing to the mirror. There was no other way out of the room. "Can one Glasswalker follow another through a glass?" Maybe they could launch a pursuit.

"I don't know."

Before Jean-Claude could invent any suitable invective, a beckoning finger of smoke caught his attention. The gray ribbon twined, like a snake charmer's cobra, from a large clay pot by the mirror stand.

Match cord!

Jean-Claude turned and bolted for the window. "Bomb!"

He leapt. A giant boot kicked him in the back, and the world turned white.

CHAPTER

Ten

The sound of the blast jerked Isabelle's head around. Smoke and fire belched from a gaping hole in the second-story wall. Bits of wood and plaster rained all over the cavalcade. Sparks wafted skyward and then faded and died, like damned stars reaching for paradise. Alarm bells pealed.

The street rang with the sounds of panic, shouting, and running. Most of the onlookers had stampeded, leaving trampled bodies in their wake, and no assailants had appeared to replace them. But where was . . . *Oh Savior, no!*

On the cobbles below the window lay a crumpled figure. His white hat and silver trim shone in the angled afternoon light.

"Jean-Claude!" Horror ran like snowmelt through her veins. *Not him. Anyone but him.* She wheeled her horse around.

A strong hand grabbed her upper arm, and a ruddy-faced lieutenant barked at her, "Get these women out of here." He pointed in the direction of her ladies' carriage.

Isabelle opened her mouth, her lips agape for one endless moment as she stared at an endless fall.

Your duty is to see to it that, no matter what else happens, Jean-Claude had said, *the princess reaches the palace in one piece.* She had to get herself to the palace. She must not fail him.

She wheeled her horse and gave it the spurs. It leapt to a gallop. He heart felt ripped from her chest. She caught up with the ladies' carriage and gave the beast its head, trusting it to keep up with its herd, not trusting herself to keep going. Going when all she wanted to do was turn back. *Not him. Please.* Never had she wanted so much to disbelieve her senses.

The wind in her face scrubbed Isabelle's eyes clean, but she could not seem to breathe. *No. No. No!* But she had to get the princess to safety.

Damn the princess. What good was she? Useless, broken, crippled.

It was only her imagination that Jean-Claude's hand was on her back, keeping her balanced, pushing her on.

The handmaidens' carriage rattled beneath the citadel's gates and across a courtyard the size of Windfall before it finally lumbered to a stop. The lathered horses stamped in their traces. Isabelle all but fell from her horse and had to grab the bridle to keep herself upright.

Guards crowded around the armored coach, lifting Vincent from the cabin. His shining breastplate was pierced and stained with blood. His head lolled like a newborn's. Valérie stood nearby, half wailing and half sobbing, her white dress soaked in blood. Several royal Aragothic servitors tried to calm her. "Princesa, please . . ."

A man wearing the sash of the king's chamberlain exchanged verbal broadsides with the guard captain in overheated Aragothic.

Isabelle gathered what remained of her wits, shouldered into the press around Vincent, and knelt at his side. How could anyone have that much blood in them? His haughty expression slumped like a candle in the sun.

Several sets of hands grabbed at her. "Get off, soldier!"

Isabelle shook the hands off. With her good hand she ripped her helmet and wig from her head and tore off the false mustache. "I am Princess Isabelle! Stand back."

Vincent's eyes fluttered open at the sound of her voice, and his gaze focused briefly on her face. "Mademoiselle. Thank the Builder." Blood was on his lips, and his voice gurgled. "Tell your father, I served him . . . defend you with my life . . . Valérie." His eyelids lowered halfway as the light of his soul guttered to a last whiff of vapor and departed on the breeze.

"Vincent!" Valérie shrieked. She fell to her knees and seized him by the collar. His blood oozed between her fingers. She folded in on herself and wept.

Isabelle backed away a step to let her grieve. He was gone, stolen by an assassin's musket ball. *A musket ball meant for me.* And if it hadn't killed him, it would have killed Valérie. All these people had chosen to stand between Isabelle and bullets.

Sobs welled up in Isabelle's body, but she choked them off. This was not the way to honor the fallen. She swallowed the slime of grief and said, "You lived for my father, but you died for me."

"Highness, please, come this way." The chamberlain gripped Isabelle's shoulders and pulled her away, but she resisted being absorbed into the converging mob of her handmaidens.

She wiped tears from her cheeks with her sleeves and spat out the first question that floated into her consciousness. "Jean-Claude. What happened to him?" The memory of his crumpled form was burned in her mind like sun glare on her eyes.

"Who is Jean-Claude?" the chamberlain asked, trying to usher her away. "You must come away; this is no place for a lady."

"No place—" Isabelle's shock and horror turned a corner into anger. She shrugged off his hand. "They were shooting at me! That *was* my place, and he took it."

"As was his duty," the chamberlain said. "Your duty was to let him."

He was right, and Isabelle loathed him for it. She bit down a bilious surge of undeserved invective and snapped, "Find out what happened to my musketeer, Jean-Claude."

"By your command, Highness," he said by way of a sop to her nonexistent authority.

"Who are you, by the way?" Isabelle asked.

The man took a step back, composed himself, and in the midst of the chaos, took a deep bow. "I am Don Angelo, Your Highness. And my job will be much easier to do if you go inside your residence, where it is safe."

Four new guards surrounded Isabelle, and she allowed herself to be marched up a flight of wide, shallow steps toward what she guessed was the entryway to her residence. No place had ever felt so strange and foreign.

She pivoted, trying to orient herself. The staircase had deposited her on a colonnaded portico flanked by an elevated arcade that ran the width of this building. Far across the vast courtyard, the rest of the cavalcade trickled in the main gate. She searched the crowd for Jean-Claude but saw no sign of him. He had lain so still . . . she wasn't ready to face that. She would *never* be ready to face that. He had always been close to hand, always willing to lend an ear, even when he was pretending to be staggering drunk.

Was there no one left of her inner circle? Even Marie would be a comfort right now.

Marie! She'd been in the coach with Valérie and Vincent. Isabelle broke from her escort and hurried back to the coach, pushing past a host of people who thought they knew better than she which direction she ought to be going. She leaned inside. There sat Marie, covered in blood, staring straight ahead, unmoving and unmoved by the carnage. *Thank the Builder.*

"Marie, attend me," she said, her voice rough with relief.

Marie clambered out of the carriage, leaving behind a clean spot on the bloody upholstery. There was blood on the seat behind where Vincent had been sitting . . . which there should not have been, unless . . . yes, there it was, a hole in the seat cushion. The bullet had gone completely through him, but alchemetal was supposed to be proof against musket balls. And that wasn't all. The bullet had first come through the carriage's open window, shattered the mirror behind which he had been hiding, and kept right on going.

"Highness!" Don Angelo said. "Please come away from there."

"Of course," Isabelle said, but the cold, clicking, analytical part of her mind could not let this mess go unscrutinized.

She pulled out her maidenblade and probed the hole in the fabric for the bullet, but it had gone all the way through the padding and into the boards. Finally, she withdrew from the coach, but only to slip around its back end.

There, bulging from the wood behind Vincent's seat, was the bullet. It had made it almost all the way out. Had it carried just a little bit more force, it would have plinked down in the street somewhere and been lost.

She plied her maidenblade and prized the slug from its resting place. It was surprisingly small, shorter than the first joint of her wormfinger, and cylindrical except where the front end had been squashed and flattened, like a mushroom cap. It was made of some bright hard metal. It was scored along its sides at an angle, as if it had been torn with tiny claws.

"What are you doing?" Don Angelo asked.

Isabelle returned her maidenblade to its sheath and tucked the slug in her belt pouch. What was she doing? Nothing she cared to explain. *A bullet shouldn't have this much . . . punch*, she thought, but it was a hunch based, she feared, more on not wanting to believe what had just happened than on any objective truth. And it was not the sort of thing to interest a proper princess in any case. After the barest hesitation, she replied, "I am going inside, where we can all pretend it is safe."

⸻

The chamber into which Isabelle was introduced—her receiving room, she was told—was richly appointed with upholstered chairs, polished companion tables, and ornamental tapestries. What it lacked were windows and mirrors. Nor were the guards on the doors ornamental. This was meant to be a secure place.

What had no doubt been intended to be a serene and gracious welcome by the female staff had already been thrown into disarray by Valérie's bloodstained arrival. The poor decoy had been settled in a chair, and a half-dozen olive-skinned, raven-haired Aragothic women hovered around her. Everyone looked up and goggled when Isabelle, in boots, trousers, and military jacket, marched in.

Her male escort, swept along in her wake, tried to follow her, but she said, "Women's quarters. Out!" She made a sweeping gesture and the men retreated. The doors clicked shut. Isabelle wanted to follow the men out, to race back into the city and look for Jean-Claude, but she had duties. Some idiot had given these women into her charge.

The Aragothic women looked back and forth between Isabelle and Valérie in confusion, but all the Célestial handmaids, even Valérie, curtsied to Isabelle.

"Rise," Isabelle said. "Except you, Valérie. You sit down. Are you hurt?"

Valérie sat but did not settle. The veil had been pulled from her face. Sweat and tears had made a mess of her makeup, but she seemed to have reached an exhausted interlude in her weeping. "Vincent was terribly angry when he figured out he had been duped. He swore he was going to gut monsieur musketeer, but I . . . I talked him into the coach." Fresh tears welled from her eyes, and Isabelle would not have blamed her if she broke down, but after a few deep breaths she said, "And everything was going well. And then there was this terrible bang, and glass went everywhere, and he jerked in his seat, and his eyes went very round. He looked surprised." She shook her head as if trying to dislodge a biting fly. The other handmaids wrapped their arms around her shoulders and made soothing noises.

Isabelle bit back a dozen questions; Valérie needed time to pull herself together, and Isabelle didn't know what to do to help. Uttering platitudes like, "You did well," or, "It's over," could hardly be a comfort to her at this point. Likewise saying something like, "Would Vincent have wanted you to fall apart like this?" would squash her flat.

Instead, Isabelle asked, "Is there something we can get you? Wine? Blankets?"

Valérie looked at her with gratitude in her eyes. "Yes, please."

"Get her wine and warmth and anything else she wants," Isabelle said.

"What about you, Highness?" asked Darcy of sergeants-are-better-than-privates fame.

"I . . ." Isabelle hesitated. She felt neither good nor exactly calm, but, instead, strangely balanced, focused. It was as if she'd climbed a steep emotional cliff and found herself on a high plateau where the view was broad and clear but the air was cold and thin. She couldn't stay in this clarity above it all forever, only as long as it took to scout a course ahead.

"I am uninjured," she said, but Vincent was dead and Jean-Claude's fate uncertain. Was she defenseless now? Whom would she turn to for counsel?

A quiet cough drew her attention to the Aragothic ladies-in-waiting, all six of whom had formed up in an arc and stood with downcast eyes, apparently awaiting her recognition, or approval, or something. On a mannequin between them was displayed an elaborate, layered gown of silk and velvet, black and red with gold embroidery. It had matching gloves and slippers and lacquered combs for her hair.

"Highness," said the first lady, "allow us to cover your nakedness."

Isabelle looked down at herself, still clad in cuirass, jacket, trousers, and boots, and tried, unsuccessfully, to contemplate the propriety-is-more-important-than-reality mind-set that could possibly consider this naked, or that being so was important at a moment like this.

But as much as she wanted to hare away to find Jean-Claude, outside was more dangerous than inside, and information was likely to come to her faster than she could fetch it. And when that information arrived, she had to be ready to receive its bearers. Being clean, polished, calm, and collected could only help.

She spread her arms and said, "Ladies, I place myself at your mercy."

When Isabelle disrobed, the Aragothic lady who pulled off her right glove nearly swooned at the sight of her wormfinger, and all the others turned slightly green.

Isabelle glowered in habitual resentment of this revulsion, but she was still too worked up to be anything but blunt. She smoothed her expression and gathered the Aragoths around, holding her hand up like a torch. "I am Princesa Isabelle, and this is my hand. Yes, it is malformed, but there's nothing I can do about that; I just have to live with it. You all don't. If you stay, be informed that I am not ashamed of it and I will not hide it. Or, if you think this makes me a monster, or if you just can't stand the sight of it, you can go with my good blessings and a letter of recommendation. I leave the choice to each of you." Probably this would come back to bite her, but right now she didn't care.

The Aragothic ladies dispersed to discuss the matter with a great deal of whispering, and Isabelle's Célestial handmaidens took over the duties of bathing her. She hated this. People got one look at her wormfinger and forgot everything else about her. Not for the first time, she wondered if she wouldn't be better off just having the whole thing amputated at the wrist. Then she could claim she'd lost it in an accident. A stump would still be unattractive, but it might provoke reactions of sympathy rather than horror.

She lowered her gangly body into the steaming bath. The hot water soothed her flesh even if it couldn't touch the shivers in her soul. How could she be carrying on like normal while Vincent cooled, Valérie grieved, and Jean-Claude's fate remained uncertain? But maybe that was her job, to be the place where fear and panic stopped, to pin down one corner of reality so that disaster did not blow all civilization away, like a loose sail.

It physically hurt to turn her attention to the future, almost like ripping free of her own skin, but if her job was to pick up shattered pieces, she had damn well better have a plan.

As Jean-Claude liked to say, "In confusion, there is opportunity," and she expected a spate of opportunists to show up on her doorstep seeking audience. She made a mental wager with herself that the first ones to arrive would be the ones who had nothing important to do during a crisis. As a survivor of the Comte des Zephyrs's court, she knew the value of identifying such parasites and avoiding them.

Would Príncipe Julio come to check on her? He was presumably nearby, but he seemed to be the only person in all of Aragoth who wanted nothing to do with her.

She was still brooding on this when Olivia, her oldest handmaid, leaned in the door to the bath chamber and said, "Highness, Artifex Kantelvar is here. He seeks an audience."

Isabelle's first thought was to rush to meet the artifex, but Kantelvar had once again failed to stop an assassin from making a try at her, this time at great cost. She would not put her vulnerability on display by being rushed. "Tell him to wait until I am dressed."

Normally it took an hour or more to get sewn into a new dress, but Isabelle's Aragothic ladies seemed determined to make up for their earlier squeamishness and had her stitched up in a quarter of that time. The threads would hold, probably, as long as she didn't attempt any radical movements . . . like sitting down. She swept from the dressing room, hugged by velvet from the waist up and flowing with silk from the waist down. The strange short-hemmed, long-sleeved jacket that she had seen Margareta wearing was called a bolero, and Isabelle had been given one of black velvet embroidered in gold.

Kantelvar stood up from the padded chair the ladies-in-waiting had provided for his comfort. His hood hid his expression and his hunch distorted his body language, but the gleam from his emerald jewel of an eye fixed on her. He made a formal bow, the joints of his quondam prosthesis softly whining.

"Highness," he said, his voice a rasp. "Thanks be to the Builder, you are safe."

"Thanks be to Vincent, you mean," she replied.

"Yes, of course, what happened to your men was unfortunate, tragic, but they—"

"Men?" The plural form gripped her around the throat and made her voice quaver. "Jean-Claude?"

"I am given to understand he entered a building that exploded, but you must not—"

"But you don't know if he's . . ."

"Dead? I have not confirmed it, but he is not my charge. You have a greater destiny, and it is my concern to see that you reach it. I must keep you safe."

"You're doing a rotten job so far," Isabelle snapped. "Why are you here now, with the assassin still abroad?"

"You asked to be kept informed."

Isabelle sucked down a deep breath to calm herself. "Yes. And now I wish to know how this assassin managed to evade your security, kill my bodyguard, and elude capture."

Kantelvar's head shook. "I have not yet had the chance to investigate the scene myself, but I am informed there was a mirror—"

"Is this Thornscar again? I though you said he would still be incapacitated."

"I very much doubt it is Thornscar, but our enemy has many resources."

"And we don't?"

Kantelvar ignored that barb. "I had my men search every room in every building along the parade route. I can only surmise the assassin moved the mirror into the room after it was searched, possibly as recently as this morning. He then entered and departed the building by way of the mirror, leaving no trace of himself behind."

Isabelle forced her anger and disappointment back into its cage. Let it snarl in the background, but she had to think. "That's not entirely true. He left a bullet. It embedded itself in the back of the coach, and I recovered it."

There was a muddy gurgle from the hump under Kantelvar's cloak, and his bent back stiffened in surprise. "What did you do with it? Do you still have it?" His voice was rough, eager.

"It's in my coin purse. Darcy." She gestured to her junior handmaiden, who fetched the purse and handed it to Kantelvar.

Kantelvar accepted the pouch with his mechanical hand. He considered the silken purse for a moment, as if it were a puzzle box, then turned and shuffled to a small table flanking the doors and began worrying the strings. "My apologies, Highness, but my fingers are not as clever as they once were."

Isabelle nodded to him to go ahead; every day, she strove to prevent people's noticing how one-handed she was.

Kantelvar rummaged through the purse and then upended it. A few coins buzzed as they spun on the table. "There is no bullet here."

Isabelle stiffened. "What? Oh damn, it was an espejismo. It must have faded, like Jean-Claude's hat." Alas, the wound it caused was not so ephemeral. Still, the timing was strange. "But Jean-Claude said his hat disappeared immediately after falling off his head, while this bullet was embedded in the wood for much longer, a quarter of an hour at least."

"Metal lasts longer than cloth does, and an object to which significant emotion is attached will last longer than an object taken for granted. If this assassin is driven by hate, he may have spent weeks obsessing about that bullet, imagining the path it would tear through flesh, imbuing it with his obsession. I doubt your musketeer was so attached to his hat."

Isabelle subsided into frustration. Up until now, the horrors of her life had been known and familiar. They had been dread certainties of abuse and humiliation, killing her slowly. Survival had been a matter of coping with what she could not hope to combat. These attacks were different, knife-quick flashes of terror and chaos, here and gone, leaving blood in their wake before she could even grapple with them. She needed some way to slow them down. She pressed her wrists to her eyes and forced herself to think.

She said, "I think the killer may have been working for the Temple."

An angry boiling noise came from Kantelvar's hump and his posture stiffened. "What? What makes you think that?"

"An accurate musket that could punch through alchemetal and iron-wood. A bullet made of hard metal with strange grooves. That was a quondam device, and the Temple takes a dim view of anyone but itself having possession of the Builder's gifts." She gave a pointed look to Kantelvar's artificial limbs. "Also, there were three sagaxes down at the harbor who spoke of rising up against me . . . and you."

Kantelvar's tension subsided and his voice came out a metallic monotone. "I know those three. They are partisans of Príncipe Alejandro, probably sent down by his wife, Xaviera, as something of a clumsy snub. No one would employ them as conspirators, though. As you noticed, they tend to leak—the tongues of warriors and the spines of jelly-floaters, though I suppose they might be useful for disseminating misinformation."

"They claimed that you are obsessed with the Reckoning and the coming of the Savior."

Kantelvar stilled into one of his thoughtful silences, then rapped his staff on the ground and said, "The Temple's whole business is preparation for the end of these degenerate times. We are instructed not to wait for the Savior, but to prepare the way. Any cleric of any rank who is not working toward that end has failed his most fundamental duty."

There was little in theology of interest to Isabelle so she turned back to the subject at hand. "Then how do you explain the musket? It could not have been an ordinary weapon."

"The Temple certainly has the only legitimate collection of quondam devices, but not all collections are legitimate. Greedy, stupid men seek to circumvent the Builder's law and usurp His power as Iav of old did. This is especially true in Aragoth, where many Temple warehouses were raided and many artifacts stolen during the Skaladin occupation. Xaviera's father had a large collection of quondam relics that he seized from the invaders. He handed a great deal of it over to the Temple, and such was the nature of the time that no questions were asked concerning any pieces he might have kept for himself. He was, after all, defending the border from a heathen horde."

Isabelle stilled her expression. That was twice in less than a minute Kantelvar had tried to direct her suspicions at Xaviera from two entirely different angles. As someone raised by Jean-Claude, Isabelle's first thought was, *I should talk to her.*

The outer door opened and Olivia bustled in, her face flushed with as much excitement and alarm as if there had just been another assassination—with at least one person dead it hardly seemed fitting to think of it as just an attempt—and curtsied before Isabelle.

Isabelle gestured for her to speak, and Olivia said breathlessly, "Your Highness, His Imperial Majesty Leon XIV, le Roi de Tonnerre, arrives via his emissary."

Isabelle was nonplussed. Over the past few weeks, she had been so caught up researching particulars of the Aragothic court that she had mostly failed to consider the Célestial presence in San Augustus. But of course Grand Leon kept an embassy here, complete with a full diplomatic staff—the ambassador's name was Hugo du Blain, though she knew nothing else about him—and an emissary, a bloodhollow le roi maintained in San Augustus for those occasions when he needed to project his presence here in person.

Her breathing came too quick and her head felt light. She'd never been given to fits of the vapors, but this was Grand Leon. His word was more like a divine proclamation than mere law. By an act of the Builder's grace he had given her birth his blessing and bestowed on her Jean-Claude's protection.

"Send him in," Isabelle said, dry mouthed. Isabelle nervously brushed her new dress smooth. Olivia opened the door and stood aside, curtsying deeply, eyes downcast.

A tall, stout gentleman, larger than Jean-Claude but of the same general shape, stepped through the door. He was clearly a man of flesh and not a translucent bloodhollow, so Isabelle reasoned he must be Hugo du Blain, the Célestial ambassador. He wore the most elaborate costume Isabelle had ever seen on a man, layers of silk and satin in Célestial blue and white, with lacy cuffs and ruffs, a broad baldric, silver frogging, and several heaping helpings of silk braid. The fact that the ensemble looked glamorous instead of ridiculous was a testament to his tailor's genius.

Du Blain swept off a hat for which an entire flock of exotic birds had been sacrificed and announced, "His Imperial Majesty le Roi de Tonnerre, Leon XIV!"

Isabelle curtsied deeply as her imperial cousin entered. Grand Leon's emissary was a skinny man, dressed all in white, a doublet and roomy trousers tucked into tall white boots, all stitched with silver and pearls. Her gut sickened at the sight of the bloodhollow, and she could not help but wonder by what criteria the man had been selected for this hellish fate. Jean-Claude always said that Grand Leon kept few bloodhollows and selected only the worst criminals to endure this fate, but was there truly any crime so vile as to justify the harrowing of a soul?

As the emissary came through the door, Grand Leon's presence swelled inside it, bulging through the translucent flesh, stretching and molding it into a new shape, taller, broader of shoulder, an expression of le roi's towering pride and indomitable will rather than his actual physical shape. The bloodhollow's shadow turned from gray to red as Grand Leon forced his sorcery through the aperture of its flaccid soul. Any Sanguinaire sorcerer who could make a bloodhollow could inhabit its body, but for most that was as far as the transfer of power could go. As far as she knew, only Grand Leon could make his bloodhollow vessel produce a bloodshadow of its own. Even the Comte des Zephyrs at the height of his powers had not been able to achieve it. Cold comfort for those through whom he had experimented.

Isabelle's heart hammered so loud that she could barely hear herself think, but she managed to avert her eyes and mumble, "Your Majesty. How may I serve you?"

Grand Leon said, "Rise, Princess, be at ease, and you, Artifex Kantelvar, though I should have expected to find you elsewhere, hunting down whoever attacked our cousin."

Isabelle rose and Kantelvar said, "I cannot be everywhere at once, Majesty, and arranging to close the holes in Isabelle's security left by the deaths of her bodyguards seemed my paramount task."

"Indeed, though I do wonder how this debacle forwards your schemes, as all such calamities seem to do."

Kantelvar said, "You know as well as I do that a good strategy ensures all paths lead to victory, but as it happens, in this case, the Temple's only concern is to ensure the continuity of Aragoth's royal line. The preservation of the saintblooded sorceries is our greatest mandate."

Grand Leon made a curt gesture of acknowledgment, and Isabelle got the impression she'd been witness to one scene from the middle act of a much longer and more complicated play. She was very much a latecomer to her own betrothal.

Grand Leon looked Isabelle in the eyes, something men other than Jean-Claude rarely bothered to do, and asked, "Are you injured? Are you ill at heart? I would treat with you, if you are able."

Isabelle's throat tightened up. The very last thing in the world she wanted to do was treat with le roi. It could only lead to disaster . . . and yet was not treating with him any worse? She had lost Jean-Claude. *No, don't think like that.* Whether Jean-Claude was dead, or alive, or standing athwart the shadow's breach, she could not fail his faith in her by balking at the first test. *If you can't survive without me, then I have truly failed you.* She would not make a failure of him, even if her heart quailed and her bowels turned to water.

She filled her lungs and said, "My heart is wounded, but it still beats. What would you have of me?"

"I would have the story of your attack from your own lips. What did you see?"

"She saw nothing, Majesty."

Isabelle didn't dare turn her body away from Grand Leon, but she risked a glance as her father strolled in. The Comte des Zephyrs wore Marie's body, his face pressing out from her ghostly features. He took up a station in front of Isabelle and bowed to Grand Leon. Isabelle's mustered courage wobbled into a familiar queasy loathing, and her tongue clove to her palate. Grand Leon might not strike her down out of pure spite, but her father would. He would silence her, punish her. He always had.

The comte filled his voice with indignation. "Isabelle was not in the coach when the attack occurred because the musketeer, of whose many offenses

I have previously made you aware, compromised the integrity of Isabelle's security arrangements by removing her from the protective perimeter. His recklessness directly resulted in the debacle during the cavalcade and the death of Isabelle's guard captain."

Outrage flared in Isabelle's heart. Jean-Claude had spent his whole life watching out for her, but who would watch over him or the shade of his honor? *Me.*

"Lies!" she spat, as if the word were made of fire. Her father could not cast his shadow at her through Marie, but he would beat her somehow. Buoyed by her anger, quivering from expectation of the blow, she stepped around the comte so as to be on equal footing with him in regard to le roi. Facts were what she had, and so that was what she deployed. "Thanks to Jean-Claude, I was nowhere near the shooting, and even if I had been in the coach, Vincent still would have been shot. As it happened, I was sitting a horse in the cavalcade and had a very good view. The shot came from a second-story window along the left-hand side of the road. The bullet punched all the way through an alchemetal breastplate, Vincent's chest, and an inch of ironwood. The only thing I missed by not being there was getting sprayed with blood. I also saw Jean-Claude leap from the back of a running horse into the window from which the shot had come, and I saw the room explode, and I saw him lying facedown on the ground afterward. After the coach stopped, I pulled the bullet out, but it was apparently an espejismo because it vanished shortly thereafter."

The comte said, "Sire, please forgive my daughter's temper. She is over-wrought and not thinking clearly. May I suggest she be allowed to retire while we discuss these important matters?"

Grand Leon cleared his throat and silenced the room. He gazed intently at Isabelle. She felt herself start to shrink and melt away like a sugar sculpture in the rain. She dared not offend le roi, and many nobles grew wrathful if proper deference was not given . . . but Grand Leon was in no way typical. He was the man who had employed Jean-Claude, after all.

What does he want? That was Jean-Claude's favorite question. Le roi wanted to use Isabelle to see to Célestial interests in Aragoth. The question became whether he would try to use her as pawn, player, or partner. Not the latter if she shrank from the comte's bullying.

Stand tall, she could almost hear Jean-Claude whispering in her ear. Riding her pain and outrage, Isabelle squared her shoulders and met Grand

Leon's gaze steadily. She did not race to defend herself verbally as a desperate woman might. She had to be both strong and reserved and trust him to read her correctly.

The corner of Grand Leon's mouth twitched in what might have been a suppressed smile, and he turned to Kantelvar. "What do you think, Artifex? Was my musketeer's ploy reckless or inspired?"

The artifex's hump gurgled, and his clicking voice said, "That which is inspired is frequently reckless. In any case, it seems not to have affected the outcome."

"An aphorism and an evasion. I should have expected nothing else. Comte, your petition is denied. We choose to include Princess Isabelle in our councils. I now assume you will point out that, until she is married, you remain her legal guardian, entitled to know her business."

"I would not presume to tell you what you already know, sire."

"Indeed. We would hear what Isabelle thinks should be done to ensure her safety."

The request caught Isabelle off guard. She was on trial, her mettle being tested. Even that was something; she'd never been acknowledged to have mettle before. *Forge it hot and hammer it hard.*

She wished for eloquence but settled for logic. "I suggest a small troupe of guards loyal only to me as a last line of defense, and a larger group of agents to seek out threats and deal with them before they get near me. I would rather confront my enemies in their bedrooms than mine."

Grand Leon said, "Your husband may wish for you to be more heavily guarded."

Isabelle tried to keep the sourness from her voice. "Despite two attempts on my life, my betrothed has made no attempt whatever to contact me, not even by proxy. For now, I must assume his indifference will continue."

"Two attacks?" the comte asked.

Kantelvar ignored him and said, "The prince is well apprised of your situation, Highness, and he looks forward to meeting you, but he is constantly observed and politics have made it impossible for him to seek you out in person."

"Which politics?" Isabelle asked. "And why does he accede to them?"

"In the interest of prosecuting the investigation, the attack against you on the ship was kept secret—"

"I had a right to know!" the comte snapped, and then he started coughing as the stress of his anger and the effort of projecting into Marie took a toll on his distant, enfeebled body. Isabelle hoped it would force him to withdraw but prayed the fit would not kill him, not until Kantelvar had a chance to resuscitate Marie . . . if that was not an empty blandishment.

"He could have sent a message," Isabelle said. "And why is he not here now?"

Kantelvar said, "Because after today's attempt on your life, and with the threat of civil war on the horizon, all the royal family currently in the city have been moved to places of refuge lest some political opportunist attempt to abort the succession debate by an assassination during the uproar."

Once again, Grand Leon coughed quietly, and the conversation stilled. "Gentlemen, if you please, we would have a private word with our cousin."

Kantelvar raised a mechanical finger as if to make a point, but Grand Leon's bloodshadow rippled, a sleeping giant on the verge of awakening, and the cleric subsided. The artifex took the comte by the arm and led him into the corridor outside with all the other servants. The felt-lined door shut with a dull thunk. A heavy and complete silence fell.

Isabelle almost wished her father had stayed; she could count on her fury at him to give her strength beyond fear. Perhaps that was why he had been dismissed.

She faced her sovereign. Suddenly the spacious chamber felt very small, or Grand Leon very large within it. She waited, trying not to shudder, wondering why he deigned to treat her as, if not an equal, at least someone worth listening to. Her wormfinger twitched in its glove, agitated.

Grand Leon gazed upon her for a long moment. She was just wondering if she ought to offer a conversational gambit when he said, "You have cultivated the gift of silence. Good. Most of my nobles prefer to assail me with opinions, requests, outrage, flattery, demands, and the occasional outright lie. Can you see the problem, from their point of view, that is?"

Since he seemed to value silence, Isabelle gave the question due consideration before saying, "Because they are telling you what they want, and therefore giving you a way to manipulate them."

Grand Leon smiled, saying neither yes or no, and then changed the subject. "The world turns. King Carlemmo is dying. I should rejoice, for his death will leave his kingdom divided and weak. Ripe for the plucking. But how to obtain it without bruising the fruit?

"Carlemmo's obvious heir, Príncipe Alejandro, is out of favor and has been exiled across the deep sky, and his reserve heir, your betrothed, is crippled and weak, almost entirely under the thrall of his mother.

"And yet with Carlemmo dead, I will have outlived my oldest rival, and all my younger ones are so tediously earnest. They are still filled with the deadly delusions of youth and power, not realizing that youth is temporary and power, even the power of sorcerer kings, is fundamentally limited. We cannot alter the skylands in their peregrinations, or the Solar in its daily journey, or the weather on which it seems all other things ultimately depend. I have ruled my empire for more than fifty years, and while I have no intention of dying any time soon, I have come to be humbled by the vastness of time."

Isabelle strove to divine a deeper purpose to this soliloquy. Was he truly baring his soul to her, or was this some official fiction? It had the grandiose stage quality of a nonpareil autobiography, but there was no doubt that he had a grandiose soul, so there was no telling.

There was a large tapestry map of Aragoth on the wall. As Grand Leon spoke, his bloodshadow flowed up and surrounded the kingdom, pressing against its borders like a crimson fist around a plum. "My nobles strain at their leads, like hounds on the scent of a wounded animal. They want to ravage the beast and gorge themselves on its flesh even before its heart stops beating." Barbs of crimson stabbed past the border into the center of the country.

As the shadow stretched, somewhere in the back of Isabelle's mind, on a level beyond normal hearing, she heard or felt screams, the echoing wails of all the tormented souls he had shadowburned. The un-sound stood her every nape hair on end. She reminded herself that Grand Leon had a reputation for sipping lightly from those upon whom his bloodshadow fed . . . but still he kept bloodhollow emissaries, one in every kingdom big enough for an embassy. Restraint was a relative concept.

Grand Leon continued, "Nor are my nobles alone. Aragoth teeters, and all the petty kingdoms around it are ready to pounce. The Vecci have designs on it, and the countryside swarms with Stalfjell mercenaries. Even the barons of Oberholz are pacing around the edges, a pack of starving wolves looking for an easy kill. All that holds them back is their mutual distrust of each other and the promise of an easier battle once the Aragoths start fighting amongst themselves, as all are convinced that they must do.

"I, conversely, have no desire for bloodshed, no yearning for useless glory, no desire to heap rewards on my nobles for being shortsighted brutes. Nor do I have any desire to have l'Empire's longest border devolve into unproductive turmoil." His shadow withdrew from the map, like an outgoing tide, and puddled around his feet. The mental howling faded from perception if not memory.

To Isabelle he asked, "What do you think?"

Isabelle spoke carefully. "I think that keeping the peace would be a good idea."

"And how do you think that might be accomplished?"

"Forgive me, Majesty, but I have barely begun to scratch the surface of Aragothic intrigue. So far, the closest ally of my mother-in-law-to-be has hired an anti-royalist to kill me so that my position may be given to his dearest enemy, and everyone seems to think this makes sense. From my outsider's perspective, it seems the only way to prevent a war would be for there to be a truce between the príncipes, but no one seems to think that such an agreement is within the realm of possibility. Indeed, you just said Príncipe Alejandro has been exiled."

"Not in so many words. Margareta had him sent to the Craton Riqueza on the pretense of performing a royal audit of the treasure ports. She wants him to be as far away from Aragoth as possible when Carlemmo dies. It is a gamble, however, because fully half of Aragoth's navy is on or about Craton Riqueza, and an extraordinary number of them are in sky dock, suffering from outbreaks of swamp fatigue, or otherwise exhibiting a noteworthy disinclination to follow orders from their fleet command—but Alejandro's proximity may well motivate them to his cause, if only because some admiral sees the chance to play kingmaker.

"Meanwhile, Margareta is hoping Carlemmo dies while Alejandro is still en route, leaving him neither here nor there when the incivilities begin in earnest. She has also taken the precaution of keeping his wife, Princesa Xaviera, in San Augustus."

"A royal hostage," Isabelle said.

"But not a very good one, from Margareta's perspective. Xaviera has proven barren, else this succession conundrum would not exist. As it stands, many of Alejandro's supporters would be happy to see her replaced with a more fecund bride, but Alejandro will have none of it."

Good for him. Isabelle liked Alejandro already, better than Julio, in fact, but she said, "And so the príncipe's allies would be happy to see his wife murdered by his worst enemy. This is more evidence that Aragothic politics are insane."

"They would settle for having her set aside as an honored and acknowledged mistress, but Alejandro refuses even that compromise."

Isabelle reflected on Grand Leon's household. The queen had died years ago, but le roi kept three acknowledged mistresses—who also happened to be the most intelligent and influential women in l'Empire—so perhaps that idea did not seem offensive to him.

She took the conversation in another direction. "It seems to me that I will be a poor hostage as well, seeing as many in Aragoth disagree with me on religious grounds and would be happy to see me given to the sky."

"Ah, but being an inadequate hostage can make you a more effective negotiator; your value will be in what resources you can offer rather than in your, shall we say, intrinsic worth."

Isabelle sensed that this was near the core of the matter le roi had been easing up to. "And what resources can I offer? Do you propose to empower me to deliver the full weight of l'Empire to my husband's cause?"

"If Margareta is willing to make certain concessions to l'Empire, yes."

For a moment Isabelle was too stunned to do anything but stare at him. She wanted to ask, *Are you serious?* One might doubt Grand Leon's purposes or disagree with his reasons, but never ever his proclamations.

Isabelle forced herself to ask, "What sort of concessions?"

"Margareta is prickly to deal with. She is clever, aggressive, and opportunistic, but she is also impatient. She has shown a tendency to mortgage the future for the sake of the present. There was even a rumor, a nasty slander I believe, that when a previous artifex offered to help make her queen to fill the gap left by the childbed death of Carlemmo's first wife, she offered up her firstborn son to the Temple in exchange. Alas, the clergyman disappeared shortly after she was crowned, so he never had a chance to collect."

Isabelle's curiosity was piqued. "Another artifex? Was that the same one who showed up at my birth?" It would have been about the right time.

Grand Leon's expression grew dark. "That is one of the details Jean-Claude neglected to procure during his scramble to salvage your life."

Isabelle winced, cursing herself for forgetting that Jean-Claude had been sent to guard her as a punishment for his incorrigible impudence. She did her best to reverse course. "How can an artifex just disappear?"

"I am informed that he attempted a crossing into Skaladin to meet with tribes disaffected by the sultan in an attempt to create a buffer between the sultanate and Aragoth. Instead, he was waylaid and killed. The most popular rumor is that one of his retinue was left alive to carry his meat back to Om as a taunt while the raiders took his Exalted metal parts as a trophy, sacred artifacts to be traded for high honor in the sultan's court."

"Do you believe that?" Isabelle asked.

Grand Leon made an ambivalent gesture. "I hear many fantastic rumors. Most turn out to be false or greatly exaggerated. Some simply dissipate like smoke. A very few prove true.

"On a matter closer to hand and nearer to the present, I deem Margareta's lust for power to rule her sensibilities. It is likely she will not object too heavily when you insist that, in return for l'Empire's support, your children be fostered in the Célestial court."

Isabelle stiffened as if slapped. In the same dialogue, le roi had told a horror story about Margareta's agreeing to sell her unborn children and then suggested Isabelle do the same. Of course, noble children were always pawns to politics, royal children ten times so, but to Isabelle, who had long believed that children were a dream out of reach, the idea of crafting a child of her flesh and soul only to send it away was revolting.

Yet this was a man whose mistresses were his closest councilors and by whom he had dozens of children, acknowledged bastards all. He could not be oblivious to maternal impulses.

"And what will you do if the queen does not agree to these conditions?" Isabelle asked.

Grand Leon said, "I doubt she will refuse. She wants to capture Aragoth intact, which will not happen if it comes to blows."

"But if she did, you must have a plan for it. Every good plan includes a contingency."

"Now you are starting to sound like Kantelvar—the man has wheels within wheels—but yes, there is an alternate plan, not as elegant, quite a bit more tediously bloody, but effective. I don't suppose you know what persistence hunting is?"

This coming from a man whom Isabelle deemed to have his own many-layered, deeply laid plans. She said, "In Gottfreid's *Eine Studie der Bar-*

baren, he describes persistence hunting as a technique used by the tribes of Nyl during the dry season wherein a large, dangerous animal is harassed continuously by a rotating schedule of hunters. Prevented from drinking or resting, it eventually collapses from exhaustion and makes for a safe kill."

Grand Leon's eyebrows rose in surprise of the pleasant variety. "Precisely so. A similar technique should work here. We grant a little aid to one faction, then a little aid to the other to prolong the war. Back and forth. Over and again. It will probably take years, but eventually the beast of Aragoth will collapse and succumb to our coup de grace. The hard part will be restraining our nobles from full commitment. They will be so eager for glory and plunder that they would likely forfeit victory to achieve it."

The proposed strategy made Isabelle rather queasy, but le roi continued, "On the other hand, if Margareta is assured of our cooperation, we can resolve the debate swiftly and decisively, capturing Aragoth mostly intact and possibly without untidy lakes of blood."

Isabelle saw the two visions of the future spooling out before her. She took the yet raw, bloody events of the day, the terror, the agony, the grief, and multiplied them a thousandfold in her mind. It beggared her imagination, and yet, she suspected, fell far short of the reality. To condone war was unthinkable.

"You ask much of the unborn," she said. "Such a heavy burden to put on babes not yet conceived, much less born. Their grandmother might not mind using them as a tribute, but the notion cuts their mother to the quick."

Grand Leon looked at her sharply, then shrewdly, his ghostly eyes glimmering like stars through a fog. He was, she realized, looking for the first time at Isabelle the person rather than Isabelle the princess, and she prayed to all the saints that bringing that facet of her being to his attention was not a mistake. Just because he was aware of women's priorities didn't mean he respected them. On the other hand, he had recognized all his bastards.

"It is not out of the question that arrangements could be made with the mother," Grand Leon said. "And I would suggest the mother consider all the alternatives. In l'Empire, she could be sure her children would be safe under the protection of a strong emperor, raised with Célestial culture, trained at the finest academies—"

"And they would make all the best Célestial friends, who are the glue that holds kingdoms together," Isabelle said. "And so Aragoth would be conquered, not by war, or even economy, but by culture."

"And does that seem insane to you, compared to what you have seen of Aragoth?"

"It sounds . . . elegant, but it would make me a traitor to my husband, to make his children tools of a foreign power."

"Ah," he said, and he scraped the underside of his chin with his thumb in a rare thoughtless gesture. "Your concern touches upon the nature of royalty and reality. Any decision we make, no matter how wise or foolish, bold or timid, will be paid for in blood and pain and suffering. If we order a road built, inevitably someone will die building it, and once it is finished trade will shift from one town to another, one man will grow rich while another will starve. If we are wise, we do more good than harm, but we can no more avoid causing harm than we can avoid growing old.

"Your decision, like so many, must eventually be phrased in terms of whom to serve. If you try to do it the other way around, to decide whom to avoid betraying, you will be ineffectual and it will drive you mad."

Were these Grand Leon's true beliefs or just a heap of steaming platitudes?

"Dare I ask whom you serve?" she asked.

Grand Leon beamed at her. "By the Builder, I thought Jean-Claude's frequent praise of your wit was excessively effusive, but I see that he in fact fell short of the mark." He must have seen Isabelle blanch at the mention of Jean-Claude's name, for he let the matter drop and went on more neutrally, "I serve l'Empire Céleste. In my youth, I served myself and thought that l'Empire did too, but that is foolish. A man must die, but an empire can go on forever. The question of the moment is, whom do you serve?"

Isabelle quailed before this question. The intensity of his gaze told her this was the fulcrum. If she spoke one way, he would confer a terrible authority on her, the right to bestow in his name all the might of l'Empire Céleste. If she spoke another, she would be relegated to the status of pawn. Either way, her whole future and mayhap the futures of countless others depended on her word . . . or his reaction to her word. Where did culpability begin or end? Did she really want to be the one to touch off a senseless war?

No. Nor did she feel any particular loyalty to Julio. To her unborn children then? But no, a parent must raise a child, not submit to it.

"I serve peace," she said. That was the only cause in this whole mess worth

fighting for. Peace for her children to grow up in. Peace to spare the suffering of tens of thousands.

Grand Leon sniffed, one corner of his mouth twitched up, and she knew
she had failed his test. How could Grand Leon respect anything so child-
ish, so naive, so weak?

"Really? Most men would have said they served me."

Isabelle's knees weakened, but she couldn't buckle. "I am not a man, and
I serve peace." She wanted no part of anything else.

"An epitaph to be carved upon your gravestone, no doubt, but it's an
impossible task. Choose another."

Isabelle felt all futures slipping away, but she would not yield. Her voice
came thick. "I think choosing another is your job now, sire."

"You defy me?" Grand Leon growled.

"I answer you truthfully," Isabelle said.

"And what will you do when I put the negotiations for an alliance between Aragoth and l'Empire in the hands of my ambassador? He will
bargain as I instruct him."

Isabelle's vision grew blurry as hot tears welled up in her eyes. "I will
continue to advocate for peace." For all the good it would do.

At last Grand Leon stepped back, and said, "Kneel."

It was all Isabelle could do to maintain her poise as she smoothed her
skirt and sank to her knees in the traditional posture of submission. If le roi
had held a sword he could have easily lopped her head off. It would not
come to that—they still needed her to breed—but she dreaded whatever
punishment he might devise. Her father had found endless ways to humili-
ate her, and Grand Leon was many times more clever.

Grand Leon placed a hand on her shoulder, the cold fingers of a bloodhollow. "Princess Isabelle des Zephyrs, imperial cousin, we hereby grant
you the position of special ambassador to the court of Aragoth, with full
powers to make peace or declare war."

Isabelle blinked hard in surprise, squishing out her unshed tears, and
looked up. "Majesty, I . . . don't understand." Was this some kind of cruel
joke?

"It means we give the negotiations for l'Empire's part in Aragoth's succession squabble into your hands. A civil war here would be a disaster. A
winnable disaster from l'Empire's point of view, but too costly by half. Peace,
though, has possibilities."

"And what would l'Empire gain from peace?"

Grand Leon gave the barest hint of a smile. "Our barons are a fractious lot, many of whom would happily see all the progress we have made turning l'Empire into a nation undone if they thought that by such calamity they could obtain one more square meter of land. Many of them have mortgaged themselves to the hilt to muster armies in anticipation of an Aragothic civil war. If they are forced to withdraw without conquest they will be broken on poverty's wheel, much easier to control than if they are allowed to glut themselves on plunder. Hence, I need a negotiator who will fight for that peace until her last breath, and I give her the might of l'Empire to commit at her will. Certainly Margareta will want l'Empire's armies at her side, and you know my terms."

Isabelle sensed the words he'd left unsaid. "Because you know I will do everything in my power to avoid actually making that commitment, because to do so will cost me my children." She had been wrong to think he didn't understand a woman's priorities. He knew exactly where her jugular was.

Before Isabelle could ponder her predicament, the soundproof door rasped open and a river of sound welled in like water through a cracked dam, a babble of voices that quickly became a flood, further churned up with the thud of marching feet.

Isabelle turned where she knelt. *What in the world?*

One voice rose above the rest: "I demand to see Princess Isabelle!"

"Jean-Claude!" He was alive! Thank all the saints! Isabelle lurched to her feet, rushed to the double doors, and threw them wide.

A quartet of guardsmen in various shades of livery, Aragothic and Célestial, bore Jean-Claude on a stretcher slung between two halberds. His face was smudged and bloody, his left arm was bandaged, and his right leg was in a splint, but his eyes lit up when he saw her. He was absolutely the most glorious thing she had ever seen. She plunged into the swirling pool of people surrounding him and threw her arms around his blue-coated waist. His age-thickened middle was reassuringly solid. "Thank the Savior! I was so . . . I thought you were . . ." Damn that taboo against expressing concern. "I will see you are granted great honor."

He folded his uninjured arm around her shoulders. "Highness, I already have the greatest honor I could ever want."

Isabelle would have liked to bury her face in his middle and weep for pure relief, but that would not make a good show. A princess was expected to be, if not detached, then certainly decorous. A momentary outburst of joy was permissible; wallowing in it was not.

Worse, saints help her, she had turned her back on le roi, a serious social blunder.

Isabelle jerked back from Jean-Claude as if she were on a hook, turned, and curtsied deeply to Grand Leon. Had she just undone all the devious trust he'd placed in her? Some nobles could be so damned touchy about the fine points of etiquette.

Jean-Claude's head swiveled around until he caught sight of Grand Leon. He swept his hat in an approximation of a bow. "Majesty, please excuse me for bleeding in your presence, but someone just tried to shoot the princess's coach and bomb me, which is rather backward of the way I would have done it, but I am thankful for his incompetence."

Apparently unperturbed, Grand Leon gestured for Isabelle to stand up. He gave Jean-Claude a look of very nearly paternal exasperation. "I can see that the decades have not blunted your enthusiasm for extravagant pain. I will want a full report on this latest calamity when you have rested, but for now, we forgive your dishevelment and order you not to exsanguinate."

Isabelle was befuddled. This seemed more like the reunion of two old friends than the tense confrontation between a musketeer and the monarch who had exiled him to l'Île des Zephyrs all those years ago. Maybe this was one of those mysterious male traditions she always found so baffling.

Jean-Claude's bearers made to set him down on a sofa, but the Aragothic handmaids, who had surged in with the rest of the crowd, rushed to cover the embroidered fabric with a rough cloth to prevent Jean-Claude's wounds from seeping on it.

Don Angelo emerged from the swirl of people and bowed to Grand Leon. "Your Majesty, we have recovered your musketeer."

"Hah!" Jean-Claude scoffed. "Do you know what they tried to do to me? They tried to sic a surgeon on me. Builder be praised I woke before he sawed any bits off."

Don Angelo wore an expression that suggested a man sucking on a lemon. "In his . . . delirium, your bodyguard threatened to shoot King Carlemmo's royal surgeon."

Grand Leon's eyebrows twitched in suppressed amusement. "Did he?"

Jean-Claude's face was ashen and haggard, but he seemed to be trying to cover up his weakness with more than his usual abrasiveness. "I'd be doing el rey a service if I did. Doctors kill more soldiers than bullets. The only reason we don't take more of them to battle is we can't get them to operate on the enemy first."

Don Angelo replied tartly, "Perhaps Célestial surgeons are in the habit of killing their patients. It is not so in Aragoth. At any rate, the surgeon managed to get the shrapnel fragments out of your leg, clean the wound, and stitch it up before you awoke and started bellowing."

Isabelle, who was too wrung out for any more excitement, raised a mollifying hand. "Thank you, Don Angelo, for granting my humble request to find Jean-Claude. It seems my faithful guardian is still quite distressed from his pain. I think he will calm down more quickly without so many people around." She made an ushering motion and took a step toward the door. Don Angelo, perforce, retreated, drawing stretcher bearers, handmaids, and other assorted hangers-on in his wake.

Isabelle said, "You may give my thanks to the surgeon, and you may both expect Jean-Claude's personal apology, once he returns to his senses. For now, I think a little peace and quiet is in order."

Yet before she could push the door closed, Kantelvar shouldered to the front of the throng with Marie in tow. The comte's visage had withdrawn from Marie's features.

Kantelvar said, "Highness, if I may be permitted."

As much as Isabelle didn't want a room full of people, it seemed unnecessary to yank Marie from Kantelvar's grasp and slam the door in his face, so she stood aside to let them both in before closing the doors on the crowd.

Kantelvar handed Marie off to Isabelle and bowed to Grand Leon. "Majesty. If I may be so bold as to question your musketeer."

"Jean-Claude is wounded," Grand Leon said. "I would not have him overtaxed."

"As you wish, of course, but the longer we wait to question him, the more time our enemies will have to cover their trail."

"He did a pretty thorough job of that with the bomb," Jean-Claude said, shifting uncomfortably on the sofa. "There was a gunshot from a second story. I leapt in through the window, hoping to surprise the shooter, but he was gone when I arrived. He escaped through a mirror."

"Are you sure?" Kantelvar asked.

"I came in through the window. Two of your soldiers came in the opposite door. There were no other methods of egress. So, yes, he must have been a Glasswalker, unless there is some sorcery that allows one to walk through walls."

"Not that I know of," Kantelvar said.

Jean-Claude waved this away. "However he got out, he left a bomb behind. I saw the fuse smoke and jumped out the window. The wall shielded me from the worst of the blast."

"Builder be praised," Isabelle said. Ever since she'd seen him lying on the street, she'd felt as if she were drowning. Now she could breathe again.

Jean-Claude smiled at her. "The next thing I knew, the damn doctor was pecking at me like a vulture. I fought him off, commandeered some soldiers, and made my way here."

Isabelle said, "Savior be praised that you were so alert and quick. But why did the assassin leave a bomb?"

"A trap for anyone who tried to chase him," Jean-Claude said. "Or to blow the mirror to pieces to prevent another Glasswalker from trailing him, if that's even possible."

"It is," Kantelvar said. "If the pursuer is very skilled. It's a moot point now; any clues that might have been in that room are either vanished or destroyed."

Grand Leon said, "And that, I believe, is all we need to know for tonight. Kantelvar, walk with me awhile and let us leave these good people to recover from their noble exertions."

"As you wish," Kantelvar said.

Only once they were gone did Jean-Claude allow his posture to sag. "Thank the Savior."

"Tonight, Vincent was the Savior," Isabelle said.

Jean-Claude winced. "I heard. I cannot say I liked him, but I did not wish him dead. Dead people are no fun to pester."

"Hah!" Isabelle laughed in spite of herself, and the involuntary spasm knocked a question loose inside of her. "Do you think he died for nothing? I wasn't even in the carriage."

Jean-Claude took a moment to answer, and he spoke carefully. "He died maintaining the illusion. The illusion was what was keeping you safe, so, no, he did not die for nothing."

Isabelle resisted the urge to sit down. The new stitching in her gown was already warping in directions it ought not. Pieces of it were threatening to slough off. "So what do we do now? All our clues vanish as fast as we find them, and we learn nothing."

"That's not entirely true. We know the killer has an accomplice; someone had to put that mirror in that room for him."

"And the bomb. Unless he set them both up in advance, then went and left his body somewhere else while his espejismo returned via the mirror. It would, as you say, reduce the circle of people in on the plot."

"True." Jean-Claude rubbed his forehead in obvious exhaustion. "But I will look for an accomplice anyway. Just as soon as I can walk."

"How bad is it?" she asked.

"It hurts, but it's stopped bleeding, and the surgeon did get all the bits out, I'll give him that much. Thank the Savior for leather and silk. Cotton and wool get all tangled up in the wound. You can't get them all out, and the wound festers around them. Silk and leather, though, they don't break up so much. They're easier to get out."

He was babbling, plainly at the end of his rope but not willing to let go. He didn't know how to quit, so he just kept going while his internal spring wound down.

"Stand down, soldier," Isabelle said. "That's an order. And get some sleep, because I will not rest until you do."

Jean-Claude's mouth opened as if to protest, but then he nodded and said, "Your wish is my command, Highness."

CHAPTER
Eleven

The morning after the cavalcade, Isabelle met Queen Margareta in an airy courtyard with terraced sides overflowing with greenery. Garden trees, shrubs, and flowers filled the enclosure with a sweet, mossy, heady perfume. Harp music came from somewhere deep in the bushes.

Isabelle crossed the courtyard at a decorous walk, bracing herself for the audience. Kantelvar lurched along at her side, bearing the scroll that held her freshly inked ambassadorial credentials.

After meeting the queen's espejismo on the *Santa Anna*, Isabelle had wondered how true her imperious image was to her incarnate reality. In fact, the flesh-and-blood queen was shorter and stouter than her espejismo, but not grossly so; the biggest change was in the quality of her skin, which in reality was somewhat oily and porous, not the color of milky starlight she had so ardently projected. *Do you think of yourself as a celestial being, Majesty?*

A small court of ladies, officials, and entertainers attended her. The only one Isabelle recognized, by dint of the silver tiara in her braided black hair, was the queen's stepdaughter-in-law, the crown princess Xaviera, whose lean, heart-shaped face was marred by a rigid expression that suggested a statue brought *almost* to life. It was generally hard to tell what the Glasswalkers were looking at with their silvered eyes, but Isabelle felt the pressure of Xaviera's gaze the instant she came into view.

Isabelle had been informed by her Aragothic handmaidens that the crown princess was far too mannish, blunt, brash, and bellicose. Isabelle was instantly intrigued—she sounded like a kindred misfit spirit—but her curiosity was tempered by the likelihood that they were destined to be on opposite sides of a civil war.

In defiance of all tradition Xaviera wore a sword on one hip and a pistol on the other. Her skirts, though elegant, were not of a standard cut and probably concealed modifications that would allow her freedom of movement. Underneath the silk and satin, she was stretched taut as a bowstring.

Notably absent, again, was Príncipe Julio. Yes, this was technically a ladies' court, but that did not mean men were entirely forbidden. Kantelvar had accompanied her in, and Margareta had a bodyguard, a knife-faced man with skin the color of chestnuts, armed with a sword, a dagger, and a brace of pistols. His high collar bore a whole regiment of dueling pins.

Isabelle curtsied before the queen. Her tongue felt like lead in her mouth, but she no longer had the option of silence's shield. "Your Majesty."

"Princess Isabelle," Margareta said. "Rise and be welcome."

Isabelle stood. "I bring greetings from my cousin, His Célestial Majesty Leon XIV, le Roi de Tonnerre. He bids you peace and prosperity."

"An awkward wish, as peace and prosperity are ever at odds," Margareta replied. "But we do not hold the message against the messenger. On behalf of my husband, His Majesty King Carlemmo II, el Rey de los Espejos, and myself, I welcome you, at long last, to our humble house."

Isabelle extended her good hand toward Kantelvar. "If I may present my credentials as Célestial ambassadress."

Margareta curled her fingers. Kantelvar clanked forward and handed the scroll to the bodyguard, who opened it and showed it to Margareta. She gave it a cursory glance and said, "Everything seems to be in order."

Isabelle felt she ought to say something, but she had no idea how to begin negotiating for peace. The only way she could see to avoid a war was if the brothers agreed not to fight, but neither one of them was accessible . . . except here through wife and mother. From everything Isabelle had heard of Margareta, she seemed unlikely to abort her grab for power, but what about Xaviera? Could she negotiate on her husband's behalf?

No sooner had Isabelle turned her thoughts in that direction than Margareta gestured to Xaviera. "Princesa Xaviera, make yourself known to soon-to-be–Crown Princesa Isabelle."

In her lap, Xaviera's hands were clenched into white-knuckled fists. "My lord and husband commands me to bring you greetings, Princesa."

Margareta scowled, and Isabelle judged it was because Xaviera had obeyed her command while simultaneously denying her authority.

Isabelle caught Xaviera's silver gaze as best she could. "I . . . Please give your husband my thanks. I pray you are reunited soon in happiness and health."

Margareta said, "Alas, that is a prayer unlikely to be answered. Xaviera does her best to project hardiness but her fitness is doubtful."

Xaviera's sinewy features grew even harder. Her reflective eyes had a blue patina Isabelle had not seen on any other Aragoth, like tarnished silver. Her painted lips were also creased around the edges like an old woman's.

"You question my fitness and yet you would let this in." Xaviera's hand jerked toward Isabelle. "Misbegotten and malformed."

Isabelle's cheeks burned.

"Xaviera! That is uncalled for," Margareta snapped, but the crinkles around her eyes were smug.

She set this up. Of course there was nothing Margareta would like better than for Isabelle and Xaviera to be at each other's throats.

Isabelle let go a long breath and began peeling off her right-hand glove.

Xaviera was riveted, but Margareta leaned forward. "Isabelle, what are you doing?"

"The truth of a thing is never as horrible as the anticipation of that thing," Isabelle said, a steady mantra in her life. She had been cursed with the title of Breaker's get since she was too young to understand anything but its hateful tone. To this day, she remembered clinging to Jean-Claude's leg, weeping herself insensible while he stroked her hair and made her say a hundred times that she was not touched by the Breaker. It ought to have been easier to deal with by now, but some types of pain just got worse over time.

She pulled her wormfinger from her glove and held it up for display. It wriggled like a worm on a fishhook.

Xaviera growled, "You are Breaker touched, unclean."

Margareta relaxed.

Kantelvar stepped up from behind Isabelle as if to shield her. "She has been tested and found untainted."

Xaviera sneered at him. "Tested by you, oh web spinner. Your threads dangle from every ear—"

"Silence," Margareta said to Xaviera. "One more outburst from you and I will have you removed."

Xaviera's hands twitched, but she kept them carefully clear of her weapons.

Isabelle cleared her throat and stepped around Kantelvar. She held up her hand and examined it as if seeing it for the first time. "The womb injury to my hand is a fact, nothing more." Then she swiveled her gaze to meet Xaviera's squarely. "People have been judging me by my hand for my whole life, as if it is the only thing about me that matters." Then she placed her hand over her belly, her womb, that organ that had failed Xaviera so bitterly and for which she had been roundly condemned. "I know exactly how much that hurts."

Xaviera caught the implication straight to the gut and recoiled into her chair. Isabelle kept her gaze fixed, trying with all her might to convey, *We are not so different, you and I.*

At last, Xaviera recovered, squared her shoulders, and addressed Kantelvar. "Your Exaltedness, I apologize. Truly none can find fault with you. You are always to be thanked when victory is to be celebrated or justice is said to be done. I believe there is not a soul in this kingdom that does not owe you some small favor." Her gaze flicked briefly to Margareta. "Some owe you their whole status and station. I am sure that the rumors that you seek to advance your own cause over all others are completely unfounded. They are merely the mumblings of those who lack your favor, as are the accusations that you grant no favor you cannot take away again, thus binding your supplicants to your will."

Though Xaviera spoke to Kantelvar, Isabelle felt the words smite her in the chest, a warning, but was it a gift in earnest or an attempt to divide her from an ally?

Margareta said, "Xaviera, you are overwrought. Go to your room and stay there until summoned."

"Yes, Majesty." Then she met Isabelle's gaze again and said, "I am pleased to meet you, Princesa Isabelle."

Heartened by this personal greeting, Isabelle decided to up the honor. "As I am pleased to meet you, Crown Princesa Xaviera."

Xaviera dipped her tiara in Isabelle's direction. She flashed a glare at

Margareta and managed to give the impression of storming out even while maintaining the proper, decorous, floating pace.

Margareta said, "Isabelle, please accept apologies on my daughter-in-law's behalf. I honestly don't know what has gotten into her. I promise she will not trouble you any further."

Which meant Margareta had not missed the armistice negotiations. She'd keep Xaviera away from Isabelle if she could. *Not if I can help it.*

The queen dismissed the other courtiers; now that they had witnessed the formal exchange of greetings, their presence was no longer required, and it seemed the queen wished to move on to more private matters. Kantelvar managed to avoid being shooed out, as did Margareta's bodyguard.

Margareta said, "Xaviera is not your problem. Her husband is. Príncipe Alejandro knows my husband favors Julio for the throne. The only thing that prevents him from declaring so openly is the fact that Julio's marriage is not yet consummated and confirmed in the Builder's eyes. Alejandro will stop at nothing to see your marriage fail."

"And yet the first assassination attempt came from your ally, Diego," Kantelvar said. "What has been done about him?"

If Margareta's stare could have incinerated its target, Kantelvar would have been nothing but a pair of smoking boots.

She said, "He remains ignorant of our suspicions. We must determine if the attempt on Isabelle's life was a personal protest, or if he has been suborned by Príncipe Alejandro. I cannot move against him until I can prove to my supporters that he has betrayed us, especially as many of them disagree with our strategy of involving l'Empire Céleste." Margareta turned her gaze on Isabelle. "It would help us to have some public guarantee of Grand Leon's support of Príncipe Julio. It is time to fulfill your commitment and pledge l'Empire's armies to our shared cause."

Isabelle retreated into the waxwork expression she always wore in her father's presence. Of course Margareta would try to get her to commit l'Empire without giving anything in return, but what could she say? *Stall. Delay.* Time was the thing no one wanted to give her. "I would prefer to talk to my betrothed first. It will be to him that any support is given."

Margareta's nostrils flared in irritation at this check. "It would help him to know what you propose."

"I must know what he expects from me, and what he intends to give in return."

"Being queen of Aragoth is not enough for you?"

Kantelvar stepped between Isabelle and the queen, raising his staff. "Majesty, Isabelle fully intends to deliver the might of l'Empire Céleste into Julio's capable hands. In the end, there is no other choice. Tonight, at the masquerade, she will have a chance to meet Julio and all her fears will be allayed."

Isabelle fumed and growled, "You have no right to promise that."

Kantelvar's hunch gurgled and Isabelle thought she heard a hiss of escaping air. He turned his head and said, "Please, Princess. You will get to meet Julio, and you will give him l'Empire's support as you have been charged to do. You have no choice. At this point we are all just dancing a gavotte through the necessary formalities. Even Grand Leon knows this, although he pretends not to."

Isabelle clamped her mouth shut rather than say something stupid.

"Give Julio his chance," Kantelvar said.

It was amazing Isabelle could feel so jilted by a man she'd never met, but she had leapt all the way across the sky on hope and faith and desperation, and still she had no place to land.

"One chance," she said. "Just one."

Margareta said, "In that case, it seems to me that this audience is premature. We will speak again after the ball. Felix."

This last was directed at the champion duelist, who stepped down from his place on the dais and escorted Isabelle and Kantelvar to the exit.

As he opened the door for Isabelle, he said in a gravelly voice, "There is nothing to be gained by delay. The sooner you commit your forces to the queen, the sooner she can convince your opponents that resistance is futile and more bloodshed can be avoided. Delay only weakens your position by making you seem feckless and indecisive."

Isabelle stiffened. "As opposed to being pliant and easily stampeded."

Felix shrugged and ushered her out. "It is a wife's sacred duty to obey."

"And do you give Margareta that same advice?" Isabelle asked.

"You are not the queen," he said, and shut the door.

Isabelle was tempted to shout through the door at him, but Kantelvar took her elbow. "Princess, come. We have much work to do before tonight."

Isabelle allowed herself to be towed along. "You told me Julio was a great swordsman, a statesman, and a sorcerer, yet everyone else seems to think of him as a puppet and a pawn."

"I told you of the man he was, and the man he could be again with your help."

Isabelle snorted. "What makes you think he wants my help? He's made no effort whatsoever to contact me. Not even a message." But as a wife she'd be expected to prop him up, and be blamed if she failed.

Kantelvar said, "Margareta was quick to take advantage of his accident to put him under her thumb. Once you remove him from her influence he should bloom into the husband you deserve."

"And why can he not extricate himself from his mother's sway?"

"Could you extract yourself from your father's control?"

That rebuke stung. "It's not the same. He is a príncipe with his own loyalists. I had no one."

"Just a King's Own Musketeer," Kantelvar said. "A man who speaks with Grand Leon's voice. He could have whisked you away whenever he wanted had he the wit to do so. Instead he chose to let you suffer in place so that he could preserve his tattered privilege."

Isabelle recoiled as if she'd been slapped. Outrage boiled in her breast. "Jean-Claude has always been there for me!" But could he have stolen her away, given her a different life?

"As you say, Highness," Kantelvar said. "I only meant to point out that you do have partisans, just as Julio does. All of Julio's loyalists have been locked away from him, but Margareta cannot lock you away from your husband once you are wed, nor can she lock you away from court. Therefore you will have the opportunity to breach the wall she has set around him."

Isabelle's mind still frothed with fury at his suggestion that Jean-Claude had only been using her as an excuse to maintain his status. She wanted to pluck the lie from the air and smash it to a million pieces. Instead, it leaked into her mind, spreading out through her consciousness like a single drop of poison in a butt of wine.

Think about something else. "Then why have none of Julio's partisans attempted to contact me, if they are so desperate to reach him?"

"They haven't taken your measure. No doubt they will do so at the masquerade tonight."

"And what if they find me wanting?"

"They won't; your destiny and Julio's are intertwined," Kantelvar said. "You were made for each other."

"What do you mean by that?" Isabelle asked.

"Let us gather your bloodhollow handmaiden, and I will show you."

Isabelle tugged away from him, alarmed. "What does Marie have to do with this?"

Kantelvar paused and turned. "Have you forgotten? I promised to revive her, and I always keep my promises."

——

As long as Jean-Claude didn't move, all the various pains in his body receded to dull background aches. The problem came when he tried to move, to lift his head off this fine pillow, or worse, to sit up in bed.

Isabelle had provided him with a feather mattress. It was far too fine a thing for him, who was used to sleeping on a straw-filled canvas mat on the floor. Or just on the floor. Or the dirt. Such luxuries as this could sap a healthy man's will to bestir himself, let alone a wounded man's.

If only there were not so much yet to be done. Isabelle's enemies weren't taking the morning off, and there were ever so many more of them than there used to be. He was going to need to take an apprentice . . . or two . . . or a dozen. Except he wasn't really the masterly type. The day he couldn't do this job himself was a day he did not want to think about.

So he had to act. Now. Pain or no pain.

Reluctantly, gingerly, he swung his legs out of bed. It was like stirring up a well-banked fire. All the embers of ache flared to life, passed through pain without stopping, and landed in agony. His leg, in particular, burned like a sap-filled log, hissing and sparking. The world swam . . .

"Señor? Señor musketeer, what is the matter?" Gentle hands steadied his shoulders and large, warm brown eyes stared into his.

Jean-Claude jerked upright and immediately regretted it, but at least he didn't pass out again. One of the Aragothic handmaids hovered before him, or perhaps "hand-matron" would be a better description. She was not old—perhaps a few years younger than Jean-Claude himself; with women, it always paid to underestimate—but not so young and blank faced as the rest of Isabelle's new servants. Did her age represent experience and competence, or simply the inability to improve her station?

Competence, he decided as she pressed a goblet into his hand and held on with both of hers until she was sure he could support the weight without spilling it. The drink was translucent white, like watered milk.

"Dream spirits," he grunted, and made to thrust it away; the stuff eased pain but brought strange visions and made men its slave.

The señora caught his hand. "It is only a very thin mixture, enough to dull the hurt but not addle your wits. Sip it slowly and maybe you will be able to get out of bed without falling over. Or maybe you would rather the surgeon see you in pain and ask la princesa to order you back in bed for a week."

"The princess, where is she?"

"The artifex took her to meet the queen. She commanded that you be allowed to rest."

"And who is guarding her?" Kantelvar's security had proved singularly inadequate.

"Royal guards. She specifically commands you to remember that you cannot aid her if you kill yourself."

Very competent. She was exactly the sort of servant whose goodwill he needed to cultivate. "Señora," he said. "May I be so bold as to ask your name?"

"Adel," she said. "Now drink."

Jean-Claude sipped. The stuff tasted vile, bitter and oily. "And how is it you come to speak in Isabelle's voice?"

"As the most experienced lady here, she asked me to. I am the royal midwife." On her purple sash was a silver pin in the shape of two interlocking rings, the symbol of her station. "I was Príncipe Julio's wet nurse before I got elevated. It is to be hoped that I will be there for the birth of his son . . . sooner rather than later."

Jean-Claude phrased his next question carefully, which is to say backward of the information he wanted. "Do you think Príncipe Julio will find Isabelle to his liking?"

Adel hesitated. "She is very smart. I think she would make a lovely queen. I think Príncipe Julio would have liked her."

"Would have?" The dream spirits were starting to take hold of Jean-Claude's flesh, taming his pain even as they made his senses tingly around the edges. Deliberately, he put the goblet down.

Adel deftly removed it from arm's reach. "He loved strong women."

"Women who fought back?"

"No. Not like that," Adel said, clearly eager to defend her príncipe but not sure how. "He once told me that so many of the people at court are just like mirrors; they show you yourself. He could not stand those people. He liked people who were like windows, or telescopes, or—or mysteries. They showed him things he hadn't seen and made him think. He said he could never call any man a friend who was afraid to slap his face. It was the same with women. I think he always envied his brother because of Xaviera."

Jean-Claude leaned back in his seat, impressed. "Princesa Xaviera is a strong woman?"

"She was raised on the border with the Skaladin Breakerspawn. Her mother once fended off a siege of the fortress at Castrella, and she swore that her daughter would learn to fence and to shoot and to ride and lead men because, she said, it is best for a woman to be able to protect her own house and honor. Since Xaviera came to San Augustus, she fences in the challenge courts and hunts with the men."

Aware that he was being gently diverted, Jean-Claude nonetheless asked, "And what does the court think of that?"

"They say it is the reason she cannot have children."

Jean-Claude grunted dismissively; he had grown up on a farm where women did hard physical work all day and still produced large families. "So Príncipe Julio would rather have Xaviera than Isabelle."

"I did not say that, señor!" Adel protested. "It is just that since his accident—" She bit her lip.

"He has lost interest in women?" Jean-Claude ventured. If Julio's manhood had been damaged—

"No. No. If anything, he is more 'interested' than he used to be, but, before, he had one or two women he would go to, respected women, discreetly."

Jean-Claude waved this along; he understood how the process worked.

"Since the accident he is . . . less discreet, and less discriminating."

"These women are more like mirrors," Jean-Claude said.

"Bent mirrors. They show him bigger than he is."

Jean-Claude frowned in distaste for Isabelle's sake, but were Julio's actions really hard to understand? A cripple who could no longer fight or hunt or engage in other masculine pursuits would want to exercise his masculinity in whatever way he had left.

Understandable or not, a man with a broken spirit would be no good for Isabelle. Either she'd spend all her time propping him up, or he'd drag her down. In neither case would she soar as she ought.

Another handmaid, younger than Adel, with eyes as wide and black as a doe's, poked her head in the room. "Señora. Don Angelo is here, and the royal surgeon, Esteban, to see the musketeer."

"Tell them I will see them in a moment," Jean-Claude said. They were here for his apology, no doubt. He did not look forward to apologizing, but Isabelle had promised, and he would not betray her word. To Adel he said, "Help me put some pants and boots on."

"The doctor is going to want to look at your leg," Adel said reprovingly.

"Then he can look at it through my pants. Look, the wound isn't hot, and if it was going to go septic, it would have done so by now."

Reluctantly, Adel helped him dress and maneuver into an upholstered chair. Even those slow, orchestrated movements brought new pain. Already, he yearned for another sip of the dream spirits. Where had she put that cup? *Away. Saints be praised.* He wondered, briefly, if Adel was married, but then quickly put the thought out of his mind. His duty as Isabelle's protector had long hampered his own romantic inclinations, and he had limited the pursuit of his primal urges to the occasional whore.

Once he was delicately arranged in a firm upright posture, Jean-Claude allowed his visitors in.

Don Angelo had come dressed to impress, wearing so many layers of fine purple silk and brocade that Jean-Claude wagered he'd doubled his thickness. His mustaches were waxed in perfect spirals. The doctor, Esteban, was a middle-sized, middle-aged man dressed in maroon robes of a more functional cut, though of an especially fine material.

Both of them gave him respectful half bows. Jean-Claude replied in kind from his sitting position. "Please pardon me for not standing, gentlemen, but my leg is still weak."

Esteban said, "I should imagine it is in agony."

Jean-Claude swallowed his distaste for the man's profession and got down to the business of this audience. "Not at all, thanks to you. Please allow me to apologize for my harsh words to you yesterday. I was quite out of my head with pain and worry for my princess, but that was no excuse for the unkindnesses I heaped upon you, and you, Your Grace."

Don Angelo hesitated, as a man prepared to besiege a fortress might do upon finding the gates flung open in welcome. After a moment of thought in which he apparently found no irony lurking in the corners of Jean-Claude's apology, he said, "Apology accepted, señor musketeer. I must say I found your dedication to your task . . . compelling."

"Indeed." Esteban smiled and a half-dozen concentric laugh lines rippled away from his white teeth. "Different people react differently to pain. It turns some men into babies, but it only makes you mad. You have the heart of a lion."

Jean-Claude liked Esteban better already. Yes, he was a doctor, but that wasn't necessarily his fault. Some jobs were inherited—like fulling or dung gathering; others involved apprenticeship at an early age. They weren't duties people necessarily wanted or enjoyed, but they had to be done. Embrace the man, despise the mission; that was the key.

"I have something for you," Esteban said.

"Not more medicine, I hope," Jean-Claude said warily.

"Memento," Esteban said. From his belt pouch, he flourished a small roll of silk that he unfurled to reveal a twisted, jagged piece of metal about the size and shape of Jean-Claude's thumbnail. "This came out of your thigh. One inch to the left and it would have severed a major blood vessel. You are a very lucky lion."

Jean-Claude rolled the lump of metal between his fingers, its jagged edges creasing his fingers. It was iron, forged and—"What's this?" He stopped rolling the projectile and stared at its largest flat face. There were molded ridges on it. He stared at the pattern they made. It was incomplete but recognizable.

"What is what?" Esteban asked diffidently, as if Jean-Claude had just rudely pointed out a flaw in a guest gift.

Jean-Claude showed it to him. "Look at this. See the raised pattern? It's a maker's mark."

Esteban's brows lifted in curiosity. "I hadn't noticed that."

"Are you sure this is the piece that came out of my leg?"

"Oh yes, very sure. Why?"

"Because before that, it came out of the Aragothic royal armory."

Don Angelo said, "That's not entirely inexplicable. The armory distributes munitions to all the city's artillery outposts. This bomb could have been stolen from any one of them."

"True." Jean-Claude leaned back in his chair. His mind kept trying to pounce on some vital clue that would lead him straight to Isabelle's enemies, only to have his inspirations evaporate in a puff of logic. Perhaps it was only weird to his drug-fuzzed mind that every last clue seemed to point in a different direction immediately before it ceased to be a clue. So was there any place the clues didn't point, or rather that they collectively pointed away from? Isabelle had a word for that, "trifangulation" or similar. It was hard enough to do that with sticks planted in the ground. With people who kept moving around, it would be impossible.

He said, "I don't suppose the royal armory would respond kindly if I showed up and asked them if they were missing any mortar shells?"

"Probably not," Don Angelo said stiffly.

Jean-Claude drummed his fingers on the arm of the chair and said, "Your Grace, may I trouble you for a crutch and a carriage?"

"Of course," Don Angelo said. "May I inquire why?"

"Because I'm not fit to ride," Jean Claude said. "And I want to have another look at that sharpshooter's nest."

⸺

By the time Jean-Claude's chaise pulled up in front of the bomb-scarred building, pain had reclaimed his leg, and he had exhausted his supply of invective on whatever misbegotten soul had invented cobblestones. As good as the undercarriage springs were, and as slow as the cautious driver had been, he still felt as if someone had been hammering on his thigh with a red-hot tenderizer. For a long moment, he just sat in the soft, upholstered seat— this was a *royal* chaise—eyes closed, contemplating amputation. Perhaps the surgeon's saving his leg had been the cruel thing to do.

But, no, this pain was temporary . . . he hoped. Esteban said he should heal nicely, if he didn't overexert himself—if he didn't do his duty. Don Angelo had suggested he send someone else to examine the building, but who else could he trust? Who else would know what to look for? Breaker's breath, even Jean-Claude didn't know exactly what he was looking for, or even that he would recognize it if he found it. That was why he had to do the looking.

He opened his eyes and stared up at the half-stone building. A large chunk of the wall was missing, and the edges of the hole were scorched and ragged, like old scabs.

The city's scavengers had already descended, scouring the street clean of potentially salable debris, everything from candlesticks to pot shards. Had they carried off anything telling?

Jean-Claude turned his attention to his driver, Mario, a quiet man with a sun-browned face several shades darker than the average swarthy

Aragoth. He had put up with Jean-Claude's agonized mutterings without comment or complaint.

Jean-Claude asked, "Monsieur, how would you like to help track down a killer?"

Mario gave him a quizzical look. "What would you have me do?"

"Put the word out that I am in the market for debris from yesterday's bomb blast. I will pay top coin for items that interest me. Potential sellers should queue up here, and I will attend them shortly."

"Señor, the scroungers, they will bring everything they can find—old bones and bits of glass—and claim it was from the blast."

"And I will send them packing," Jean-Claude said. "I am looking for just one thing."

"And that is?"

"It's a surprise." *Even to me.* Likely he'd find nothing of interest, but he had to try.

The street was packed with people moving hither and thither on their own business, and even the royal seal on the side of the chaise granted little reprieve from the press. There was a general clockwise motion to the action. Jean-Claude hefted his crutch—the damned thing made him look old and decrepit—and debarked on the left side of the conveyance to take advantage of the flow. It was like stepping into a very lumpy river that bumped him around in a direction that only averaged forward.

With no small relief, Jean-Claude stepped up into the entry niche of the bombed building. It was a tenement, something else he had failed to notice yesterday. Had anyone talked to the owner yet? That should have been Kantelvar's first stop. Instead, he was playing courtier to Isabelle. If there were a prize for being somewhere else when the action happened, Kantelvar would have won it. Well, that wasn't quite true. He had fought Thornscar aboard the *Santa Anna;* he just hadn't done a very good job.

The apartments were built in a square around a courtyard centered by a tall pole strung with pulleyed ropes that did double duty as guy wires and washing lines. A dozen or so women and thrice that many children bustled about their daily chores, glancing up at Jean-Claude only for the oddity of his appearance. He asked the first one he encountered where he might find the building's owner and was directed to the bombed-out room.

Jean-Claude considered the problematic stairs and toyed with the idea of sending an urchin to fetch the owner down to him. Alas, he wanted to have a look at that room himself, so he lurched, step by grimacing step, up to the second floor.

Jean-Claude found the owner and a gang of carpenters in the damaged room, using jacks to install a brace so that broken timbers could be replaced. There were holes in the floor and ceiling to match the ones in the walls. What was left of the floor was smeared with blood from the guards who had not gotten away. Jean-Claude quietly said the soldier's prayer on their behalf—just in case it mattered—and turned his attention to the man who was directing traffic. "Monsieur, might I have a word?"

The man turned and paused long enough to stare Jean-Claude up and down. His sweaty face went a bit paler. "You are the man who escaped. Señor, forgive me. I did not know—"

"I am not here to accuse you of anything . . . yet," Jean-Claude said with just enough bite to make the man wince. "What I want to know is, who occupies this room?"

"No one. These rooms have been empty for weeks."

"Rooms?"

"This one and the one next to it." He pointed through a hole in the wall where the mirror, now a shattered spray of glass, had stood. "The owner raised the rents, and I haven't been able to fill them."

"You're not the owner?" It was true, the man didn't look nearly rich enough. "Who is?"

"Duque Diego."

Of course. If Duque Diego wanted to take another shot at murdering Isabelle, he had to provide his killer with a platform from which to strike, and a couple of empty rooms filled the bill nicely. Too nicely. Kantelvar's protests of secrecy aside, Duque Diego must certainly have known he was suspected of the first assassination attempt, and what sort of idiot leaves such an obvious trail back to himself? Not a man like Duque Diego. Of course, if this assassin wasn't Diego's, then the choice of this corner apartment for the shooter's perch might have been purely coincidental. Or it might have been that someone else knew Isabelle's defenders knew about Diego's first attempt on her life and therefore picked him as a convenient subject for a frame. His ownership of the building could mean anything, or nothing.

Jean-Claude asked, "Has anyone else come asking questions like these?"

"Two men came last night from the Temple inquest. I told them everything I've told you."

Jean-Claude grunted; those would be Kantelvar's men. "Did they examine the room?"

"The searched the whole building and took away two men."

"Were they witnesses or suspects?"

"I have no idea, señor. One does not question the inquest."

"We'll see about that." He was going to have some pointed questions for Kantelvar when he was done here. *And why am I here?* If there had been any clues left after the bomb blast, odds were they had been taken by Kantelvar's men, stolen by scavengers, or trampled by the repair gang.

He searched the sharpshooter's room as best he could with the work gang in the way. The bomb had blown away an ox-sized hole in the floor and in the slat-and-plaster wall. The smell of gunpowder lingered. He poked through the wreckage with his crutch. It was all wood and plaster and straw. Then he moved to the room next door. The mirror frame and most of the glass had ended up in small pieces on this side of the wall. There were some pot shards. Frustration extruded its slimy tentacles into his brain. *What am I looking for?*

He wished he could have brought Isabelle with him, or at least her perceptions. She observed things so closely that even inanimate objects seemed to talk to her. Jean-Claude was better with people. People wanted to tell you their secrets. Secrets were only secrets because they were important to the holder, something to be obsessed about. A secret that wasn't important was just a memory. All you had to do was find the right place to apply the pry bar, and secrets would come flying out of wherever they'd been wedged.

"You are the musketeer?" came a thick, drawling voice from behind him. Jean-Claude hobbled around to face a square-shouldered man with dark eyes set slightly too close together. He wore a red doublet with ripped sleeves, slops, and high boots. He carried a rapier at his side, and a main gauche.

"Who wants to know?" Jean-Claude asked, intrigued. Everything from the man's sword to his casually aggressive stance marked him as a hired blade. Though Jean-Claude still wore his own sword, he was acutely aware that he was not at his best. Should he call for the custodian, or Mario? He wanted the man to talk, which was much more likely if he perceived Jean-Claude as helpless.

"I have a message for you," the fellow said, stepping into the messy room. His eyes were very hard despite his neutral tone. Not good.

"Very good," Jean-Claude replied, groping for his money bag as a means to readjust his grip on his crutch. "How did you know to find me here?"

"Followed you from the citadel," said the swordsman, his hand drifting nonchalantly to his rapier's hilt.

"I was hoping you'd show up. I assume the message is payment on delivery?" The thought of money had to distract a mercenary. "Who sent you?"

The swordsman hesitated. "He is a man with a scar." He drew a line down his cheek.

Thornscar. Jean-Claude's heart thudded so hard it almost drowned out the pain in his leg. Not dead or discommoded after all. "And what did he have to say?" He shook a few coins into his hand.

"He said you were a nuisance." The mercenary drew his sword. It was a silky movement, not sudden or jerky. A man who wasn't expecting it might have been flummoxed by its smoothness, its body-language illusion of peace. Jean-Claude had seen men run through by such ploys before they ever realized their danger.

The swordsman lunged. Jean-Claude flung his handful of coins in the man's face. The man flinched. It skewed his aim. Jean-Claude twisted. The blade ripped through his doublet but only creased his skin. He surged off his good leg, swinging the crutch as a cudgel down on the crook between the man's neck and shoulder. The meaty shock reverberated up Jean-Claude's arms. The swordsman's eyes rolled up and he pitched forward to his knees. Jean-Claude came down on his right foot. His wounded leg buckled and he sprawled on the floor. Red sparks swirled before his eyes, and white-hot agony burned up his leg.

Behind him, the swordsman convulsed, vomiting onto the floorboards. Jean-Claude was not in much better condition. Even though he had been expecting pain, it took him a dozen precious heartbeats to force himself up on hands and his good knee. His whole body shuddered, but he balanced well enough to plant his crutch and thrust himself upright, and none too soon; the swordsman finished retching and gathered himself to stand.

Jean-Claude brought the crutch down on the back of the man's head. He slumped like a dropped pudding. "Nuisance, am I?" he said between racking breaths. "I'll give him nuisance."

By this time, the landlord-caretaker and his crew had taken note of the ruckus and hurried into the doorway, shock on their faces. Jean-Claude jabbed his finger at the caretaker. "You, señor. This is the second time I have been attacked in your building, and you will have my undying curse if you do not aid me now. I want this man tied up, securely, and somebody fetch my driver."

Several very busy minutes later, the bound swordsman had been loaded crossways on the floor of the chaise. Jean-Claude sat over top of him, resting one boot on the back of his neck. His vision still swam as if he were sky sick, but his stitched-up wound had not started bleeding again. Maybe after today he'd be able to let it rest and heal properly.

To the building's nervous caretaker, he said, "If anyone comes asking after us, we've returned to the citadel."

The caretaker gave profuse assurances that he would pass the words on precisely.

Mario flicked the reins and set the coach in motion. "Is this the surprise you were expecting?"

Jean-Claude closed his eyes and tried not to feel the carriage jostling. "I had hoped to draw my adversary out, or why else would I have come back?"

Mario's eyebrows rose. "Risky."

"I was the best bait I had to offer." Better to be thought a clever madman than a lucky fool. "Once we leave sight of the building, take us around another way and head for the docks."

—

Jean-Claude steeled himself against nausea as he limped up the gangway onto the *Santa Anna*, Mario and their prisoner in tow. Captain Santiago met him on deck, a quizzical expression on his face.

The captain raised a curious eyebrow. "Señor musketeer, you are truly the last person I expected to see here. You have made your distaste for skyships quite plain."

"And so this will be the last place anyone will come to look for me," Jean-Claude said. "I am in need of a private location to interrogate this man."

Santiago scowled. "You know I can't allow that. This is a royal courier and—"

"This man was hired by the man who tried to burn your ship out of the sky. I hope to follow his lead back to his employer."

Santiago skipped a single beat and then said, "I will have the turret emptied. The noise of repairs in the hold should serve to mask any screams you may elicit."

The swordsman squirmed and shouted muffled protests through his gag.

"Thank you, Captain," said Jean-Claude, lurching onto the deck. Thank the Builder the ship was not heaving right now, or Jean-Claude would have been joining it.

"Welcome aboard."

Navigating the steep, narrow stairs taxed Jean-Claude's strength and patience, and climbing back up was going to be worse, but eventually he and Mario, with the help of two burly sailors, bumped and banged the swordsman into the *Santa Anna*'s belly turret and secured him to a turvy mast.

Jean-Claude dismissed the sailors, but Mario took Jean-Claude aside and said, "I must stay. If he had managed to kill you, it would have been on my head. Don Angelo ordered me to keep you safe."

It was Jean-Claude's turn to be surprised. "I would not have warranted he prized my life so highly. Did he say why?"

"For la princesa's sake."

"That is good to know. I thank you." But did Don Angelo mean for Mario to be a guard dog or a scapegoat?

Mario's expression soured. "I have not done a very good job so far. When he finds out I failed to prevent you being attacked—"

"So don't tell him. In fact, I recommend you don't mention this little incident at all. I won't, and our friend there sure as doomfire won't, either."

Mario looked relieved. "What are you going to do with him?"

"I'm going to start by talking to him. How it ends is up to him." Jean-Claude ripped the gag out of the swordsman's mouth. The man glowered at him—his close-set eyes were pits of hatred—but he held his tongue.

Jean-Claude sat down across from him on the butt of a cannon. "So, señor . . . I don't believe I caught your name."

"Nufio," he muttered.

"Ah, very good. Señor Nufio, shall I present you with your options, or shall we skip the preliminary threatening and get right down to you telling me what I want to know?"

"What happens if I answer your questions?"

"As soon as I verify the veracity of your story, you will be set free on solid ground. If you lie to me, we leave out the part about solid ground. A man proven to be dishonest once is not to be trusted a second time."

The swordsman took a moment to mull this over, but only a moment. "He didn't pay me to die. What do you want to know?"

"The man with the scar who hired you to kill me; what was his name?"

"He called himself Thornscar."

"And how did you find him?"

"He found me. He came into the Cog and Crank, dressed rich and hooded like a monk. Said he'd heard of me, had a job for me."

"And how did you see his scar if he wore a cowl?"

"I could see his chin and his cheek. It was a really big scar. The rest was in shadow."

"Who told him about you?" That would be the next step in Jean-Claude's chain of pursuit.

The swordsman shook his head. "I don't know. Could've been anybody. I have a reputation."

And you're not a big thinker, so you didn't bother to ask. "And how much did he offer you?" Jean-Claude asked, teasing the man's money pouch from his belt. The swordsman shot Jean-Claude a look of fury but was wise enough to refrain from arguing the point of theft.

Jean-Claude opened the purse and found a tidy sum in silver coins, enough to set a wise man up for a year, or a fool for a week. "Impressive. And with such an amount being offered, it did not occur to you that I might be dangerous?"

"He said you were wounded, crippled."

Which he could have learned from anyone who saw the blast. "Was he carrying a weapon?"

"He had a sword—didn't look comfortable with it, though, but his bodyguards did."

"Bodyguards?" The picture forming in Jean-Claude's head kept drifting farther and farther from the Thornscar he'd encountered in the ship's hold. As Isabelle had informed him, the man who'd attacked them en route didn't even have a knife, much less a sword. This latest incarnation of Thornscar hired others to do his work for him. That spoke of money. And wouldn't bodyguards be *inconvenient* for someone who wanted to remain hidden?

"Two of them. Professional soldiers by their look."

"Was Thornscar injured in his left arm?" Where Jean-Claude had thrust his main gauche.

"Huh? No. He had a bit of a limp, though."

Jean-Claude shook his head. Unfortunately, he had no idea if damage done to a reflection would be mirrored on the body, or if it would show up as some sort of phantom pain, or not at all, and he could have acquired a limp anywhere, as Jean-Claude could attest.

"How were you supposed to pick up the second half of your payment?" Jean-Claude asked. "And don't try denying it. These arrangements are always half on proof of kill."

"He said nail your hat to the Temple door, and he'd find me."

"Well then," Jean-Claude said merrily. "Let's try it and see what happens."

Twelve

Isabelle clung to Marie's cool, dry, translucent hand like a sailor clinging to a line in a gale. In truth, she did not need to hold her friend at all to get her to follow along, but the mad hope that their mutual torment might soon come to an end was a wind in her face. She had suppressed that hope ever since Kantelvar had presented it. It couldn't happen. It wouldn't. She was a fool to let herself be drawn in, her long-dead dream rekindled. Yet now that the moment was upon her, the pressure seemed ready to erupt into something physical that would fling Marie away from her.

"Where are we?" Isabelle asked as Kantelvar led them down a long, dusty, deserted corridor somewhere in the bowels of the citadel. "You said we were going to the Temple." A public place. Instead she'd been guided down what she thought was a shortcut into what turned out to be a warren of abandoned corridors. If she'd known they were going this far out of the way she would have insisted on a bodyguard.

"We are," Kantelvar said. "When the citadel was built, it swallowed up much of the old city, including a Temple that had stood here since the days of Rüul. Carlemmo's father knocked the upper levels flat and built that stupefying edifice in the square to replace it." He snorted contempt for the gleaming complex that stood across from Isabelle's guest residence. "But the Temple's vault remains, and I make use of it from time to time. It will serve our purposes well today."

Isabelle stopped and the pall of dust she'd been trailing wafted by her. "There is no reason to do this in such a hidden place."

Kantelvar clanked two more steps before stopping and turning. "This is where my equipment is. If you wish, I can have my equipment removed to your quarters, thought that will take time, and it may be difficult to re-create the precise conditions required for the treatment."

"What conditions would those be?" Isabelle asked.

"Silence, stillness, and complete, uninterrupted darkness. We must sep-arate the subject from her shadow. When a Sanguinaire creates a blood-hollow, he leaves a piece of his bloodshadow diffused through the victim's shadow, like a single drop of ink diluted in a bucket of water. The resident bloodshadow then feeds on the victim's soul, like a parasite, just enough to keep it alive without destroying the host. Most of the time, the host's spirit weakens and is ultimately devoured. That is why it is so remarkable that yours has lasted so long and has even thrived. You must have put in an extraordi-nary amount of work."

Isabelle's chest swelled a little at this praise, but she squeezed it down. Marie wasn't cured yet. "But Marie has been in the dark before." Shutting her in the dark was the one sure way to make sure her father was not using her as a spy.

"For how long? An hour? A night? The bloodshadow can survive that. Indeed, a lifetime of darkness would not be enough to dislodge the barb; darkness only weakens it and leaves it vulnerable to shriving, which is done with a solution of soul ash, moon resin, the pollen of several rare orchids, and the spores of a gloom fungus in a medium of alkahest."

"How did you find this cure?" Such a complex potion could not have been hit upon by accident.

As he so frequently did, Kantelvar took his time answering. "The Risen Saints and the Firstborn Kings had powers that modern sorcerers could only pine for. The saints who possessed what we now call Sanguinaire sor-cery could make what they called Satrapae Umbra, Shadow Lords, like bloodhollows except that they retained their own free will when not being directly possessed. It was counted a high honor for a clayborn to be chosen for this role. They served as ambassadors, scouts, and champions for their masters. They could even borrow a portion of their master's power. And when their term of service was done, or when they became too old, crippled, or weak, it was customary to shrive them of the barb and its burden. The recipe for the shriving agent was never precisely written down, but the gathering of the ingredients was mentioned in some of the Remnants and Ghost Tales."

Isabelle frowned. "I've never heard of any of that." How many times had he answered one of her questions with a reference to some ancient work or hidden knowledge she had no way to verify?

Kantelvar made a metallic snort. "The Temple has enough to do sorting out the Builder's truth from the Breaker's heresy without releasing all of its accumulated apocrypha into the world. *The Book of Instructions* contains only those revelations proved to be true."

"Your experiments demonstrate the efficacy of the cure, surely." Unless he was lying.

"Two experiments so far, only one successful. More to the point, do you honestly think Sanguinaire society would appreciate it being known that there is an antidote for their favorite poison? No. As degenerate as they have become, they are still the Builder's chosen and their authority over the clayborn must remain absolute. Now, are you coming?"

Reluctantly, Isabelle resumed following him. He brought them into a section of the palace made of older stone where the blocks were set tightly but without mortar and the floor was dished from great use.

"Do you mean that no one should find out about Marie being cured?"

"If it works, we will claim it is the Builder's miracle," Kantelvar said. Another pat answer. Isabelle knew the technique well, for she had often used it to shut down conversations, to defend herself in her father's house.

Her father. He was one more link in the chain that had brought her here. "Could you have shriven my father's bloodshadow?"

"The red consumption is not the same as being bloodhollow," Kantelvar said, which was neither yes nor no.

Isabelle's stomach quivered with nerves. She'd survived Grand Leon's audience by being agonizingly honest, Margareta's by being compassionate and stubborn, but she had no idea how to get around Kantelvar's relentless obfuscations.

"I suppose what I'm curious about is why didn't Father ask you to save him from the red consumption when he first bargained to give me away?" Le Comte des Zephyrs cared for nothing more than his own life.

Kantelvar's hump gurgled, which it seemed to do when he was agitated. What kind of bizarre mechanism did he have under there anyway?

"Because he didn't have the red consumption at the time," Kantelvar said.

Isabelle seized on this. "I remember Hormougant Sleith talking about it with my father, some bargain he'd made." Right before he'd hollowed out Marie.

"Sleith . . . I . . . yes. Very clever, that was the same bargain."

"But that was twelve years ago," Isabelle said, a welter of new questions boiling up in her head. "How could he have known then that I would be offered to Julio now?" Twelve years ago, Príncipe Alejandro hadn't even been married to Xaviera, much less been vexed by her infertility. King Carlemmo had been healthy.

"Your father only agreed that . . . one of my order would choose your marriage partner. Who that partner would be had not been decided."

Isabelle seized on this new revelation. "Who are your order?"

"A consortium of sorts, dedicated to the preservation of the saint lines."

"And by 'preserve' you mean 'breed.'"

"Yes."

Isabelle imagined he was telling the truth, if not all of it. She stewed in irritation. The notion of marriage to a man who apparently had no interest in her turned even more bitter in the context of its being arranged by a clandestine conspiracy for the sole purpose of her being a broodmare, like a damned animal. Bearing children might have been a duty, but it was not the whole breadth of her being. She had her math and her philosophy. She'd been entrusted with the power to unleash or withhold the armies of l'Empire Céleste. She only got to keep her children if she stopped the war. Yes, but turn that logic around.

"I will not consent to bring children into being in the middle of a war," she said. "If you want my help you will have to help me convince Julio and Alejandro not to fight."

Kantelvar stopped, his hump sloshing. His neck hinges pinged as he turned his emerald gaze upon her. "And will you consent to the project if that miracle can be accomplished?"

Isabelle felt as if she'd leaned on a solid wall only to have it crumble to dust. His lack of resistance to the idea stunned her. "That follows," she said, and then took a leap more of hope than faith. "Yes." If Aragoth was at peace and she was married to Julio, children were naturally part of the plan . . . even if it wasn't purely her plan.

"Done," Kantelvar said with a voice like a gavel. He turned into yet another dusty side corridor. Isabelle followed, feeling she had missed something vital. A little way along was an iron-banded door set into a niche in the wall. He touched the spiny tip of his staff to the door. There was a spark, the smell of lightning, then a chain-rattling noise before the door groaned inward. Beyond was a cramped stone landing and a narrow spiral stairway curling down into darkness. A dry musty smell wafted up from the depths.

Isabelle balked at the threshold—this looked far too much like a tomb to her—but if Marie was to have any hope of ever being freed from her curse, it was down these stairs, and Isabelle had not come all this way not to take the final step. She lifted the hem of her skirt and eased onto a narrow, crumbling stone, guiding Marie after her.

Kantelvar came in behind them. The door boomed shut. Total darkness filled the stairwell and Isabelle had to suppress a shriek. If she slipped now and tumbled, she might fall forever, or at least far enough to break her neck. But something clicked and the tips of the spines on Kantelvar's staff glowed brilliant green. The points of light made traceries in the air whenever the staff bobbled. The shadows before Isabelle roiled like steam, but she picked her way down and down, legs aching with the care of placing each foot carefully on the slippery slivers of stone. At the bottom of the stairs, past another landing, another thick door opened with a spark from Kantelvar's staff and he stiffly bowed her into a large, dark room. She made out two thick columns supporting a tall arch.

Kantelvar touched his staff to an alchemical lantern high on the wall. It came to life with a soft *poomph* followed by another and another farther along.

Revealed to her widening eyes was a room the size of a Temple nave, forested with granite pillars graven with ancient icons of the Risen Saints. The groin-vaulted ceiling was painted, beneath a layer of soot and grime, with fantastic scenes, beginning with the fracturing of the cratons at the breaking of the world and running all the way to the founding of the great city of Om at the inception of the Final Age.

Closer to hand was a long table piled high with books, and beyond that rows of shelves stacked with more tomes, alchemical instruments, beakers, redactors, crocks of strange compounds, chests, and quondam artifacts. Isabelle turned in a slow circle. There was a true ice crucible, an alchemical forge, a printing press twice the size of her own.

Oh, I want this place. Her pulse leapt at the thought of all the knowledge hidden down here and all the philosophical experiments that a woman might perform well out of the sight of disapproving eyes. She could give Lord DuJournal so much more to write about.

A glint of emerald light in a corner caught her eye. "An omnimaton!" It was a clockwork machine in roughly human shape, with bones of the same coppery substance as Kantelvar's limbs, and muscles made of telescoping silver tubes, just like Kantelvar's right arm and leg. Its flattened, clamshell-shaped head was set directly on its shoulders. A single cyclopean eye set in the leading edge of the clamshell glowed a dull green.

Isabelle veered toward the device, drawn like iron filings to a lodestone. "I've never seen one intact before. I thought they were all destroyed when—"

"Don't touch it!" Kantelvar snapped, his voice sharp as a knife.

Isabelle halted, her hand close enough to its metal surface to feel it coldness. It was like standing in the doorway to an icehouse. "Why not?"

"Because it reacts badly to being touched. When I found it, it was much more greivously damaged. It took me ages just to restore its inner spark. Alas, its behavior is still erratic. The last time it was provoked, it reduced a man to a thin paste."

Isabelle took a cautious step back. "How did you repair it? I thought nobody really knew how these things worked."

"No one does. Nobody really understands how black powder works, either, but that doesn't stop anyone from building cannons. Over the centuries, the Temple has retrieved enough functional quondam mechanisms to make at least an educated guess where the pieces are supposed to go and which fluids need to be present in what proportion to make certain things happen. Where possible, we compare our experimental results to the *Instructions* for confirmation, but even that is not the same thing as understanding."

Isabelle hesitated; *The Book of Instructions* was the Temple's holy book, its secrets forbidden to women. Isabelle had therefore made a point of reading it cover to cover, painstakingly translating every passage from the Saints-tongue into la Langue until she had a better grasp of the saints' language and of Temple lore and doctrine than most clerics.

"Do the *Instructions* contain information about omnimatons?" she asked as innocently as possible; she did not recall any passage devoted to them.

"It's in one of the lesser-known apocrypha, the *Twelfth Book of Fragments,* cantos eight to twenty-seven." He pulled a thick book from the shelf and thumped it down on the table.

Isabelle's blood thrummed with new excitement; she'd never been able to get her hands on a copy of the *Fragments.* Yet in case Kantelvar's bringing out the book was some sort of test of her moral rectitude, Isabelle repressed an urge to open it up and leaf through it. "I'm afraid it wouldn't mean much to me."

Kantelvar drummed his fingers on the book and scrutinized her with his unblinking emerald eye. At last he said, "Come, let us see to the bloodhollow."

Kantelvar led Isabelle, who had never let go of Marie's hand, into a small side chamber with a rope-sprung bed with a thick mattress and several blankets. Kantelvar had Isabelle arrange Marie in the bed while he adjusted an apparatus made of copper vessels, glass spheres, and lots of brass piping on a stand by the bedside.

"This matrix will deliver the infusion. The great unknown in this experiment is whether the subject's soul will respond to the opportunity or whether it has atrophied over the years. The fact that the subject has matured physically during the intervening decade is hopeful but not necessarily predictive."

As he spoke, he bathed Marie's arm, located a vein, then jabbed in a needle that was connected to a tube leading to the still.

Isabelle said, "You aren't going to leave that in there, are you? She'll take fever!"

"Everything has been properly cleaned. I have some experience with this. Corruption is possible but not likely. It's a risk that must be taken." He tied the first needle down and moved around to her opposite side. By then, Marie's blood had percolated all the way through the device and was starting to return through a second hose-and-needle. Kantelvar waited until a steady trickle of blood was coming out of the needle and then jabbed it into a vein in her opposite arm. The transparency of her skin at least made the veins easy to see, and the returned blood flowed through her glassy flesh like dark ink in a stream.

He said, "Now, if you will please instruct her not to fight the needles or pull them out . . ."

There followed several minutes of adjustments and fiddling wherein Isabelle summoned every scrap of hope and encouragement she possessed and whispered it into Marie's ear. Finally Kantelvar took her arm and led her from the room, extinguishing the alchemical lantern, shutting the door, and plunging Marie into darkness.

Now that the process had begun, Isabelle's heart should have felt lighter, but instead it was heavy as lead. She folded her arms to stop herself from fidgeting, wishing there was something productive she could do; anything would be better than nothing. What if Marie could not be revived? What if there was no hope at all? Then what? Should she continue as she always had, treating her once-friend like a precious but fragile heirloom, or should she take the hard step and a draw her maidenblade across Marie's throat? The very thought made her ill.

She asked, "When will we know if the treatment is effective?"

"I don't know. I've never dealt with a victim who has been entangled for so long. It could be anything from hours to weeks—"

"Weeks!" Isabelle was appalled. "But I can't leave her alone. She needs someone to feed her and—"

"Be at peace. It will be taken care of. You are no longer alone," Kantelvar said, his mechanical voice nearly guttering out as he softened it. He reached out with his fleshy hand to touch her shoulder in what was probably meant to be a gesture of reassurance. His fingers were gray and clammy as a corpse, with bruised-looking nails. She recoiled, her skin shrinking away from him.

Kantelvar hesitated, his hand in midair, before self-consciously withdrawing it up his voluminous sleeve.

Isabelle turned away to stifle her revulsion. *Hypocrite.* How could she ask people to accept her deformity if she did not return the favor? Indeed, she was usually fascinated by the strange and grotesque, but Kantelvar's attempt at compassion, at familiarity, was more disturbing than all his obfuscations.

Leather scraped on wood. Isabelle turned in time to see Kantelvar heft the copy of *Fragments* he had put down earlier and weigh it in his hands. "Did you know one of your ancestors helped compile this?"

Thankful for relief from the blighted silence, Isabelle said, "No, who?"

"Saint Céleste."

Isabelle puffed a noise of disbelief before her math skills caught up to her. "Well, that was hundreds of generations ago. If her children had children and they survived, she must have thousands of descendants by now."

"Yes. I believe every single living Sanguinaire is related to her by some degree, but you are her only living direct maternal descendant. She had two sons and one daughter, who took her name, as was their tradition. The younger Céleste in turn bore a daughter, and so on and so forth down through the millennia, to your grandmother to your mother to you."

"How can you possibly know that?" Isabelle said, thrilled and appalled at the same time. To think that she was the direct descendant of an ancient heroine was like a childhood fantasy come true. In stories, such omens and portents always came complete with some grand destiny. But to think that Kantelvar actually believed such nonsense cast doubt upon his sanity. "It's been two thousand years, genealogies get fabricated, people are unfaithful, women are raped—"

"But blood will out," Kantelvar said. He hefted a small chest onto the crowded table, extracted from it an ornate rod about the size of her finger, and presented it to her.

A tingle of excitement ran up her spine. It was clearly a quondam artifact; shadows played beneath its metallic skin, as if the metal itself had a pulse. She'd never so much as touched such a prize before. Gingerly she took it. It was warm to her skin and heavy as gold. One end was tipped with a bulb the size of her thumb joint and the other with a half loop about the same size. The shaft was covered in rows of characters that seemed to be extruded from the surface. One row read "Isabelle des Zephyrs" in the Saintstongue. The others were all in strange characters that Isabelle did not recognize.

Seeing her name on this odd trinket made all the hairs on the back of her neck stand up. "What is this? And what is it supposed to prove?"

"It is a blood cipher, and it will tell you your lineage," Kantelvar said. "Just press the round end to your thumb?"

"Why?"

"Because that's how it works."

Isabelle wavered. She did not trust Kantelvar, but he clearly wanted her alive and in good health to have Julio's children. He could not simply make her disappear, and she'd never used a quondam artifact before.

Curiosity took the reins before reason had worked out all the details, and she touched the tip of the thing to the pad of her thumb.

It stung her, sharp and hard. She yelped and tossed the rod away. The cylinder arced across the room, caromed off a pillar, and rolled under the table. A dot of blood welled up from her thumb.

"What did it do?" she gasped, her pulse racing with fear. "Poison?"

"Not at all," Kantelvar said, lurching around the table to retrieve the fallen device. "It just needs a drop of your blood to decipher. A man's seed is a special form of blood that carries the spark of life into a woman's womb. It mixes with her blood, half to half. This admixture precipitates from the mother's body to form the child. The child is therefore half its mother and half its father."

He gave the blood cipher's head a twist and plunked it down on the table. Instantly it set up a high-pitched whirring hum. Seams opened up in its sides and it sprouted four insectile legs. From inside the crate came an answering buzz, and dozens of blood ciphers scuttled out. The swarm converged on the blood cipher bearing Isabelle's name and all the metallic bugs crawled over one another, touching tips and tails in a boiling hive.

Isabelle edged closer, sucking her pricked thumb.

Suddenly one of the bugs reoriented itself to the vertical and all the other bugs swarmed up it, branching out two by two until it formed a tree over a meter tall. A family tree. Kantelvar leaned in and stared at the base. "This is you . . . yes. Just as I thought. And this is your mother and your grandmother." He traced her lineage back through five generations of mothers.

"And if you activate this one," he said excitedly, pointing at her three-times-great-grandmother Giselle, "it goes back five more generations, and so on until we get back one hundred three generations to Saint Céleste herself."

Isabelle marveled at the device—what a magnificent machine—almost as much as the information it so elegantly displayed. She leaned in close to get a look at how the ciphers hooked up to one another—how in the world did they communicate?—and read her name again, only more information had been added: Isabelle des Zephyrs, l'Étincelle.

Isabelle was not given to fainting fits, but this made her dizzy. This had to be wrong. She was unhallowed. She most surely did not possess l'Étincelle, Saint Céleste's power to breathe life into the lifeless.

Impossible. She very nearly blurted the word aloud, but Kantelvar didn't know she could read Saintstongue.

She quickly followed the branch up to her mother: Vedetta des Zephyrs, Sanguinaire, and her father . . . Her father? The man listed as her father was Lorenzo Barbaro, Fenice.

Isabelle's mouth dropped open and her blood ran cold with shock and disbelief. Surely Kantelvar had to know it was wrong. Unless it wasn't.

Assume it's true. She was more than happy not to be related to the cruel and vicious Comte des Zephyrs, but who in all the world was Lorenzo Barbaro? The Fenice ruled the city-states of Vecci. She had never met one, but she had seen paintings of men and women clad in brilliant feathers, like scale armor, each one sporting an elaborate mask of feathers and a great crest of plumage on their head. They were said to be stronger than a team of oxen and tough enough to survive grapeshot unscathed.

Was Lorenzo Barbaro still alive? Did he know of Isabelle's existence? Did she have any other siblings? Did her father . . . le Comte des Zephyrs know he had been duped? He would have killed her for sure . . . or would he?

What if creating Isabelle for Kantelvar's conspiracy had been the deal from the very beginning? What if the comte had known from the start that he was to raise a cuckoo? His contempt for her needed no explanation—he was cruel to everyone—but it would explain why no other match had ever been made for her, why there had never been talk of a nunnery, of getting rid of her for any price. She was already spoken for. And from there it was not hard to guess what her father had gotten in return. The name des Zephyrs, the rank, and the title all came with the skyland, and that had been his wife's dowry. And if there was one thing Kantelvar and his ilk seemed to be good at, it was brokering marriages.

"Is something the matter?" Kantelvar asked.

Isabelle stiffened. He hadn't meant to show her this. He hadn't announced her supposed sorcery or her paternity. He wanted to show her, but he didn't want her to know.

Her mouth dry as dust, she asked, "Can it do this for anyone?"

"It can track anyone for whom it has a sample to compare."

"So it had to have samples from both my parents?"

"And all four of your grandparents."

Perhaps the sudden heaviness in Isabelle's chest was the weight of history settling behind her breastbone; if Kantelvar's astonishing claim was true, someone had been tracking her ancestry for more than two thousand years. Was the conspiracy that old? It seemed impossible, but so did at least three other things that had happened to her today.

She tried to school her face and glanced at Kantelvar, but he was staring enraptured at the genetic tree, like an artist staring at a vision he was struggling to bring into the world. This was his obsession. He'd brought her here to show her this, but also to show himself, to make absolutely sure of his facts.

"This is fascinating," she said. *Question his obsession, push his lever.* "But this grand lineage seems an inheritance without property."

"No." Kantelvar's voice came out a rusty groan and he shuddered like a sleeper waking. "There is destiny." Almost unconsciously, he reached out with his gray hand and stroked the cover of the *Fragments.* The answer was there, so close she could touch it. So far away.

"What destiny?" she breathed, as if she were blowing on the ember of a candle trying to get it to light. How badly did he want to tell her?

Kantelvar shook his head slowly, his cowl swinging. He withdrew his hand from the book. "To carry on the line. Until the Savior comes."

Isabelle looked back and forth from the artifex to the family tree. *No. Not until the Savior comes. Until the Savior is created.* That's what all this was about. The Temple admitted to only one prophecy, "The Savior will come," and Kantelvar's order was trying to force destiny's hand.

Isabelle's blood felt like icy slush in her veins. If Iav's transgression, seeking the secret of life, had caused the Breaking of the world, how much worse must be the attempt to shortcut humanity's redemption?

"What happens next?" she asked aloud. How close was Kantelvar to his goal? Did he imagine that Isabelle would deliver the foretold redeemer?

"We get you back to your handmaids to prepare for the masked ball." Kantelvar twisted the blood cipher with Isabelle's name on it, and the whole tree collapsed in a brief rain of cylinders. He scooped them into the chest and then stepped toward the door. "Come."

The book lay unattended. If she could grab it up . . . but no, he'd surely see her. She could not sneak it out from under his sight.

From under his mind, then.

"May I have this?" she asked, resting her fingers ever so lightly on the cover. "If Saint Céleste was truly my greatest-grandmother, I would like to have something of her to think on."

Kantelvar hunched in alarm, but his voice was its usual monotone. "Leave it. You would not be able to read it in any case."

Summoning every ounce of calm she possessed, Isabelle let her fingers slide across the leather cover and down the spine. Fear churned her bile to a froth, but she kept her voice calm and reasonable. "Reading isn't the point. It's an heirloom, something that was touched by her hand, now by mine. A memento." She eased the book from the table and cradled it to her breast, praying like an Iconate that the saints would aid this mad deception.

Kantelvar raised his hand as if to ward her off, but hesitated and then lowered his arm. "As you wish, Highness."

Elation thrilled through Isabelle's veins as she followed him out of the room. She felt like she was clutching a powder keg with a lit fuse to her chest. She hated abandoning Marie, but what choice did she have? She had to give Kantelvar's potions time to work. She had to make it to the masquerade and meet her husband-to-be. She had to talk to Jean-Claude, and she had to find a spare secret moment to read this book!

—

A space narrow, dark, and so stuffy that the air tasted of vomit, the Cog and Crank tavern had little in its favor as a venue. The one-man play in progress, which Jean-Claude titled *Bait for a Villain*, with the swordsman Nufio in the leading role, made up with longevity what it lacked in variety. Nufio had done little but moan and clutch his belly since Jean-Claude had fed him a concoction of herbs guaranteed to induce stomach cramps, telling him it was a slow-acting poison. All he had to do to earn the antidote was stay put until Thornscar or his proxy showed up.

The Solar had settled on the rooftops, the matinée performance rolling on into the evening. Jean-Claude had just dealt himself yet another hand of cards when the rickety door banged open, then fell off its frayed rope hinges. A quartet of Temple guards in wheat-yellow doublets burst through, bringing the performance to a premature close.

Every patron shrank in their seat except for a couple who tried to flee out the back, only to encounter a pair of guards coming the other way.

A guard with sergeant's stripes barked into the sudden silence, "We are here for Nufio Tellarez." Several people reflexively flicked their gazes at the incapacitated swordsman.

"Breaker's balls," Jean-Claude muttered. It was a whole afternoon wasted, or was it? He'd been expecting someone to come looking for Nufio, and someone had. Had this been the plan all along?

In theory, Nufio would only have nailed the hat to the door if Jean-Claude were dead. And who better to receive that signal than someone inside the Temple. Kantelvar? Jean-Claude resisted making that leap, as tempting as it was. The Temple was a vast organization, a stateless nation with its own factions and internecine quarrels. As Isabelle was wont to say, follow the evidence where it leads, and right now his evidence was being bundled out the door.

Jean-Claude waited a slow thirty count after the guards had left, then slapped down a winning hand of cards, swept the pot into his coin purse, and limped after them.

The Solar had sunk behind the rooftops and inky shadows quickly washed the color from the cobbled channels of the city's streets. A few meters along the way the Temple guards shackled Nufio in the back of a wagon. Jean-Claude crossed the street at a hobble, too slowly to give the guards any cause for concern, at least until he got to the alley opposite, after which he limped at speed. On the next street over, a cul-de-sac, awaited Mario and the chaise.

"Señor musketeer." Mario waved in what he likely imagined was a surreptitious manner.

"Mario, are you a sight for sore legs. Mount up. The Temple has Nufio and I want to know where they're taking him."

"Of course, señor."

Jean-Claude was about to embark the chaise when he noticed a ragged figure curled up on the floorboards. Rheumy eyes peered at him from under a hood made of layered rags. "What's this?"

"I's Tony," said a voice that had traded several teeth and part of a tongue for an extra helping of slobber. "I has what you're looking for, good sir."

Mario said, "You said you would pay good coin for refuse brought from the blown-up room, and this fellow spent all day tracking me down. He was incredibly persistent."

"Top coin, he says, but only if it's real. Tony's is real. Tony was first." His breath smelled of rotting teeth and cabbage.

"Well, let's see it, then." The way today was going, Jean-Claude didn't expect much.

"Top coin," Tony insisted, holding out a cupped hand.

Jean-Claude displayed five copper coins in one hand and drew his main gauche with the other. "I will give you these coins, but what you show me had better be genuine or I will have them back with a tithe of your skin to boot. Do you understand?"

Tony quailed but managed to stammer, "Y-yes."

Jean-Claude drizzled the coins into Tony's hand, probably more wealth than he'd seen in a year. Quicker than a conjurer's trick the coins vanished and Tony produced a few twisted bits of brass. "Here, here. Take!"

Mario spat in disgust. "You followed me around all day for that, mongrel?"

But Jean-Claude took the bits and examined them closely. "Hinges," he said at last. "These were brass hinges." If he just unbent them with his mind, he could see the shape, and they were covered in gunpowder smudge. "Tony, where did you find these? Where in the room?"

Tony stammered, "M-mirror. On the mirror frame they was."

"And did you bend them getting them off?"

"No. No, they was already like that."

Jean-Claude gripped a hinge that had been bent nearly in half and prized it apart, revealing a chunk of iron that had embedded in it. Metal from the bomb, just like the metal the doctor had extracted from his leg.

"Thank you," Jean-Claude said, and put his main gauche away. "Don't drink it all in one place."

Tony scuttled off like a reef crab with a broken leg.

Jean-Claude climbed aboard the chaise. "A bunch of Temple guards just left the Cog and Crank with Nufio. Let's find out where they're going."

Mario flicked the horses into motion. "What does that brass tell you it doesn't tell me?"

"It tells me that whoever killed Vincent was no Glasswalker."

"I don't understand," Mario said.

Jean-Claude grinned, his blood coming up. "How do you hide a hole in a wall?"

Mario shrugged. "You could cover it up."

"Yes, with a curtain, or a mirror, but then if someone looks behind the curtain or the mirror, they see the hole. But if you planted a bomb in the room, it would blow the wall to smithereens."

Mario's brows drew down in puzzlement. "Then you'd have a very big hole."

"Exactly. The small hole would be invisible." He could see the progression of events. The sharpshooter in his nest shot at the princess, lit the fuse on the bomb, opened the mirror on its hinges, and escaped through the other room. Any witness who wasn't killed by the blast would see only an empty room with no other means of egress; in a land ruled by Glasswalkers, it would be easy to assume the shooter had gotten out through the mirror.

Yet where did this brilliant insight lead him? It did nothing to suggest who was actually behind the cavalcade attack. The only fact with a name attached to it was that Duque Diego owned the building. That smelled of a stalking horse, but Jean-Claude would investigate the man anyway.

Mario had no trouble locating the Temple cart or following it up the hill to the citadel, where it lurched to a stop before the great Temple across the courtyard from the royal palace. It was a vast wheel of a building with six chapel wings extending from a central hub capped with a huge brass dome. A dozen alchemical floodlights illuminated the hemisphere, making it seem as if the Solar, swollen and sullen, had come to rest on the roof.

Even after dark, the pilgrims, scholars, and other worshippers came and went through the doorless entrance. Jean-Claude joined the flow, following the guard sergeant inside. The Aragoths had certainly spared no expense on this edifice. The walls were lined with a series of alcoves painted on the inside with vibrant frescoes, each depicting the life and deeds of a particular saint. There was Cynessus the Blind, the first to awaken from the long sleep in the Vault of Ages. She was the last person ever to gaze on the Primus Mundi and the only one to witness the breaking of the world, for which sin her eyes had been withered in her skull.

There was Saint Cerberus the silver eyed, first and greatest of the Glasswalkers, or perhaps the last of an elder breed. The artist here had naturally depicted him as first and greatest of all the saints, with several other prominent figures showing him deference.

On and on they went, probably weaving together some greater narrative for people who were impressed by that sort of thing. Jean-Claude's quarry turned down a side corridor. Jean-Claude followed without breaking stride.

The hallway was short, with a door at the end, where an all-too-familiar voice from the other sided rattled, "Enter."

Jean-Claude put on a lurch of speed just as the guard heard him coming and turned.

"¡Alto! This is—"

"Crown business," Jean-Claude said automatically. Never mind which crown. He barged past the guard and into a room that looked like a cross between a clerk's office and an alchemical workroom. A chandelier hung with humming alchemical lights provided harsh, brilliant illumination. The walls were lined with bookshelves, pigeonholes, and glass-fronted cabinets filled with brass instruments, crystal beakers, vellum scrolls, pots of slimy worm-things, a jar of what looked like eyeballs, and even the occasional book.

In the center of a horseshoe-shaped desk in the middle of the tile floor sat Kantelvar, his clockwork fingers drumming a tinny tattoo on the desktop.

On the desk before him lay Jean-Claude's much-abused hat, now with a hole in it from being nailed to the Temple door.

"Artifex Kantelvar, why did I know it would be you?"

Kantelvar said, "Jean-Claude. How . . . unexpected."

The guard rushed in behind Jean-Claude, drawing a dagger. "I said stop! Exaltedness, my apologies. I'll remove this ruffian."

Kantelvar held up a warding clockwork hand. "That won't be necessary, Sergeant. Jean-Claude is, in fact, the person we have been looking for."

Jean-Claude kept his attention fixed on Kantelvar. "A private word, if you don't mind."

Kantelvar said, "You may go, Sergeant."

The sergeant said, "Are you sure that's a good idea, Exaltedness?"

"Not entirely," Kantelvar said. "But diplomacy does have its place."

Jean-Claude waited until the sergeant had taken himself out and said in a lower tone, "Just what in blazes are you up to?"

Kantelvar steepled his fingers. "If by that you mean why did I send my men to the Cog and Crank, I should think that would be obvious. I was looking for you."

"Why?"

Kantelvar said, his voice grating, "Because your safety was in doubt. Princesa Isabelle asked about you this afternoon. My men followed your trail as far as the building where the assassination attempt took place, where they learned you had been in an altercation with a local thug. They were told you had returned to the citadel, but you were not here. Fearing that you had been set upon, a search was launched, but to no avail.

"Then one of my contacts in the local Temple informed me that a reprobate named Nufio Tellarez had nailed a hat to his door. He thought it was a nobleman's hat; you see, it had no reflection. I recognized it and sent my men to search for Nufio, who is known to wallow at the Cog and Crank. Now, I believe, it is your turn."

Jean-Claude looked for a chair, saw none, and so leaned on the desk. "I was looking for Thornscar." *And I found you.* "I might have found him if your men hadn't stolen my bait."

"Perhaps if you could be persuaded to share your plans with me, we might stop tripping over each other. I've wasted considerable resources looking for you that could have been looking for Thornscar."

"I'll take it under consideration. Where is Isabelle?" He wanted to ask her if she'd asked the artifex to look for him.

"At the masquerade by now, which, I must point out, you are ill dressed to attend, unless you intend to arrive as a bad smell."

Jean-Claude considered the spectacle he'd make, stumping into the ballroom, ill kept, lurching, and smelly. It would almost be worth it, if not for its casting Isabelle in a bad light. "No, I think not." Right now he needed about a dozen things to make him human again, starting with a bath. "I shall retire for the evening." He clapped his much-abused hat on his head and limped out the door.

The warm night air tickled Jean-Claude's skin and made him itch. He passed by the gaol wagon, which was still waiting at the bottom of the steps. Nufio lifted his head and gripped the cage bars. "Antidote," he groaned. "Please."

Jean-Claude shook his head wearily. "I didn't poison you, dog, just gave you a bellyache. Stick your finger down your throat and puke it up."

The swordsman's eyes rounded. Waves of surprise, relief, and fury rolled across his face. "You unholy bastard. Breaker take your balls!" Then another wave of pain hit him and he doubled over.

Jean-Claude said, "A word of advice, friend. The next time somebody offers you money to kill a King's Own Musketeer, turn it down."

———

Getting dressed for the masque was an epic event, not helped by the fact that Isabelle fidgeted through the washing, the powdering, the painting, the primping, the fitting of layer upon layer of petticoats and a corset that assumed she had no further use for her internal organs.

Right now she didn't care about the Aragoths and all their ridiculous squabbles. She just wanted to look through that book. Maybe she was wrong. Maybe there was nothing in it but disconnected fragments, as its title implied. Or it might tell her why the blood ciphers thought her father was not her father and why it labeled her l'Étincelle. She had no powers . . . although she supposed it was possible to be an unhallowed l'Étincelle instead of an unhallowed Sanguinaire, a difference that made no difference, surely.

At last her handmaids were done touching up everything but the train of her skirt, which she wouldn't put on until she was ready to board the coach. She thanked the handmaids and complimented them profusely before shooing them out the door.

"But, Highness, the coach is waiting," said Valérie, more subdued than usual; she was still rattled and grieving, but she was sticking to her post.

"Then I will be fashionably late. I just need a moment to compose myself. Alone. It's not as if they can start without me." She bustled Valérie out, closed the felt-lined door, and hurried to her desk. The *Fragments* awaited her. She opened it to its first page. It was handwritten, but definitely not two thousand years old. The pages, though yellowed like autumn leaves, were not so dry as to crack under her touch.

It was, thank the saints, written in Saintstongue and not some more esoteric language. The text of the first page read, ". . . fluctuations in the underlying aura . . . primordial infinitesimals are generated . . . ," which was annotated with a description that went on much longer than the passage itself of where and when the fragment had been found.

She tried not to get stuck wondering what primordial infinitesimals were and flipped another page, and another. The book was long and there was no way she was going to get through it all tonight. Did she have to put the answer together in pieces? Was there an answer? She needed more time.

The book was well worn, its tooled leather cover warped, the rough edges of its paper stained from the oil of many fingers. Maybe he had a favorite passage, something he kept returning to time after time.

She closed the book and set it, spine down, on the table, then let the covers fall open. There was the telltale crack of a broken spine, and the pages spread to reveal a longer passage much stained, smudged, and scribbled upon.

Isabelle stifled a cry of triumph; there was no guarantee this passage held what she was looking for, but she dove in:

I, Saint Céleste, inscribe this argument in defense of my beloved and innocent sister, Ur-Saint Iav.

Isabelle stopped and read the line again, and again, as if her eyes and her mind must have been playing tricks on her. Never had more heresy been encoded in a single sentence. Saint Céleste was Iav's sister? Iav who had tried to steal the secret of life from the Builder. Iav who had unleashed the Breaker and shattered the Primus Mundi. And Saint Céleste named her innocent? Impossible.

Or was it? If this was a true transcription of the actual words put down by Saint Céleste, one of the blessed few who had survived the Primus Mundi, could Isabelle discount her words? If Céleste was her greatest-grandmother, then that made Iav her greatest-aunt.

With trembling hands Isabelle traced the rest of the passage. Much of it was broken and much more written in a technical language she had no way to decipher, words that no longer had meaning because the theory behind them had been lost. Near the end of the passage were a few clear uninterrupted lines.

Iav's hypothesis was correct. Heritable minutiae are neither infinitely elastic nor divisible. Given the limited number possible stable corpuscular sets, it is plausible to infer that the decay of sorcery need not be inevitable and the tendency toward malignancies can be reversed by outbreeding with the clayborn. Not only did her limited experiments with wild crosses show no evidence of corruption, but the extra degree of motility provided by the exosomes enabled the emergence of novel phenomena. The most enticing possibility is the manifestation of a higher order of sorcery . . .

Isabelle felt as if she had entered a trance or a dream. It was no wonder the Temple had not included this fragment in the *Instructions;* it contradicted every belief they espoused. Sorcerers breeding with the clayborn produced abominations . . . and what was an abomination but a novel type of sorcery that its wielder did not know how to control? Something as unfamiliar and powerful as unbound sorcery could be terrifying, and people had a very difficult time distinguishing between frightful and evil.

The last line of text was broken.

. . . with the ability to transmute . . . on a scale hitherto deemed impossible . . . could lead to the salvation of . . . manifest in a single individual . . . that which was promised . . .

A single individual. This was what drove Kantelvar and his ilk, breeding sorcerers down through the centuries. Combining, back-breeding, narrowing all the bloodlines down to two.

Julio and I. The understanding of exactly what Kantelvar wanted of her stunned all other thought from her mind. *My child. The Savior.*

The door to her room opened with a soft swishing noise and Valérie said, urgently, "Highness. It's time to go."

Quaking with reaction, Isabelle shut the book. Yes. She needed to concentrate on other things, to clear her mind. She had been expecting politics to rule her life, not prophecy. She needed to talk to Jean-Claude about this.

Later. Right now she had a social duty to perform, a betrothed to meet, and a war to avert.

On her way out the door she said to Valérie, "If Jean-Claude comes back, ask him to wait for me. I need to talk to him."

"Are you well, Highness?" Valérie asked. "You look pale."

"Just nervous," Isabelle said. "Going in front of all those people. I feel like a prize heifer at a county fair." And that was the least of her worries.

—

The chaise rattled about halfway around the vast courtyard and dropped Jean-Claude off in front of the three-story edifice that was serving as Isabelle's guest residence. He mounted the steps to the porch and met Valérie, who had come out to greet him.

"Jean-Claude, welcome," she said. Her voice was husky from crying.

He doffed his battered hat to her. "Mademoiselle Valérie, good evening. Is Princess Isabelle here?"

"She's gone up to the masque. She begs you to stay and wait for her."

Jean-Claude grunted. "I will do better than that. I will meet her at the masque. There are people there I need to talk to." Isabelle and Duque Diego chief amongst them.

She escorted him into the house. Her face, ordinarily rosy and cheerful, had a gray color and wore a pinched expression. Her hands were knotted together before her belly. "Have you caught the man who shot Vincent?"

"Not yet," Jean-Claude said. "The investigation is less straightforward than I'd like."

"When you do catch him, spit in his eye for me." After a moment she added, "You may not have liked Vincent, but I did."

Jean-Claude touched his hand to his heart. "You have my word, mademoiselle." Vincent had been an ass, but he'd been an honest ass, and Jean-Claude could see why Valérie might find that attractive.

She nodded in satisfaction and her hands unclenched. "Builder keep."

"Savior come." Two servants helped him inside to one of the silent rooms—perhaps it was because of the noise of the city, but the Aragoths seemed to have a passion for quiet rooms—and poured him a steaming bath. The hot water stung like the Breaker's own venom until the heat finally seeped deep enough inside him to start working on his muscles.

He was just starting to loosen up when the door opened and Adel padded in, bearing a basketful of drying cloths and pots of ointment. "Good evening, señor musketeer. Are you enjoying your bath?"

"Indeed, madam," Jean-Claude said. "A bit too much, I'm afraid, but I am almost finished." He needed to get up, dry off, get dressed in a silly costume, and attend Isabelle at the masquerade.

He made to lever himself up, but Adel placed her hands on his shoulders and pushed him back down. Water sloshed over the sides of the tub. "Not so fast. La princesa gave me explicit orders that you were to be well cared for. I would not wish to earn her displeasure by sending you off to meet her looking like last week's laundry." Before he could protest, she dug strong thumbs into his shoulders, bringing painful heat to the knots therein. He gasped in agony very close to ecstasy.

"Mon dieu, woman, you have the hands of a saint."

She kneaded his tired muscles like bread dough. "I certainly hope not. I would hate to have them wind up in some reliquary when I am finished with them."

Jean-Claude laughed. "Fear not, good saint, your secret is safe with me. And I would love to endure your ministrations, but I really do have duties I must perform."

"And what would you do at the masquerade, protect Princesa Isabelle from disingenuous conversation? No one is going to assault her in the king's presence. Far better for you to take care of yourself now so that you are ready when she does need you."

"I need to talk to people there."

"The masquerade will be going on until dawn, and the longer you wait, the drunker your quarry will be."

Jean-Claude grumbled at this logic primarily because it was irrefutable. He was exhausted. "Ten years ago, I would have just been hitting my stride at this time of night."

"Hmmm . . . the trade-off of age is supposed to be energy for wisdom. One hopes you have not been shortchanged."

"Did I mention you have the Breaker's own tongue?"

She laughed. She rubbed his shoulders and then let him out of the tub, but only far enough to lie on a table where she could cover him in heated blankets and massage his aching back.

"You know, you really don't have to take this trouble for me," he said.

The pleasure he took chopping the knees out from under the high and mighty was matched by his distaste for imposing himself on the humble.

"Tame your worries. It is my pleasure to ease the hurts of one who works so hard to protect Her Highness's interests, though you will weary me if you do not relax."

"My apologies, madam, but my mind cannot stop its tumbling."

"Then speak of pleasant things. Tell me of your princess as one who knows her well."

Jean-Claude released a long, slow breath. "Tell you of Isabelle? I do not have that much time. She is . . . wonderful."

"She is certainly very clever."

"Hah. Conjurers and shysters are clever. Scholars and priests are learned. Composers and artists are inspired. Isabelle is brilliant. She looks at things and sees them in ways that no one else does." And if he said too much more, he would implicate her in the heresy of engaging in pursuits reserved for men, so he changed the subject. "What about your Príncipe Julio?"

"When I knew him best, he was always very high spirited. Not just un-afraid but eager for challenges. The quickest way to get him to do something was to tell him it couldn't be done. And he was so competitive. He had to be the best at everything. Running, riding, shooting, fencing. He was always pushing himself past his abilities."

"A typical boy, then," Jean-Claude said.

"Oh, but it was frightening how often he succeeded. He taught himself to mirror-walk when he was only eight, when most children don't even get their silver eyes until they are twelve or their instructions until they are fourteen. It scared the queen his mother half to death."

"Mothers are inclined to be upset when their boys try to kill themselves," Jean-Claude allowed. "I nearly drove my poor mam to fits."

Adel laughed. "And you haven't changed a bit since then, as I can see, but that's not how I meant it. Queen Margareta wasn't scared *for* Julio. She was afraid *of* him. More than once I heard her call him the Breaker's child, and it wasn't just a mother's fits. She was terrified, like she'd found herself leashed to a great dog turned vicious."

"And was he vicious?" Jean-Claude asked.

"Never that I could see. He was just *intense*. But he was always kind to me and his servants never feared him, not even the whipping boy."

"They still use whipping boys here?" Jean-Claude asked, incredulous.

"Queen Margareta resurrected the practice."

Jean-Claude asked, "And how often was this whipping boy plied in his trade?"

Adel hesitated thoughtfully. "Not very often. In truth, most of the transgressions for which he suffered were manufactured."

"By whom?"

"Hmmmm . . .'Tis a delicate subject."

"It goes no farther than my ears."

"By the queen, then, if you must know. She couldn't lash out at Julio, so she vented her wrath on poor Climacio."

"And what did Julio think of that?"

"He hated it, but there was nothing he could do about it."

"Ah." Jean-Claude's opinion of Julio rose at the idea that he was capable of feeling compassion for the lowly.

"What about Artifex Kantelvar?" Jean-Claude asked. "When did he become involved in the príncipe's affairs?"

"Him, I do not know. He used to keep to his own palace up in the mountains. He never came to San Augustus until he showed up to officiate at Alejandro's wedding. That was about five years ago."

Jean-Claude wished he could draw some nefarious conclusion from that, but who better to officiate at a royal wedding than a Temple artifex?

Adel continued, "A lot of people think his Exaltation drove him mad."

Jean-Claude grunted. Exaltation was the name of the ceremony in which some high-muckety yellow-robe got his limbs lopped off and replaced with metal bits to bring him closer to the Builder's clockwork perfection. "I imagine they'd have to be mad to start with." On further reflection he added, "Mad in what way?" And who would be in a position to judge?

Adel made a shrug that rippled down her arms and across his back. "It's just gossip. Folk said he was always more interested in money than the Builder's work—absolve thy sins for a fee. I heard he got one of the up-country lords to hand over a whole fief to pay off some scandal, then kicked all the farmers off it and put sheep on instead. He even had his own trade fleet."

"More profit than prophet," Jean-Claude said. Indeed, that didn't sound much like the Kantelvar he knew, more slimy than cunning. "And now he's different."

"Oh yes, much more around town. Much more political. He even helped

Duque Diego's son get married to Lady Noelia, and that set off a feud between Duque Diego and Noelia's uncle Don Blanxart, who had meant to marry her off to someone else."

"Why is that important?" Jean-Claude asked. He had never needed to know Aragothic society before.

"Because Duque Diego used to support Príncipe Alejandro, but Don Blanxart is Xaviera's brother, so Duque Diego was forced to either back down or switch sides."

"So he switched sides," Jean-Claude said. "Leaving us with a political mess today."

"I don't know all that much about it. I was more interested in the married couple."

"And how are they doing?" Jean-Claude asked.

"He accused her of cuckolding him and had her thrown from the coastal rim."

Jean-Claude's heart thundered with outrage. Much too little much too late. "And was that villain ever punished?"

"He was tried before the king. Don Blanxart wanted him thrown in the Hellshard, but Carlemmo stripped him of his name and banished him instead."

"A result I am sure made no one happy," Jean-Claude said; it certainly sickened him. If all of this was true, Kantelvar was at least partly responsible for the tensions in Aragoth today. Was there anything he did not have his clockwork fingers in?

At last, Adel rubbed the last kink out of Jean-Claude's back and changed the dressing on his leg. He felt like melting into the table. If only he could remain here for perhaps a decade. Alas, duty called, and after a suitable amount of time to let the good work set, she let him up.

"We must find you a costume," she said. "Something fabulous."

Jean-Claude bit his tongue on the first three suggestions that came to mind: a beggar, a donkey, and a dog. He wasn't going just to tweak noses; he had to make Isabelle look good. "I will wear my high-court uniform— that's the white one with all the silver trim—and a suitable mask. I doubt anyone else will be going as a musketeer."

CHAPTER

Thirteen

The royal palace's huge courtyard was filled with coaches of every shape and size. An army of drivers, footmen, grooms, and stable hands milled about, making sure the animals were both relaxed for a long stay and ready to go at moment's notice.

Isabelle's coach pulled to a stop in front of the Hall of Mirrors. It had taken longer to carefully bundle her and her acres of white silk into the coach than it would have taken her to walk the short distance, but a princess of the blood royal did not arrive on foot.

The footman opened the door and Isabelle poured out in a cascade of lace, like the foam at the bottom of a waterfall. Her gown was trimmed with silver and vented to show layers of crimson beneath. Her wig was done up in an elaborate coiffure threaded through with strands of rubies and pearls. For her face, she had chosen the most diaphanous of all possible veils, barely more than a wisp of fabric, and, for the sake of the masquerade, a "mask" of paint in the form of a white Solar burst centered on the bridge of her nose, its rays spreading up to her hairline across her eyes, over her cheeks, and down to her chin. She must make the Aragothic court's first, critical impression of her a good one. Tonight and forever hereafter, she represented not only herself, but all of l'Empire Céleste, and l'Empire did not trip over its own skirts.

Isabelle's personal guard, Vincent's men bedecked in l'Empire Céleste's blue and gold, fell in behind her as she mounted the red-carpeted steps. She wished Jean-Claude were at her side. She clung to his assurance that she could manage her own affairs, despite all evidence to the contrary. If she couldn't handle this social venue on her own, then she had no business being here no matter what Grand Leon's, Margareta's, or Kantelvar's schemes required.

Her mind was still a whirlwind as she rearranged the facts surrounding her betrothal to fit the new context of Kantelvar's breeding program. The emerging pattern was girded with corpses. Kantelvar had shoehorned Isabelle into this marriage by having her selected as an alternate to Lady Sonya de Zapetta—the less controversial choice—but in order to ensure that her wedding came to pass, Lady Sonya had to die. Kantelvar had blamed that on Thornscar but only *after* Isabelle's ship had been attacked. Could Kantelvar have murdered Lady Sonya? Yet even that would not have been enough to secure this marriage.

Presumably Julio had been part of the conspiracy's breeding plan, his history as distorted as hers. His birth had only come about because an artifex had helped arrange Margareta's marriage to Carlemmo after his first wife died, and now Carlemmo himself was dying, a necessary prerequisite for Julio's ascent and a civil war. Did Julio have any idea of the part selected for him? Did he approve of it?

If Kantelvar's conspiracy was consolidating all the bloodlines, including those of the ghostbred saints, like Saint Céleste, they would have had to manipulate pairings going back hundreds of years at a minimum. How many other lives had they bent and twisted to this singular end? It was a great mural painted in blood, a great play choreographed to try to force the prophecy to come true. It turned Isabelle's stomach, but she had not an iota of evidence to prove any of it, nothing except the book, and that could mean anything. If she tried to put it forward as evidence, Kantelvar could claim she'd stolen the book and modified it or even printed it herself.

No one outside the Temple knew what was in the *Fragments,* and she had no way of knowing who within the Temple was part of the conspiracy. She needed the blood ciphers. She would have to sneak back to Kantelvar's sanctum and recover that chest of quondam clockworks. Jean-Claude would help her. He would have some idea of how to drag the conspiracy into the light of day.

With difficulty, she forced her attention to the matter at hand. She had a great deal of business to conduct this evening. First, she had to meet Carlemmo and plead with him to pick a successor. Surely if he cared about his grandchildren, he would not oblige his sons to fight each other. She also wanted to take Duque Diego's measure. Kantelvar had pointed him out as an enemy, blamed him for Thornscar's attack, but was it a true warning against a real enemy, or was he trying to cut her off from potential allies? It might possibly be both. But the most important meeting of the night, the one that held the most promise and terror, would be with Príncipe Julio.

The very thought of meeting a stranger and calling him betrothed filled her stomach with razor-edged butterflies. What would he be like? Why had he ignored her? Was he a dupe in Kantelvar's scheme or a partner? Did he have any affection for the brother he seemed destined to fight? Too many questions. She levered herself forward with the knowledge that a single truth was less overwhelming than a thousand formless fears.

The two-story-tall, peaked double doors of the grand entrance had been thrown wide. Inside, every wall and pillar was lined with silvered glass, which made the vast space seem even larger and more crowded and distorted than the reality. The marble floors were done in a pleasing abstract design of white, black, and gold tile. Overhead, dozens of alchemical chandeliers blazed, their harsh light cutting night's shadow into tiny slivers that scuttled about under the cover of ladies' skirts.

As Isabelle crossed the threshold, her skin tingled with the light touch of sorcery. The building, she had been told, was warded against unauthorized magic; only those specifically permitted by the king could work their sorcery here. As a consequence, a mirrored hall full of Glasswalkers was actually one of the least sorcerous places in the kingdom.

A line of musicians in purple livery raised long trumpets with pennons bearing the symbol of the Aragothic crown and blew a silver-throated fanfare. A herald raised his voice. "La Princesa Isabelle des Zephyrs, of l'Empire Céleste!"

Inside, a hundred conversations hushed. Isabelle emerged into a wonderland of fantastic costumes, of glittering faeries and sulfurous demons, fiery dragons, fierce gryphons, and other rare beasts. The competition for most ostentatious display of wealth and talent had reached a sartorial crescendo, straining toward a climax of silk, satin, and stitches.

The Comte des Zephyrs had hosted his fair share of feasts, balls, and ceremonies, and Isabelle had thought them grand to the point of gaudy, but they were as nothing to the tableau before her. It was as if she had stepped into a world of demigods, where reality was rearranged at whim, and it was all she could do to keep from gawking like some provincial milkmaid. *I am l'Empire, and l'Empire does not gawk.*

The sea of fantastic frippery parted before Isabelle, and a pair of young ladies stepped into the aisle. They curtsied and then proceeded slowly and decorously before her, strewing flower petals from large baskets as they went. The crowd made a collective leg to Isabelle as she passed, as if she were a stiff breeze causing a field of grass to bend. When had she acquired such force? She fought to keep herself from scurrying forward to release the tension; l'Empire did not scurry. This courtesy wasn't really directed at her, but rather at the powers she channeled through her blood and rank.

At the far end of her long walk, on his throne atop a broad dais, King Car-lemmo waited. He was not a tall man, but he had a powerful frame that had been withered by disease, leaving a frail and bony husk. His skin—what she could see of it—which should have been swarthy, was a sickly shade of gray. From a gold chain about his neck hung a reliquary of Saint Cerberus, a quondam metal cylinder in which the living eyes of the first Glasswalker saint were held, a symbol of sorcerous divinity. Around his crown, he wore an elaborate headpiece in the shape of a skyship of the line, a calculated reminder of how Aragoth's power and wealth derived from her formidable navy.

Isabelle's nervous gaze skipped over Queen Margareta and landed on a lean man in royal purple wearing a silver medallion bearing the royal heraldry and the marks of cadency befitting a second son. His posture was languid, almost bored, and the upper half of his face was obscured behind the jeweled scales of a wyvern mask.

Julio. My betrothed. She tried to make the name and title fit the figure before her, but a wide, thin-lipped mouth and a narrow chin weren't enough to hang a label on. A pox on whoever had come up with the idea of masquerade balls. How was she supposed to be properly introduced to people if she couldn't see their faces?

She arrived at the foot of the dais. A pair of Temple censer bearers detached themselves from the wings and walked slowly around her, wafting her with a heady, pungent incense. A sagax in a golden robe embroidered with carmine clockworks planted himself between Isabelle and the king. He was one of the fellows who had taken offense at her existence upon her arrival at the docks, the one who had claimed Kantelvar was deranged by his vision of the Savior's coming. Did he have any idea how right he was? Dared Isabelle speak to him? *The enemy of my enemy can give me information on my enemy.* Yet she dared not reveal the exact nature of Kantelvar's scheme, for the sagax would surely see that the easiest way to defeat Kantelvar was to remove Isabelle.

The sagax chanted in the Saintstongue, pronouncing the words roughly and mechanically, as if by rote rather than meaning, pleading with the Builder to sanctify an unclean woman to stand in the presence of Carlemmo, who was His power in the world. He monotonously reiterated the Temple's assertion that Iav's sin had somehow corrupted all women, enfeebling them body, mind, and soul. *My many-times-great-aunt.* And she was innocent . . . or at least Saint Céleste had defended her. On a level below reason, Isabelle felt she was the damned saint's partisan, if for no other reason than any argument a woman made against this presumption of corruption was invariably rebutted with, "If you were a man you would understand this, but you're a flawed woman, so you can't."

Apparently satisfied that Isabelle was not going to vomit up a swarm of locusts on the spot, the sagax finally withdrew.

Isabelle curtsied to the king and summoned up her voice. It cowered in the back of her throat like a dog hiding under the bed in a thunderstorm. She dragged it out and brought it to heel. These were not her words but an agreed-upon formula: "Your Majesty, I bring greetings from His Imperial Majesty Leon XIV, le Roi de Tonnerre, of l'Empire Céleste. In his name, and for the sake of everlasting peace and friendship between our kingdoms, I present myself, my life, and my blood, to reinforce the strength of your line." Somehow the words seemed bigger and heavier, more important than when she had practiced them in front of her handmaids.

The king stirred, but his voice seemed to be coming from far away, as if he were calling back to her from halfway down a lonely road. "Princesa Isabelle des Zephyrs, your offer is well made and graciously accepted. Rise and be welcome. All hail la Princesa Isabelle."

The crowd voiced a dutiful cheer. Likely more than half of them were privately outraged about the gross breach of tradition her marriage represented. How many in that faceless crowd still plotted her murder? And might all the masks, with their promise of anonymity, tempt her enemies to strike at her tonight?

Carlemmo gestured Isabelle to an empty chair beside Julio's. The príncipe watched her warily from behind his wyvern mask, hunching into himself like a wounded animal holed up in a cave. His left leg was noticeably stiff, the amputated limb disguised with a boot, the buckles of the prosthesis poking out from his garters. His breath reeked of wine.

With a sinking heart, she curtsied to him and tried to speak, but her mouth had gone dry; this was the man to whom her fate was forever tied, a sulking, drunken stranger in a mask.

"Príncipe," she managed, barely more than a whisper.

"Your Highness," he said in the careful tones of someone rummaging for misplaced syllables. "You are even more beautiful than I had been led to believe."

"Thank you, Highness." She had a hundred things she wanted to talk to him about—politics and prophecies, intrigue and murder—but none of them involved her appearance. Also, she wished his gaze would've lingered at least a moment on her face. She made perfunctory obeisance, then took her chair.

Music resumed, and the crowd began to mill. A herald called out for the commencement of public ceremonies and all the most important nobles began queuing up in order of social rank. One by one they would ascend the steps, greet her, exchange rote pleasantries, and present her with gifts. Judging by the sheer number of nobles present, it was likely to take hours, and every last one of them would be judging her.

Would Lorenzo Barbaro be in the queue? What would she say to him if he was? *Do you remember a time you spent with Vedetta des Zephyrs? Did you know you have a daughter?* She supposed revealing herself as a bastard would be one way to extract herself from this marriage trap, if she were willing to sign her own writ of execution in the process.

She turned her mind from the mystery of the past and tried to think how best to persuade Julio to attempt reconciliation with his brother. She did not believe in prophecy, but Kantelvar did, and he seemed to be trying to arrange for its conditions to be met.

"Look at them," Julio muttered to no one in particular, the words muffled in an alcohol-scented fog. "Lord of the Ten Gates all the way down to the royal rat catcher, every pendejo with a title to hide his name behind, bowing and scraping to el rey in public and wagering on the hour of his death behind the curtains. Boy-buggering whoreson. Cloth-of-gold sack of shit."

It was impossible to tell toward whom these imprecations were directed.

Isabelle steeled herself and pushed a question onto the field. "And what happens when your father dies?"

Julio snorted like a man waking from a dream and finding himself in a gutter. "I suspect we will all be horribly killed."

This was not the sort of answer Isabelle had expected, but it seemed like a good enough opening for her petition. "If you don't think you can beat your brother, why not come to an accord with him? Surely avoiding bloodshed is in everyone's best interest."

Julio cast a doleful eye upon her. "What makes you think there's going to be a fight?"

"I . . . just assumed there would be some sort of struggle."

"No doubt," he said, "but riddle me this, oh unlucky princesa. What is messier than a civil war between two brothers?"

"I have no idea." Indeed, Isabelle felt adrift in this conversation.

"A civil war with no brothers." Julio took a drink. "If there is one brother left, he wins. If there are no brothers left, it's a free-for-all."

Isabelle was appalled at this insight. The Savior was supposed to be born into a time of universal war, but Julio could not be killed, at least not right away, not until Kantelvar was convinced Isabelle was with child. Did he know that was the plan? She dared not broach the subject until she had some idea how he would react.

"Then why don't you treat with your brother?" she asked.

"What would be the point?" Julio said. "They say the dead give no testimony, but wills can be faked; competing wills are even better. Damned spring-wound spider thinks I'm too stupid to figure it out. Thinks I'm just his puppet."

"Kantelvar," Isabelle said. "Do you understand his scheme?"

That evoked a humorless chuckle. "I have no idea what he thinks to gain. All I know is that he talks to everyone, generally about what they want and how he can help them get it. The people he seduces become the careful gardeners of their own lies."

"What did he offer you?"

Julio gave her a wary look. "He never offered me anything. No promises to keep that way. Just a pawn with no open moves, waiting to be sacrificed."

"Then you must change the rules."

Julio shook his head. "He is not two moves ahead. He is two games ahead."

Isabelle's spirit sagged under the weight of his listlessness and of all the lies she had been told about him. This was not a man who had ever set out to be the greatest sorcerer in the world, or the greatest swordsman. He would be no help to her at all unless she could turn his apathy into a tool.

"Then shall I bargain with your brother on your behalf? If I can persuade him—"

Julio made a shooing gesture. "Make whatever bargain you like— it won't matter—but for the Savior's sake, can we please talk about something else?"

That was as definitive a commission as she was likely to get, but she imagined he would stand by any deal she made if it saved his sorry hide.

She shifted into rehearsed small talk. "Were you named after King Julio the Just?" That was a name she had picked up from her readings, one of the feudal kings who had fought the Skaladin to a standstill during the long occupation.

"No, I was named after my grandfather Julio, the Duc de Bosque de Dolores."

Isabelle translated the name: "The Forest of Sorrows." And a connection clicked in her mind like the hammer of a flintlock being cocked.

Her skin went suddenly cold and she must have been staring into the middle distance, because Julio asked, "Are you ill?"

She blinked hard and then asked, "The Forest of Sorrows. Is that still in your family?"

"Yes."

"For how long?"

"Ah . . ." Julio pulled at his chin. "I think we've had it for a few centuries. It was one of the few places the Skaladin never conquered. Why?"

"Nothing," Isabelle said, not trusting her own conclusions, not trusting Julio. Kantelvar said he had revived a bloodhollow in the Forest of Sorrows, which meant it had been ruled by Célestials, which meant either Kantelvar was lying or the revival had taken place over two hundred years ago. Impossible. Kantelvar could not have been creeping around that long; even if his quondam clockworks were somehow keeping him alive, someone would have noticed.

Even as she grappled with this deduction, a herald announced her first supplicant, Duque Ramon de la Gallegos Diego.

Isabelle's head snapped around and her gut knotted as the man who had used her brother to arrange an attempt on her life approached. She pasted on her most professional smile and forced herself to breathe steadily.

Diego was not a looming nightmare giant, but rather a man of average height with above-average thickness. His mask was that of a dragon, the emperor of all fell beasts. It was not a terribly subtle message, but then, she gathered his ambition was well-known. Like all his kind, his eyes were pure mirrors and she could see her distorted reflection in them.

Yet whatever emotions he felt toward Isabelle, his manner and tone were entirely reserved as he made a leg to her and said, "Your Highness, I bid you welcome; your presence brings hope to us all. Please allow me to present you with this small token of my esteem." He lifted a narrow box of polished wood from a pillow carried by his servant and held it up to her in his large, meaty hands.

Isabelle forced her good hand to remain steady as she accepted the box and thumbed it open. Inside lay a vellum scroll fastened with a ribbon and a wax seal bearing the Diego coat of arms.

The herald announced, "The deed to Monarch's Cove." A murmur of appreciation rolled through the crowd. Apparently this was a good gift.

Diego said, "For your own use, unattached to any dowry."

Isabelle forced a smile. "Your Grace, I thank you for this. I hope to use it well." That was all diplomacy required or protocol permitted, but she could not let the exchange go so easily. "And my condolences for the loss of your friend."

Duque Diego's expression was unreadable behind his dragon mask, but he remained stiff just a fraction too long before saying, "It is a loss everyone should mourn." He turned his gaze on Julio, then bowed himself out.

Isabelle barely had time to wonder what he meant by that cryptic response before her next supplicant stepped forward, and the next. Servants circulated bearing silver trays laden with hors d'oeuvres and goblets of drink. Somebody poured Isabelle a chalice of strong wine. She calculated the size of her bladder relative to the length of the line in front of her and resolved to sip slowly.

An elegant parade of high nobility greeted her. Some were subtly hostile, others guardedly enthusiastic. Everyone brought gifts, though none so grand as Duque Diego's. Julio supplied acerbic if not terribly useful commentary about most of them. "He has the manners of a saint but a manor in disrepair." "No, that isn't a mask; he really does have a nose like a pig."

"Please, Julio. My poor mind cannot absorb your wit." Jean-Claude was fond of mocking nobility, but at least his observations were clever and useful. "Don't you care what your future subjects think of you?"

Julio frowned at this mild reproof and slouched deeper into his chair. "Long have I observed this . . . game." He waved a languid hand at the assembly. "And I have come to the conclusion that a king does not and cannot command his subjects to behave. If everyone cleaved strictly to the rules, a balance would be reached, which would not be so bad for those on top, but would be intolerable for those being cooked on the bottom of the pot, and since there are more on the bottom than the top, they would soon cease to put up with it. The king therefore stirs the cauldron of courtly intrigue. He gives his subjects very subtle incentives to misbehave and taxes them for the privilege. This well-dressed rabble couldn't care a fig what I think of them so long as they believe I can give them what they want."

Isabelle had not evolved a response before a familiar shuffling figure caught her eye. Kantelvar entered the hall without fanfare and made his way directly to el rey, who was holding court with his favorites. Kantelvar cut through the line and leaned forward to whisper a few words in Carlemmo's ear.

Carlemmo nodded and made a little "go ahead" gesture with his fingers. The artifex limped around behind the throne and headed in Isabelle's direction. He had worn clothes cut to show off his clockwork limbs and polished the quondam metal until the telescoping tubes, coiled cables, and ball joints gleamed under the alchemical lights. Everybody he encountered stepped quickly out of his way, and at least two made signs against the wicked.

Julio groaned at his approach. "So much like a winter wind he is, squeezing in through every crack and bringing a chill."

"Highnesses," Kantelvar said, bowing. "I see the intended couple have finally been introduced. I trust all is well."

"Well enough," Julio said tightly.

Isabelle's bottled indignation leaked into her voice. "Indeed, Príncipe Julio has completely supplanted my expectations."

Even shadowed by his hood, Kantelvar managed to give her a wilting look.

"What have you for me tonight?" Julio asked. "Some new and incomprehensible subterfuge, another wallow in the dregs?"

Kantelvar's emerald eye gleamed balefully beneath his hood. "No, Highness, but, if I may, I have news for your soon-to-be wife."

"I pray it is not as grim as most of your news," Isabelle said. *Or as strange as your secrets.*

"Indeed not, Highness," Kantelvar said, bowing to her as much as his crooked spine would allow. "I come to inform you that your musketeer's meddling has cost my investigation in time and resources. May I humbly request that you require him to cooperate with me?"

Isabelle could think of few worse ideas than putting Jean-Claude under Kantelvar's direction. "Jean-Claude is not mine to command. If you don't want him treading on your toes I suggest you tell him where you intend to put your feet."

"He is an impediment to discovering your enemies."

In other words, he's getting in the way of your schemes. "Nevertheless, he stays." And the sooner she could speak to him the sooner they could drag this mad scheme of Kantelvar's into the light of day.

"As you wish, Highness." Kantelvar bowed himself out but lingered, like an unfinished chore, behind the dais, to what purpose Isabelle could not discern. She did not like having him there and had to resist the urge to fidget.

Another petitioner came, and ten-score more, until the last of Aragoth's highest nobility had made their official welcome and the foreign dignitaries lined up for their turn. There was a dour, heavyset mercenary general from Oberholz, and a sleek, goateed one from Vecci, and several more from other surrounding states. So many of the Aragothic nobles had supplemented their native troops with foreign mercenaries in anticipation of a civil war that they amounted to about a third of the armed men on Aragoth's native soil. It seemed a dangerous proportion to Isabelle, even with as little as she knew of warfare. She referred dinner invitations from both generals to her staff to sort out and schedule appropriately; if she accepted every dinner invitation she had received tonight, she would bloat up to the size of a leviathan.

The herald announced, "The mathematician Lord Martin DuJournal."

Isabelle very nearly choked on her wine. For a moment, it was all she could do not to cough or sneeze the stinging liquid out her nose. The effort of holding it down brought tears to her eyes, blurring her vision and making it impossible to see the man who claimed the identity of her nom de plume.

The man announced as DuJournal had taken a quick step forward as if to assist her, but a pair of guards blocked his way. He was tall and lean, and he wore a mask of autumn leaves and stag's horns, a depiction of the lord of the hunt. Behind his mask, his eyes were green, and beneath it, his mouth was framed by short whiskers the color of wheat.

I am DuJournal! The adventuring mathematician was hers, her alter ego, her creation. She was the one who had conceived him, gestated him in the womb of her mind, given him life on paper, and sent his adventures out into the world.

"Isabelle, are you poisoned?" Julio asked.

She shook her head. "It just went down the wrong way. Thank you." She coughed into a handkerchief and glared into the imposter's eyes. *How dare you . . . whoever you are?*

More importantly, why had this man chosen DuJournal for a disguise? To get her attention, clearly. She had never made any secret she was DuJournal's publisher, but she always maintained that she had never actually met the man, instead receiving his manuscripts by post. It added to his air of mystery.

Had this imposter discovered her secret? If so, why announce himself to her in this way? Did he mean to blackmail her? The Temple would not hesitate to drag her right out of the ballroom to be blinded and deafened if they knew she had been engaging in forbidden scholarship . . . but this DuJournal could hardly expose her as the author of those books without also exposing himself as an imposter surely not welcome in the royal court.

Stifling outrage, she gestured the fraud forward. "Lord DuJournal," she said civilly; she was good at civil. "What a surprise. I never expected to meet you in person. Your writings always expressed disdain for court life." She wanted to have him clapped in irons. Alas, she would learn nothing from such a move. Far better to engage him, wrap his strings around her fingers, and tug them ever so gently to find out where they led. That was just the sort of thing Martin DuJournal would do, and she was not going to let an imposter beat her at her own game.

DuJournal bowed. "Your Highness, I would not have missed the chance to meet you even if this ball were being held in the Halls of Torment. Allow me to humbly thank you for your kind patronage of my poor works. I regret my greeting gift is not so grand as to be commensurate with your generosity, but if there is any little way in which I may be of service, it would be my honor."

Clearly this was an opening not to be missed, but rage drove all inspiration from Isabelle's head. "What do you imagine you can do for me?" *No, that isn't what I should have said—*

But the fraud pressed on, undeterred. "No challenge so far is beyond my reach. After all, it was I who proved Holcomb's Theorem, which was thought unsolvable."

Isabelle's hand clenched on the arm of her chair. *Liar, I proved it. Me.* Even with all her practice enduring abuse in her father's court, it was a special effort to keep from springing from her seat and throttling him. Her father had hated her for something she wasn't. The imposter was trying to steal something she was.

After a steadying breath, she said, "I shall think on it. Tell my secretary how you may be contacted."

The fraud bowed himself out, and Isabelle continued receiving people whose faces she could not see and whose names she could not remember. She could not understand how some people seemed to enjoy a state of rage. Rarely had she felt more powerless. A bloodshadow might have paralyzed her body, but with uncontrolled anger her mind seized up.

As the hot iron slowly cooled, she considered the distinct possibility that the fraud might not be acting entirely on his own account. To be invited to a party like this, a lowly Célestial mathematician would have needed a sponsor to introduce him. To Julio she whispered, "Do you know who supplied DuJournal with an invitation?"

Julio said, "No, but Kantelvar might."

"Someone *other* than Kantelvar."

"Ah. Yes. Don Angelo would know, or rather his secretary would."

Then she would have to speak to Don Angelo as swiftly as possible. By the time the last petitioner finally bowed himself away from her, Isabelle's spine was stiff and her backside sore. She was ready for motion. At some unspoken command, the floor cleared, and the orchestra that had been providing background music for the lumbering ceremony came together for something more exciting.

To Julio, Isabelle said, "Shall we take the first dance?" It was tradition.

"Alas, I have but one left foot." He knocked on the hollow wooden shell that filled his right boot. "It's all I can do to get around on my cane." He gestured to a polished walking stick that had been innocuously propped against the side of his chair all evening.

Isabelle winced at her faux pas. "My apologies." She settled back in her seat, disappointed and relieved at the same time.

"Have no fear," Julio said. "I shall have my second escort you." He snapped his fingers and a polite young man appeared to lead Isabelle out on the floor. The queen, too, took a substitute partner in the form of Duque Diego. King Carlemmo slouched in his seat, hardly more than a skeleton buried in layers of purple velvet. Kantelvar clanked up and began whispering fiercely in Julio's ear.

The music struck up. Isabelle was not the world's best dancer but neither was she the worst, and tonight she gave the exercise her all. It was not easy to manipulate her prosthetic hand through the necessary clasps, but Julio's second showed her to her best advantage.

Diego led Margareta around the floor as if he were directing troops in a complex drill. Their lips moved in conversation, but neither one of them was pretending to smile.

The second dance rolled around, and Isabelle had no shortage of willing partners, but she was not at all surprised when Diego cut in front of a junior member of the nobility. "Your Highness."

"Your Grace," she said through gritted teeth. Saints, she was not ready for this conversation, for any of this intrigue, but the moment was upon her, a duel of wits at slightly less than arm's length.

She was actually taller than Diego, though he outweighed her considerably. She got the impression his hands could crush stone. His presence was not as expansive as Grand Leon's, but nearly as heavy.

They exchanged only pleasantries as the dance floor filled up, but when the music began, he asked, "Who do you serve, Highness?"

He was a military thinker, Isabelle decided, and this was his first sally, not a main thrust. "I am not sure I understand the question."

"Do you serve Aragoth or l'Empire Céleste? Whose interests do you hold dearest to your heart? Your family's?"

Isabelle smiled sharply. It was the second time she'd had this conversation, albeit with different men for different reasons. "I serve peace."

"The problem with peace is that it cannot defend itself."

"That is why it has me." She wasn't sure precisely where these fierce words were coming from. Perhaps it was the faceless swirl of the masquerade, or perhaps it was her banked fury after the conflagration of rage, but the thrill of battle was upon her. She didn't know if she was wrong or right, only that she must win. This must be how Jean-Claude felt all the time.

"Do you intend to defend all of Aragoth by yourself?" Diego asked.

"Of course not, but men of action must be led by men of virtue, else there is no honor, merely chaos and barbarism. If your lord and master ordered you to put away your sword, would you do it?"

"There is the tricky matter of who my master is," Diego said.

"El Rey de Espejos," Isabelle said.

"But when Carlemmo is dead, who will be el rey? That is the matter that must be settled."

"And if the brothers can decide it between themselves, will you honor their decision?"

Diego did not answer until very nearly the end of the dance. His expression was closed, like a man playing thwarts in the dark, trying to picture the whole board and every possible configuration. *We both are: white princess tilts with black duque.*

At last he said, "It is unfortunate you could not identify the man who boarded your ship."

Isabelle's heart raced. Was Diego truly unaware that his operative had been named, or was he merely fishing for confirmation? Could she split the difference?

"I would know him if I saw him again," Isabelle said.

"Truly?" Diego asked, and then danced a few more thoughtful beats. "In that case, this conversation is premature. It will be more fruitful on the morrow. My secretary shall contact yours."

He timed his statement to the last bar of the song, giving Isabelle no choice but to curtsy and back up a step. He strode from the dance floor before she could recapture him, going where? To warn his operative perhaps? Isabelle wished she had someone to follow him. Where was Jean-Claude when she needed him?

The next dance started, and Isabelle was forced to concentrate on giving a good impression of herself to her partners and all observers. It was not long until the faux Lord Martin DuJournal slithered into her dance queue. He wore a pleasant expression, and his eyes sparkled with an inner humor that made her want to throttle him. He was laughing at the world, and most specifically at her, like a brazen thief wearing stolen jewels to the very house he had burgled.

Yet if she refused him, she gave up a chance to learn what he was about. She tamped down her bile as he took her hand and led her through the first steps of a one-partner dance.

"Have you become suddenly greedy, milord?" she asked. "An introduction and now a dance. Much loftier men have gotten much less from me."

He said in la Langue, with the accent of a man educated in Rocher Royale, "Dire need calls for desperate measures. I have news I must present to you in person and in private."

"You have my full attention." And an outsized portion of her loathing; DuJournal was *her* creation. Did the imposter actually know that?

They stepped through a complex dip and exchange before he said, "This is not the place for such proofs as I have to present."

"Proofs of what?" she said. "Your identity? We both know you're not the real DuJournal."

"If such a man even exists," he said without breaking rhythm. "Which I am inclined to doubt. Of course, after my appearance here tonight, very few other people will be inclined to doubt it, which is a favor I grant you free of obligation."

"Then what do you want?"

He twirled her around to face Kantelvar, who was now deep in conference with Julio and Queen Margareta. Oh, to be a flea on one of those curs to hear that conversation.

"Have you any idea what drives yon artifex in his scheming?"

Isabelle's heart skipped a beat, her fury arrested by the possibility that this imposter might have information she could use against Kantelvar.

"Which scheming?" she asked. Who knew how many plots the man had?

DuJournal said, "I am told that he promised Margareta her son would be king, and he also promised Príncipe Alejandro that Julio would never sit upon the throne. It is said he always keeps his promises, but I simply fail to see how two such promises can be compatible."

"Of what concern is it to you?" Even if what he said was true—and she wasn't about to take a fraud at his word—the idea that Kantelvar might be playing both flanks against the center was not exactly news.

"Because he made a promise to me as well in return for a favor I now regret." His tone was stiff and somber.

"And what does it have to do with me?" Isabelle asked.

"Because you are the fuse in the powder keg with which he means to crack the world."

Isabelle's head felt light. Did he know of Kantelvar's breeding program? Could he confirm his intent to conjure the Savior? "How much do you know of his plans?"

The music stopped.

DuJournal cursed under his breath and whispered, "Allow me to meet you after the ball, and I will bring you proofs of his villainy."

He bowed and she curtsied. At the bottom of the move she whispered, "And will you tell me then who you really are?" If he agreed to meet with her after that, then she knew he was serious, or at least desperate.

His eyes narrowed but he replied, "All will be revealed."

"Then I shall arrange it with my secretary." The overworked Olivia, who had been saddled with the task of plotting out Isabelle's social obligations in one-minute increments.

Isabelle danced the rest of the evening proficiently but without feeling. Her mind raced down paths of reason but kept stepping in puddles of madness and confusion. What had seemed a mere political dispute mixed up in a family tragedy had grown and transformed into something that had no name, no center. Builder, but she wanted Jean-Claude and she wanted him now. Only to him could she speak without hesitation or reservation.

At last, midnight struck, the dancing stopped, the orchestra fell silent, and the circulating servants stilled as the clock tower bells boomed. When the last echoing gong had died away, the crown herald took Isabelle's arm and escorted her with a brace of royal trumpeters to the foot of the dais. It was time for the unmasking.

The trumpeters raised their silver clarions and blew a clear shrill blast that made Isabelle's ears ring and chased away the weariness of the hour. Then the herald raised his voice to a penetrating yet musical pitch and announced, "His Royal Majesty el Rey de Espejos, King Carlemmo II."

Carlemmo stood, shakily. For a moment, Isabelle feared he would not be able to stand all the way up without assistance, but his regal will would not be denied, and, with a modicum of grace, he removed his skyship mask. At the sight of their king revealed, the whole audience made obeisance, bowing and curtsying and removing masks.

Yet it was not the king's visage that made Isabelle gasp. It was Julio's. When her betrothed removed his wyvern mask, she could but stare in shock and dawning horror, for she had seen him once before, staring up at her from her own sketchpad aboard the *Santa Anna*. It was the face of the man who had tried to burn her ship from under her. Julio was Thornscar.

CHAPTER
Fourteen

It was lucky that Isabelle's throat constricted at the sight of Julio's face, or she might have screamed. The man who had tried to kill her had been sitting right next to her, chatting with her, lying to her.

She took a step away from him. Her lips peeled back in revulsion. This could not be right. She'd only ever seen Thornscar in a drawing by her own hand. Could she have made a mistake? No. Jean-Claude and Vincent had both confirmed the picture's accuracy. Besides, what were the odds against so perfectly capturing someone by accident? This was the same man . . . except this man had no scar, no ragged welt running down the side of his face. She should have seen that sooner.

Scars could be concealed by clever makeup, or created by it. But the scar was his namesake. Would he fake that? Why not? Give yourself a nom de guerre like Thornscar and a scar is all people will look for . . . except he hadn't given himself that name.

Julio gazed upon her avidly; his drunken leer magnified her loathing. She jerked her gaze away, only to have it land on Kantelvar, still flanking the dais, watching her from the green-tinged shadows of his cowl. A hot spike of anger jabbed through the web of her confusion. He was the one who had named the saboteur Thornscar. How dare he ambush her like this? Did he think she wouldn't recognize her would-be killer?

Comprehension hit like a thunderbolt. Of course he did not expect her to recognize Julio as Thornscar. He didn't know about the portrait. He thought she was ignorant of her attacker. But surely he must have realized that Jean-Claude would recognize the prince. Jean-Claude *and* Vincent. But Vincent had been killed before he ever got a look at the príncipe, and Jean-Claude had nearly died, and Kantelvar had taken the purse with the bullet, except he had found no bullet. No, he had *made sure* there was no bullet, so no one would doubt that the shooting had been done by a Glass-walker. He was trying to remove the witnesses, the only people he thought could discover his plan.

Isabelle was dimly aware that everyone in the ballroom was staring at her. She was still standing at the foot of the dais, in full view of the crowd, and she must have looked stunned and ready to faint. She faced the king and curtsied deeply—curtsying to a king was never the wrong thing to do—and tried to plan her next move, or her first move in a whole new game.

"Rise," Carlemmo muttered.

Isabelle straightened, slowly, majestically, drawing out the moment like a ballet dancer. She made eye contact with King Carlemmo. "Thank you for this glorious welcome," she said. "A celebration like this should go on forever." She paused a beat for effect and swept the crowd with her gaze. "Or at least until dawn."

That small, safe jest drew polite applause and resulted in a resumption of the music. Isabelle glided away from the dais, gave Olivia the word to add DuJournal to her schedule, then sought out Don Angelo, who seemed to be the king's man and no other's.

He beamed at her and gave a polite half bow. "Highness, how may I serve you?"

"Two things," she said, drawing him away from the group with which he had been mingling. "First, I would have you seek out my musketeer. I have a task I need him to perform."

Don Angelo's silvered brows drew down. "Is something the matter, Highness?"

"Nothing," she lied. "It is a personal matter between me and his master, for which he is the only suitable go-between. Will you help me?"

Don Angelo looked as if he wanted a better explanation but said, "Of course."

That was a relief. If she was right, Kantelvar had murderous intentions toward Jean-Claude, and he must be warned. And if there was some other truth, she would still feel happier knowing he was safe.

"And the second thing. Might you tell me who invited that mathematician, Lord DuJournal, to the ball?"

"Has he offended you, Highness?"

Isabelle still didn't like anyone stealing her work, but if the imposter could help her expose Kantelvar's schemes to the world she'd let him keep the name. "Quite the contrary. It was very thoughtful of his patron to invite someone with whom I might speak in my native tongue. I wish to thank the patron personally."

Don Angelo brightened at this. "In that case, it is my pleasure to tell you that his invitation was given to me by Princesa Xaviera."

Isabelle was nonplussed; that was an entirely unanticipated angle. Contrary to rational expectations, Princess Xaviera had been the least of Isabelle's concerns. Did this mean that she knew about Isabelle's literary double life? If so, sending a DuJournal imposter was a strange way of showing it. Or was Xaviera also a dupe of the imposter?

"Where is she now?" Isabelle asked. The seat Xaviera had occupied earlier was empty, and she was not to be seen on the dance floor.

"She does not share your enthusiasm for our celebration," Don Angelo explained. "She has retired for the evening."

DuJournal seemed to have disappeared as well, though now that everyone was unmasked, she had lost her one real point of reference for most of the guests. Kantelvar had also disappeared. She disliked having him present, but his absence made her cold with dread. What could he be plotting now?

To Don Angelo she said, "And if you could please have someone summon Kantelvar for me? I have had a thought pertaining to his investigations that I would share with him personally." Even if Kantelvar refused her summons, the fact that he had people looking for him might deter him from doing anything diabolical. She wished she could have someone go check on Marie, but she had no precise idea where her hollow friend was.

And then she was back to dancing—it was the safest place she could be—and thinking. Diego had put Thornscar's mirror aboard her ship. He had to know about the prince. Was he trying to help Julio thwart Margareta and Kantelvar by killing his potential brides? Isabelle felt like she was one obstinate variable short of an equation. No matter how she turned it around in her head she kept coming up with a tautology. She needed one more factor. One more substitution.

Substitution. One expression that serves exactly the same purpose as another.

She looked up at Julio. A man without a scar. A man with a wooden leg who would have been no good at all running up and down stairs in a burning ship.

"Oh merde," she breathed.

—

Jean-Claude sucked in his gut as Adel buttoned his doublet, snowy white with silver buttons in the shape of the thundercrown, epaulets, and lots of silver braid. Formal uniforms were a lot like coffins, in Jean-Claude's opinion; both were methods to present stiff old sticks in public. He'd rather have been trolling the unlit streets, the taverns, the filthiest gutters stocked with the lowliest scum of the world than spending one minute amongst the oh-so-noble throng, but tonight, for Isabelle's sake, he had to put on the proper show.

Adel examined him. "You must have cut quite a dashing figure in your youth."

Jean-Claude put on a pained expression. "Are you implying I no longer do?"

"Hah! Time has made you more solid than dashing, I think. A redoubtable profile."

"Mademoiselle." Jean-Claude smiled. "No man's pride may survive your scrutiny."

Her eyes twinkled. "Oh, but, señor, I have not had the opportunity to scrutinize your manly pride." Jean-Claude's eyebrows rose. It had been a very long time since he had been propositioned so; the women in Windfall had quite given up on him. He had always been so preoccupied with guarding Isabelle. And was he any less so now? Hardly, but Adel seemed to move in the same layer of pressure that he did. She might understand . . . or she might have an ulterior motive, perhaps trying to peel him away from Isabelle or divide his loyalty. Not that Adel seemed the type, but he had not known her long or well, and, for Isabelle's sake, he simply could not take chances.

Sluicing himself with self-deprecation, he said, "Alas, I doubt it would be able to answer your call. It has been some years since the regiment has mustered." Thank the Builder for a codpiece that covered his lie. He bowed over her hand but did not kiss it.

"Oh." She flushed with embarrassment and retreated to more formal tones. "Builder keep you."

"Until the Savior comes." He took up a polished walking stick, donated by Don Angelo; made his way out of Isabelle's chambers; and girded himself for the hobble to the grand hall. At the front door, he was very nearly bowled over by a royal page coming the other way.

"Oh, excuse me, señor," said the child. He was about to brush on by when his gaze focused on Jean-Claude. "Are you the musketeer? I am supposed . . . I mean, Princesa Isabelle invites you to attend her."

Jean-Claude chuckled indulgently. "Very good, boy. As it happens, I am heading that way now."

"Oh. Uh, if milord pleases, a coach awaits."

"I have become fond of coaches in my old age." Jean-Claude followed the boy into the torch-lit night. A whole fleet of conveyances ringed the courtyard like ships in a harbor. The creak of wood and leather and the grunting, snorting conversation of horses underlay the muted, mingled gossip of servants.

At the foot of the steps awaited a dark coach. Jean-Claude asked, "How did Princess Isabelle know I was here?"

"I don't know, señor; I don't get explanations, just orders."

Jean-Claude grunted. "You and me both, boy." Isabelle would want to know what he had learned about Thornscar and Nufio. She would be particularly keen to hear his deduction about the hinges. He only wished he had more of substance to share with her.

A footman in royal livery opened the door to the coach and stooped to lower the carriage step. Jean-Claude's wounded leg throbbed, and he hesitated, contemplating the vexing problem of which foot to climb with. The footman rose smoothly and swiftly, his hand blurred. The truncheon slammed into Jean-Claude's gut just as he lifted his unwounded leg. Agony doubled him over, his planted leg buckled, and all breath left him in a gasp. Strong arms prevented him from falling, and someone slapped a moist rag to his face. Vapors stung his eyes. He couldn't hold a breath he didn't have. Against every command of his will, his body rebelled and sucked down a lungful of the rag's vile poison.

Jean-Claude twisted in his attackers' grip, but his boots slipped on the cobbles. He had no leverage. He wanted to cry out, but his face had gone numb, and his tongue was a dead snake bloating in his throat. The light of the torches bubbled and blurred. The colors and patterns of the night smeared. The world turned upside down and he fell toward the sky.

—

The opportunity for Isabelle to gracefully exit a party held in her honor did not come until King Carlemmo himself declared weariness a little after third bell, by which time Isabelle's eyes were crossing. She'd spent most of the night evolving ever-wilder speculations about Julio and/or Thornscar. Could they be long-lost twins, or was one some strange doppelganger conjured by Kantelvar's eerie arts, or, or, or . . . She couldn't remember four words she'd said in the last few hours, or whom she'd said them to, and she was going to have a terrific headache when she woke up, assuming she ever got to sleep. Despite multiple appeals to Don Angelo, she had received no news of either Jean-Claude or Kantelvar.

The exodus from the ball took place in order of rank so that the greater might not be inconvenienced by the lesser. In less civilized times, dickering over the order of precedence had been known to lead to duels. Tonight, it merely produced bluster. Thus did civilization advance. The king and queen departed first. Isabelle made a curt farewell to Julio, who might have been Thornscar—had the intruder on the ship been missing a leg?—and took herself off quickly.

Stifling yawns, she mounted her carriage and returned to her chambers. The night guards outside her doors saluted. Though she had drunk but a little, her brain was a fog of indistinct faces and half-remembered names. Her body wanted nothing more than to strip out of these hot, heavy clothes and collapse in a comfortable bed for a week, but she called for Valérie instead.

Her handmaid appeared with remarkable alacrity for someone who ought to have been asleep. "Highness, how may I serve you?"

"Has there been any word from Jean-Claude?"

Valérie looked puzzled. "He left here several hours ago. He was going to find you. Some of Don Angelo's men came looking for him shortly thereafter, and we sent them back to the palace."

Isabelle's heart faltered at the dread possibilities that simple statement implied. Had Kantelvar gotten to Jean-Claude first? Isabelle resisted the urge to run out in the courtyard and shout the musketeer's name. "Has anyone else come by?"

"No, Highness, just the guards changing an hour ago."

"Send a runner to the palace," she began, but who to contact? Don Angelo had not told her that Jean-Claude was supposedly on his way, but perhaps his scouts had not given him the complete message. He remained her best wager. "Tell Don Angelo that Jean-Claude has been waylaid." If it turned out not to be so, she would live with the embarrassment. "And send another runner to the dock, to the berth of the *Santa Anna*, find Captain Santiago, and do whatever it takes to put him on retainer."

Valérie's eyes grew round. "Are you running away?"

"Not yet, but I want an avenue of retreat if it becomes necessary." Nothing in the Aragothic court was what it seemed, and she would be damned before she married a man whose doppelganger had tried to kill her, at the behest of an apparently ancient artifex who might have killed Vincent and been complicit in Jean-Claude's disappearance.

Valérie nodded, and her expression became sharper. "Is there anything else?"

"No." Except there was. "Yes, curse it. I have to find Marie."

"Don't you know where you took her?"

"Yes, generally, but this place is a maze."

"If you are in danger, you will need guards."

"I'll take some of Vincent's men. Nobody from this household should go anywhere without a companion, including you."

"I'll rouse the others," Valérie said with a decisiveness the warmed Isabelle's heart. Thanks be that her ordeal hadn't broken her.

Valérie disappeared into the waiting ladies' bedroom. Isabelle stumped through her vestibule to her bedroom on legs that felt like wooden pilings. The door, with its padded edges, shut with a sound like a pillow being squeezed. Silence enveloped her, so thick and heavy that she imagined she could hear the alchemical lamp flames whispering to each other. It was by far the quietest space she had ever inhabited, not just noiseless, but armored against sound. She made her way to the trunk at the foot of her bed, unlocked it, and extracted the pistol she had worn yesterday as a guard. Jean-Claude had shown her once how to load a pistol. She meticulously repeated the process now, powder, wad, and shot. She closed the lid of the trunk and tucked the pistol in the sash round her waist.

"It is good for you to arm yourself," Kantelvar rattled.

Isabelle spun so fast she felt like she'd left all her innards facing the other way. And there was Kantelvar, with that huge hump on his back, bent over and leaning on his staff. And there was a hole in the floor next to him, a secret trapdoor. How had he moved so silently?

"There is going to be a war," he said. "A war like no other in history, a conflict that will draw in all the kingdoms of the world and consume them to the last ash, and you must be protected from it."

Isabelle judged that she was closer to the outer door than he was, and she had the pistol. She put her hand on its grip. "And how can you know that?"

"Because I have worked very hard to arrange for it to be so. Carlemmo will die, his true heir and his false heir will vie for the throne, and between alliances I have brokered and greed that needs no help to grow, the whole world will be sucked in. Only then, when chaos consumes all civilization, will the world be ready to receive the Savior. Only then will the Builder be compelled to yield him up through you."

As jaded as she had become to Kantelvar's assertions, this prediction stunned her in its audacity and scope. "You can't force the Builder's hand just by arranging events to resemble the outcome of a prophecy."

"Can I not? I have been bidden, commanded, condemned to this course. Céleste herself bade me redeem her word."

"You? But Saint Céleste died over sixteen hundred years ago." Just when she thought Kantelvar could not get any more lunatic . . .

The artifex shuddered and his hump gurgled. "She did not tell me how long it would take. Did she think I would refuse? For a thousand years I waited and watched as the world grew corrupt and the Builder's holy blood thinned in the veins of each new generation. His sorcery grew weak, and His will was forgotten, and Céleste's prophecy went unfulfilled, a prophecy she had given only to me. To me.

"Only then did I realize she had given me the prophecy not to watch for, but to construct and complete, and so I have reordered the heavens. All of the bloodlines have been distilled and concentrated into just two lineages, two people who hold the blood of all sorceries. Julio the false prince, the changeling raised by Margareta's hand. Her taking him in exchange for her true son was my price for arranging the queen's ascendancy."

Isabelle knew she ought to run, but Kantelvar had made no hostile move. While he remained content to squat there rattling and spewing madness like an overboiling kettle, she might chance to learn something useful to thwarting him.

"Julio is not Margareta's son?" Isabelle was less surprised than she should have been; she'd been surprised so many times she'd lost the capacity. "So he is not Carlemmo's, either."

Kantelvar scoffed. "What matters the blood of a mongrel king when Julio has the pure blood of true saints in his veins? You are both descended without dilution from the saints. Your blood is as pure and potent as that of the Firstborn Kings."

Isabelle slowly reached over to her desk and drew the portrait of Thornscar out of her portfolio. She displayed it to Kantelvar. "How do you explain this?"

"Unfortunately, when I told Julio of his destiny to be the Savior's father, he responded irrationally. He called me mad and threatened to expose me, though, being a changeling pretender, it would have meant his own death. I had no choice but to confine him until it is time for him to do his duty. He resisted, and that was when I marked him with that scar."

"Wait," Isabelle said, feeling she'd missed a turning. "If Julio is Thornscar, and Thornscar is confined, who sits now at Margareta's side?"

Kantelvar chuckled. "His name is Clìmacio, Margareta's actual son, and an unhallowed wretch to boot. He spent the last twenty years as Julio's whipping boy."

"But he looks like Julio's twin."

"The Risen Saints left gifts. Primal Clay, the very stuff from which the clayborn were fashioned. Clìmacio was sculpted to be Julio's exact replica, a true changeling."

Isabelle recalled the false DuJournal saying Kantelvar promised Margareta that her son would be king, and also promised Príncipe Alejandro that Julio would never sit upon the throne. He'd also promised Isabelle he'd help her make peace between Julio and Alejandro. She saw now how all three of those things might be literally true, and without any of Kantelvar's marks knowing what they had actually bargained for.

"But Thornscar, the real Julio, found out a way to escape you through a mirror. He came straight from wherever you have him imprisoned; that's why he didn't have a weapon. He didn't attack me at all, he was trying to kill you, but he failed. You detonated the orrery with your lightning, then you blamed Lady Sonya's death on him to confuse the issue. Then you killed poor Vincent and tried to kill Jean-Claude with that bomb because you thought they were the only ones who could make the connection between Julio and Thornscar. You didn't count on this." She shook the portrait of Thornscar.

Kantelvar made a palm-up gesture, as if granting her the point. "You are so much like she was. So clever. You are mostly correct, except that I have, in fact, finally succeeded in disposing of that meddlesome musketeer. He will trouble us no further."

Isabelle's skin chilled like a threefold winter. "No. Not Jean-Claude."

"Do not mourn him," Kantelvar snarled, his voice creaking like an overstressed mast. "He is the villain. He is the one who has kept you from your destiny all these years. If he had not stopped me from taking you from your parents when you were born and placing you in a position to be married to your destined mate without any fuss, then this complex marriage never would have needed to be arranged, and the blood required would never have been spilled."

Outrage rang in Isabelle's voice. "How dare you blame him for *your* wickedness."

Kantelvar rose from his crouch. "Céleste bade *me* bring the Savior into the world. She entrusted the Builder's most sacred work to *me*, and I will see it done. I swore to her. I. Swore!" He pulled back his hood to reveal his corpselike visage, his waxy gray skin stretched over a distorted, hairless skull. His emerald-green eye burned with the cold light of madness.

Kantelvar's voice rasped from the grille. "I am the Builder's breath, the word He whispered to the universe to make His will come true. Sixteen hundred fifty-three wretchedly long years ago, I swore I would not rest until the Savior came. Little did I know—indeed, how could I have possibly understood—what that would mean."

Isabelle tried to wipe dread and dismay from her face. Kantelvar had cracked an axle, and his wheels had come completely off. She had to get out of here. She had to summon help, right now.

"I think I need a drink." She turned and strode, not too quickly, for the doors. All she had to do was slip out and set guards rushing in to bring this whole scheme crashing down. Damn her curiosity; she should have bolted long ago, just as soon as she had enough of an admission from him to justify arrest.

"Highness, don't go." Kantelvar's voice carried a double edge of threat and despair.

"I'll be right back," she said. *With lots and lots of reinforcements.* Her heart hammered, and the air had gone thick as lamp oil. When did that door get so far away?

"I'm afraid I must insist." Kantelvar's words were like a knife blade against her neck.

Isabelle wrapped her hand around the butt of the pistol. "Just stay put." She willed him to obey.

Damn, she needed to let go of the gun to work the door latch. She opened her grip.

There was a bright flash and a pop. An electric needle jabbed its way from her crown to her soles. Excruciating pain followed instantly by total numbness. She didn't even have time to scream. Her whole body twitched, and she slumped forward, her face dragging down the padded door. Her good hand clenched and unclenched spasmodically.

Across the room, Kantelvar took several deep, hollow breaths, like tearless sobs. Isabelle tried to extend herself into her body, but there was no response from anything between her toes and her tongue. Kantelvar limped slowly to her side. His shadow loomed over her, and her blurry vision could barely make out his hand wrapped around his quondam staff. Its spiny tip smoked with vapors from its discharge.

"The secret passage wasn't the only reason I chose this room for you. It is soundproof and, to the extent that such a thing is possible, proof against sorcery as well. No one will ever know what has transpired here."

Bastard! She willed violent death on him, but that was useless. She had nothing left but a mind, so she had to use it. If his trap was so secure, why was he nervously rattling off the details? What was he missing, and how could she exploit it?

Kantelvar flipped her onto her back and she stared up at the ceiling, her mouth agape, very much, she imagined, like a landed fish. Kantelvar bent down and stroked her cheek with desiccated fingers. "You look just like her—Saint Céleste—so beautiful, and you have her mind, sharp as a razor." His metal fingers traced the line of her jaw.

Isabelle thrashed uselessly inside her own skin, trying to find a way to the surface, even as Kantelvar pressed a stinging cloth to her face. "Breathe this. Things are about to happen that you don't want to be awake for."

CHAPTER

Fifteen

Color and sound swirled around Jean-Claude like currents in a raging flood. Smears of red, stripes of gray, and flashes of yellow barked and yowled and buffeted his awareness from all sides. He'd been poisoned. He was not entirely sure he was not dead. This place of vicious, viscous, shapeless colors and cruel sounds seemed a likely candidate for the Halls of Torment.

Through the mud of noises assaulting his awareness something like voices came: "Oove im dow ere." "Ike a sac v suet." "Ake is other leg." "Eave ho!"

He tumbled. Something bashed his shoulder, his head, his poor leg. Pain spread through his body like cracks through drying mud. Pain was good. It meant he still had flesh and life.

He came to rest on a floor, facedown, more or less. His fingers discovered splinters. A wooden floor. He smelled vomit. It might have been his own. That dull thudding noise might have been footsteps. Judging by how he'd tumbled, somebody had thrown him down a flight of stairs. He had to get back to himself, but firm shapes refused to resolve out of his colorful blindness.

"Prop 'im up."

Two sets of hands grabbed Jean-Claude by the armpits and heaved him upright.

He tried to say, "Good evening, gentlemen," but his voice was a gurgle. He squeezed his eyes shut and shook his head, but it only lolled like a newborn's. No wonder babies squalled, feeling this helpless.

"Prop 'im up." Several pairs of hands lifted him from the floor. "Make this quick." They dropped him on what felt like a bench. One of them kept hold of him to prevent him from sliding down. He tried to flex his hands, his arms, but they might as well have been sacks filled with mud.

Think. He couldn't die like this—who would look after Isabelle?—but why wasn't he already dead? They could have used a lethal poison or stabbed him when he succumbed to a nonlethal one. Perhaps they wanted to interrogate him first. He hoped so, because that meant he would be able to talk.

One of his captors splashed something on his face. It was sticky and tasted like ale.

"You're wasting good drink!" complained one voice.

"Gotta make it look right," said another. "Knifed in a tavern, see?"

So it *was* to be murder, after all, but why bother with misdirection?

"Bah," Jean-Claude sputtered, barely loud enough to be called a sound.

"I think he's waking up," said one of the men. "Stab him now?"

"Still limp," said another one. Jean-Claude thought he could sift at least three voices, though he was sure he was only picking up about half the words.

Jean-Claude tried again. "Ransom." It wasn't the most subtle hook he'd ever thrown into the creek, but he was short on inspiration, and these didn't seem like the brightest fish.

A wide, blurry face loomed before Jean-Claude. "What did he say?"

"Don't listen to him." Someone pulled the wide face away. "He's addled."

"Ransom," Jean-Claude muttered. His voice was becoming steadier, but too slowly. "Worth more alive than dead. Much more."

"We're not interested in ransom. Besides, you're just a soldier. No money."

Jean-Claude's pulse raced even faster. His mind was clearing more swiftly than his vision. "No soldier. King's Own Musketeer. The princess's favorite. I'm the one who knows where her dowry's hid." He willed them to take the hook.

"Dowry?" a third man asked. Stupid. Stupid man.

The blade of a knife, cold and sharp, pressed against his throat. "Tell me about this dowry, and I'd better like what I hear, or it'll be the last thing you ever say."

Not much of a bargainer, are you? "The dowry of a royal princess, for the most important wedding in a century. It's a gift from Grand Leon, three chests of Craton Riqueza gold, Aragothic gold recovered from a hulk of an Aragothic treasure ship. To be returned as a gesture of goodwill." Would these thugs recognize the acceptable political code for captured booty? Probably not. He mourned an elegant detail lost on a dim audience.

The blade scraped Jean-Claude's skin. "Where?"

The pain and fear churning through Jean-Claude's mind slowly cleaned the gunk from his system. The pulsing fog resolved into three vaguely man-like shapes, dark splotches moving against a lighter background. "A shipment from Rocher Royale. Coming in tonight. Ship called the *Weirgeld*."

"He's lying," spat another, more skeptical thug. "Just gut him and be done with it."

"You don't want the password?" Jean-Claude flexed his fingers and they responded, but slowly.

"Tell me," said the thug with the knife.

"Why? Just so you can kill me afterward? That doesn't sound like a good bargain."

"Don't listen to him," said the skeptic. "He's trying to put the wind up us."

Knife boy said, "Tell me the password or you'll die slow instead of quick."

The world of Jean-Claude's perception slowly congealed toward familiar solidity. "You don't want to do that. If I give you the right password you will all be very wealthy men, but if I give you the wrong password, bloody chunks of you will be fed to the pigs. The only way you could be sure of getting the right password is if I am there with you to give it."

The skeptic said, "Joseph, this is not what we're being paid for. He's lying, and even if he's not, you think there's any way he'll give us gold once he has his friends around?"

Joseph, the knife man, growled in frustration.

"There's one way you lads could come out ahead," Jean-Claude said. "If you could get the password out of me, and one of you kept me under guard, the rest could go collect the gold. One of you approaches the ship while another keeps lookout from a safe distance. If anything bad happens, then the lookout runs back here and you can kill me any way you like."

Joseph wavered, and a third, hitherto silent shape said, "It could work." Jean-Claude willed them all to come into focus, but the universe was non-compliant to his wishes.

"I don't like it," said the skeptic, almost plaintively, as if greed were slowly strangling his good sense. "And Thornscar said kill him here."

Thornscar again! The man seemed to be everywhere, damn his eyes.

Jean-Claude shoveled on another layer of horseshit. "Ah, so Thornscar is paying you a pittance to do his dirty work, while he collects a princesa's ransom. You take all the risk, and he gets all the reward."

"I say we kill him now, like we agreed to do."

Perhaps it was Jean-Claude's wishful thinking, but he sounded like a man willing to be talked out of it.

"But what if he's telling the truth?" Joseph said.

"Money doesn't do a dead man any good," said the third.

"You should have thought of that before you took up with Thornscar," boomed a new voice from the formless space behind the kidnappers. The men whirled and stared, momentarily paralyzed with surprise. A firearm bellowed, spitting flame and smoke. One thug fell. The skeptic reached for a knife, but a green blur came through the smoke and pricked his throat with a rapier thrust. Crimson blood sprayed. Joseph tried to run, but the green blur leapt after him.

"Don't kill them all!" Jean-Claude tried to yell, but the smoke choked him. He heaved with all his might and managed to achieve nearly a sitting position before collapsing backward and toppling off the bench. There was a heavy thump from the direction in which Joseph had fled.

Jean-Claude rolled to his belly. His boiling humors had finally scoured away enough of the grime from his eyes that he could make out individual planks of the rough wooden floor. He had pushed himself slowly to his knees, trembling with the effort, when a strong hand gripped him under the upper arm.

"Come on, old man, let's get you up."

Jean-Claude jerked away from the grip, twisted, and landed on his rump, staring up into a blurry face with blurry blond hair. "Who are you calling old?" He might curse his age, the creeping weakness that stole in with every passing moment, but he did not give anyone the right to notice it. And what of this blurriness? Would it pass, or was he to be crippled like some sexagenarian with cobwebs across his eyes? The idea was too terrifying even to think about.

The figure raised his hands in a gesture of supplication. "No offense intended, monsieur, but you seem to have been drugged. May I offer you my hand in friendship? My name is Martin DuJournal."

Isabelle's nom de plume? What new quackery was this? Whatever the case, Jean-Claude was not about to let a good rescue go to waste. "Pleased to meet you. I am Jean-Claude, His Célestial Majesty's King's Own Musketeer, and I thank you for your timely assistance. How is it that you stumbled across this little tête-à-tête?" *And why in the world do you care?*

"I attended Princess Isabelle's masquerade, but I had left the ball and was on my way to her domicile to await a promised audience when I witnessed your abduction. I followed these ruffians and used the distraction of your fascinating repartee to approach them undetected."

"Why didn't you simply summon the palace guards?"

"Because I was not at all sure whose side they would be on."

Jean-Claude grunted by way of acknowledgment. Yes, the kidnappers had been in possession of royal livery. Had Thornscar suborned someone in the royal household? Breaker's balls, but the man was inconsistent in his resources and his methods.

"And what compelled you to involve yourself in my troubles?" Jean-Claude asked.

Martin replied cheerily, "For one thing, what they did to you was entirely dishonorable, and I could not stand to see such a crime committed to one of my countrymen. For another, you are Princess Isabelle's favorite, and I thought rescuing you might increase my stature in Her Highness's eyes."

"Indeed." This man was a liar, a trickster, and very interested in the princess. Another problem. Another lead into another one of Aragoth's factions perhaps. "She is generous with her thanks, but she will be very interested to hear how you came to know the name Thornscar." *And DuJournal.*

"From the mouths of your assailants. I thought it might startle them to hear it."

"Are you saying you'd never heard it before?"

"Should I have?"

"Perhaps not." For all the havoc Thornscar caused, there were an awful lot of people who had never heard his name. He ought to have existed in the storm cloud of gossip, if not as a lightning bolt of fear, then at least as a distant rumble of rumor. Yet the only people who seemed to know his name were minions he had recently employed. None-too-bright minions, in fact. Someone who employed such people should be known *about* even if they were not known.

He asked, "And you wish an introduction to Princess Isabelle?"

Martin produced an insolent grin. Jean-Claude could tell it was insolent from the way it gleamed through the fog of his vision. "I already have an introduction. She has invited me to attend her to discuss a matter of mutual interest, a math problem of sorts."

Jean-Claude coughed a laugh; he could imagine Isabelle's chain of thought on that one, and he would have been willing to pay for the privilege of seeing her dismantle the monkey who sought to steal her best clothes—even if she did it in the foreign language of math—just so long as he was there to protect her from any violence an exposed fraud might seek to commit. "So you are a mathematician?"

"Au contraire; I am *the* mathematician, the world's foremost master of numbers."

Jean-Claude chuffed. "Not shy."

"Fortune favors the bold. It is well-known that she has a fine appreciation of the intellect and an awareness of the importance of mathematics—she published my monographs, after all—so I seek her patronage. Speaking of which, if I am going to take advantage of this opportunity, we should get you back to the citadel."

Yes. His whole body ached, and he could still barely see. "You didn't kill all of these scoundrels, did you?"

Martin prodded the limp forms with his boot. "I am afraid I was over-zealous."

Conveniently silencing any testimony they might have been able to give, but there was no point in criticizing DuJournal on that score; the man had saved his life, or at least interrupted his would-be murderers. It was not outside the realm of possibility that this entire scenario, from kidnapping to rescue, was nothing more than a ruse to get DuJournal close to Isabelle, but the man apparently already had an appointment, assuming that wasn't also a lie. A few words with Isabelle should straighten that out.

"To the citadel, then," Jean-Claude said.

DuJournal eventually heaved Jean-Claude onto the bench seat of the very same coach that had stolen him from the royal citadel, then lifted the team to a quick trot. To Jean-Claude's dismay, the Solar was rising; he had been out all night. The light came up from the direction of the harbor today, painting the world with broad strokes of rose and cream.

The thugs had taken him far down into the city, because even with the right of way granted to a royal coach, it was almost full light by the time the citadel loomed into view. Jean-Claude squinted ahead and was happy to note that his vision seemed to be clearing up at last; the looming blur before him resolved into the royal citadel's gatehouse.

Two guards detached themselves from their posts. "¡Alto! ¿Quien va alla?"

Martin reined to a stop. "It is I, Lord Martin DuJournal, returning stolen property"—he thumped the coach—"and, not coincidentally, the most excellent Jean-Claude, His Célestial Majesty's musketeer."

The first guard's eyes rounded and he faced Jean-Claude. "The musketeer? Señor, your papers, please."

Jean-Claude leaned forward apprehensively. "Why? What is the matter?"

"We must identify you, señor. Please, no offense is meant."

Jean-Claude patted his belt for his pouch, but it had gone missing. "Blast. They must have been stolen when I was waylaid."

"I will vouchsafe for him," Lord Martin said, presenting his own passport. The guard examined the papers with due diligence and entered them in his logbook.

"Something *is* wrong," Jean-Claude said. "Guards are never this meticulous until *after* disaster strikes. Has something happened to Isabelle?"

The guard returned the papers and favored them with an ironic look. "I gather she has mislaid her favorite musketeer. She's got the whole royal household and half the city guard looking for him." He bowed them through the gate.

"Cheeky bastard," Jean-Claude muttered, not disapprovingly, as DuJournal piloted them through the gate tunnel.

No sooner had they entered the courtyard than a frantic acolyte burst from the Temple complex to the right side of the vast square. "Help! Help! The artifex! Somebody help!"

Jean-Claude hesitated, for he recognized Kantelvar's adjutant from his last trip to Kantelvar's demesne. As much as Jean-Claude needed to return to Isabelle's side, this looked like a situation disinclined to wait on his convenience. He jabbed his finger toward the Temple. "Go!" But DuJournal had already snapped the reins and whistled the horses into a quick trot.

By the time the carriage rolled to a stop at the foot of the Temple steps, a crowd had gathered, and two yellow-cowled sagaxes were half-guiding, half-pursuing the frantic secretary back inside. Jean-Claude dismounted, caught his balance, and then lurched through the press. A trio of Temple guards wearing yellow tabards and carrying halberds were forming a cordon, demanding the crowd move back and announcing unconvincingly that there was nothing to see.

Jean-Claude headed straight for the man in the middle, who raised a hand to thwart him. "Señor, I apologize but—"

"King's business!" Jean-Claude declared, stepping smartly around the outstretched hand.

DuJournal caught up with him at the doors. "You're going to earn that poor fellow a demotion."

"Then maybe he'll learn to do his job." Jean-Claude followed the sagaxes and the secretary up a staircase to Kantelvar's office. Jean-Claude's chest tightened with more than mere exertion. As much as he disliked the artifex, he'd be no use at all dead.

The sagaxes pushed open a tall, narrow door graven with images of cogwheels, axles, and springs. Jean-Claude slipped in after them.

Inside, the clerics stood aghast, staring at Kantelvar's desk. Jean-Claude squeezed between them, and there lay Kantelvar—at least, Jean-Claude surmised it was he by his robes—spread-eagled across the massive wooden surface. He had been hacked to bloody pieces; his clockwork arm and leg were missing. Blood overflowed the desktop and made a great puddle of the floor. It was still wet. This had happened recently, within the hour.

"Can anyone confirm this is Kantelvar?" Jean-Claude asked, startling the artificers, who had been too transfixed to take notice of him.

"Who are you?" asked one of them indignantly.

"The one asking intelligent questions. How can you be sure this is he when he never takes his cowl off?"

"Not in front of outsiders." The artificer skirted the blood slick and leaned over to lift the cloth from the corpse's face. He revealed the waxy gray visage of a corpse with a hole through his right eye socket all the way to the back of his head.

Jean-Claude recoiled. "What is that?"

"That is Kantelvar," said the second sagax.

Jean-Claude shuddered deep inside. Perhaps there were worse fates than growing old. He turned to the secretary. "How did you find him?"

The man stammered, "I-I just came in to deliver some papers, and there he was."

"Was the door locked?"

"Yes, but—"

"Who has keys?"

"He does, and I do, and so does the lord chamberlain."

"Is there any other way out of here?" Just because Jean-Claude didn't see another door didn't mean there wasn't one.

"Not that I know of."

Just then, a dull thud stunned the air, like the distant impact of a giant's hammer. It reverberated up through the floorboards, shaking dust from the rafters and rattling the mechanical devices littering the shelves.

"What in the Builder's name?" DuJournal muttered.

"That sounded like a mortar shell," Jean-Claude said. It had been twenty-five years since he'd last felt one detonate, but it was a sensation not easily forgotten.

An alarm bell sang, a desperate warning. Fire! Fire! A dozen more bells joined in, a symphony of urgency and terror. Jean-Claude hurried to the window. Across the square, smoke and flame belched from the windows of Isabelle's residence.

"Isabelle!" Jean-Claude's heart twisted in a horrible knot. He bolted from the room and all but toppled down the stairs. DuJournal took his elbow and hustled him out the door and into the coach. They shot across the square in a rattle of hooves. People vomited from the princess's building, coughing and gagging from the smoke. Jean-Claude debarked and fought his way upstream, his wounded leg crumpling at every step. "Isabelle!"

Two women stumbled through the doorway. Jean-Claude recognized Adel, who was coughing and sputtering and half-carrying Olivia, whose face and hands were burned to blackness.

"Adel! Olivia!" Jean-Claude reached to help her support Olivia.

Adel fell to her knees in a paroxysm of hacking. Olivia reached up with one hand that was little more than bone and grabbed Jean-Claude by the collar. Blood and serum sprayed from her lips along with the words, "Princess. Room."

Jean-Claude felt as if he had been harpooned, a massive pronged barb pierced straight through his chest. No. No. Not this. He laid Olivia down and scrambled for the doors. Strong hands grabbed him by the shoulders and tried to spin him around. "Monsieur, wait! You can't go in there."

"Unhand me!" Jean-Claude turned and rammed his fist into DuJournal's groin. The mathematician fell with a yelp, and Jean-Claude hurtled through the doorway. Black smoke, stinking of scorching meat and burning wood, enveloped his face, choking and blinding him. He dropped to his hands and knees. Beneath the smoky pall, a dozen figures lay sprawled in death, suffocated or trampled. Jean-Claude crawled past them. Flame filled the corridor beyond the foyer, greedy worms of heat gnawing on the wood. Tapestries blazed and sheets of flame danced across the carpets. The heat broiled Jean-Claude's face like dragon's breath.

"Isabelle!" he cried, and the smoke reached down his lungs. *No! Not her. Please, Builder, not her. Take me!*

Something grabbed Jean-Claude's feet and hauled him backward. His face scraped along the floor. "Princess," he gasped, "Isabelle!" He tried to kick his way free, but his legs did not avail him. Cool air seared his lungs as he was dragged into the courtyard and pinned fast. Several people piled on top of him as greedy fingers of fire claimed the entire residence as their own.

—

The fire burned for a day and a night before the royal and city fire brigades managed to put it out. To add insult to grievous injury, the sky unleashed rain three hours after the blaze was extinguished, and the downpour hadn't abated in the three days since.

Wrapped in heavy oilskins, and accompanied by DuJournal, Jean-Claude hobbled in numb desperation through the wreckage of the residence. The building had been reduced to a blackened shell. Bits of the outside wall remained upright, but the whole interior had collapsed down to the ground. Recovery crews worked day and night, clearing a path to where Isabelle's chamber had been, but progress was slow. So far, fifty bodies had been recovered from the massive building. The fire had spread so fast that few escaped.

Jean-Claude had inspected all the bodies recovered so far. The worst of them were unrecognizable, charred husks curled into fetal balls, but none of their clawed hands had Isabelle's distinguishing digit.

Jean-Claude staggered through a muddy black slurry of ash and debris, picking his way carefully around broken timbers and splashing into holes where the stone floor had cracked from the heat. Before she died, Olivia had managed to convey that she had been looking for Isabelle, but when she opened the door to Isabelle's chamber, the room had exploded.

Adel, still abed with the drowning lung from the smoke, had described a blast like a bomb that had thrown Olivia across the room. "It all happened so fast," she wheezed. "There was an explosion and then suddenly the whole world was on fire. Isabelle's room looked like the inside of a forge."

And then Jean-Claude had gone back to losing his mind. He'd stood on the porch of the infirmary in the rain and slowly ripped his fancy, soot-stained musketeer's uniform into shreds, strip after strip, until those threads that remained were too small even to be used as bandages. A musketeer was all he'd ever been. He'd been so proud. Of the king's blessing, of raising Isabelle, of being too damned clever by half. What damned good had it been? What a fool. What an ass. *Why her and not me?* When there were nothing left but shreds, he threw the sodden tangle in the gutter with the rest of the filth.

Yet nobody had said Isabelle was dead. Nobody dared. They hadn't found her body—until an hour ago they hadn't even found anything from her room—and until they did, the forlorn shadow of hope remained, a whisper against a howling gale of despair.

Amongst the courtiers, accusations of blame had begun to fly. When something like this happened, someone had to be blamed, but nobody wanted to be the one accused, and the best way to avoid that was to accuse someone else. Several members of Queen Margareta's faction tried to pin fault on Jean-Claude—where had the musketeer been when Isabelle was attacked? Out carousing, no doubt—and only Lord DuJournal's persistent defense had kept him from being thrown in a dungeon on an accusation of murder.

Not that disgrace mattered anymore. Jean-Claude had failed his master, his child—the child of his heart if not his loins—his maker, and his soul all at once, and he hadn't even managed to acquire a fatal wound doing it.

In the end, he had only one duty left to perform. To find her, and to find

266 — CURTIS CRADDOCK

the one who had done this. To wrap his fingers around the villain's throat and hurl him from the sky cliffs.

On the fourth day after the fire, with DuJournal at his side, Jean-Claude splashed into what was left of Isabelle's bedroom. He did not know why the imposter accompanied him—what purpose could Jean-Claude serve for him now?—but he was glad for the company.

The area underneath the princess's chamber was only now being uncovered by salvage teams being overseen by Don Angelo. Standing under a military rain tarp, surrounded by aides de camp, in the midst of the soggy destruction, the gray-haired nobleman looked like a field commander on the battlefield of the damned.

Jean-Claude ducked under the overhanging canvas and doffed his soaking hat. "Your Grace, may we join you?"

"Of course," he said solemnly. He offered wine, which neither accepted, and then said, "I am grieved. Princess Isabelle seemed a very worthy woman."

Jean-Claude had thought he had no tears left, which didn't account for why he had to fight back a fresh wave of them. *Enough.* "She was that and more." His voice was rough, and not just because of the smoke damage. "By your leave, we would like to witness the recovery."

"Of course," Don Angelo said.

As they turned away DuJournal whispered to Jean-Claude, "Did you know his daughter was once destined to be Príncipe's Julio's bride?"

Jean-Claude hesitated, planting his walking stick in a puddle. "Lady Sonya?"

"No, no. This was years ago. When Príncipe Julio was an infant, he was betrothed to Doña Angelina, who was a year his senior. She was sickly for years and finally died about two years ago. "

Another woman murdered. Jean-Claude shook off the assertion as baseless. Sometimes people got sick and died; he had seen it many times. Besides, even if she had been killed, what good did it do him to know it? He had failed his charge.

"Your Grace!" came a cry from the work site. Two dozen wet burly men had stopped hoisting fallen beams and clearing away rubble. They clustered around a pile of wreckage near what once had been her writing desk, and the foreman called again, his voice strained between excitement and horror. "Your Grace, I think you ought to have a look at this."

To Jean-Claude's mind, that could only mean one horrible thing, and he limped into the space where the room had been with a sick anticipation.

The foreman pointed. Jean-Claude's gaze followed his direction to a pile of charred timbers, and there, sticking out of the wreckage like one more torched fagot, was a dismembered limb, a lady's scorched and blackened arm, with one wormlike finger.

Jean-Claude's whole world went black. How he remained standing, he could not say, for all his strength had fled, and time went very queer. The next thing he knew, the searchers had found the rest of Isabelle's body. She'd lost a leg and an arm, and her face had been completely scorched away. Jean-Claude shuffled along after them as they loaded her onto a makeshift catafalque and carried her to temporary shelter under a tarp. One of Don Angelo's aides said something about the possibility that Isabelle had accidentally knocked over a candle. "A tragic accident."

Jean-Claude gave the aide such a glare as made the man retreat a full step. "She had alchemical lanterns, not candles, and this was no accident."

Jean-Claude's hand clenched the head of his cane, but braining the liveried staff would do him no good. He stuffed grief and despair and rage and every other emotion down into the pit from whence nightmares came. What use had he for feelings? What right had he to grieve, he who had failed so completely? Nothing could undo the crime. Nothing remained of his service but to hunt down its perpetrator.

Jean-Claude stalked into the remains of the building and stared around, looking for he knew not what. Isabelle would have been able to survey the room and tell him a dozen unusual things about the fire, about the way it burned and what that meant about whoever started it, but Jean-Claude was not so gifted. Yet perhaps others with more talent than he could be brought into service. DuJournal was already in the room, examining bits of charred wood, sniffing them.

"What are you doing?" Jean-Claude asked.

"Trying to figure out how the fire got started," he said. "The princess was found near her desk, which means she wasn't in bed when she died, but if she was awake, she could have escaped before the smoke overwhelmed her."

"She might have been asleep at her desk," Jean-Claude said, playing the Breaker's advocate.

"Hmmm—possibly," said Martin. "But no mere candle started this fire. Smell this." He tossed Jean-Claude a piece of burned wood.

Jean-Claude sniffed it dubiously and his nose wrinkled at a sharp stench, oily but stinging even more than vinegar. "What is it?"

"Unless I miss my guess, it's some sort of oil spirits, spilled all over the place. It would be perfect for getting a fire started."

"I thought a bomb caused the fire."

"I haven't found any bomb bits. Things look to have been burned rather than blasted."

"Then what caused the explosion?"

"Sometimes that can happen when a fire burns in a closed room. Fire needs air to mix with its phlogiston. I read a monograph by Gregor Von-Orn that hypothesizes that once a fire has used up all the air in a confined space, it lies dormant until, say, a door is opened, then it flares up explosively. Isabelle would have been at her desk. Then a fire started and burned and she succumbed to the smoke and fell to the floor. And then Olivia opened the door, and that caused the blast and spread the fire. I can't say for sure, but the furniture inside the room seems in place, if not intact, which means the blast was mostly *outside* the room."

Jean-Claude grunted—it all sounded like hocus-pocus to him—but followed along with the story. "If the blast was outside, how did Isabelle lose her arm?"

"That is a very good question. With your leave, I would like to examine her body."

Jean-Claude's gut knotted at the thought of this stranger pawing over Isabelle's corpse. It was indecent, but Isabelle . . . it was exactly the sort of thing she would have thought to try. Jean-Claude said, "You *will* treat her with respect."

"The utmost." DuJournal bowed low and took himself out, leaving Jean-Claude alone in the drizzle. He poked around through the ashes. He didn't understand empirical philosophy. Fire didn't have motives or reasons. It just was what it was. The natural world didn't make mistakes. People did. Except whoever had murdered his princess hadn't made enough mistakes, or Jean-Claude hadn't been clever enough to spot them.

His walking stick jammed and twisted against something in a puddle that was deeper than it looked. He jerked the stick in consternation and popped an oblong object from the murk. He blinked, and saw a cavalry officer's pistol half-submerged in a hole in the floor. He knelt and picked it up. If it was not the same pistol he had given Isabelle on the day of the cavalcade, then it was an identical twin. The barrel was cracked at the base, a sure sign of a backfire—like what might happen if a loaded pistol were left in a burning room.

He frowned and imagined the room as it had been. There was the wreckage of Isabelle's bed, and the pistol had been in the trunk at its foot. The trunk that was no longer there. There was no remainder of it, no debris. Could the workers have taken it out already? Could the murderer? Why?

Jean-Claude went back to basics. Catching the killer was his duty, as empty as it seemed. How did the murderer get in and out? There was only one door. The walls had been burned down to mere stubs. Jean-Claude walked the perimeter, looking for what would have been empty spaces indicating secret passages. Alas, if such existed, their defining boundaries had been obliterated in the building's collapse.

So assume just one door, and the chamber beyond had been filled with handmaids and guards. Could one or more of them have been complicit? Half of them were dead and therefore difficult to question. So further assume that a guilty handmaid, being forewarned about the fire, was one of the escapees. Were they all accounted for? He seemed to recall talking to each of them in the last few days. So, had all the dead ones been positively identified, or . . . wait.

Realization struck Jean-Claude like a crossbow bolt. He stood in the center of the room and turned a complete circle, peering through veils of rain, probing every cranny for something that was not there.

There was one handmaid unaccounted for. *Marie.* She wasn't here. There was no corpse. So where was she? Most people wouldn't even think to account for a bloodhollow. Bloodhollows weren't people. They were part of the background, a piece of functional furniture. They didn't count, except to people like Isabelle and therefore Jean-Claude. So where had Marie gone? Was she the instrument of the murder, controlled by the Comte des Zephyrs? But no . . . he stood to gain nothing from Isabelle's death, and even if he did use Marie as a murder weapon, why not just let her burn along with everything else? Marie had left this room or been taken, but why and by whom? Whoever it was, it was a mistake, a loose thread, if only Jean-Claude could find some way to tug on it.

"Monsieur musketeer," DuJournal shouted to be heard over the drumming rain.

Jean-Claude hobbled quickly to the mathematician's side and carefully tipped the brim of his hat so that it did not drizzle on Isabelle's remains. DuJournal knelt by Isabelle's side. Jean-Claude still found it hard to look at her blackened husk, but the spirit of the hunt gave him strength. He would find her killer, even if it took him until the end of time.

"What have you found?"

DuJournal flexed his fingers, as if preparing to snatch a burning brand from a fire. "I think . . . the princess did not have foul breath."

"What is that supposed to mean?"

"Look at her mouth."

Jean-Claude had to hold down his gorge, but he bent to look where DuJournal was pointing. Isabelle's skull had shattered in the fire, and the flesh had been burned from her bones, but her teeth remained. They were yellowed and blackened. "I see nothing," he admitted.

DuJournal pointed at a group of molars that were black and deeply pitted. "This isn't burn damage. This is jaw rot. This woman, whoever she was, had rotten teeth and terrible breath. Princess Isabelle did not. I danced with her the night of the fire."

The implication stunned the breath from Jean-Claude's body. He hardly dared embrace the logical conclusion lest the reprieve be snatched away. At last he whispered, "She's alive."

"Or at the very least, this is not her," DuJournal said.

"But someone wants us to think it is." Jean-Claude's mind raced, and understanding heaved up like a leviathan from a cloud bank, vast and frightful and unexpected. "It's all misdirection. Breaker's balls, I'm such a fool."

"What are you talking about?"

"This is not a murder; it's a kidnapping." And if it was a kidnapping, that meant Isabelle was alive, bless the Savior. Without food or drink or sleep, Jean-Claude felt he could live a hundred years on that knowledge alone. "Someone meant to kidnap Isabelle, but they wanted everyone to think she was dead so no one would look for her."

"But why? The dead give you no political leverage, and you can't collect ransom on a corpse," DuJournal said.

"Not for ransom, for something else, and I would give a lot to know what that 'else' is. But first they had to get rid of me, so they kidnapped me and tried to make it look like I'd been gutted in a tavern. Nothing mysterious about that, just a stupid foreign drunkard dying a drunkard's death. No one would ever investigate such a death."

"No one except Princess Isabelle; she had the whole city looking for you."

"Yes, but while I was supposed to be dying in a tavern, Isabelle was abducted. The kidnapper wanted to avoid pursuit, but he knew he'd be hunted unless everyone thought Isabelle was dead, so he set the fire and left another corpse in her place. One burned corpse looks pretty much like another, except for Isabelle's . . . oddity."

DuJournal said, "Bones survive fires, so he took the only course open to him. He amputated her deformed hand and left it for searchers to find."

An impotent fury swelled in Jean-Claude's heart. Someone had maimed Isabelle, vandalized the most beautiful, precious girl in the world. And whoever had stolen her intended to keep her, else why the cover-up? He had to find her. *Idiot!* He had already wasted four whole days feeling sorry for himself. But there was no time for additional self-recrimination now.

DuJournal looked thoughtful. "But if we'd found her with just a missing arm, we might have been suspicious, so this mysterious kidnapper cut off the corpse's leg for verisimilitude, because two missing limbs looks more accidental than just one. Ironic."

"Yes, he counted on people accepting the obvious explanation. He didn't count on you looking this poor woman in the mouth."

"So you were kidnapped in order to be murdered, and Isabelle was murdered in order to be kidnapped. Very symmetrical. But that still doesn't tell us who did it. Or why."

"You are correct, but I do know who might know why."

"Who?"

Jean-Claude frowned, wondering afresh who DuJournal worked for. He did not want to give his next quarry any warning; neither did he want to let DuJournal out of his sight. "Come with me and I will show you."

CHAPTER

Sixteen

The coach Jean-Claude had borrowed from Don Angelo rattled and splashed its way along San Augustus's winding, rain-slicked streets. Jean-Claude willed it to go faster. Every step taken slowly for the sake of care was another instant lost in his search for Isabelle. People didn't become lost by distance but by time. Events did not hold still, and the courses of lives were buffeted and twisted by events no empirical philosopher could calculate. Where was Isabelle, and what was happening to her? She had to be absolutely terrified.

"Do you mind telling me where we are going?" DuJournal asked.

"To visit Duque Diego," Jean-Claude said.

DuJournal's eyebrows lifted. "You think he knows something about Isabelle's disappearance?"

"I intend to find out."

"What makes you think he will speak to you?"

"I will demonstrate to him that it is in his best interest to do so." He flashed a sideways look at the imposter, still wondering who the man was working for and what he wanted. "You do not have to accompany me, of course."

"Builder forbid I would miss an opportunity to introduce myself to a great nobleman."

"On your head be it."

The coach halted under the portico outside Duque Diego's city residence, a stand-alone house in an expensive quarter. It was built to a tasteful scale but clad in ostentatious marble.

Jean-Claude marched up the broad steps to the main doors as if he had an army at his back instead of an imposter. He hoped persuasion would get him an audience with the duque, but if not, Jean-Claude had other means. One of the more specialized classes in the musketeer academy was penetration without detection, taught by a man with the title "master of the rooftops" whose final admonition with every mission was, "And don't get caught." Jean-Claude found himself wishing that the academy had not been such a long time ago, or that he had not spent so much of the intervening decades loitering in taverns. He was out of practice.

Just as Jean-Claude was about to rap on the door, it swung open and a steward liveried in black, red, and gold appeared. He bowed them in and said, "Señor musketeer, be welcome. Duque Diego has instructed me to inform him whenever you should happen to arrive. Happily, he is in residence at the moment. May I ask who is your guest?"

DuJournal grinned at Jean-Claude. "Do you get the feeling you are expected?"

Jean-Claude said, "This is Lord Martin DuJournal, mathematician, swordsman, and gadfly."

The steward took their sodden coats and their swords. In l'Empire Céleste, disarming a King's Own Musketeer was tantamount to disarming le roi, but in Aragoth, he was just another foreign soldier.

A pair of menials scrubbed the muck from their boots. Jean-Claude would have sooner gone barefoot than had any poor drudge kneeling before him scraping his boots, but no representative of Grand Leon went barefoot like a peasant, and, as one of his musketeer instructors had pointed out many years ago, "If they don't clean your boots, then they have to scrub the whole floor."

The steward led them into a lushly appointed library. Jean-Claude did not have the sort of mind that could peruse a man's book collection and deduce everything there was to know about the inner workings of his mind, but he looked around anyway. The books were certainly impressive, leather-bound volumes in various colors, some with titles sewn, stamped, or embossed on their faces, but most without. A few large, old, hand-calligraphed volumes were chained to the wall at a broad writing desk. A few upholstered chairs sat before a fireplace, and paintings of people Jean-Claude didn't recognize filled in the gaps. Judging from the wear on the upholstery, the place got used, but how much time did Diego himself actually spend here? Maybe his housekeeper spent a lot of time in here knitting when Diego was away.

The door on the far side of the room opened, and a silver-eyed, thickset man in a fine doublet, tall boots, and slops—Diego, presumably—strolled in. He folded his left arm behind his back in the position Jean-Claude always thought of as the please-put-me-in-an-armlock pose. He made a point of dismissing the two armed guards who accompanied him. The guards took up stations outside the door, a subdued but unmistakable declaration that, while they were all civilized people, violence remained an option. Diego glanced at the philosopher impersonator and said, "You are Princesa Xaviera's man, are you not?"

DuJournal doffed his hat in a sweeping bow. "Lord Martin DuJournal, mathematician, swordsman, and gadfly, at Her Highness's service."

That answered the question of who DuJournal worked for, and opened up a whole slew of other questions, such as, what had the other princesa retained him to do, precisely? It made sense that Xaviera would have wanted to open up a line of communication with Isabelle while she was alive, but why had her minion lingered when everyone thought Isabelle was dead?

Diego turned his silver-eyed gaze on Jean-Claude. "And you must be the musketeer." Jean-Claude braced himself for some sly mockery of his competence, but Diego only said, "I present you and your king with my condolences," which was almost worse.

Jean-Claude did not say, *You tried to kill her yourself, you goat-sucking whoreson,* nor did he let that emotion anywhere near his expression. "I shall bear them to him, personally. Before I return home, however, I must conclude my investigation. Sadly, a few sizable holes remain. I was hoping you might help me fill them, in the interest of—completeness."

Diego raised one salt-and-pepper eyebrow. "Completeness? Not justice?"

Jean-Claude produced a mirthless smile. "The only true justice is in the crime that is foiled before it is committed. That twisted thing the law calls justice is little more than revenge by committee. Completeness only asks that the whole story be told. All I want to know is, why did Thornscar want to kill Isabelle?" That danced nicely around any suggestion of impropriety on Duque Diego's part.

Duque Diego had been reaching for a goblet of wine on the sideboard. He paused with his fingers on the rim and gave Jean-Claude a puzzled look. "Thornscar?"

Jean Claude would have sworn the man's surprise was unfeigned, but how could Diego not know his own assassin's name? "The man who attacked the *Santa Anna* and tried to kill Princess Isabelle."

Diego looked like he was going through some quick mental shuffling of his own. "Did he call himself that?"

Jean-Claude answered warily. "In fact, he did not. The name was given to me by another." By Kantelvar, in fact.

Diego asked, "And did you see this supposed would-be assassin?"

"Face-to-defaced-face," Jean Claude said.

Diego drummed his fingers on the sideboard. "And I suppose you have some accusation to lay against me in the matter of the attack?"

"None that the authorities to which you bow seem to care about," Jean-Claude said, glumly aware that he was not leading this conversation, though it seemed to be meandering in an intriguing direction. "Though you might do well to distance yourself from the burning of Princess Isabelle's residence."

"Your concern for my welfare is touching. I assure you I had nothing to do with setting fire to your princesa's chambers. That foul deed belongs to another. I know not who. I am only surprised no zealot has stepped up to take credit.

"I have not seen the man you call Thornscar since the night he bade me have a mirror placed aboard the *Santa Anna*."

At least Jean-Claude now knew what Diego was fishing for. "What name did you know him by?" Jean-Claude asked, and it felt like flakes of rust were dislodging from his brain. "And what hold did he have over you that *he* could compel *you* to that act of sabotage?" Diego as the cat's-paw in someone else's scheme was backward to Jean-Claude's expectations. He cast a glance at DuJournal, who was as intent on the conversation as a cat on a mouse hole.

Diego turned and gave Jean-Claude a sharp, direct look. "First answer this. At whom was his attack aimed?"

"At Isabelle," Jean-Claude said.

Diego shook his head. "Of what significance was a crippled, deformed, unhallowed princesa from a fading power? She had no inherent worth."

Jean-Claude had no sword, but his heavy cane would make a fine club, and he imagined he could stave this arrogant pig's skull in before his guards could intervene.

DuJournal placed his hand upon Jean-Claude's shoulder. "I am sure Duque Diego is only asking you to look at the attacks from Thornscar's point of view. Who was his target?"

"Kantelvar," Jean-Claude realized aloud; the artifex was the only one who had actually been attacked. "He attacked Kantelvar and failed. That's when he turned tail and fled. But why in the Breaker's Torment . . ." The question died on his lips as his brain got on with the business of exhuming his assumptions to take a better look at their desiccated corpses. If Kantelvar had been the target all along . . . "Just who in the name of all the saints were you helping?"

Diego took a defensive swig of his wine and said, "I am not completely sure."

"Are you saying you helped someone you didn't know sabotage a diplomatic mission?"

"I am saying that the situation is more complex than you grasp, but you are bound to stumble over the truth eventually, so it would be best for everyone if you found it unfractured. Come." He turned and strode through another set of doors into a drawing room. It differed from the library mostly in that it had more paintings and no bookshelves. There was a gated alcove with comfortable chairs and a full-length mirror in it, suitable for receiving a sojourning Glasswalker.

Duque Diego said, "Señor musketeer. Allow me to introduce you to His Highness Príncipe Julio de Aragoth." He gestured to a painting.

Jean-Claude's eyes rounded. The face was the same one he had confronted in the *Santa Anna*'s hold, only absent any scar. Jean-Claude's thoughts lurched and spun like a skyship in a hurricane as he revised everything he had learned to balance around this new center.

DuJournal looked equally surprised. "You're saying Julio attacked Kantelvar? Why?"

Duque Diego glowered at the painting as if willing it to yield up an answer to those very questions. "One night, over a month ago, I was roused from sleep in the hours of the dead and summoned to this very chamber by a man, an espejismo I instantly took to be His Highness Príncipe Julio, except that he still had his leg and his face was marked with a great scar. He was dressed in servant's garb, and he quivered in horrible distress. He was so pale, I thought he must have been stabbed, but there were no fresh marks upon him. I asked him what had happened to him, and he said he had been betrayed. I asked him by whom and he said, 'Everyone, my whole family, but Kantelvar most of all.'

"I asked him what he meant, and he asked me when was the last time I had seen him. When I told him that I had seen him that very morning, he became even more distressed. He told me that he had been kidnapped months ago, an attack arranged to look like a hunting accident. He fought back against his attackers, and that was when he acquired his scar. He said, 'The man you saw today, the man who has been your príncipe for the last nine months, is a fraud, an imposter, a marionette placed there by Kantelvar in a bid to usurp the throne.'

"Needless to say, I was aghast, but such an outrageous accusation could not go unchallenged. Did he have any proof, any evidence of his legitimacy or his alternate's fraud? He gave such proofs as speech alone may deliver. He answered every question I posed to him, no matter how subtle, yet even then I was skeptical. Why had he not gone to his father with this; why come to me? At that point, he became as bitter as winter and said, 'My father is delirious. My mother wields the power there and she plots against me. There is no one in the royal household I dare trust, and even if I did, Kantelvar has spies everywhere, and my body is under his power. If he guesses I have found a way to escape him, it will mean my death.' At last he persuaded me that with my help he could acquire such proof as to banish all skepticism.

"He said he had a plan to unravel the plot against him, expose the traitors, and prove his own true identity. All he wanted from me was to use my contacts on the Île des Zephyrs to put a mirror on board Princesa Isabelle's ship, a service to which I reluctantly agreed."

Jean-Claude did his best not to sneer. "And what did he promise you in return for this favor? What tipped the balance? Or was it merely that you hoped he might dispense with Isabelle? Either he might have killed her or proved the marriage contract fraudulent. Whether he is the real príncipe or not, he was in a position to solve a problem for you."

Diego's face darkened. "Julio's marriage to Princesa Isabelle would have been a disaster for Aragoth."

"But once she was gotten rid of, you could sort out the problem of the príncipes at your convenience. So you gave your visitor what he wanted, but then it all went wrong. The attack on the *Santa Anna* failed, whatever its mission was. The scarred príncipe never came back, and you've been searching for him ever since."

"He said he was being held by Artifex Kantelvar, but now Kantelvar is dead."

Jean-Claude felt suddenly light-headed, as if the floor had dropped out from underneath him. Dozens of small clues suddenly lined up and came to attention like a regiment of lazy soldiers when a sergeant barked a command.

"Breaker's blood," he muttered.

Both DuJournal and Diego gave him puzzled looks.

Jean-Claude reviewed his clues and grinned. "Who is the one person who is never a suspect in a murder?"

DuJournal arched his eyebrows. "A riddle, monsieur?"

"Oh, better than that," said Jean-Claude. "This rides right through the land of Riddle and into the duchy of Hoax."

"Explain yourself," Diego said.

"The victim." Jean-Claude bumped his fist into his open palm while he gave throat to the idea boiling in his brain. "The victim is never a suspect in a murder."

"That was not an explanation," DuJournal pointed out.

Jean-Claude backed up to get a running start at his inspiration. "There were only three people who actually saw the man who boarded the *Santa Anna:* Vincent, me, and Kantelvar. Well, there was one more, but nobody counts a bloodhollow. Kantelvar knew his game was finished if either Vincent or I made the connection between Príncipe Julio and the boarder. Kantelvar had to get rid of us, and he had to frame a third party for it. He invented the name Thornscar on the spot and left the convoy in a tearing hurry. He had to secure his captive and set up a trap for the witnesses. It was only after he left that we discovered your involvement, Duque Diego, otherwise he probably would have gone after you as well.

"After that, everything falls into place. The attack on the cavalcade killed Vincent but missed me. He tried two more times to kill me after that, but thanks to DuJournal, I'm still above ground."

Diego looked thoughtful. "You say Princesa Isabelle did not see the intruder, but she knew what he looked like. When she saw Julio's face, I swear she nearly fainted."

Jean-Claude straightened up and grinned. "Yes. Isabelle used her blood-hollow's memory to draw a portrait of the assassin, but Kantelvar didn't know about that. So on the night of the masquerade, Isabelle finally got a look at Julio. If Kantelvar saw her reaction as you did he immediately realized she'd recognized his deception. His intrigues were doomed, so he took the only course available to him. He kidnapped Isabelle and faked both their deaths."

Diego's face slackened in surprise. "You think they're alive? I saw Kantelvar's corpse!"

DuJournal said, "You saw a corpse that looked like his. We saw a corpse that looked like Isabelle's, but it turns out to have been a fake."

"Yes," Jean-Claude said, "that's the crux of it. He was trying to throw us off, make us think there was nothing left to search for, but he missed again. We already know he's faked Isabelle's death."

"Actually we don't know that," DuJournal said. "It could have been someone else, parties yet unknown."

"It could," Jean-Claude said, "but I don't believe it and neither do you."

"Touché, but what I don't see is why. Why would he go through all the trouble to bring Isabelle here, only to fake her death?"

Jean-Claude said, "I'll warrant he wants to drag l'Empire Céleste into the imbroglio everyone is sure must happen when Carlemmo dies."

Diego made a derisive sound and looked to a map displayed on the wall. "L'Empire's troops have been massing along our borders for months. I think they require no encouragement."

Jean-Claude said, "Right now, Grand Leon is 'allowing' his barons to occupy the frontier. That means they're all doing it at their own expense, bleeding money by the day. He was counting on Isabelle to broker a peace between Julio and Alejandro, so that he will not have cause to unleash them. If there is no war, he can recall them back to their own territories, much poorer for their ambitions, much easier to control. But news of Isabelle's death adds injury to insult and must be avenged. If you want to stop that from happening, we need to find Isabelle."

Diego rubbed the back of his neck, clearly frustrated. "Even if both príncipes were here, I doubt their followers would accept a peace between them. Everyone is too far extended. I happen to know that at least three of my fellow duques have mortgaged their estates to arm and equip their forces. They cannot afford not to fight."

DuJournal said, "It seems to me that, for the moment, you are a man without a faction. You can hardly be sworn to Julio if you do not know which Julio is the true príncipe. Indeed, you cannot allow either of them to take the crown."

"Si," Diego said. "And that is one reason I am grateful to see you, Lord DuJournal. You are Xaviera's man." He paused, staring into space as if searching the horizon for some sign of cavalry riding to his rescue. When no promising dust clouds were forthcoming, he snapped his finger and a servant entered carrying a silver platter on which lay a small, tightly rolled scroll wrapped in a black ribbon. Diego lifted the scroll and presented it ceremoniously to DuJournal. "If you will please bear this to Princesa Xaviera."

"From your hand to hers," DuJournal said.

"And what is it?" Jean-Claude asked.

"A declaration of submission," Diego said. "Without precondition. I place myself at her husband's service and at his mercy. Julio must not be allowed on the throne, not while any doubt lingers as to his legitimacy."

"I shall go at once," DuJournal said.

"Go carefully. Margareta and her subordinates are utterly committed to victory. She must either put her puppet príncipe on the throne or face the Hellshard."

DuJournal said, "Then we'll just have to present them with duplicate Julios; then they'll face the same dilemma you do. They won't dare back either of them. It will be easier for Alejandro to offer them amnesty if they turn on Margareta."

"I doubt it will be that neat," Diego said, "but a quick war is better than a prolonged war, and this gives Aragoth a better chance than the alternative. What I still don't understand, though, is how Kantelvar thinks to profit."

"I don't know, but there's one person left who might." Jean-Claude turned his attention to DuJournal. "When you deliver that petition to Xaviera, ask if she can arrange an audience for me with her brother-in-law, the one with the wooden leg."

"What makes you think he'll expose himself to you?" Diego asked. "I questioned him extensively, and he survived every question I put to him. It makes me doubt I chose the right príncipe."

"I have leverage; you don't," Jean-Claude replied. Or at least he could pretend he did. To DuJournal he said, "Have Xaviera tell Julio that I have a message from l'Empire Céleste. Imply that it is an official message, too delicate to be routed through the ordinary channels."

DuJournal nodded. "That can be arranged."

DuJournal took his leave and Jean-Claude returned his attention to Diego. "I have one more question. Where was your man's corpus when his espejismo contacted you? Surely you tried to follow him back to his point of origin, or at least asked where he was being held prisoner." Wherever Thornscar had been kept was likely where Isabelle had been taken.

"He did not know. He had been rendered unconscious when he was taken there, and the place had no windows. He said it was somewhere very cold, and I believe him, for his espejismo's breath steamed in the air. I tried to follow him, naturally, and he tried to lead me, but the portal at the other end . . . I have never witnessed anything like it. He said he had managed to cast his espejismo through his reflection in water. That is an art that has long been lost to us, but after what I witnessed, I believe him, at least about that. One moment, he was there in the Argentwash, and the next, gone. He did not pass into any speculum loci I could detect, though I searched for hours. It was as if he had vanished into mist."

Jean-Claude swore under his breath. Someplace cold and windowless could be anywhere: a mountaintop cave, an icehouse cellar, a skyland in the upper air. Isabelle could be lost forever, gone like an exhalation, completely beyond recovery.

He could not think like that. There was still too much work to do. "By your leave, I have another errand to run."

Diego looked puzzled. "Aren't you going to wait for DuJournal to return?"

"No, but I would be much obliged if you would let him know to find me in the royal infirmary."

"Are you injured?"

"Only my pride and vanity for having been so blinded for so long. Yet, if I am to confront the false príncipe, it behooves me to first find out who he is."

—

Jean-Claude limped into the palace infirmary, where a few of Isabelle's household staff still convalesced. Despite a long wall of open windows, the whole room stank of ruined meat, bile, pus, soap, and stinging tonics.

If Diego's tale was true, somebody had been impersonating Julio for months, and so effectively that Diego doubted his own judgment as to who was who. The circle of people who knew the príncipe well enough to mimic him that convincingly had to be tiny, and Jean-Claude thought he knew someone who might be able to winnow the list down even further.

Adel sat, doubled over, on a padded bench, coughing dark flecks of blood into a white cloth. Her swarthy face had gone pale as soured milk, and her flesh seemed to have shrunk around her bones. Her plight sent an ache through Jean-Claude's soul. She was good and kind, and he hated having been suspicious of her even in the course of his solemn duty.

Jean-Claude eased himself down beside her. "Mademoiselle."

Adel turned a rheumy gaze on him and a brief flash of happiness darted across her face. Her voice came as a hoarse whisper. "Jean-Claude, what are you doing here?"

"I came to see you," he said, half the truth. By every oath he had ever sworn to le roi and to Isabelle, he ought to press his questions on her immediately, but she deserved better, and if there was not some higher justice that commanded compassion, then there bloody well ought to have been. "I see that you are out of bed."

"Oh, yes." She beamed weakly, like the sun through a dense fog. "Now if the cursed doctors would just let me get back to work—" A spasm of coughing interrupted her bravado, and Jean-Claude wrapped a tentative arm around her shoulders. She leaned into him and he held her tight to his chest as she expectorated blood, serum, and bits of rotted lung. When the spasm passed, she leaned her sweating forehead against his chest. Fever heat rolled from her in waves, and tears rimmed her eyes.

"Why did you come to see me?" she asked.

Jean-Claude fought back an urge to lie, to make Adel the center of the universe, at least for a few moments. "I need to ask you a question about Príncipe Julio," he whispered in her ear. "I think someone may have betrayed him."

She stiffened, but with anger, not disbelief. "Who?"

"That is what I hope you can tell me. Did he have any servants who went away or disappeared about the time he had his riding accident?" Whoever replaced the príncipe must have studied him closely, and the only sort of person who could know the príncipe that well and still be able to disappear without drawing undue attention was a servant. Every nobleman *knew* servants ran away at the drop of a hat; it was one of those *facts* that no amount of evidence to the contrary could refute.

"Servants? No, not that I can think of."

Jean-Claude gritted his teeth. There had to be someone. Someone whose appearance had somehow been altered to match the príncipe's.

"Someone with a bad leg," he guessed. Why else maim the puppet prince except to cover up some deformity? After all, Kantelvar had been willing to cut Isabelle's arm off . . . a fact that made his vision red with rage.

Adel looked up at him in surprise. "Climacio," she said. "He had a club-foot. He ran away a month before the accident."

"The whipping boy?" The idea stunned Jean-Claude with its pure vindictiveness. Kantelvar needed a pawn to replace Julio, and he had offered the job to Climacio; what better way for a whipping boy to get back at the whole family? Replace the prince, assume the throne, disgrace the queen. It was an ambitious revenge, more than a whipping boy might conceive, but easily the sort of thing Kantelvar might have invented, the means to some greater, more twisted end. But how was such a deception possible?

"Did Climacio greatly resemble Príncipe Julio?"

"No, why?"

"Just a thought," Jean-Claude said, and a major hole in his speculation. Yet either Julio had to have a twin nobody knew about, or someone had to have been altered to resemble Julio. A Goldentongue glamour could disguise one's appearance, but they tended to be temporary effects, not the sort of thing one could rely on for months.

Adel huddled against Jean-Claude, shuddering in her distress. "I am sorry. About la princesa."

"Nay nay, take comfort. She is alive." That particular secret would be all too safe with Adel, he feared.

Adel gasped in a way that had more to do with surprise than suffering. "Truly?"

"She is kidnapped by the same villain who betrayed Julio, and I seek to find her."

"Even so. Good news."

Jean-Claude embraced her through another long shudder. It was cruel to trouble her further, but there was yet another question she might be able to answer. Would she not take some comfort, even now, in serving the príncipe and princess?

He said, "But we do not know what became of Marie, Isabelle's blood-hollow handmaid."

Adel said nothing for a long moment, and Jean-Claude thought she might be too lost in her own pain to respond, but at last she said, "La princesa took her. With the artifex. Don't know where. She came back alone."

Jean-Claude denounced himself as a dunderhead. Kantelvar had promised Isabelle to lift Marie's curse; it was an obsession she could not resist, her biggest blind spot.

Someone cleared his throat behind Jean-Claude. He turned to find DuJournal standing there and cursed his inattentiveness; that could have been an enemy. Indeed, it might still be.

But DuJournal said, "I think I know where the bloodhollow might have been taken. There's an old Temple not far from the guest residence. It was razed years ago, but the basement vaults are still there."

Jean-Claude wanted to ask, *And just how do you know that?* but decided not to kick the messenger in the teeth.

"Someplace dark and cold without windows?" he asked.

"Yes, indeed."

He shifted his weight to stand but then remembered Adel. "Mademoiselle . . ."

She stirred and eased away from him. "Go, Jean-Claude, rescue your princesa."

He stiffly stood and bowed to her. "I will return, mademoiselle," he said. *It will be too late, I fear, but I will return.*

She smiled at him again. "I thank you for your concern, brave musketeer."

Tears obscured Jean-Claude's vision. He groped for DuJournal's shoulder and allowed himself to be guided from the room, Adel's racking cough echoing in his ears.

CHAPTER

Seventeen

"Who designed this madhouse?" Jean-Claude said as DuJournal led him through a maze of dusty rooms and corridors, antechambers and staircases filled with clinging cobwebs. Leaving Adel to her fate had been inevitable and needful, but it left him in a foul humor.

"Half a dozen different architects, each with his own rampant ego, all at the same time, without any sort of effective oversight," DuJournal said dryly.

"Wasteful," Jean-Claude said.

"On purpose," DuJournal said. "The gold and silver being brought back from the colonies were swamping the kingdom. Carlemmo threw as much as he dared into roads and harbors and ships and aqueducts, but there was still too much. The value of the doubloon was starting to dissolve, hence this extravagant money sink."

Jean-Claude tried to bend his thoughts around the idea of a kingdom with too much gold, but right now he hadn't the mental resources. "So how far is this Temple vault?"

"Not far." They took a right-hand turn. No hesitation. Jean-Claude wondered, not for the first time, if his guide was leading him into a trap. He made sure to do a bit of extra limping, just in case he needed DuJournal to underestimate him.

"I take it you've been here before," Jean-Claude said.

A pause before answering and then, "When I first began my service on Princesa Xaviera's behalf, I followed Artifex Kantelvar down here in an attempt to discern his place in the scheme of things."

A lie, Jean-Claude thought, or at least the truth dressed in beggar's clothes. Clearly DuJournal had been down here often enough to know the place. He had quite probably been looking into Kantelvar, so what omission was he troweling over?

"When did you start working for Xaviera?"

DuJournal chuffed and said, "A few months ago."

A few months and already he knew the minutiae of this sprawling project that had been going on for decades. "And did you manage to arrange for me to have an audience with the false prince?"

"Yes. Xaviera is arranging it now."

Jean-Claude took note of the informal use of the princesa's name, a liberty he took with no other noble except Julio. "I can only assume that her interest is primarily in seeing the imposter exposed."

"Hmmm. Yes. I suppose it must be. At the moment, though, she has more immediate worries. King Carlemmo did not wake up this morning. He still breathes, she says, but she fears his spirit has already left him."

"Damn." Jean-Claude's guts coiled nervously. "Why have I not heard this before?"

"Margareta is keeping it hushed while she moves her forces into position for the coup. Her enemies have already been warned and are making countermoves. It's only a matter of time now before someone decides that shooting first is better than being shot."

They reached an intersection where the dust on the floor had been disturbed by the passage of several sets of feet. It was impossible to say just how long the footprints had been there. So dead was the air that the dusty plume of Jean-Claude's passing hung in space behind him, as persistent and obfuscating as a bad rumor.

Jean-Claude grunted and squatted down by the tracks, briefly wondering if his creaky old knees would allow him to get up again. He made out four sets of tracks, one male, two female, one too large to be human.

DuJournal made a hissing noise through his teeth and looked around nervously. "That's an omnimaton."

"I thought they were all destroyed in the cataclysm."

"The Temple has rebuilt a few, and if there's one loose in the corridors then we are in grave danger. Any one of them is worth a whole platoon of soldiers."

"What would I do without good news like that?" Jean-Claude grumbled. He pointed to the tracks. "Looks like they came from that way."

"That's the direction of the old Temple."

"Carefully then." Jean-Claude readied his pistol and cursed the need for his cane. DuJournal shifted his lantern to his off hand and drew his sword, and Jean-Claude noted the maker's mark just below the quillons. That weapon came from one of the most renowned sword makers in Aragoth. Jean-Claude almost sighed as the pieces of one mystery lined themselves up neatly on the game board of his mind: victory in two moves, though this was not the opportune moment to push his pawns.

A brace of fears yoked Jean-Claude's heart as they skulked down the hallway, listening for some sound more ominous than their own breathing and muffled footsteps. First, that some trap would snap them up unawares before they reached Kantelvar's hole; second, that they would find the hole empty and all trace of Isabelle lost. The foot tracks and the column of dust that followed them like a parade of stealthy soldiers suggested that this place was forgotten, but surely if Kantelvar had intended to hide down here, he would have found some way to obliterate these footprints.

At last they reached a locked side door through which all of their quarry had passed.

"This is the place I remember," DuJournal whispered. "There should be a stairway beyond this. I know not what awaits us at the bottom."

Jean-Claude's doubts grew. Surely Kantelvar would not leave any place important unguarded. So either there was a guard he could not see, or this place was not important. Even so, it must needs be checked. Jean-Claude put away his pistol and drew his knife, sliding it into the crack between door and jamb. The lock was new, but the door was old and the gap quite roomy. While he worked at prizing the bolt out of its hole, he said, "The question is, what do you hope to find? It occurs to me that it is in Príncipe Alejandro's interest to see the false prince unmasked—and I don't mind being the cat's-paw for that—but it does not serve him to see either the real Julio or Isabelle recovered."

DuJournal took his time answering. "Aragoth gains nothing from Princess Isabelle's death. In fact, returning her intact to l'Empire Céleste would be to Alejandro's great political advantage, and I would gladly help you with that."

"Which leaves only Julio," Jean-Claude said. "As much as Alejandro would like him out of the succession debate, having him missing would only serve to destabilize his rule. Missing heirs and heroes give the opposition a figurehead around which to rally. The fact that this figurehead is insubstantial only works to their advantage, for that which is not corporeal cannot be destroyed. It therefore behooves Alejandro to wish Julio's corpse to be discovered, conveniently murdered by Kantelvar before he could be rescued. That leaves only one contender for the throne."

DuJournal fidgeted with his sword. "Better that Julio should be rescued, I think, and held at least for a time. Once the imposter is exposed, and Artifex Kantelvar is implicated, support for Julio's marriage to Princesa Isabelle will evaporate and Queen Margareta's faction will collapse."

Jean-Claude twisted his knife one last time. The bolt popped out and the door glided open on well-oiled hinges. Beyond, a spiral stairway corkscrewed down into darkness. There was no dust on the floor here, but a breath of cool, damp air brushed his face. No sounds of habitation rose from those depths. The place felt abandoned.

Jean-Claude ushered DuJournal forward and waited until the man swung his foot out over the decline. "I defer to your judgment on Julio; he's your brother, after all."

It is not quite possible to spin in place while walking forward down a winding stair, but the man who styled himself Lord DuJournal tried it anyway. He might have tipped backward and tumbled down the stairs had not Jean-Claude seized him by the doublet and pulled him back onto the landing.

"Príncipe Alejandro, I presume."

The man's eyes narrowed, but all he said was, "How did you know?"

"I probably would not have suspected anything, except that I have met the real DuJournal, and you look nothing alike. After that, it was just a matter of summing up the peculiarities. You work for Xaviera, but she does things for you, and you speak her name with tender familiarity. You know this place like someone who has lived here all your life. Your sword is of the finest maker in all Aragoth, and so on and so forth."

"And, just now, if I had spoken against Princesa Isabelle—"

"You would be at the bottom of these stairs. For what it's worth, I much prefer this outcome."

"As do I," Alejandro said dryly. "But how do we proceed?"

"As before," Jean-Claude said.

"But why reveal that you know my secret, if not to blackmail me?"

"Because keeping up the pretense of ignorance is as bothersome and inconvenient to me as your disguise is to you. We cannot work together if we are both investing effort in maintaining the fiction of your rather excellent disguise. By the way, how are you managing to not have silver eyes, and to pass amongst your own courtiers without so much as a hiccough of recognition?"

"A glamour talisman of the highest order. It even disguises my accent. The Goldentongue who made it for me charged a small fortune. Fortunately, I have a large fortune that Margareta has not yet figured out how to confiscate."

"I had heard the citadel was warded against such magic."

"Against unauthorized sorcery. Being a member of the royal family, I am authorized."

"I would have thought Margareta would revoke your permission."

"She can't. The mechanism that provides the protection is from the Primus Mundi."

"Ah, so you know how to use it, but nobody knows how it really works."

"Exactly. I do know there's a pecking order of sorts and she can't interdict me." Alejandro made a sweeping gesture toward the stairs. "I think I should prefer it if you go first."

Jean-Claude lit an alchemical lantern and stumped down the stairs. Trusting Alejandro with his back was a risk, but a minor one. This was a man who rejected fratricide even for the prize of the throne—not just a nobleman, but a noble man—but he might need a moment to recover from the shock Jean-Claude had given him.

Down the stairs and past another landing they found a heavy door ajar. Beyond it Jean-Claude was surprised to see a vast round room with carved granite columns and a painted ceiling. It was lined with mostly empty bookshelves and workbenches. A wide table took up the center of the room. The place looked to have been emptied out in a hurry, and a variety of oddments had been left behind: a few books; some broken glass; bits of brass, iron, and copper; a few pieces of clockworks. Unfortunately, no one had left behind any princesses. The only other exit was a curtained doorway on the far wall.

"Evacuated," Alejandro observed, emerging from the stairwell behind him.

"It was a shot in the dark to begin with," Jean-Claude said, wondering who precisely he was trying to console. This had been his best lead, and now he would have to fall back on trying to wring information out of Climacio, and do it all before San Augustus became the world's largest graveyard.

There came a squeak from behind the curtain.

Jean-Claude froze and listened.

"Help." The voice barely hung together long enough to reach Jean-Claude's ears. "Help me. Please." It was female, young, but ghostly hollow. Only years of professional caution saved him from racing through the curtain. Breaker only knew what sort of ambush lay beyond.

"Who is that?" he called.

"Monsieur Jean-Claude, is that you?"

"How do you know my name?"

"Your voice. I remember. You took me and Izzy home." She sounded like her voice was rising up from the bottom of a well.

Jean-Claude felt the world spinning. "Marie?" How was this possible? "Hold on, child!"

Jean-Claude flew past the first curtain into an antechamber with another heavy curtain at its opposite end.

"No light," the Marie voice called from behind the second curtain. "No light, please."

Jean-Claude halted, staring at the curtain and then his lantern. "Why not?"

"It will make the bloodshadow come back." Her voice was eerily devoid of the emotion her words should have carried.

Alejandro joined him in the antechamber.

Jean-Claude said, "Tell me what happened."

The Marie voice spoke in a monotonous rhythm. "I don't know. It's all mixed up. I remember you brought us back to the château, and we went to see the comte, then there was a nightmare and I couldn't wake up. I tried and I tried to wake up but I couldn't. And then the artifex stuck needles in my arms and said no light, and everyone went away, and then I woke up, and I called for help and nobody ever came."

Jean-Claude braced himself against the wall as his mind fought to catch up with the story. Marie was alive. Well, she'd always been alive, but now she was awake and aware. He thrust his lantern into Alejandro's hand and said, "Get this out of here."

Alejandro seized him by the elbow before he could get away. "What if this is a trap?"

"Then I have fallen for it. Twelve years ago, I failed this girl. I failed her more absolutely than I have failed anything in my life, at least until I lost Isabelle. I told her I would make her safe, and then le Comte des Zephyrs turned her into a bloodhollow. So if it pleases Your Highness, wait outside, and if I do not return, you may assume whatever you wish."

Alejandro nodded solemnly and took himself out. Jean-Claude tugged at the flap of his jacket and squeezed as gently as possible past the second set of curtains. The room was black as a hatful of soot. It smelled of urine and feces. How long had she been trapped in here? In the dark. All alone.

"Where are you?"

"On the cot," the Marie voice said. It was horrible not being able to see her, like talking to a ghost. He followed the sound of her voice and ended up barking his shin on the frame of the cot and biting back words that were inappropriate to use in the presence of ladies. Jean-Claude felt his way along the cot until he found a human foot. It twitched under his fingers, but she did not cry out.

"Sorry," he said, and felt her shift on the cot, sitting up, or trying to. Her fluttering fingers brushed his, and he clutched her hand. Living skin, but cool and papery, dehydrated.

"Are you a dream?" she whispered, and he felt ashamed for his own trepidation.

"I am real," he said.

"Thank you," she said in that same vacant tone, but when she reached for him, he gathered her into him, hugging her around the shoulders as she squeezed him. She shook like an autumn leaf. As feeble as she was, it didn't take long for her to exhaust herself, and he replaced her on the cot. He plied her with water from his skin. Not too much. She'd have to come back slowly. The same with food. She'd also need clean clothes and linens, things that made humans feel human. And he would have to figure out what to do about these tubes stuck in her arms.

"Do you know what the pipes are for?" he asked.

"Kantelvar said they were going to filter out the comte's bloodshadow." As feeble as she was, she already sounded better for having water in her.

"You can remember things Kantelvar said to you when you were having your nightmare?"

"I can remember everything," she said, "but it's hard. It's like going down a deep hole and it's hard to climb out. I feel like I'm going to slip and fall and get stuck forever."

Jean-Claude grimaced for the cruelty in which he must now engage. As much as he would have liked to stay and cosset Marie, there was too much else to be done. She had to be provided for, which meant leaving, and he still had to find Isabelle, which meant he needed every scrap of information he could get.

"I need your help," he said. "Kantelvar kidnapped Isabelle. Do you know anything about that?" He wished he could be more specific with his question, but he had no idea what Marie might have seen.

Marie was quiet for a long moment, and Jean-Claude, with his hand on her shoulder, could feel tension quivering through her. At last she said, still in that ethereal voice, "Izzy used to cry herself to sleep because of me. I'll try."

Spoken without reproach, those words nonetheless drove a spike of pain into Jean-Claude's heart.

Marie took a deep breath, like a swimmer about to dive to the bottom of a lake, and then went very still. He held her hands as she dove into the murk of memory. He found himself holding his breath. Was she going to come back? Must he sit by while yet another woman slipped through his grasp to her doom?

She gasped and shuddered; a sound like the last hiss of a boiling kettle passed her lips.

"Marie, are you injured? Can you hear me?"

"Yes." She clung to his arm. "Isabelle and Kantelvar brought me here. Isabelle was worried about me. Then they left. Later he came back. He was in a hurry. He kept shouting at someone who didn't answer. 'Pack this up. Take it to the *Voto Solemne.*'"

Jean-Claude had to stifle a surge of pure vicious joy at this. This is what he had been looking for: the name of a ship. Finding one ship in the deep sky would be like finding the proverbial needle in the wheat field, but at least he knew which wheat field and which needle.

Marie continued in an exhausted monotone. "And then he left, too. And then I woke up, and I knew I shouldn't move, because Isabelle gave me instructions about the lights and the tubes before she left. I called for help. And then it was quiet until you came. And now you're going to leave me, too."

"I will come back for you," he said. That was the second time today he'd made that promise. He hoped this time was not as futile.

"That's what Isabelle said."

"Kantelvar kidnapped Isabelle. I'm going to get her back." No oath he had sworn before Grand Leon had ever had such conviction.

It was physically exhausting for Jean-Claude to drag himself out of the dark room. Twelve years ago, he had delivered Marie to her enemies. For the intervening decade, he had counted her as dead, and now he must abandon her to the darkness, at least for a while.

To Príncipe Alejandro, who had been gathering the remnants of the sanctum's contents onto the table, he said, "Your Highness. I must beg a favor."

"An attendant for the girl. Done. I can barely begin to imagine what she has suffered. I will send one within the hour. Within the quarter hour, be it within my power to do so."

"No light," Jean-Claude said.

"Of course." He drummed his fingers on the table. "Have you ever noticed how it is possible to be horror-struck by the pain of one person and simultaneously oblivious to the travails of thousands?"

"I am but a simple musketeer," Jean-Claude said. "Caring for one person is quite enough burden for me. To care so deeply for thousands and still be sane would require the fortitude of a saint."

"With answers like that, I can see why Grand Leon keeps you around." He handed Jean-Claude his lantern and they started up the stairs. "Are you going to tell me what she told you?"

"Are you going to tell me what you found in the gleanings?"

"You first."

"The name of a ship, I think, that Kantelvar used to carry Isabelle away."

294 — CURTIS CRADDOCK

"Hah! We have him, then. We can locate him using the registry at the Naval Orrery. It has a chartstone from every ship flagged out of Aragoth."

"You are assuming this ship is flagged out of Aragoth, and under the name I was given, but you are right that it's worth a try."

"If it does not have a chartstone in the Naval Orrery, then it would risk being challenged by our picket ships. I doubt Kantelvar would want to take that chance, so that's half your problem solved."

"And what did you find?"

"A candle stub." He produced the waxy stump and began rolling it over in his fingers.

"And what's so remarkable about that?"

"Nothing in and of itself, but this place has sconces for alchemical lanterns, so it has no need of candles, and this is finest beeswax, and this"—he flipped the stub up to display an indented pattern on the flat end—"is the maker's mark for a chandler in Castrella, my wife's home province."

"And she brought her candlesticks with her when she moved to San Augustus."

He nodded, looking progressively more worried the more he fondled the waxy remnant. "It's possible to poison candles, you know. Dip their wicks in certain solutions of arsenic, for example."

"But that candle is spent," Jean-Claude pointed out, "and I have heard no rumor that she is ill."

"No. Just barren." And now his eyes burned with suspicion. "And hopeless in her distress at being unable to conceive, she prays at her altar every night, burning candles just such as these."

Poisoning herself. Jean-Claude was beginning to think that was Kantelvar's style. "And Xaviera's infertility gave Kantelvar the leverage he needed to bring Isabelle into play and give Julio a plausible claim to the throne, a plan that has now thrown all four shoes."

"Now the imposter that sits at Margareta's side finds himself backfooted. He believes both his chief conspirator and his bride-to-be are dead."

"Unless he is in on it," Jean-Claude said.

"I doubt he'd agree to making Isabelle disappear. More to the point, I know Margareta wouldn't, and she seems to be pulling the imposter's strings. They'll be in an absolute panic."

"So what's their next move?" Jean-Claude asked.

Alejandro's face grew still in thought. "He'll want to level the battlefield. Xaviera."

"Wait. How does removing her help him? Your faction has been begging you to set her aside so you can remarry. Getting rid of her would be doing your side a favor."

Alejandro glowered at him, but Jean-Claude said, "I am thinking from his point of view, not yours."

"She still works as a hostage against me," he said. "Even if the rest of the world would discard her."

Jean-Claude said, "Just be sure you don't commit yourself too quickly to rash action. One of my academy instructors had a saying: 'When you hitch up a team of four, make sure fear and anger are not in the lead.' I have frequently served Isabelle best by not being at her side."

They reached a four-way intersection. Alejandro stopped and perforce Jean-Claude did as well. "Your point is taken, but with my father on his deathbed, I must make sure my wife is removed from the pretender's reach, as I should have done before. Damn that leaving her in place was so useful." The príncipe pointed down one corridor. "If you follow these footprints, they will lead you as surely as I can to wherever Kantelvar went."

Jean-Claude scowled at the indicated path. "No doubt those tracks lead to an empty berth where a skyship once was, and I cannot walk on air. I need to visit the Naval Orrery, and I need a ship to pursue Kantelvar, and for those things I need your help, Highness. As much as it pains me not to bay and chase like a hound on the scent, I must take my own advice and turn aside to assist you."

Alejandro accepted that with a nod and led him down a different path in the maze.

Both of them were covered in dust, gray as ghosts, by the time they emerged into the light of one of the citadel's forecourts. Tall, straight walls gave the impression of walking through a canyon. The rain had finally quit, but the yard was still pocked with puddles. Golden light splashing off the upper third of the walls told Jean-Claude it was late afternoon. They had been down in that maze for most of the day.

Alejandro said, "We will fetch Xaviera and send a minion to tend Marie, then we'll make our way to the orrery."

But no sooner had they thrust their way into one of the citadel's occupied sections, a broad hallway with glazed windows and parquetry floors, than a guardsman in royal purple livery hailed them. As it would have seemed suspicious to run away, and as Jean-Claude would have lost a footrace in any case, he merely shared a worried glance with Alejandro qua DuJournal and contrived to greet the approaching guardsman with no more than a look of mild curiosity.

"How may we help you, Sergeant?" DuJournal asked.

"Señors, the queen commands your presence. You are requested to accompany me."

Jean-Claude patted his jacket, causing clouds of dust to fly up. "If you are sure Her Majesty would appreciate being exposed to us in this disheveled state."

No hesitation. "It will not be a problem, señors."

Damn. Jean-Claude had not expected to escape the audience, but the alacrity with which the guard disposed of the usual assiduously enforced niceties was alarming. They allowed themselves to be led briskly into the heart of the royal wing. Servants of various types scurried on their errands like mice with a cat on the prowl. By now the whole staff must have known of el rey's downturn. The usual buzz of a busy household had been reduced to frantic whispers.

They came soon to the gold-inlaid outer doors of an audience chamber. A pair of guards divested them of weapons. The doors opened onto a room that was small only in comparison to the scale of the citadel. Mirrors inset in doorwaylike arches in the walls managed to make it look labyrinthine and busier than it was.

Queen Margareta, already draped in voluminous robes of mourning black, sat on a throne atop a dais. The false Príncipe Julio sat to her left. His wooden posture could not quite contain a nervous twitch in his fingers. On Margareta's right stood a thin man with a waxed mustache and a red doublet. He had the silver eyes of a Glasswalker, but his skin was dark and mottled. A wide nose and thick lips gave the impression of a wider man pressing out from within a skinnier one. His hand rested lightly on the pommel of his sword. There were more guards than a friendly audience required, and more than a diplomatic audience would have allowed, and their postures were close and aggressive.

Jean-Claude's pulse thudded harder. He and DuJournal were marched forward by a pair of flanking guards until they reached the foot of the dais. DuJournal bowed to Margareta, pointedly ignoring Julio, a fact which neither of them seemed inclined to protest. Jean-Claude probably should have made some obeisance, but his stiff neck was acting up. He folded his arms across his chest.

Margareta said, "Lord Martin DuJournal. You and your accomplice, the Célestial musketeer Jean-Claude, stand before us today guilty of conspiracy and treason against the crown of Aragoth."

DuJournal looked surprised, but was it contrived or real? From his angle, Jean-Claude could not tell. His own response was muted by his expectation that something like this was going to happen. The king was dying and neither side of the succession debate was likely to pass up the chance to blame it on the other. Even if the king had been hit by lightning, some culpability would have been invented and weaponized. The only question was why Margareta had chosen this venue to make this accusation. It was a private audience, therefore not intended to make a political point, and yet if not to make a political point, why go through the motions? She could have had the both of them rounded up and thrown into prison or executed on the spot. In the chaos that was brewing, two extra corpses would hardly be noticed.

DuJournal said, "Perhaps Your Majesty would care to explain—"

"The king, my husband, is dying, and it has been discovered that your patron, Princesa Xaviera, is the murderess. She was caught red-handed this afternoon dripping vile poison into the king's unconscious mouth. She has confessed her crime and further revealed that she was acting at the behest of her husband, who was carrying out the program himself before he was dismissed from the capital."

DuJournal held together fairly well under this onslaught of slander and lies. "That is tragic, Majesty, but what has it to do with me?"

"You are the disgraced princesa's agent, the go-between by which she keeps in contact with her traitorous husband."

DuJournal huffed in disbelief. "As you said yourself, he was sent away. Furthermore he is a Glasswalker; he can contact her any time he wants."

"But he did not leave. His ship was intercepted this morning and boarded, and he was found to be missing. The captain of the ship confessed that Príncipe Alejandro had departed the ship soon after it set sail, returning to San Augustus in direct defiance of the king's command. He is now hiding somewhere within the city, making plans to contest my son's rightful ascension to the throne. Xaviera confessed that she was using you to spy on the royal court for him. For that you are condemned to death."

DuJournal said, "Your Majesty, I mislike your idea of a trial. Even a saint could not defend himself against such a nebulous allegation. What message do you think I carried and when? Where is your proof?"

Jean-Claude did his best to be invisible. As vile as Margareta's lies were, they were a masterpiece of the form, outrageous enough to be interesting, plausible enough to be believable, grounded with facts at the periphery even while being vaporous at the center. It was almost a pity they were wasted on an audience that knew better, though perhaps Margareta meant to use DuJournal as a sounding board to test for holes in her narrative.

"Silence!" Margareta snapped. "A trial for a foreign spy, and one guilty of attempted regicide? Preposterous. The only reason you live is you may yet have some minor utility."

"Let me guess: you want me to fetch Príncipe Alejandro for you, as if I knew where he was."

Jean-Claude crowed inside at the thought. With a little luck and a well-greased tongue, he might walk out of here in DuJournal's shadow with a mission to help him find himself.

"If you do not know, then you will find out, and when you do, tell Príncipe Alejandro that his beloved wife has been placed in the Hellshard, and will remain there until he submits to justice and confesses his crimes against the kingdom."

DuJournal took a half step back, and his face went so pale that even the dust on his cheeks looked dark in comparison. An inarticulate gurgle rose in his throat.

Jean-Claude had heard of the Hellshard, a bit of quondam sorcery left over from the Primus Mundi. It was supposed to be an implement of unspeakable torture, and the mere mention of it had winded Alejandro. Unfortunately, the queen's right-hand man also noted this, and with a flick of his wrist he impelled two pairs of guards to brace DuJournal and Jean-Claude's arms up behind their backs. It was all Jean-Claude could do to resist twisting from their grip and making a fight of it, but there were ten of them, all professionals. Perhaps if he were ten years younger, he would have tried it, and if he were twenty years younger he might have succeeded, but four decades of hard use blunted any edge he had once possessed.

Instead, he let out a piteous whimper and slumped to his knees. "Mercy!" The guards relaxed their grip rather than be dragged down with him.

"Felix?" asked the queen.

The silver-eyed swordsman stalked toward DuJournal like a cat. "Surely you saw his pain, Majesty, when you spoke of Xaviera's fate. No indifferent hireling is he."

Jean-Claude said, "You put a woman in the Hellshard. Did you expect him to be indifferent?" His best chance of getting out of here was still in DuJournal's wake.

"You were," Felix pointed out, though without taking his mirrored eyes off DuJournal.

"I'm a well-known degenerate. Too many years of hearing bad news gives one scar tissue on the soul."

Felix ignored him and pressed in on DuJournal until they were nearly nose to nose, or at least nose to chin, for DuJournal was that much taller. From a metal pouch on his belt, he withdrew a ring. It was the size of a splayed hand and looked to be made of a flat black stone. He brought it up to eye level. DuJournal's gaze fixed on it.

Felix smiled a razor of a smile and said, "And would sir care to know that I put la princesa in the Hellshard myself? That I poked her hand through this key ring and watched her unravel like an old sock as it drew her in? Oh, how she screamed. 'Alejandro! Alejandro!'"

DuJournal surged against his captors' grasp. "Bastard!"

As quick as a striking snake, Felix's opposite hand whipped out with a slender chain of dark, jagged-looking metal and looped it around Du-Journal's throat. When the two ends touched, DuJournal's face blurred like fresh ink smeared across a page and then washed away, revealing another face, swarthy, strong jawed, and mirror eyed, beneath.

Felix stepped back and made a flourish like a sculptor unveiling a statue. "Behold, Your Majesty, my design has worked even better than I anticipated. Cold iron trumps glamour and reveals the bait as the prize. Sometimes the old methods are the best."

The false Príncipe Julio cringed back in his seat, but Margareta leaned forward, her face stern but her eyes shining gleefully. "Well done, Felix. This is better than I could have hoped for. Truly we have the Builder's own blessing."

Alejandro settled but did not sag. His jaw was clenched, and his eyes burned. "Traitress. Murderess. Do not think you will sit easy on your stolen throne."

"Silence. There is no one left to contend with. You will confess to treason and regicide before the Sacred Hundred or your wife will remain in the Hellshard until her very soul is flayed to ribbons."

Felix held the stone ring up to his ear and said, "Even now I can hear her wailing."

From there the negotiations proceeded with a gut-wrenching efficiency. Both players had seen the endgame and nothing remained but to play it out, and for Alejandro to hope for Margareta to make some inattentive mistake. He said, "And what guarantees do I have that you will release her if I do what you say?"

Margareta smiled thinly. "The Hellshard will only hold one person at a time."

"Take her out now, hold her someplace else if you must, and I will do as you say."

"You are in no position to bargain," Margareta said. "You will do as you are told, and you will be grateful for our mercy. If you offer any resistance— any at all—we will leave Xaviera in there until her soul is rendered unto dust and blown away in the wind."

Alejandro sagged, daunted if not defeated. "Assemble the Hundred," he said.

Margareta leaned back in her seat. "In time. My husband is not dead yet, and it would strain credulity to punish you for an incomplete crime. You will be held in solitude until he breathes his last, which may yet be several days."

"But Xaviera—" Alejandro cut himself off.

"There will likely be little left of her by then," Margareta purred. "Unless, of course, you choose to expedite the matter. If so, you will be led to Carlemmo's chambers and a dagger provided for the purpose."

Jean-Claude had never seen such mortal horror on a man still standing upright. Alejandro might have absorbed defeat, even disgrace, but this wickedness overwhelmed him.

"My father—" he choked.

"Is dying anyway," Margareta said. "Slaying him now does him a mercy, saves your pretty wife's soul, and prevents the kingdom tearing itself apart in open war. It is in fact a noble sacrifice you make, one life for thousands."

"Three lives at least," Jean-Claude said. "Carlemmo's, yours, and Xaviera's, because if you think Margareta is going to let any of you live—"

A soldier's boot slammed into Jean-Claude's stomach. Pain doubled him over and he vomited on the parquetry.

While he was heaving his guts, Margareta said, "Dispose of him. The whole world will know how Grand Leon conspired with Alejandro in this murder."

Jean-Claude forced himself to laugh. Margareta was an imaginative liar, but she was too impatient. More importantly, she thought she was better at it than anybody else.

Not so, Jean-Claude swore. Aloud he said, "Yes, go ahead and dispose of me. Slay the only man who can save your scheme from disaster."

Margareta scoffed at him. "Kick him again. Harder."

The kick was harder, but this time Jean-Claude was ready and curled himself around the boot. "Have you not wondered about your great enemy, the one who slew your pet artifex and Isabelle on the same night?" As close as he could figure it, Kantelvar had been the driving force behind Margareta's schemes, perhaps nurturing her native ambition into the monstrous thing it had become. His sudden absence had been like stripping the muzzle off a vicious dog.

"Harder!"

The kicker aimed at Jean-Claude's head, but he took most of it on his forearm.

"I know where he is!"

The kicker lined up for another go at Jean-Claude's head, but Margareta stayed him with a flick of her fingers.

"Where?"

Jean-Claude took his time pushing up to his knees. "The Naval Orrery."

"Where at the orrery? Who is he?"

"The orrery is how I will find him. The who is a subject for further negotiation." *Because I am inventing this as I go.*

Felix said, "Pay him no heed, Majesty. He is only trying to save his pale, ugly hide."

"Quite correct, Majesty," Jean-Claude said. "I am trying to save my skin. That is why I came here today. After Isabelle's death, my life is forfeit if I return to l'Empire Céleste. I therefore seek employment elsewhere. Aragoth is the most prosperous kingdom in the world, and is likely to remain so if it can avoid tearing itself apart in civil war. And you, Majesty, are the most powerful patron in the kingdom. I therefore thought to win your favor with a gift, but what gift suits a queen, except perhaps her greatest enemy's head on a pike? Alas, instead of gladness and honor, I am met with scorn and abuse."

Alejandro looked at him askance, and Jean-Claude could only hope the man was as honorable as he seemed.

Felix said, "Your Majesty, trust not the traitor. One who has betrayed another will betray you as well."

Jean-Claude smiled inwardly, for arguing about his character was infinitely easier than arguing about his facts; character was such a pliable thing. "And whom have I betrayed, sirrah? My disgrace comes not from disloyalty but from defeat. Protecting Isabelle was my singular duty and I failed, as any man may do. Alas, Grand Leon is not merciful toward merely human frailty and I have no wish to serve him as a bloodhollow. Queen Margareta is said to be more pragmatic, and more in need of allies. Thus I seek an elegant solution, securing a new position for myself by means of revenge on the man who robbed me of Isabelle and you of Kantelvar."

Margareta said, "Who is this enemy you speak of?"

"You mean your lapdog here hasn't told you?" Jean-Claude pointed at Felix with his nose. "Surely with all the resources at his disposal, he could have done more in the last four days than capture poor Xaviera."

Felix's face darkened with anger, but Margareta said, "Felix's actions are not at issue here. Nor will I tolerate any more circumlocutions. Answer the questions put to you or die."

"Does that mean I won't die if I do answer?" Jean-Claude said.

"That depends how well we like the answers."

"That hardly seems fair. I can only guarantee truth, not happiness."

"The name. Now!"

"As you wish, though the name alone will do you no good." And now the big gamble. Every good con involved making the mark think he'd figured out the trick. The question was how much the queen knew about Kantelvar's most recent activities. "Thornscar."

The queen scowled, but the hitherto-silent Príncipe Julio started in his seat.

Jean-Claude addressed the false príncipe. "I see Your Highness recognizes the name." If Jean-Claude guessed aright, Kantelvar had tapped him to play the part of the fictional assassin when he hired Nufio to murder Jean-Claude. An assassin with a limp, and bodyguards.

Margareta wheeled in her seat. "You knew about this? You!"

Julio shrank from her anger. "No. I mean I know the name, but I did not know this." Cautiously, like a male spider approaching a hungry female, he leaned toward the queen and whispered urgently in her ear. Jean-Claude could not imagine Kantelvar would have trusted such a cringing creature with the truth, only with the cover story.

Margareta's eyes narrowed and then rounded. She brushed Julio away and returned her attention to Jean-Claude, watching him over steepled, pudgy fingers. "Tell me about this Thornscar."

Jean-Claude held his glee close and tight; the hook was set. "There's not much to tell. The name itself seems to be a nom de guerre. He is a man who had a grudge against Kantelvar and all his works, including Isabelle's marriage. The only other target I know of is a man I haven't been able to track down yet. At least I assume Clìmacio is a man's name."

The false príncipe, now fully absorbed in the conversation, did not manage to suppress a twitch at the mention of that name. *Score one for Adel, bless her.*

"I suggest, therefore, that your best and simplest option is to use this unfortunate individual as bait in a trap."

"Clìmacio is dead," Clìmacio said. "He died months ago."

"Ahh," Jean-Claude said, contriving to look disappointed. "So much for the simple solution."

Margareta said, "You claim to know where this assassin is."

"No. I claim to know how to find him, but for that I will need the Naval Orrery."

"And how do you intend to use it?"

"To find his ship, of course."

"He is lying," Felix said. "He should not be let out of this room with blood in his body."

Jean-Claude glared at Felix. "Thornscar killed Isabelle, and I will see him dead! By my hand!" He returned his attention to Margareta. "In this, our causes align perfectly. Let me slay this man for you."

Margareta tapped her fingertips together, and Jean-Claude bit down hard on his tongue. He could do no work on the queen that she could not do better herself. She must have been going mad trying to figure out who had apparently killed Kantelvar, and now her false prince had confirmed that the assailant was real. And what if she refused? There were still ten guards in the room. If he could take the man behind him in the throat, he could snare the man's sword. And how would Alejandro react? That he had not yet tried to sell Jean-Claude's secrets for his wife's safety was hopeful.

At last the queen said, "I would sooner trust a scorpion in my boot than your intentions."

Jean-Claude tasted victory. She was hooked. "I, on the other hand, trust your intentions implicitly. There is nothing you wouldn't do to secure your position, and you cannot afford to leave Thornscar gliding in the wind. In this we are utterly aligned, or do you really think I want him to escape? He murdered my princess." Jean-Claude had no trouble conjuring rage to back his words, only in restraining it.

Margareta's face contorted with the ferocity of some inner battle. As a traitor and a conspirator herself, she was primed to see plots everywhere. If most people judged the world by the view they saw in the mirror, how much worse must it be for a Glasswalker sorceress?

"You will go to the orrery," Margareta said. "You will find this Thorn-scar's ship."

Jean-Claude exhaled in authentic relief and bowed to her. "Your Majesty is most wise."

Felix spat, "This is a mistake. He is dangerous."

"That is why you will go to guard him and ensure he does as he has promised. And if he complies, you will bring him back unharmed. In the meantime, Alejandro and I have a visit to pay to his father."

CHAPTER
Eighteen

Isabelle clawed her way through a fog of pain and fever. *Where am I?* Her bones felt like hot coals cooking her flesh and blistering her skin. Was this how a cut of beef felt on the spit, roasting in its own juices? If there was any part of her that did not ache, she could not name it. *The vaporization point of self equals the limit of suffering as it approaches agony.* Call it Isabelle's first theorem of pain. She hadn't thought it possible to feel worse than she did after her father set his bloodshadow on her.

It was humbling to know she had been wrong.

The last thing she remembered was the stinging bite of the vapor filling her nose and her lungs. And then a darkness full of sharp-edged, rasping dreams, and screams, and now—

The creak of heavy ropes under tension reached her awareness, and not all of the heaving and dipping in her gut was a product of her uneasy flesh. She really was being tossed slowly up and down.

Skyship, she surmised, and the implications of that were enough to force her upward, outward through the haze of sickness. *Kantelvar.* The artifex had kidnapped her and now they had left San Augustus, left the Craton Massif. She was en route to whatever stable he meant to breed her in.

She opened her eyes—they felt glued shut and only opened partway—and found herself in a ship's cabin. Thick-glassed portholes let in a thin, watery light, but even that poor illumination stung her brain like a thousand tiny needles. She was bundled in blankets and tied into a hammock that was wrapped around her like a sausage skin.

Cold air scraped at her face, chilling her fever sweat, and her breath steamed. Where had this winter come from? But she knew the answer to that if only the pudding of her brain would set up properly. *Altitude.* A few thousand extra meters of elevation turned summer to winter. A few thousand more made men delirious right before it turned them into frozen corpses. Kantelvar was insane in the lower sky. How much worse would the upper airs make him?

Isabelle tried to shrug her way out of the blankets. If she could just get her hand free, she could undo these ties, which looked as if they'd been put into place to keep her from thrashing in her fever.

A sharp pain knifed up her right arm when she tried to press out with her elbow. She grabbed her right arm with her left.

She grabbed a stump.

A stump!

Horror flooded her veins as her left hand crawled, spiderlike, over the place where her right arm should have been, seeking something that wasn't there and finding a metal stub instead. Kantelvar had removed her arm at the shoulder. Saints in Paradise, he'd *dismembered* her. Disbelief and denial flooded Isabelle's mind. Her gorge rose in pure visceral terror, and she only barely managed to roll herself far enough to vomit over the side of her cocoon. The convulsions seemed to go on forever, even long after she'd run out of bile to disgorge.

One good thing about the retching was that, by the time she was done, she was too spent for panic. No wonder she ached with fever. Amputation was surely one of the greatest insults a body could endure.

Why did he disarm me? Kantelvar might have been completely mad, but he never did anything without a reason. If he'd wanted to cripple or contain her, he would have taken her *good* hand. Why take the *abnormal* hand?

Understanding struck her nearly breathless. He'd cut off her identifying mark, and she could think of only two reasons for that. Either he wanted to conceal her identity—from whom?—or he wanted to convince someone else that she was dead. She imagined her absolutely identifiable bloody stump dropped somewhere near her chambers. Her countrymen would cry murder, and Grand Leon would demand justice, but Carlemmo would die, and the Aragothic court would fracture and begin fighting amongst themselves. The mercenaries from Oberholz and Vecci would pick sides and draw their home powers into the fray, and Brathon would take the opportunity to challenge Aragoth's overskies influence. All the powers of the world would descend on Aragoth like wolves on a wounded bear. Blood would run in rivers. Kantelvar would have his age of ruin, and she . . . did he honestly expect her to *comply* with his wish that she bear some unfortunate child that he could twist into a counterfeit Savior?

Surely he must realize she would oppose him at every step, and just as surely he had accounted for her resistance, just as he had accounted for everything else. He had been planning this for more than a thousand years. He had to have contingency plans for every conceivable opposition, which meant that to thwart him, she had to do something inconceivable.

She certainly couldn't do anything while she was hanging here like a smoked ham. The straps around the hammock clearly hadn't been arranged to prevent escape, or they would not have been placed so that she could, after a short eternity of squirming, shrugging, and sweating, get hold of the first buckle with her teeth. She worried the leather and brass like an exhausted terrier. Her neck strained, and her jaw ached, and her stump burned with fresh agony every time it hung up in the folds of the blankets, but she did not relent. Tears and drool and sweat were streaming down her face by the time she worked the first buckle free.

One down, four to go.

Ah, but now she worked her good arm loose, unlatched the next buckle, and peeled off the blanket to see what had become of her starboard limb.

The arm had been cut off just below the shoulder. The stump had been covered with a cap of quondam metal, a gleaming hemisphere that swirled with shades of pink and purple and glittered with motes of firefly light. There was no obvious seam where metal ended and flesh began; the one flowed smoothly into the other like twilight into full darkness. It was so strange and unexpected, she even forgot her horror in the fascination of it. She ran her fingers over the metal and found it smooth and warm and sensate. How could that be?

The fever heat that had filled her awareness slowly ebbed, as if her waking allowed a pent-up reservoir of pain to drain away.

She finished unbuckling the straps; not as easy as it should have been without her right wrist to use as a brace. She might not have used her crippled hand for much, but she used her right *arm* all the time.

She swung her legs out of the hammock opposite the direction of her vomit and tried to stand, but the deck rocked, her knees buckled, and she reflexively tried to catch herself with an arm that wasn't there. She sprawled across the planking like a dropped jelly-floater, gritting her teeth against the white, sharp pain where she'd banged her stump. Perhaps she ought to just lie here for a moment, catch her breath, and gather her strength.

And then what? She was certainly no physical threat to Kantelvar. She was not going to be able to overpower the ship's crew, lock them all in the hold, and sail this ship back to San Augustus by herself. Persuading Kantelvar to turn back from the culmination of sixteen centuries of obsession did not seem likely, either.

She wanted Jean-Claude to rescue her, but Kantelvar had said Jean-Claude was dead.

No.

But what if he was telling the truth?

No!

But Jean-Claude never would have let this happen to her. Over his dead body, he would have said. He was her oldest and dearest friend. He had raised her, served her, protected her against the whole world. Why? She was not his child, his blood. Because of her, he'd never taken a wife. Because of her, he'd never had children of his own. *Because of me.* And now he was gone. A flush of sweltering grief filled Isabelle's chest and boiled up behind her eyes, forcing out tears as no physical pain could. And in the dry tinder of her soul, anger sparked a flame.

Kantelvar, I will kill you for this. I will see you dead.

But how?

Something inconceivable.

Isabelle carefully, stiffly, picked herself up and searched her surroundings. From a set of hooks on the ceiling hung several glass bottles with tubes dangling from them, just like the ones Kantelvar had poked into Marie's arm. Each was filmed with a thin residue of saints only knew what concoctions, and there were bruises on her arm where clearly needles had been. Had he been keeping her alive or asleep? Where in the world was this ship?

She wobbled to the porthole. It was amazing how unbalanced she felt without her right arm. She leaned against the cabin wall, sucking down deep drafts of thin air, and peered out through the thick glass, but there was no sight of land, only endless banks and shoals of clouds.

She tried the cabin door and found it locked. *Damn!* But what else did she expect?

She shivered. Outside the heavy blankets in the hammock, she'd been left with nothing but a light linen shift that was insufficient for this cold weather. She retrieved a blanket and a strap from the hammock, draped the fabric over her shoulders, and tried to belt it at the waist, another process frustrated by her lack of a limb.

Breaker's blight! If only she still had her wrist. She couldn't quite bend far enough to use her stump for a brace or lever on the buckle. *Stretch!* A hair-raising tingle raced down her neck as her mind sent commands to muscles that were no longer—*there*.

An invisible, intangible force pressed the belt buckle to her waist. What's more, she could feel the metal against her nonexistent wrist. She gasped in astonishment and let go with both . . . hands? The sensation vanished. The belt and buckle fell to the floor.

Isabelle looked down at her left hand, open in front of her, and her stump. She hadn't imagined that. It had really happened. She had touched the buckle with a hand she didn't have. She had heard tell of soldiers who had lost limbs but retained some sensation from those truncated appendages, an itchy foot on a missing leg, or a trick elbow on a missing arm. Phantom limbs, they were called. What if this sheath, this quondam metal, or whatever potions Kantelvar had fed her from those vials, somehow made those sensations real?

What if this is sorcery? Kantelvar's blood ciphers had claimed she was l'Étincelle, that she had the power to animate the inanimate. But how could that be? How could she have gone twenty-four years without manifesting any sorcery at all? Had it been dormant all this time? It was true that some sorcerers needed prodding to awaken their powers. Her father's methods were well founded even if his application of them was needlessly cruel. Might it be that bonding with this strange metal had been enough to rouse hers from hibernation?

Or was it just a property of the metal itself? Kantelvar needed Isabelle to live in order to complete his plan, but he had cut her arm off anyway. He must have been confident of her survival, which meant he must also have been confident in his surgical technique, which included the metal sheath. That suggested it was an operation he had done before, perhaps the same operation that was performed on clerics having their limbs replaced with clockworks in the ceremony of Exaltation. That would explain how Kantelvar and other priests who wore quondam prostheses controlled them.

But she didn't have a prosthesis, just a stump, yet she'd pressed the buckle to her belly.

Exactly what caused this phenomenon was a question for later. Right now the only thing that mattered was whether or not she could exploit it. Isabelle knelt and extended what would have been her right arm to the buckle. *Just push*. Nothing happened. She closed her eyes and tried to remember what it felt like. A tingle down her spine and along her arm. The cap on her stump hummed with a vibration she felt deep in her bones. Out at arm's length, the ghost of her wormfinger twitched.

Her wrist brushed the buckle. *Yes!* She held on to the sensation and bumped the buckle around the floor, trailing its strap. She used the front, back, and sides of her invisible, intangible limb. *That's it. That's the way*. She opened her eyes and almost lost it, but she could feel its presence, its shape in the air.

Like a kitten obsessing over a shiny button, Isabelle swatted the buckle around the cabin until she was satisfied she could do it on a whim. It was too bad she had manifested a phantom wormfinger instead of a whole ghostly hand, but this phenomenon seemed to be taking advantage of her body's memory of its missing flesh, and it could not remember sensations it had never experienced . . . unless it could be trained to *imagine* that sensation. She knew what it felt like to flex the fingers of her *left* hand. Could she *imagine* that on the right?

She closed her eyes and placed her phantom palm on the buckle. *Imagine a hand there, a thumb jutting out, four fingers spreading*. An electric shiver raced down her neck to the stump of her shoulder. She felt more than heard a buzz like a thousand ants tiptoeing across the metal surface. She pushed past the distraction. Imagined her hand closing on the button. *Don't think about flexing, just . . . flex.*

The buckle budged. The weight of it pressed against her imaginary fingers and thumb. She lifted. Abstract muscles contracted though there was nothing for them to pull against. The buckle came off the floor. The tingling burrowed deep inside her and settled into her bones. A faint light leaked in through her eyelids.

She opened her eyes and gasped. Pink and purple light limned her stump, like the stormfire that caught on the masts of ships during a squall. The strange glow extended, sketching the shape of her phantom arm in the air. A glowing mist of pink and violet filled the volume, and glittering motes of rose and lilac sprang to life in the mist. She might have been wearing a glove made of stars in a nebula. And in the grip of those stars hung the buckle.

"How extraordinary," she breathed. She swished the buckle around, marveling at the feel of it, fascinated by the cold sparks that sprayed and spiraled away from her arm whenever she moved it. This was l'Étincelle, it had to be . . . and that fact had more implications than she could begin to consider right now.

She dropped the buckle and picked it up again several times, just to be sure she could. Her phantasmal fingers were as clumsy as a toddler's, but perhaps ease would come with practice. She tried to pick up the belt by the leather, but no matter how she focused, her spark-flesh passed through leather as if it weren't there.

She moved on to grabbing other things. Her spark-hand passed right through the wooden planking, the blanket fabric, and her own flesh, but found good purchase on a metal sconce and the glass from the portal. So what did all these things have in common? Fabric, wood, and flesh were or had been living things, whereas neither metal nor glass ever had. It was a correlation that bore further investigation.

Now that the spark-limb had manifested, it showed no inclination to disappear. Every sorcery had its blazon: crimson shadows, silver eyes, a crest of feathers instead of hair, or . . . this.

And if she could not find some way to rid herself of it, she could never return to civilization. L'Étincelle was not one of the canon sorceries. No one would recognize it as a saintblooded gift. The Temple would dub her an abomination, and for that the remedy was Absolute Confession, excruciation unto death.

No doubt that was part of Kantelvar's plan, to bring forth her blazon and thereby isolate her from all possible allies, to convince her beyond all hope that there was no way out for her, just as he had done to that wretched imposter on the throne.

Change the Rules, she had told him, a participant in the ubiquitous delusion that other people's problems were easier to solve than one's own.

So make them someone else's problems. Even if she had no future, others might, Jean-Claude and Marie first and foremost, and her handmaids and everyone else who had been kind to her. She would not leave them a future of war if she could help it. If she could not return to Aragoth, if she could not warn them of Kantelvar's manipulation, she must get someone else to do it for her.

Príncipe Julio. If indeed Kantelvar intended to breed her to the not-actually-a-prince, he had to take her to wherever he was standing stud.

Having a goal was good, but it did not tell her how to reach it. She sat in the corner of the cabin, her feet braced on the chilly floor, massaging her face with her flesh-hand. *Think!* She had no other weapon but her mind. *What is inconceivable? To Kantelvar?* She could not overpower him, nor, she admitted ruefully, outwit him. He had arranged everything to force her to capitulate, to bend to his will or be broken. He had blocked off every possible retreat.

Or was that the answer? Isabelle's head came up and she stared into space with the same tentative extension she felt when a new proof suggested itself to her imagination. If only she could reel it in without breaking the gossamer thread of reason.

Deep in his warped and bitter mind, Kantelvar expected her to fight him. He did not expect her to give up. Her capitulation was inconceivable. So what if she inverted the equation, agreed wholeheartedly to his plan, dragged him forward instead of pulling him back? He would not have prepared for that. Once she had the bit in her teeth, she would run as far and as fast as she could. Could she snatch control from him?

It was not a game she was well equipped to play, but she had no better idea. Besides, a plan like this would make Jean-Claude . . . cackle. The idea twisted her mouth in a painful smile, but it also gave her the strength to shove off the floor. She adjusted her blanket cloak and knocked loudly on the cabin door. Several minutes of repeated hammering finally brought footsteps to the door.

Keys rattled in the lock. Isabelle checked her posture and steadied her nerve. The door swung inward on well-oiled hinges. She stopped it with her foot when it was just wide enough to see out. An artifex stood beyond.

Not Kantelvar, was her first impression. Though he wore the Temple's saffron and a deep cowl and carried the artifex's quondam staff, this man was tall and straight and lacked mechanical appendages. Yet it was in Kantelvar's voice that he said, "Good day, Your Highness. I am glad to see you awake at last."

"You've changed," she said. She had no trouble keeping her tone harsh. She had to convert to his cause quickly, but not so fast that he doubted her sincerity.

Kantelvar chuckled, an eerily familiar sound, and pulled back his hood to reveal an unfamiliar face, square jawed and blunt nosed, but festooned with a sapphire lens where his right eye ought to have been, and his mouth sewn in a circle around his speaking grille. Long angry incisions, crudely stitched together, radiated from the implanted metal. His left eye was glazed and unfocused. His head had been recently shaved, and a segmented metal tube ran from the base of his skull, down the back of his neck, to a large backpack.

Isabelle had thought there was nothing left in Kantelvar's repertoire of madness that would shock her, but this left her throat tight. *His mind is in the machinery.* That was how he had survived since the age of Rüul, passed down from artifex to artifex with occasional stopovers in other useful clerics. His hosts thought they were being Exalted and honored by being conjoined with the Builder's mechanisms, when in fact they were being hulled out like an apple infested with a worm.

He said, "The body you saw was not the first I wore, or the second, or the sixteenth. The flesh is not made to endure as the soul is. When muscles rot and bones break, they must be exchanged. Céleste promised that the Savior would come. I must redeem her word. The prophecy must be fulfilled. She promised she would come back to me."

Kantelvar's ardor gave Isabelle an extra chill. He had been serving Saint Céleste for over sixteen hundred years, and he expected her to return. Oh, unfortunate woman if she did, for who could live up to so much accumulated expectation?

"What happens to those whose flesh you conscript?" Isabelle asked. Was Kantelvar's latest victim still alive inside his skull, awake and aware of what had happened to him? His left eye swiveled and seemed to focus for a moment on Isabelle, an expression of despair rippling across that side of his face, before swiveling away again.

Kantelvar said, "My hosts are volunteers, eager to pledge their souls to the Builder's service."

Isabelle felt like someone had knotted her innards in their fists. She wanted to scream, to run away, but there was nowhere to go, no exit but forward down the gullet of madness.

She said, "Let me guess. By now, everyone in San Augustus thinks we're both dead. You chopped my arm off because that's the surest way to identify me, and you shed your old skin like a locust. It was the only way you could be sure of making a clean escape." And if it had worked, no one would *ever* come looking for her.

"Very good," Kantelvar said as if to a pupil who had just solved a difficult conundrum. "Can you deduce what happens next?"

Isabelle summoned her court face, the mask of indifference that had served her so well in le Comte des Zephyrs's house. "I imagine Carlemmo will die and there will be a war. What happens to me is, of course, entirely up to you."

On that carefully balanced note, Kantelvar's expression twitched rapidly between a scowl, a smile, and a grimace. It was a lot like watching lightning in the clouds, random, spasmodic, and violent. He didn't have good control of this new visage, which only made sense. If having a phantom arm took some getting used to, having a whole new body must have been especially problematic.

Finally, Kantelvar smoothed his face and said, "You have a destiny—"

"At the moment, my destiny seems to be to freeze to death. I don't suppose you managed to bring me any clothes." If she could engage him on purely practical concerns, perhaps she could segue into acceptance of his plan.

Kantelvar hesitated a heartbeat. "Of course, but it will require you to let the door open."

Isabelle didn't want him in the room with her, but it would be impossible to win his trust if she showed her fear.

She stepped back. Kantelvar moved aside, and an omnimaton, the one she had seen in Kantelvar's workshop, entered the room, carrying her trunk. The clockwork man looked most like great a copper skeleton with viscera made of cables, gears, cogs, and springs. Its chest and shoulders were clad in a carapace of coppery plates. Its head was a clamshell atop its broad shoulders, a metallic hillock set with a single gemlike orb that she could only think of as an eye.

As the door opened, Kantelvar's gaze fell upon her spark-arm. Kantelvar's quilted-together face was, as always, unreadable, but his backpack gurgled excitedly. "L'Étincelle," he breathed, the word leaking from his voice tube like a ghost loosed from Torment. "Your sorcery."

Isabelle resisted the urge to recoil from his interest. *Don't demur, debut.*

She turned her rotation into a ballroom pirouette and extended her arm in a graceful wave. "Is this your work?" she asked. "It's beautiful." And she was surprised to find that it was true. Its pure aesthetic delighted the eye despite the mutilation it represented.

"It is your birthright," he said. "The shadowburns your father inflicted upon you before your maturity served to suppress it, but his influence has been expelled, as it was with your handmaid." He gestured to the tubes and bottles on their hooks.

It was all Isabelle could do to keep the yelp from her voice as she asked, "Marie, where is she?" *Please let her be on the ship.*

"There was not time to collect her. I am sorry."

Boiling outrage nearly shattered Isabelle's reserve. *You just left her there! Stowed away in a lost dark closet with no one to feed her or care for her!* It was all she could do to keep herself from launching herself at him and trying to claw his mismatched eyes out.

Instead, she ate her fury and said, "I hope you have plans to replace her."

Kantelvar hesitated. He had not been expecting such coldness from her. "Indeed, when we arrive at my aerie, I will provide you with a suitable handmaid."

As if that would atone for his sins. "And when will that be?"

"By sunset," Kantelvar said, drawing back into his usual, carefully clipped mode of speech. He gestured to the trunk. "When you are properly attired, the door is unlocked. I suspect you will want to explore the ship and assure yourself of its safety. When you are ready, I will be in the chart room." He bowed himself out.

Isabelle leaned against the door, shaking with rage, but she dared not let it out. She had to cultivate pliancy and feign ambition. Not for the first time, she wished for Jean-Claude's silver tongue. Her musketeer could talk birds out of their feathers and make the outrageous sound not only plausible but sensible, while she had trouble holding anything in her mouth that she did not also hold in her heart.

She waited for her fury to subside, then tried the door. It opened onto the quarterdeck, which was strung with an amazing spiderweb of ropes and pulleys, rigging even more complex than an ordinary skyship's. The extra ropes were gathered at a single station amidships, manned, or rather machined, by the omnimaton. From there, the machine could do the work of twenty men without ever leaving its post. Someone could really disrupt the ship's operation by fouling those lines, but to what good end? Kantelvar was taking her where she needed to go.

She considered her spark-arm. If l'Étincelle sorcery revolved around giving life to the inanimate, the omnimaton surely counted. Might her power allow her to control the machines?

Alas, her sorcery was a phenomenon with no theory behind it. She felt no instinctive connection with the clockwork man, and she hardly dared experiment. The last thing she needed was to have another limb or three ripped off. Indeed, it occurred to her that she didn't need limbs at all for the service Kantelvar wanted from her. She imagined herself limbless and bloated with child and shuddered in disgust. Sometimes it didn't pay to have a vivid imagination.

A frigid breeze curled itself around her bare legs and chased her back inside. She opened the trunk and found her clothing the way she had left it. It took her some time to get herself dressed, especially since only one hand would interact with her clothing, and it was trembling with fatigue. She ended up looking like something a hurricane had thrown together, but it kept the cold out and the wind off. She found herself mentally sketching out ideas for a mail glove to wear on her spark-hand so she could use it to manipulate the otherwise inaccessible class of soft objects.

Kantelvar had said he would await her in the ship's chart room, and she really did want to go in there and get a look at the ship's orrery—hopefully, she could discover where she was relative to where she had been and where she was bound—but first she wanted an unimpeded look around.

She climbed up onto the windswept deck of the sloop, where the high, cold sky raked thin, icy fingers through her unbound hair, and the pale gray light of evening stung her eyes. She peered over the rails, but the Craton Massif was nowhere to be seen. How far away was she? Did anyone down there have any inkling where she had gone? Was there anyone left to care? She clung to the idea that Jean-Claude was still alive, looking for her. To believe anything else was utter despair. She said a solemn prayer for him, wherever he was.

Stopping every dozen paces to catch her breath, she explored the ship from stem to stern. It had no launches that might be used to escape. She found Kantelvar's cabin, the armory, the powder magazine, and the keel chamber barred, but beyond that, her captor seemed content to allow her parole. She found holds provisioned for a long voyage, stores of lumber, sailcloth, tar, paint, and all the other things required to keep a skyship functional. Practically every barrel contained some potential for sabotage—if she was willing to destroy the ship she was standing on—but now was not the time for such grandiose gestures.

She made her way to the chart room and, in the absence of anyone to announce her presence, rapped on the door.

There was no answer. She tried the latch. The door glided open on soundless hinges and she entered once more into quiet dimness, though neither so quiet nor so dark as the hold, owing to the emerald glow of the orrery's simulacrasphere and the sibilant whisper of the aethervalve matrix under the pedestal.

The orrery was larger and more complex than the one aboard the *Santa Anna*. Its green-glowing, aether-filled simulacrasphere was wider than Isabelle could have stretched with two arms. The cubic expansion of volume with radius meant this display was a hundred times more detailed than the courier ship's had been. Hundreds of blobs and specks of light floated in the tank, each one representing an individual ship or skyland. The great number and minuscule size of the images meant that Kantelvar had increased the scale to include as much of the deep sky as possible.

Kantelvar, hunched before the main instrument battery, did not immediately stir at her entrance. Bent over like that, with his hood pulled forward and his gurgling hump ascendant on his back, he looked a great deal more like the Kantelvar of old.

That hump had to have something to do with his serial immortality. Perhaps it was the seat of his consciousness, some kind of soul bottle. If that were true, if she could gain control of it, she could force him to unravel his own schemes.

Unfortunately, she had barely padded halfway across the room when the mad artifex lifted his cowled head. "G-goood d-day, Cél—Isabelle." His voice was low and muddy.

Had he just confused her with Saint Céleste, or was he merely waking from sixteen-hundred-year-old dreams?

Kantelvar came around from behind the orrery. "I take it you have satisfied yourself of the ship's integrity?"

"It does not seem likely to fall out of the sky. Where are we bound?"

"To my aerie, a skyland in the upper reaches."

"Uncharted, I assume."

Kantelvar chuckled. "No. If it was uncharted that would risk some fool coming along and discovering it. It's just mislabeled. It was originally discovered by a merchant explorer with an eye toward selling its location to the highest bidder. I appropriated his chartstone from him and distributed the shards to all the skyfaring nations, along with a description that labeled it a broken reef, a very dangerous navigation hazard, an effective bit of occultation if I do say so myself."

Isabelle smothered a grimace. So there was a chartstone shard in the fabled Naval Orrery at San Augustus that *could* lead a rescuer straight to her, if anyone was even looking for her, but instead showed her destination as a place to be avoided.

"And that is where my husband awaits, the man who tried to kill you. Don't you think that will be a little awkward?" Julio, Thornscar, or whoever he was, ought to be a viable ally against Kantelvar, if she could convince him she too was Kantelvar's enemy. Hard to do if she pretended to be Kantelvar's ally.

"Fear Julio not. He is defeated. He escaped from confinement once, but not again. Ere your marriage is consummated, he will have had a change of mind."

Isabelle was about to ask how Kantelvar could be so sure when understanding and loathing hit her all at once. She stared at the metal tube leading into the back of Kantelvar's skull. Except it wasn't his skull. It was the skull of his current body. Kantelvar's *mind* was in that gurgling hump in his backpack. "You're going to take Julio's body," she breathed.

"Julio made that choice of his own free will when he decided to oppose the Builder."

Isabelle had never experienced sky sickness, but she imagined it paled next to this gut-sick, soul-deep dizziness. Kantelvar had expressed a deep devotion to Saint Céleste, but what if it was more than that? What if this was infatuation, an unfulfilled, unrequited desire, a festering obsession of sixteen hundred years? He wanted to prove himself to her across the millennia, to fulfill her prophecy and win her favor . . . her love. Now, in Isabelle, who apparently resembled her down to her sorcery, he had finally found . . . what? A proxy? A reincarnation? He meant to complete the circle, become the father of the Savior and the husband to his beloved.

By the Savior—the *real* Savior, not the abomination Kantelvar envisaged—she would not . . . she would rather die than be taken by this man. She would sooner throw herself from the rail and fall forever into the Gloom. But that was not the plan. The plan was to take his plan and run with it. If he really imagined Isabelle the reincarnation of Saint Céleste, his long-lost love, then she ought to be able to use that to her advantage.

She said, "I should speak with Julio before you . . . decant him."

"There would be no point—"

"Is there not?" Isabelle asked. "He tried to murder me aboard the *Santa Anna*." This was not true, but it was the official fiction.

"And I will not give him the opportunity to try again," Kantelvar said, so caught up in his own lies that he'd forgotten that Isabelle knew better.

"Yes, you will be there to protect me," Isabelle said, "but I have a right to confront the man who tried to kill me."

"To what purpose? He is full of lies and deception, and he will only try to confuse you. Nothing he says can be trusted."

"Damn his lies," Isabelle said. "I don't want to question him, but I cannot very well spit in his eyes after they become your eyes." It was pure fabrication, but this struggle was not about the truth. It was about obsession and desire and madness.

Kantelvar twitched. He must have been suspicious of her enthusiasm, but he couldn't resist drawing her deeper into his fantasy where Julio was the villain of the piece. "That might . . . be arranged," he said.

"As soon as we make landfall."

Nineteen

The Solar had mostly dissolved into the hazy horizon by the time Isabelle and Kantelvar debarked the sloop onto the ice-rimed quay of his estate's tiny harbor. Despite the omnimaton's inhuman skill, it had taken the better part of the afternoon to make a safe approach to the slowly spinning, slightly wobbling column of rock. From a distance, the skyland's wobbling movement looked innocent, even comical, like a child's top just starting to come off its balance. But the very fact that one could observe its complete rotation in less time than it took to enjoy afternoon tea meant that, up close, it was a mountainside whirling by at a brisk running clip, carrying enough force to smash any incautious ship to flinders.

The whole skyland couldn't have been more than two kilometers in diameter, all of it jagged and barren with patches of snow. The mooring cove was little more than a crack in the side of the mountain. The only building Isabelle could see was a turret that squatted at the top of a short narrow stair at the end of the quay. The rest of whatever this place contained must have been underground.

There was a moment, as Kantelvar stepped from ship to shore, that

Isabelle almost thought she could grab him by his hood, give him a shove, and send him tumbling into the bottomless sky, but an omnimaton stood between them, ready to intervene, and even if she did manage to tip him over, it would not necessarily improve her situation. Without any way to control the omnimaton that ran the ship, she would succeed only in trapping herself here.

The moment passed, and Isabelle followed Kantelvar onto the ice-glazed stone and up the slippery stairs. Her breath steamed, and the wind clawed at her motley skirts. Her heart hammered even from the minimal effort of climbing the steps. There wasn't enough air up here. Kantelvar took her into a narrow crevice, through an even narrower door of thickly banded wood, and into a dark, round, low-ceilinged chamber. It was an improvement over the outside only in that it was out of the wind. The stones seemed to have absorbed more than their fair share of the cold and were greedy to exchange it for the heat of her body.

"Is it always this frigid in here?" she asked. "I cannot raise a child in a glacier."

Kantelvar said, "The interior is more comfortable." He gestured toward a short, barrel-vaulted corridor that terminated at a massive stone slab. The slab rested in a groove in the floor and was abraded with great curved striations. She deduced that the stone itself was circular, a great wheel that could be rolled back into the wall.

Before she could turn her mind to the mechanism by which this might be accomplished, Kantelvar raised his staff and spoke ancient words in the Saintstongue. *"And there will be a haven secure against ignorance and depravity."*

There was a hiss and a clank like steam boiling under the lid of a kettle, and the door rolled away. A breath of warmer air from inside caressed her face and melted the frost that had started to form on her eyelashes. Kantelvar bowed her into an antechamber with rolling stone doors at either end and a partially reconstructed omnimaton stationed in an alcove between them.

The machine was little more than a metal torso, a clamshell head, and a single arm that connected to a gear train that operated the doors. How did Kantelvar control the machines? This one seemed to want a passphrase, but would it take such a phrase from anyone, or was there some other element required? Was it the staff? This omni-doorman could not have seen the staff when Kantelvar first brandished it.

Kantelvar said, "*From this fortress at the end of all things, the Savior shall appear.*"

The inner door opened and Kantelvar gestured Isabelle through.

The doors rolled shut behind her with a scraping noise like the sealing of a tomb . . . her tomb, for this was where he meant to bury her, to impregnate her and plant her like a bulb from which the flower of some wicked salvation would spring.

A thick, frigid darkness enveloped Isabelle until Kantelvar rapped his staff on the ground and the head of it crackled to life, filling the room with a pale green glow. It was a foyer of smooth-fitting, polished stone with marble benches for seating, rather like a courtyard nook but without any access to the sky. If Kantelvar had his way, she would never see daylight again. The idea made her cold to the core.

Isabelle started as the room's interior door creaked open and a slim woman entered. She had soulful eyes and skin so pale that it might never have seen the sun. She wore a gray livery and a coif that did nothing to enliven her aspect. Kantelvar said not a word but made a quick, complex gesture. The woman turned, smiled brightly to Isabelle, and offered her a deep curtsy.

Kantelvar said, "This is Gretl, my thrall. She will serve as your handmaid until a permanent one can be obtained. She's a deaf-mute. I'll teach you the signs you need to command her, but for now, to let her stand up, you should lift your left toe."

Isabelle pulled the hem of her skirt back and flicked her toe up. Gretl stood up at once and watched her attentively.

Isabelle asked, "How many servants do you have?" Slaves of a cruel master could be potential allies. Indeed, the mere fact that people lived here meant certain logistical necessities had to be met. The icy rock outside was no place to grow food. Were there regular shipments of provender from the outside?

"Six infelix patrueles, all unhallowed," Kantelvar said with the proprietary enthusiasm of a man describing his flock of prize sheep.

Isabelle translated the Saintstongue, "'Unfortunate cousins'?" Then she grimaced, because she wasn't supposed to know that language.

But Kantelvar was too caught up in his narrative to notice. "Yes, your cousins in fact, by some remove, the last withered branches of failed hybrid lines."

Isabelle felt she'd been slapped, but of course Kantelvar would not have trusted all his breeding efforts to just one bloodline. Isabelle must have had dozens of cousins she didn't know about . . . mustn't she? "Why 'unfortunate'?" Even asking the question filled her with dread, as if by knowing the answer, she might somehow be responsible for it.

"Culls," he said. "Hybrid sorcery tends to be messy. Only a few from each generation manage to pass multiple lineages down intact, and the more lineages are combined in one body, the smaller the chance for success. Unless they are unhallowed, killing the failures is the most merciful thing to do. They can't control their sorcery, you see, and the Temple would hunt them down as abominations and subject them to Absolute Confession."

Isabelle sickened as though she'd swallowed clotted blood. How many had he slaughtered that way? He would have murdered her, too, if she'd failed his test. "What made me any more of a success than Gretl?"

"Your blood was the final proof, but I knew it the moment I saw you grown up. Céleste lives in you, and of course your sorcery only confirms it. The first l'Étincelle in nearly two thousand years."

The ardor in his voice made Isabelle shudder, and she pulled her cloak more tightly about her shoulders.

"Are you still cold?" Kantelvar asked.

"We should confront Príncipe Julio," she said. She had to keep moving, had to keep alert for that instant she could throw him off balance.

"As you desire." He gestured her toward the open doorway and the long, dimly lit tunnel beyond.

Isabelle dreaded pressing deeper into this spider's trap, but there was nothing to be gained by going back, even if she could. She forced herself to stride through the door as if this cave were her castle. With Gretl padding silently behind, Kantelvar escorted her by storerooms, a library, a kitchen, a mess hall, and a few dozen closed doors concealing who knew what. A spiral stair twisted down into the black heart of the rock and emerged into a long, slightly curving corridor that bent out of sight to the left. Several doors adorned the right-hand wall.

Kantelvar stopped at the first door and peered through a grate in the door before unlocking it. "These are Príncipe Julio's chambers, or were before he proved himself untrustworthy." He admitted her into a lavishly appointed suite, with a large bed draped with embroidered covers, and an

elaborately carved desk with paper and pen laid out as if to compose a letter. A padded chair with an ottoman, a chest of drawers, an armoire, and tapestries depicting hunting scenes completed the fit-for-a-príncipe main room. To the left was a bathing chamber and to the right a locked door. Before it stood another omnimaton, man shaped but squatter and more cylindrical than the one that piloted the ship. It was missing one of its arms below the elbow. Its green gemstone eye flickered erratically as if reflecting distant lightning. Kantelvar displayed his staff and said in Saintstongue, *"Warder at Oblivion's gates, stand aside."*

For half a heartbeat nothing happened, then the omnimaton darted aside. It moved so swiftly that it blurred and caused wind to swirl in behind it, then stopped so still and rigid that it was all but impossible to imagine it could move at all.

Isabelle skipped backward with a startled gasp that had hardly begun by the time the warder's movement was complete.

If ever the omnimaton had been shaped by mortal hands, surely they had been driven by a mind with a wicked and unnerving sense of humor, for who could look upon such a juxtaposition of suddenness and stillness without great trepidation?

Kantelvar ignored her startlement and put his hand on a locked window flap in the door. "This is the príncipe's reduced cell. I warn you, he can be quite vulgar and he tends to spit."

And who wouldn't, if they were treated like an animal?

Isabelle said, "I understand."

Kantelvar unlatched the window and looked in. "Príncipe—huh?"

Suspended across the window was a scrap of dirty white cloth on which had been scrawled, in a brownish pigment, "No me tendrá."

You will not have me, Isabelle translated.

"Julio, what is this?" Kantelvar ripped the cloth from its frame.

There came no answer from within and the room was dark. A whiff of stale and breathless air coiled out around Isabelle's face.

"Julio, show yourself," Kantelvar said, his voice grinding like poorly meshed gears. "This gains you nothing."

From the darkness came a soft creak, almost like a rope under tension. Isabelle tried in vain to peer through the blackness, to draw some form from the shadows. What if he had been desperate enough to choose the last resort?

"If I must drag you out of there, I will, but it will go badly for you," Kantelvar said, the whine of his gears growing louder with rising alarm. He ignited the spiny tip of his staff. The heat of it made Isabelle recoil and its brightness nearly blinded her. She blinked away tears and squinted through the view slot.

A pair of feet dangled half a meter off the floor. She lifted her gaze. Julio's hands were bound behind his back, and his scarred face was bent forward around the leather belt that hung him from the lamp hook in the ceiling. His swollen tongue bulged from his mouth, and foam dripped from his lips.

Isabelle gasped in horror.

Julio twitched.

"He's still alive!" Isabelle cried. Or at least there was still some reflex left in him.

Kantelvar cursed, fumbled at his belt for a key, and jammed the toothed metal wand into the keyhole. He yanked the door open and rushed in, Isabelle close on his heels.

Julio twitched on the end of his line, tongue lolling. Kantelvar tucked the spiny-headed staff in the crook of his arm and drew a long knife from his belt. "I'll cut him loose. Catch him as he comes down. He's no good if his brain dies."

Isabelle wasn't sure how she was supposed to catch anyone with just one hand, especially a man who weighed half again as much as she, but she grabbed his shirt to pull him close as he fell.

Yet before Kantelvar could swing and cut the strap, Julio dropped. The belt around his neck flapped loose, and he landed in a crouch. His hands came free of their bindings. Their fake bindings.

Isabelle just had time to realize it was all a trick before the príncipe spat out the swollen tongue and lunged at Kantelvar. No scream or snarl betrayed his rage, only a blade-sharp gleam in his silvery eyes as he grabbed for the staff. Trapped in the momentum of her intent, Isabelle heaved on Julio's shirt. He jerked against her grip, yanking them both off balance. Isabelle stumbled and let go.

Julio's grab came up short. Kantelvar staggered back. His wide-eyed surprise gave way to a scowling rage harrowed with grooves of fury. "Breaker's get!" He drove the spiny tip of his staff into Julio's shoulder, and webs of lightning twined around the príncipe's body.

Julio's limbs jerked, and the sparks dragged an agonized shriek from his throat. He collapsed in a twitching heap but still managed to curse Kantelvar. "Heretic! You defile the Builder!"

"I serve the Builder!" Kantelvar roared. His sapphire eye blazed. He smashed the spiked ball down on Julio's leg and jolted him again. "I gave you a chance to join me. I showed you the destiny He has for you. You would have been the father of the Savior. But you turned your back on Him!" He raised his staff to strike again. Flecks of blood fanned from its tip.

Aghast, Isabelle lurched between them, spreading her uneven arms. "Don't! We need him alive." She was painfully aware she had inadvertently foiled his escape. If not for her clumsiness, Kantelvar might already have been subdued and they might have been discussing how to get off this skyland . . . if Julio hadn't killed her. If he hadn't thought she was Kantelvar's fellow conspirator before, he surely did now. Damn.

Kantelvar's whole body trembled with fury, but the fire behind his monocle dulled to a sullen blue ember. He slowly lowered the staff. She proffered her hand as a balm to his temper. He took it and relaxed ever so slightly. His skin was hot and slimy, like a slug that had been basking on a warm stone.

"You are correct," he said, though Isabelle barely heard him over the thundering of her heart. She smiled into the face of madness and prayed his unholy eye could not see her loathing.

"Won't," Julio gasped. "I won't be your puppet."

Kantelvar glowered down at him. "You have abused every privilege I have given you and done everything in your power to thwart the Builder's plan. You are a foreskin on destiny's prick and you will be cut away."

Julio sneered at him, "So much for your boast that you never take a host unwilling."

Kantelvar leaned in more closely and growled, "Believe me. You will serve the purpose for which you were spawned and you will do it willingly. By the time I am done with you, you will cut your own skull open and beg me to spoon your brain out like a custard."

Isabelle recoiled from his madness. She felt light in the head, but she held on to her composure. "I have seen enough," she said. More than enough. For a lifetime.

Kantelvar bent and picked up the tongue Julio had spit from his mouth. It seemed to be a sheep's tongue. Kantelvar towed Isabelle out and snapped a command to the warder. The omnimaton slammed the door with such a shuddering force that dust fell from the ceiling.

Kantelvar stalked toward Gretl, who stood wide-eyed by the outer door.

Kantelvar brandished the tongue. "And how did he get hold of this? Water and gruel, that was all he was to have, slops for the swine that he is!"

Gretl backed out the door, her eyes round with terror and bewilderment. She made a series of rapid hand gestures that winged into a gesture of defense as barbs of green lightning danced between the spines of Kantelvar's urchin-headed staff.

Kantelvar raised the weapon to strike. Isabelle touched Kantelvar on the shoulder—she could not stand to see one more person put to the spark— and said, "I would thank you not to damage my handmaid. I am sure she was an innocent dupe." Or maybe, if she was very lucky, Gretl had been Julio's coconspirator, a rebel in Kantelvar's house. It was a tempting wish, brilliant and fragile as a soap bubble. "She is only a deaf-mute, after all."

Kantelvar trembled with his fist on high, then slowly brought his staff down and extinguished its electrical flickering. He turned to face Isabelle. "You are right, of course. Julio is a silk-tongued beast, an inflamer of desire and a corrupter of hearts. A churl such as Gretl could hardly resist him."

Gretl clasped her hands before her breast and gave Isabelle a heartbreaking look of thanks.

"I, for one, found the príncipe entirely resistible," Isabelle said. She had to seem Kantelvar's partisan and keep his attention away from Gretl.

Kantelvar took her hand in his muculent grip. "Yes. You see him for the beast he is."

Isabelle resisted the urge to draw away from his corpselike touch. He wanted inside her, body, mind, and soul. It would be like being eaten alive by maggots.

"My dear friend," she said—a calculated honorific, friendly but not too intimate; it gave him something to hang on to and yet left him something to work for—"I'm afraid all this excitement has left me flustered. I would be most grateful for a bit of peaceful quiet." She needed time to think and to figure out how to communicate with Gretl.

"Of course, Your Highness," he said. "I will show you to your chambers."

"Not a bare cell, I trust." She prayed.

"For the mother of the Savior, never." His yearning tone made her want to gag.

Kantelvar sent Gretl off with a brief hand gesture, then led Isabelle through a web of tunnels to a well-fitted door carved with a relief depicting the Annihilation of Rüul and the death of the last of the Firstborn Kings nearly seventeen centuries ago. Astounding to think Kantelvar had been alive at that time. He might have witnessed it, or even caused it. Had his madness been in full bloom back then, or had it taken centuries to distill to this fatal potency?

What must the world have looked like to him? After only twenty-four years, Isabelle already took so much for granted. Often she did not pause to notice the spring of grass beneath her feet, and more than one full moon cluster had gone by unremarked. How faded and gray must the world have been to one who had already seen more than half a million sunrises? Was anything at all real to him save the light of his burning obsession?

Kantelvar opened the door and introduced her to a set of rooms sumptuously albeit eclectically appointed. At the touch of his staff, several bright alchemical lanterns humphed to life, revealing a trove of fine furniture and trappings she guessed he had collected over the long centuries of his life. There were intricately embroidered Skaladin pillows, faded tapestries from the First Empire of Om, spotted rugs made from the hides of long-extinct saber cats, marble candlesticks in the early-period Messigonean style, and a vast bed that might once have belonged to a Nybian god-king but was adorned with a midnight-blue baldachin from an Irisian saint's chapel. They were not antiques in the usual sense but mementoes of Kantelvar's vastly extended life. One couldn't keep this much history in one's head; there wasn't room.

"It's . . . stunning," she said honestly. And he was trying to stuff her into the middle of this museum, as if by surrounding her with things of the past he could blend and brush her onto the canvas of his memory and pretend she had been there all along.

She turned slowly, opening herself to the room. If there was any way short of spending a thousand years to get to the root of his madness, it might be in this mausoleum of his memory. Her gaze settled on a painting, actually a fragment of a fresco that had been carefully chiseled from a wall and set into a gilt frame.

In the center of the composition stood the stylized figure of a woman in pale robes and a hood that covered her face down to her nose. The golden icon embroidered on her tippets revealed her to be Saint Céleste. A slight smile graced her lips and her left hand was raised in benediction, a peaceful gesture. Around her were arrayed a half-dozen other figures, all very small by comparison. Two carried jugs, one a newborn colt, one a falcon, one an open book, and one knelt at her feet, clutching at the hem of her skirt. The whole painting was cracked and discolored, yellowed from a coat of old varnish that had prevented its crumbling away altogether.

Fascinated, Isabelle drifted toward the artwork. Much of the surface was obscured by black smudges. Only Céleste and the kneeling supplicant had been kept meticulously clean. Isabelle raised her hand but did not quite touch the kneeler.

"This is you," she hazarded. Kantelvar had said he'd been there from the beginning.

Behind her, Kantelvar let out a rattling breath and whispered, "You *do* remember."

Isabelle swallowed hard. She pasted a smile on her face and turned. "Of course." He thought she was Céleste, her second coming. *Oh, wretched woman, what sin could you have committed to have earned this sort of obsession? Were you kind to him? Did you give him hope so bright that it seared his soul?*

Kantelvar bowed to her, as he had always deferred to her, echoes of the supplicant. "I am glad you approve. I will leave you to rest and see to it that refreshments are brought to you. In the meantime, I must make Julio secure."

Kantelvar left. The door closed. Isabelle slumped against the wood, as if her slight weight could hold out all the forces arrayed against her. She rubbed her hand on her dress, trying to wipe away the cloying sweatiness of Kantelvar's touch. By the Builder, she'd give her other arm if only Jean-Claude would come rushing in, preferably with a whole cadre of musketeers at his back. He could not be dead. Must not. The thought choked like dust in her lungs, but she refused to believe it.

Yet even if Jean-Claude was alive somewhere, there was no way he could find her here. And Marie was abandoned in darkness. And Julio was chained to a wall. *Builder help us; I am the last reserves.*

So think! Her mind was her personal pride, a well-oiled machine . . . a delicate clockwork easily thrown out of balance, never meant to be shaken or stepped on like this.

Simplify. That's what Lord DuJournal would say. So what if the imagined command came to her now in the voice of the imposter? It was still good advice.

She had to stop the war. So simple to say. So out of reach. At the very least, she had to get a message off this skyland, something on the order of "Stop, stop, you've all been tricked!" If she could get Julio to a mirror, he could send his espejismo to do that job, but Kantelvar had just gone to strengthen his captivity. Would Kantelvar begin torturing Julio right away? And what would Julio do if she managed to free him? Even if the príncipe wasn't convinced she was Kantelvar's conspirator, he might still murder her just to thwart the breeding program.

Isabelle pressed the heel of her thumb to her temple, trying to rub out an incipient headache. Never had her mind felt like such a blunt, squishy instrument. She was tired, hungry, weak, and sore. *I can't do this. I don't know how.* But there was no one else and no more time.

An arrhythmic knock on the door nearly startled Isabelle out of her skin and she jumped away from the door. Was Kantelvar back already? How much time had she wasted? She wrapped herself in the same stony impassivity that had seen her through so many potentially lethal audiences with the Comte des Zephyrs and said, "Enter."

Strangely, the knock repeated itself again, three beats, then one, then four, before the door glided open. Gretl bustled in and curtsied low while holding up a tray bearing an assortment of delectables and a ewer of wine. Isabelle surmised that, being deaf, she had been trained to knock her special knock and enter rather than waiting for permission.

Isabelle lifted her toe, giving the poor girl permission to rise. Gretl gave her a broad, carefully blank servant's smile that made Isabelle shudder. *There, but for the Builder's grace, stand I.*

Gretl proffered some light pastries with candied fruit and a crystal flute of Célestial wine, pale and sparkling. The pastries' fresh-from-the-oven smell set off desperate urges in the primitive root of Isabelle's mind, and she nearly pounced on the tray. It felt like she hadn't eaten in years. No wonder her head was so muzzy. She spent several minutes gorging far too quickly to appreciate the confectioner's art. The flaky things seemed to turn to vapor before they hit her stomach, leaving her far from sated. She needed real food, not these lacy teases.

"Do you have any meat?" she asked. Then she remembered Gretl was deaf, but the woman bobbed her head in understanding.

Isabelle's brows wrinkled in puzzlement. "Can you hear me?"

Gretl made an emphatic negating gesture, but then pointed to her eyes and thence to Isabelle's mouth.

"You can see my words?" Isabelle said, being careful to enunciate.

Gretl bobbled her head again, a sparkle peeking out from behind the mask of simplicity that shielded her eyes. Isabelle was abashed; she, more than anyone, ought to know that a defective body did not mean a dull mind. But just because Gretl could understand her didn't make her an ally. If anything, it made her a danger.

Isabelle asked, "Why didn't Kantelvar tell me this?"

With her free hand, Gretl mimed pulling a hood over her head. She covered her mouth and shrugged. Kantelvar's mouth was a grille. He had no lips to watch.

"He doesn't know." And it would never occur to Kantelvar that someone like Gretl could be any more than what he made her to be. So how much loyalty would she have to a master who treated her like an omnimaton?

The question, she realized, could only be answered by experiment. "Please bring me real food and water, and then we will talk."

CHAPTER

Twenty

Isabelle wanted to curl up around the plate of cold meat and cheese Gretl brought in and hiss like a cat at anyone who thought they might steal a morsel, but that would have been counterproductive. Instead she bade Gretl join her. The other woman warily sat down on one of the old embroidered pillows.

Over the course of an hour, with Isabelle dreading every moment to hear Kantelvar's approaching footfalls, Gretl demonstrated a wide repertoire of hand signs for Isabelle to absorb, like reading semaphore, only much faster. Isabelle wished she had more time to explore this technique—could these ad hoc gestures be formalized? Could they be adapted for the one-handed "speaker"?—but that was a question for later. If there was a later.

"How did you meet Kantelvar?" Isabelle asked.

Gretl paused, her hands pressed palms flat against each other below her naval. Her expression was bland and her gaze was distant, as it frequently was when she was figuring out how to express herself to someone not fluent in her silent language.

She tapped herself and then made a round belly gesture for "mother" and a beard-stroking one for "man," presumably "father." Then she made a stooped pantomime that meant "Kantelvar" followed by a bit of purse jingling and an exchange of coin.

"Your parents sold you?" Isabelle was appalled. The comte had sold Isabelle before she was even born, but of course she hadn't been his to begin with.

Gretl shrugged and made a stomach-clamping gesture and pointed to her mouth, pantomiming hunger. Desperate families did desperate things.

The real question, she supposed, was, "Why did Kantelvar keep you when he has not kept so many others?"

Gretl shifted uneasily, looked at her hands, looked away. Isabelle all but held her breath; it hadn't seemed like a horrid question but Gretl's expressive fingers curled into fists.

After a moment of profound stillness, Gretl drew herself up, unclenched her hands, and pointed to Isabelle's stump. She mimicked Kantelvar and then she mimed a sawing motion. Then she touched her eye and made a plucking motion, and made a chopping motion against her leg. Then she tapped herself and pantomimed fitting on a prosthetic limb and sewing up split flesh.

When she was done she stared at Isabelle with the dismal look of a subordinate expecting reprimand.

Isabelle took a moment to digest it all. "You help him when he changes bodies." Clearly, Kantelvar could perform the transfer on his own, but that didn't mean it was the ideal way to do it.

Gretl made a brief affirmative nod and shrank back as if expecting a reprimand.

"That must be horrible for you."

Gretl stared at Isabelle with a look of incomprehension that made Isabelle wonder what she'd said wrong. Then Gretl's eyes overflowed with tears, and she buried her face in her hands, sobbing.

Poor woman. Isabelle wrapped her arm around Gretl as Jean-Claude had so often done for her. She could not imagine what life must be like for Kantelvar's captive servants that such a simple statement of truth could unleash such a flood of pain.

It took several minutes of pouring herself out before Gretl was ready to make eye contact again, but when she did her expression was more open, attentive rather than wary.

"I'm going to stop him," Isabelle said, to which Gretl did not reply. "He's going to set the whole world on fire if I don't."

Gretl gave her a doubt-filled look and made an untangling gesture. *How?*

"First I need to talk to Julio." In truth, that was about as far as her plan had gotten, but if she could get him out of his cell and on her side, he'd be able to send his espejismo to take a message to his allies. At this point, even a message to his enemies would be preferable to letting them all be duped into war.

Gretl pointed to Isabelle, made a negating gesture, and used her slipper to draw a line in front of the door.

"Kantelvar never said I couldn't leave this room," Isabelle said; the imperative to stay was merely implied.

Gretl winced and shook her head in an emphatic no. She made a slash across her cheek to indicate Julio, then Kantelvar locking him in manacles, and the omnimaton standing guard.

"He's guarded," Isabelle said. "Yes."

Gretl pointed to the clock on the wall. It read the ninth hour. She pointed to the tenth hour, made the Julio sign, and made a throat-cutting motion.

Isabelle's hand flew to her heart and for a moment breath wouldn't come. She had to rescue Julio now.

"You take him his food. How did you get past the omnimaton?"

Gretl shook her head again and made the Kantelvar sign, the throat slashing.

"I'll deal with Kantelvar," Isabelle said, a promise spun from sheer need rather than any stronger silk. "But I must know how to pass the warder."

The way Gretl pursed her lips gave Isabelle the impression her sanity was in doubt.

Isabelle held on to her patience and gave Gretl what she hoped was her most somber and serious look. "Do you know what's going to happen next? After Kantelvar murders Julio and takes over his body, he's going to rape me until he gets a child on me. He thinks I'm the reincarnation of Saint Céleste, and he wants me to bear the Savior." Her hands balled into fists so tight that her left arm shook and her spark-arm threw off wisps of violet steam. *Not while I have strength to fight.*

Gretl looked appalled, but not, Isabelle noticed, dubious of the claim.

"And when he's done with me he's going to move on to the rest of the world. He has set in motion events that will start a war to end all kingdoms and destroy all peoples." This would sound completely mad to anyone who did not know Kantelvar. "There's no one left to stop him but me, and I need your help." She unclenched her fists and made a gesture of supplication.

Gretl's already pale features were washed out as old laundry and her nimble hands had knotted like the roots of an ancient tree. Yet though her eyes were round with fright, she nodded strongly and curtsied to Isabelle, a transfer of fealty. Isabelle had no oil with which to anoint Gretl, so she touched her lightly on the head and bade her rise. *And now I am responsible for you, too.* But what was one more soul on her conscience at this point? What is one more ice crystal in the groove of a fracturing rock?

From behind her apron Gretl withdrew an amulet in the shape of the Omnioculus, the all-seeing eye peering out from the center of a gearwheel. She brandished it and pantomimed the warder standing aside.

Isabelle held out her hand and Gretl passed the talisman over.

Isabelle weighed the object in her hand. "If Kantelvar needs you to help him change bodies, what prevented you from just waiting until he detached from a host and then putting the knife to him?"

Gretl made a grim face and shook her head. She made the sign for Kantelvar and then bumped the back of her head with her fist. That was where the tubes came out. She pointed to the bed and pantomimed someone lying on it, Kantelvar standing over them. She went to the hump on her back, drew out another tube, and attached it to the body on the bed. The new body stood up, walked around the old body, and pulled the tube out, at which point the old body collapsed to the floor.

"I see. He's always in direct control of the proceedings." Every variable accounted for, damn the man.

Gretl nodded in the affirmative.

It hardly mattered; she couldn't wait for Kantelvar to drill into Julio's skull before she acted. The clock on the wall ticked inexorably away. "We need to go now. Will you show me back to Julio's cell?"

Gretl squared herself up to a servant's proper posture and opened the door. Isabelle confronted the darkened hallway. It felt like standing on the edge of a precipice with nothing left to do but jump. Kantelvar was out there, and omnimatons, and Julio, and she was not ready for this.

Jean-Claude would have chivalrously suggested it was just the thin air that made her breath short and her heart pound. By all the saints, but she missed him. She had to do him proud. She smoothed her skirts and forced herself past the threshold.

Now that Isabelle was in motion, she felt as if she were riding a rock-slide, her only hope to stay on top of it and pray there was enough left of her to crawl out of the wreckage at the end. Dread waited around every corner. Would she bump into Kantelvar in the hall? How would she excuse herself to him? What if he went to her chambers and found her missing, the prize exhibit absconded from the museum? What reason might she give him for leaving her suite after she had pleaded exhaustion? Surely he could locate her by the stink of her fear.

Yet, though she heard the echoes of distant activity, ghostly voices and mechanical clanking, they encountered no one in the passages.

A short eternity later, they arrived at the suite of rooms that contained Julio's cell. Isabelle listened at the door but heard nothing. Surely Kantelvar would be talking if he were in there. Julio made him rave.

What if Kantelvar had already taken Julio away to be prepared for his surgery? All too vividly, she imagined Kantelvar plucking Julio's eyeball out and taking a chisel to the vacant socket. A hammer blow and the príncipe's body would jerk and lie still. *Not yet.* There was still time. She kept repeating that in her head like a prayer.

Isabelle depressed the latch and eased open the door. There was no reaction from within. No sound but the creak of the hinges. The omnimaton stood at attention next to Julio's cell door, a hulking armored skeleton of quondam alloy. It gave no sign of noticing her, though who knew what processes went on behind that great cyclopean eye.

Isabelle turned to Gretl, who all but clung to her skirts. "Please stand watch outside. Give your knock if anyone comes along." Though how such a little forewarning might help Isabelle, she had no idea.

Gretl nodded and closed the door behind Isabelle. Isabelle forced herself to stand erect. The damned warder must already have known she was present and cringing wouldn't help.

"Julio," Isabelle said, but her voice came out a harsh croak. She gathered herself and tried again, more clearly: "Your Highness Príncipe Julio."

There came no answer. Had he already been taken to be prepared?

Isabelle drew out the amulet and held it before her as if warding off an evil spirit. Slowly she approached the door. Could the omnimaton sense terror? Its glassy eye, throbbing with an internal light, was the only indication of . . . "life" was the wrong word, but she could not very well use the word "animation" in reference to something standing so incredibly still.

She came within arm's reach of the machine.

The omnimaton moved so quickly that it blurred. When it came to a stop, its singular three-fingered hand had closed on the door handle.

Isabelle flinched uselessly. If the thing had been inclined to attack, it could have had her head off her shoulders before she could blink.

With a series of abrupt twists the omnimaton twisted the door handle and opened the door. It didn't seem capable of moving at anything other than blinding speed and seemed to be trying to average its movements out so that it didn't shatter the door. The result was a staccato series of still lifes that ended with the door ajar just far enough for Isabelle to enter without scraping her shoulders.

Isabelle held her breath and eased past the machine into the cell.

"I see Kantelvar was right about you," came a soft, harsh voice from the gloom.

Isabelle's head whipped around. Príncipe Julio sat slumped in a far corner, his hands shackled and bound by chains to iron loops set in the walls above him on either side. His face, downcast and obscured by lengths of tangled black hair, was pale and dingy as old snow. His silver eyes were sullen. His posture, sagging like the last sack of potatoes after a long winter, radiated defeat and despair, but Isabelle was chary of deception. *Fool me once, shame on you; fool me twice . . . I think not.*

"That depends on what he told you," Isabelle said.

"L'Étincelle, the long-lost sorcery of Saint Céleste," Julio said. "A fine birthright to bestow upon the Savior."

Isabelle's hackles rose, but she kept her temper at bay. She had no time for anger or fear or any other emotion, no matter how they scratched and whined.

"You accuse me falsely," she said. "Kantelvar is my enemy, and I shall not complete his project." Which meant that in the unlikely event that she lived through this, she could never marry Julio. Indeed, with all these sorceries lying dormant in her veins, she hardly dared contemplate children at all . . . but those problems presumed a future out of reach.

"I do not accuse you of being his partisan," Julio said. "Only his puppet. We are all his puppets. The only question is, what does he want from this— what is your word?—tête-à-tête."

Isabelle resisted the urge to turn around to check if Kantelvar had come up behind her. Instead, she approached his corner, the swirling maroon glow of her spark-arm painting faint pulsing shadows on the walls. Julio blinked and shuddered as if even these dim flickers burned like flecks of molten iron. Up close, his cheeks glimmered like tarnished silver, the aftermath of quicksilver tears.

To defend herself against accusations of being manipulated would be futile, so she took a different tack. "Perhaps Kantelvar has a goal for this meeting, but that does not preclude me having one as well. I need you to help me stop this war he has planned. If I can get you out of these chains and out of this room, can you get your espejismo back to San Augustus? I need you to put this before Carlemmo—"

Julio's expression remained stony but there was a hitch of suppressed grief in his voice. "It's too late. My father . . . Carlemmo is dead. Kantelvar administered the last dose of the poison before he snatched you away. He's dead and the war of the príncipes has begun."

Isabelle's breath came short as the one thread of hope she'd been holding was ripped from her fingers. She could not be too late. There must still be time, but once the first pebble fell, was there any way to stop the landslide?

No. She would not believe it. Not without more proof than Kantelvar's word. She would keep fighting.

Julio said, "Kantelvar wants to hollow out my head and use my body to get a child on you, which he will call the Savior. That child must never be born, but at this point I can do nothing to prevent it. That means the fatal deed must be in your hands."

Isabelle recoiled. "Are you saying I should kill myself?"

Julio looked appalled. "No. I do not envy you the choices you have left to make, but I would not ask such a sacrifice of you, even if your life were mine to command."

His alarm faded into a dull, hot determination, a banked coal waiting for the breath of air. "I ask only for your help. I have no wish to be Kantelvar's vessel, or the tool he uses to rape you or unmake the world. You won't even have to strike the blow yourself. I had the mute smuggle me some leaves of queensmercy. They're under my blankets." He gestured to a pile of rags in the far corner. "Just put them where I can reach them and leave."

Isabelle struggled for balance in her mind. "I came here to free you, not murder you."

"You will be freeing me. When Kantelvar invades a body, the original owner does not die, not completely. He is mangled, shoved aside, crippled beyond saving, and cut off from the flesh that was once his, but he does not die. Some part of him lives on, a helpless witness to the atrocities subsequently performed under cover of his exalted name. I beg you, do not condemn me to that fate."

Despair clawed at Isabelle's heart, but she did not relent. "But what about the war? Aragoth needs its príncipe."

Julio grimaced. "I . . . am not a príncipe of Aragoth." His gaze flicked to the corner of the cell where lay an inert heap of blood ciphers. "My father is not my father. Even my name is not my name." His hands balled into white-knuckled fists. "I am a changeling and both Climacio and Alejandro know it. They have no reason to treat with me."

"What about everyone else? Surely the presence of a third príncipe must give the nobles cause to doubt the rightness of their position."

"There is no time for such a ploy. Kantelvar intends to force himself upon me within the hour, and he will force himself on you shortly thereafter. That must not happen."

Isabelle's hands balled in frustration, her spark-hand throwing motes of light. "Do you want to die so badly?"

"I do not want to die at all," he said, "but—"

"No more buts," Isabelle snapped. "If you want poison you can fetch it yourself after I get you out of these." She reached for Julio's chains. She had no key, but maybe her spark-hand could manipulate the locks on his manacles.

Julio flinched. "Stop!"

Isabelle froze. "Why?"

"Kantelvar commanded the omnimaton to kill anyone who tried to either harm me or set me free."

"And poisoning doesn't count?" Isabelle asked incredulously.

"It only understands Saintstongue, and it's used to people leaving things for me to eat. It wouldn't know the difference until it was too late."

Isabelle warily backed up and turned to regard the machine. Could she give it an order?

Easing away from Julio, she held up the amulet and spoke in the Saintstongue, "*Warder, hear me and obey. Set Príncipe Julio free.*"

Isabelle half expected the machine to rip her apart, but it gave no sign of noticing her.

She asked, "Did he give any special words to it? A verse from the *Instructions,* maybe?"

"Aside from the Saintstongue, the only other consistency I've noted is the staff. I think it's connected to the machines."

"Which is why you tried to grab it."

"That and I didn't want him shocking me with it."

Isabelle straightened up and carefully approached the omni. "What exactly did Kantelvar say to it?" Every statement he uttered, and every deal he made, was all about word games and slicing meaning very thinly. Was it too much to hope that he might have given similarly precise commands to his mechanical servants?

Julio squeezed his eyes shut as if trying to remember. "He was speaking in Saintstongue, '*Neither unchain him nor allow him to be unchained without my permission. Likewise, neither harm him nor allow him to come to harm.*'"

Isabelle reached up to smooth her veil, realized she wasn't wearing one, and settled for tugging her collar. The machine wouldn't heed her, wouldn't let her remove Julio, and wouldn't let her harm him . . .

"Ah!" Inspiration struck with the same thrilling terror as striking a match in the dark and finding oneself in a gunpowder magazine.

"You have something?" Julio asked.

Isabelle's pulse raced, but she quelled the urge to act. *Think first.* She thought she could persuade the omnimaton to get Julio out of the cell, but what then? She had seen no indication of individual volition in any of the omnimatons she'd encountered so far, but the tasks they performed had to involve some level of decision making. "Can these things think for themselves?"

"Not as such. They seem to have some measure of comprehension, but no free will or individual motivation. Why?"

"Say an omni is in the middle of a task, and Kantelvar orders it to do something else. What happens when the interruption is over?"

"It goes back to what it was doing before. Where are you going with this?"

Isabelle chewed her lower lip and muttered, "He didn't actually order it to keep you in the room."

"I would think that was implie—wait, where are you going?"

"I have an idea!" Isabelle called over her shoulder as she squeezed by the omnimaton into the abandoned bedroom suite. She ripped the fine linens from the bed, took an ancient tapestry from its hanger, and rushed back into the cell, making a pile against one wall. She made more trips into the bedroom, clearing the way with Gretl's Omnioculus amulet, bringing back more sheets and clothes from the bureau, antique chairs, paintings by the old masters. She heaped a thousand years of irreplaceable history into a pile as high as her waist. Even with just one arm to shuttle this mostly once-living material, it couldn't have taken her more than a few minutes, but under the omnimaton's soulless watch it felt like a year. Thank the Builder the machine seemed utterly disinclined to question her motive for this redecorating project.

Julio, on the other hand, watched her frenetic gathering in evident alarm. "What in the name of Torment are you doing?"

"Getting you out of here." She met his gaze. "Do you trust me?"

"Do I have a choice?" His voice almost squeaked.

"You could opt to be Kantelvar's vessel."

"That is *not* a choice."

Once more, she darted into the bedroom, pausing only to listen for some noise heralding Kantelvar's approach. She could hear nothing but the hammering of her own heart. She snatched an alchemical lantern from the wall and returned to the cell.

Julio's silver eyes went wide. He surged against his chains. "What? No! Are you mad!"

"No, just desperate." A very fine distinction, as it turned out.

Isabelle backed up to the far corner of the room. She pulled the glass stopper out of the lumin gas reservoir with her spark-hand. The hypervolatile liquid quickly began to vaporize, spewing a jet of vapor, like steam from a teakettle, but colder than ice. She hurled it at the wall above her pile of kindling.

The glass shattered. The phlogiston core ignited.

The bright green flash knocked her on her backside and punched the breath from her lungs. Purple sparks rained down around her. She dragged herself up in time to see flames erupt from the heap of oil paintings and cobwebbed tapestries. Black smoke billowed and spread across the ceiling.

"Mad witch!" Julio screamed, or something like it. Isabelle's ears rang with the bang.

The omnimaton sprang into action. Emitting an ululating, earsplitting shriek, it began stamping at the spreading flames. Isabelle faced the omnimaton and jabbed a finger at Julio. How would it react to her as the fire starter? In the Saintstongue she shouted, *"Do not permit him to come to harm!"* Could it even hear her over the racket of its own alarm cry?

The omnimaton hesitated, but its stomping had only spread the fire. It blurred to Julio's side, pinched the iron chains between two massive fingers, and yanked the rings from the wall as if the stones were made of talc. Still shrieking its alarm, it hefted Julio like a child and hauled him from the room in a series of rapid jerks. Isabelle followed as smoke poured from the door. Surely that wail had roused the whole aerie. They had only heartbeats to be away from here.

Unfortunately, the omnimaton did not stop outside the cell. It smashed through the outer door as if it were made of papier-mâché, then dashed into the hall and down the corridor.

"Damn." Isabelle hadn't anticipated that. She hiked her skirts and gave chase. She sprinted by a stunned-looking Gretl, who joined the pursuit.

"What now?" Julio barked. He squirmed futilely against the omni's gargantuan strength.

"I don't know; I'm making this up as I go!"

The machine accelerated, swiftly outdistancing her.

"I think it's taking me to the infirmary," Julio called, his voice faint amidst the clangor, just before the omnimaton disappeared with him around a long bend in the corridor.

The infirmary. That made sense as a standing order, one of Kantelvar's endless, interwoven contingency plans. If the príncipe had to be pulled from his cell due to injury, the most logical place to take him was the infirmary, the surgery, where Kantelvar was now making ready to butcher his brain. Builder's breath, all her stunt with the fire had done was accelerate his execution.

Isabelle followed the receding noise through what seemed like kilometers of corridors, around corners, up a stairwell. The noise had brought the denizens of the place out of their holes and they were running hither and yon, though purposefully, without panic, as if they had practiced for this. None of them seemed to be going her way. She was hurrying along yet another dim gray tunnel, gasping for breath in the thin air and nursing a stitch in her side, when the noise suddenly stopped.

A half-dozen side corridors led off this one. Which one? She leaned against the wall and listened but heard no sound louder than her own labored breathing. And what would she do when she found him? She could not fight Kantelvar and his machines.

Just then Gretl caught up with her. She waved for Isabelle to follow and darted into one of several identical-looking side passages.

Isabelle followed her along a short hallway to a small infirmary. A row of empty cots lay along one wall, and there was an arched opening at the far end. Weird grainy shadows flickered beyond the archway to the accompaniment of a high-pitched whine. Just inside the infirmary, Gretl stopped, quivering, at the very end of her courage's tether. Isabelle laid a reassuring hand on her shoulder, then crept by her, down the aisle. Her own fear made the air thicker as she approached the archway, until it was like pressing through water . . . mud . . . tar. Beyond that opening waited Kantelvar, and somehow he would know what she had done. He would be furious, his wrath would be terrible, and there were far worse things he might do than kill her, but she could not leave Julio in his hands.

She peered through the archway, and it took a moment for the scene to resolve itself in a way that made sense. In the center of the room, Julio was strapped facedown to a table with his head in a vise that restricted all movement. At his head stood Kantelvar, his hood cast back, revealing the glittering apparatus of his false eye and the still-angry flesh of his recent surgery.

On the table between the two men squatted a bizarre omnimaton. In shape it was most like a spider, with four telescoping, spindle-like legs connecting to a central hub. From the top protruded half a dozen metallic tentacles, each tipped with a different tool.

Dangling beneath the hub, between the legs, was a transparent bottle filled with a cloudy liquid . . . and the rotting remains of a head. Kantelvar's head. His skin, what little remained of it, had sloughed free of his skull, and his eyes were bloated and putrefied, his tongue swollen, his lower jaw missing entirely.

Isabelle's skin felt cold and slick as ice. This was the gurgling hump Kantelvar hid under his robes and in his pack. This was the seat of his consciousness. Through hundreds of lifetimes he had survived like this, a pickled grotesquery. And he had done it on purpose, done it to himself.

One flexible tendril was still fixed to the back of the skull of Kantelvar's most recent host. Another gemstone eye oversaw a nest of tentacles making Julio ready for surgery, shaving the back of his head and injecting his skin with some vile potion in preparation for drilling through his skull.

At the far end of the room the warder omnimaton gave its report to Kantelvar's current host. Its central eye glowed, and the air before it shimmered. Fine corpuscles of greasy light coalesced into a sort of animate sculpture suspended in air.

It was a half-sized, translucent image of Isabelle's conversation with Julio. She could see her lips moving, but the only sound was the whir of the omnimaton's gears. It was like watching a painting made of raindrops, wet and streaky, but still gut-wrenchingly recognizable. Soundlessly, her image piled kindling against the wall of Julio's cell. A wave of irrational guilt washed through her, as if she had been caught in some wickedness. She watched herself set the kindling alight. She winced in memory of the bang. And there was Julio's rescue from the omnimaton's point of view. It yanked the chains from the wall and carried him from the room.

A soul-curdling wail yanked her attention to Kantelvar. His host body was bowed and trembling as if in pain, his visage contorted with rage. His ordinary eye streamed with tears.

Isabelle drew back out of view and turned to find Gretl, on her second dose of bravery, creeping up behind her. Her face was drawn taut as a sail in a hurricane.

Isabelle mouthed, "I'll try to draw him away. You free Julio."

Gretl swallowed hard and nodded.

Isabelle steeled herself. This was a bad plan, but she had no time for a better one.

Isabelle stepped into the room. "Kantelvar!"

His sapphire lens fixed her with a murderous stare. "Traitress!" he spat. "How could you? How dare you?"

Isabelle leaned back, to turn and run, but Kantelvar's arm jerked like the spring-arm of a rat trap. The urchin tip of his staff flashed. A snap of lightning scribed a jagged path through the air and smote her in the chest. Her whole body convulsed, and she collapsed, twitching.

"He is your husband!" Kantelvar shrieked. "Your destiny!"

Spittle drizzled from Isabelle's lips even as she fought for control of her thrashing limbs. He'd gone over the edge. She had to bring him back.

Kantelvar rounded the table toward her. Arcs of lightning formed a menacing gloriole around the staff head, and his voice was the whine of a wounded animal. "He is your lord and master, the father of the Savior!"

"N . . . nmmmnm . . ." Isabelle couldn't get her jolted tongue under control.

"You tried to kill the Savior! You would have doomed the world to an eternity of chaos." He sparked her again, and she convulsed, banging her head on the floor and her arm on the table leg. Her shoulder nearly wrenched from its socket.

"S . . . stop. P . . . please . . . m-mercy . . ." She had to make him start thinking again. Thinking took time. She had to delay him until . . . what? There was no legion of musketeers to come riding over the hill. She could not best Kantelvar with force, he was impervious to reason, and he knew more about guile than anyone alive or dead.

"You dare to beg?" Kantelvar shrieked. "After everything I have done for you?"

Kantelvar raised his staff again, but Julio, facedown on the table, made a muffled shout. "And you, oh spider, are about to kill the Savior's mother!"

Kantelvar paused, arrested in the middle of a bestial snarl. He rounded on Julio, the cable on the back of his head whipping like a sheet in a gale. "Silence, you thrice-over traitor."

"Madman!" Julio said. "You very nearly killed your own broodmare."

Isabelle got her legs under her. It felt like worms of lightning were burrowing through her flesh. Kantelvar had clearly misinterpreted her actions in the cell as an attempt on Julio's life rather than an attempted rescue. To him, life was a never-ending cycle of betrayal and revenge in which he was both orchestrator and victim.

"Julio tried to kill me," she improvised. "He tried to burn my ship out from under me. I hated him for that. I could not stand the thought of being his wife, with his body close to mine, his flesh inside me."

Kantelvar returned his attention to her, a thin, translucent mask of control stretched across his burning madness. "But only *his* seed can sire the Savior."

Reason had no hold on him, but his vision sank its hooks to the bone, this dramatic revenge he had plotted on the world. *Give him Céleste!*

Once again she invoked her Saintstongue: *"It is not the seed that makes the Savior. It is the soul! Your soul, my love. That is what I have waited for all these centuries, and that is why you brought me back."*

Kantelvar's expression went slack with shock and wonder.

Is this what you've been hoping for all this time? A great woman's affection?

Poor, poor man. Isabelle smiled beatifically at him and spread her arms. *"Come, my valiant champion. Receive your triumph."*

Kantelvar's human puppet stumbled toward her. Even the spidery machine leaned in. Somewhere in the depths of his mind, he had to know he was being beguiled, but the part of him that *wanted* was ascendant over the part of him that thought. He croaked something in the Saintstongue too thickly accented for her to make out anything except, *". . . reflection times."* No, make that, *"memory of . . . through the ages."* Builder's breath; who ever thought the fate of the world would rest on her ability to conjugate in a dead language?

"It was your memory and your love that kept me alive," she said. How long would this trance hold? She had to pull him close. It was like trying to reel in a leviathan with a length of sewing thread.

A piteous rage filled Kantelvar's voice. *"You required excessive diligence."*

I made him wait too long. He didn't just want Céleste's attention, he wanted to be worshipped as he had worshipped her. She bowed her head and did her best curtsy on wobbly legs. *"I am sorry, my champion. I was weak and fearful, but you have remade the world for me. I am forever in your debt."*

Her legs gave out, but she made sure to land in an artful heap at his feet. *"Can you ever forgive me, my lord, my love?"* Now, if only he would bid her rise . . . if only she had the strength.

While she was staring at her distorted reflection in Kantelvar's polished boots, he brought the spiny tip of his staff down so close to the back of her head that the proximity of the sparks made her neck hairs stand on end. His body's breathing was deep and hoarse, as if he were trying to draw air down a well of a thousand years. Should she kiss his boots? Perhaps later she would feel some humiliation in this prostration, if she was lucky enough to have a later, but for now, it was only a means to a chance, submission as a means of control.

Finally he stroked her hair. A purely physical shudder ran down her spine. Could he tell the difference between a quiver of revulsion and one of desire? Then he knelt before her and gently lifted her chin until they were nose to patchwork nose. His cheek glistened with tears, but his sapphire eye burned. *"I forgive you."* He leaned forward, and Isabelle, realizing what he wanted, gave it to him. His lips had been sewn into a rigid circle around his speaking tube, which jutted forward like a brass tongue. She kissed the obscene protrusion. The grille was rough on her tongue, and the abused flesh around it hot and rancid with leaking serum. His arms encircled her ribs and he lifted her easily to her feet.

Even as her mouth accepted his grotesque intrusion, she raised her spark-hand and drove it through his skull. Her phantom flesh passed harmlessly through living skin, bone, and brain, but not the wire filaments permeating his gray matter or the solid metal tube of his oculus. The metal bit against her ethereal flesh. The shock of it jerked Kantelvar back. The sharp edge of his mouth tube took a strip of skin from her lip. His ordinary eye went wide, the pupil gaping, a dark fathomless window into the abyss. His arms fell nerveless to his sides and the spiny-ended staff fell away. She grabbed the ocular tube and gave a great yank, back and forth, like shaking a hen's egg and scrambling the chick inside.

The host's corpse crumpled at her feet. For a moment, she could do nothing but stare, eyes wide and mind stunned, as all the terror she'd been suppressing flooded through her. Her knees wanted to buckle. Her gut wanted to heave.

The umbilical tentacle shivered and then yanked back hard, ripping itself out of the back of the host's head in a spray of brain and bone.

The spider-thing whipped its other tentacles at her. She lurched out of the way. The tentacles gouged great grooves in the stone wall.

"Let me up!" Julio shrieked, his voice brittle with panic. A half-dozen straps held him down. Kantelvar's spider positioned an auger-tipped appendage over the back of Julio's skull. The tool spun with a whine like a giant hornet.

Another tentacle lashed at Isabelle. She gave ground. Razor-tipped appendages sliced air a centimeter from her nose. Kantelvar couldn't stretch any farther without abandoning Julio. It made a surgical incision in the skin on the back of his skull.

At the other end of the room the warder waited. Isabelle dove for the staff on the floor and prayed that it was the talisman by which his machines recognized their master.

Pain exploded in her thigh. Blood sprayed as a whirring blade opened a long gash in her leg.

Isabelle rolled to her knees, brandished the staff at the warder, and pointed to Julio. *"Remember your orders! Let nothing harm him!"*

The warder blurred into motion, smashing into Kantelvar's spider. A tremendous bang shook the air. The concussion kicked her in the side and knocked her into a wall. The constructs wrestled, like a kraken grappling with a black behemoth in the abyssal Gloom. The spider coiled its appendages around its assailant, trying to pin its arm long enough to ram the spinning, screaming auger through its central eye, but the warder lifted it from the ground and smashed it into the wall so hard that the stone cracked and rocks clattered from the ceiling.

Isabelle lunged to Julio's side and tore at the bonds holding his head. Another thunderous impact shook the room. Tearing metal screamed. A fan of razor-sharp splinters sprayed across the room. A needle pierced Isabelle's left shoulder, and the pain shattered her concentration. She slipped and landed heavily on Julio's back, covering him by accident. *By the Builder, you had better be worth it!* She forced herself up and plied the bindings with both hands, ghostly fingers fumbling on the metal buckles, sweaty, bloody flesh sliding on the leather straps. *Calm. Calm. To go faster, work slower!* Hard to do with her heart roaring like a cannonade. She ripped a strap free and then another. *Too slow.* And then Gretl was there on the other side of the table, unstringing Julio as fast as she could, bless her bold heart.

Isabelle ripped the last strap off Julio's head and moved on to his torso, arms, ankles. The whole world became a gauntlet bounded by metal monstrosities and barred by tongues of leather pierced by brass. The floor shook and folded, stone cracking and rolling as if in agony. Cracks raced up the walls and chunks of rock fell from the ceiling. The omnis were but a haze of glittering, oily edges. Julio screamed, but his words were lost in the din. Finally she loosed a buckle and found nothing else to grab. Done! Julio slithered from the table just as a falling slab of granite smashed it flat. Gretl grabbed him by one shoulder, Isabelle seized the other, and they propelled him from the room, a plume of gray dust rolling in their wake. Behind them, the machines continued their battle even as the room caved in.

Pain jabbed Isabelle's shoulder at every step, but they didn't stop running until they stumbled and nearly killed themselves pelting down a flight of stairs. They heaped up against the far wall of the landing and slid to the floor, backs to the stone. Isabelle panted, trying to catch her breath.

When the rasping sensation of sucking air into her frosted, burning lungs finally lost its grip on her attention, Isabelle took stock of her surroundings. The noise of the mechanical battle above had died down to a distant ringing, like a manic percussionist in a forge, accompanied by the occasional thumping quiver of the floor and the crunch of falling rocks.

Eventually the thundering stopped. A thin pall of freshly ground dust floated down the stair and settled around them.

"Do you think they destroyed each other?" Isabelle asked.

Julio, sitting on her left, shook his head. "Or buried themselves. I don't know. They're notably persistent." He had somehow thought to grab Kantelvar's staff when he fled. Did he know how to use it? What would he do with it?

Beyond him, Gretl sat hunched over with her head between her knees, panting, but not apparently injured. Good.

Julio focused his mirrored eyes on Isabelle. "Has anyone ever mentioned that you're completely mad?"

Isabelle laughed. She would have laughed at anything just then. Unbearable coils of tension unwound like clock springs loosed from their housing. She laughed until she cried, then coughed, and finally hiccoughed to a stop.

When she lifted her hand to blot tears from her eyes, a jab of pain reminded her of the shard in her shoulder. Blood trickled from the wound, and every little motion scraped the jagged thing against her bone. That shoulder was going to be a mess, even if she didn't die from an infection. "I think I need an infirmary," she said, and then laughed again, drunk on pain and horror.

Julio's brows drew down in concern. "We should get that out of you."

Isabelle clamped her hand on his forearm as the world rippled, peaks and troughs of light and darkness washing through her consciousness. "I need you to go to San Augustus. Stop this war."

"First, Highness, I'm going to make sure you don't bleed to death."

Isabelle felt consciousness slipping away, eroded by waves of shock and trauma, but she refused to yield it up. "Let Gretl get the shard. She's a surgeon."

Julio looked doubtful.

Isabelle squeezed his arm. "Trust me. Trust her."

Julio turned and tapped Gretl on the knee, drawing her attention to the wound. Gretl's eyes went round and she shouldered into the narrowing circle of Isabelle's vision. She gently peeled Isabelle's clammy fingers off his arm and probed the flesh around the shard in her arm.

Isabelle clenched her teeth and used her spark-fingers to help stabilize the ragged splinter and prevent its tearing any more flesh as Gretl teased it out of her shoulder. A long animal whimper escaped her throat, and pain forced her awareness deeper and deeper until the world was little more than a pinhole at the top of a bottomless, dark well. Only her need to focus on the shard kept her from slipping all the way into unconsciousness.

With a whispered slurping sound, the quondam metal exited her skin. She gasped with relief and then groaned with the certainty that the pain that remained was hers to keep.

—

Isabelle woke to jostling and thence to pain. Her whole body ached, like burned-out acres of forest after a fire. Her left shoulder still felt like it had a burning arrow stuck through it. There was a dampness in the air like fog. She was lying supine. Covered in a blanket. The ceiling above was little more than a roughhewn blur of rust-colored light.

The sound of movement drew her attention. Julio dragged a heavy crate across the floor. Gretl followed him with an alchemical lantern and a lantern hook. The cut on the back of his head had been stitched up, but his collar was stained with blood. He seemed to be setting the crate up as a weight to hold the lamp hook with the alchemical lantern suspended over a dark pit.

Isabelle forced herself up onto her elbow, trying to get a better look. Every movement she made provided evidence that not moving would be a fruitful alternative to explore. She groaned. Julio and Gretl set aside their project and hurried over.

"Princesa," Julio said. "Don't try to get up."

"What's going on?" Isabelle asked. "Where are we?"

"In the aerie's Temple, making preparations to depart."

"What about Kantelvar?"

Julio gestured to her left. A few meters away lay the tangled wreck of the spider jar. All but one of its legs had been ripped off, and its various tentacles reduced to stumps. The single remaining leg twitched occasionally, like the last limb of a crushed insect. Amazingly, the bottle with Kantelvar's decaying skull inside seemed undamaged.

"Do you think he's still alive in there?" she asked.

"I hope so," Julio said. "Alive and screaming in impotent rage."

That thought made Isabelle queasy. A clean death would have been better. One didn't torture frothing dogs; one put them out of their misery. "We should dispose of him, throw him off the sky cliff." Though perhaps even the long fall wouldn't kill him.

"No good," Julio said. "Even with the staff I couldn't open the outer doors to get to the ship and there's no guarantee we could control the ship even if we could reach it."

"You couldn't . . . how long was I unconscious?"

No longer eclipsed by despair, Julio's manner was brisk and resolute. "An hour or so. I was going to have to rouse you soon if you didn't come around. I need to know if you know where this skyland is. The last time I escaped, I was unable to inform my allies where to come rescue me. I know we're on an uncharted skyland, but I was unconscious when Kantelvar brought me here and there are no windows."

"This skyland is not uncharted; it's mischarted. It's listed as a reef, about four days off the coast between Aragoth and l'Empire Céleste, and very high up."

Julio cursed. "A reef. Of course. Damn. I had Duque Diego looking in all the wrong places."

"Just how did you escape? I assume Kantelvar left you no mirrors."

"Let me show you," he said, extending his hand to her. His grip was dry and strong, his fingers lean yet blunt. Calluses on thumb and forefinger spoke of countless hours with a sword in hand. She'd heard he was a great swordsman, but that was the sort of thing one always heard about royalty. His calluses proved he was at least serious about the discipline. As she recalled, Climacio's hands had been softer. *All those little clues we miss.*

Isabelle permitted herself to be assisted. Her balance was wobblier than she liked it, but at least she didn't tip over. The Temple was a six-sided room with a domed ceiling overhead. Kantelvar had stuck as close to the traditional designs as possible. There were niches carved in the wall wherein had been placed icons of all the Risen Saints. In the center of the space, directly beneath the center of the dome, was a wide pool of dark water. Isabelle could not imagine that a skyland this small had a natural spring, so this had to be the outpost's cistern. The only thing missing from the standard layout was an oculus in the roof.

Aside from its sacred design, the room seemed to have been given over to practical use as a storehouse for the aerie's supplies. There were shelves upon shelves of dry goods and tools, though Isabelle imagined anything vulnerable to the damp was stored elsewhere. There were also shelves loaded down with odd fragments of twisted metal, strangely colored glass, and partial pieces of quondam machinery.

Gretl handed Isabelle a mug of water, which she gratefully downed. The chill of the liquid reminded her body of the gelid humidity. She shivered.

"Is there a cloak you could bring me?" she asked.

Gretl gave a positive hand sign and hurried off.

Julio used the lamp hook to hang the alchemical lantern low over the water, pinning the hook in place with the heavy crate. The bright light in the dark room turned the surface of the pool into a smooth mirror.

"I didn't know Glasswalkers could send their espejismos through water," Isabelle said.

"It was a common practice during the Saintstime, but the technique was lost after the annihilation of Rüul. I'm the only modern sorcerer powerful enough to manage it, or at least the only one who dares." Pride lifted his shoulders. "The reflection isn't solid and there's no speculum loci behind it to latch on to. Even Kantelvar thought it was impossible, or didn't think of it at all, or he never would have left me the opportunity."

"So what do you intend to do when you get there?"

Julio stared at nothing for a moment, his face grim, as if reviewing a decision. "I'm going to approach Duque Diego."

"He's the one you went to before, the one who had a mirror placed aboard my ship so that you could attack Kantelvar."

"Yes. His name is a byword for honor."

Feeling woozy, Isabelle sat down on the crate by the edge of the pool. Her brows knitted in puzzlement. "Why? I thought he had recently switched factions."

"Yes, but Aragothic politics is like a peasant dance; people change partners all the time. Diego stands firm on the rule of law. His favorite son and named heir was accused of murdering his bride. Diego believed his son to be innocent, and it was widely believed that my father would spare the son to avoid offending Diego. Instead, Father accepted the judgment of the court and had Diego's son destroyed. Diego might have raised his banner in rebellion. Instead, he renewed his vows to the king. No one has had the cojones to challenge him on his honor since then."

Isabelle mulled this for a moment. "So he is your perfect ally. If you can convince him to argue your case to Margareta's supporters—"

"No," Julio said. "Didn't you hear? He values the rule of law. Once he learns . . . what I am, he will be compelled to turn me over to whichever príncipe he chooses to support. I believe I can convince him to swear fealty to Alejandro and turn me over as proof of his sincerity."

Isabelle's eyes narrowed in suspicion. "Are you still trying to get yourself killed?"

"No," he said. "That was never my preferred option, but it seemed the only one left to me. I . . . underestimated you. As for my current plan, I like my chances better with Alejandro than with Margareta. We were close once, before Kantelvar poisoned our shared cup, and Alejandro has every reason to spare my life. If he holds me up as a counterexample to Climacio, it will bleed away Margareta's support, and may significantly shorten the war."

Isabelle ran her mundane hand through her short-cropped hair and found it matted with blood. "I swore to Grand Leon that I would find a way to prevent this war."

"It isn't possible to prevent something that has already begun," Julio said grimly.

"It must be," Isabelle said. "There can't be a war if no one fights. They have to choose it, and they're fighting over a lie."

"No. The lie is just the most recent excuse for them to do what they've always done. Aragoth is divided in more ways than you know. There are feuds and rifts that go back centuries, even through the Skaladin occupation. The grandchildren of nobles who made bargains with the invaders are still considered traitors by the grandchildren of those who did not. Slights and injustices are handed down like precious heirlooms. My father was fully occupied stamping out these feuds wherever they flared up. Even opening up the Craton Riqueza for exploitation could not consume enough of their enmity to abate the hostilities. If anything it made them worse. Aragoth needs to change, even if that means letting the great houses drink each other's blood until they the choke on the clots."

"And how much of that blood do you want to drink?" Isabelle asked. "If you really want to change the world, try not going to war. Accept the fact that in the end, nobody gets to win. I've been reading your history, and it's almost nothing but war. There is no way more war is actually a change. To say that peace exists only at the whim of war ascribes peace no strength or value save as a respite for the beast to lick its wounds before rampaging again. That is certainly how Kantelvar saw the world. I therefore stand against it, against him. I say peace has value. It is worth striving for, risking for, sacrificing for."

"If I can bring Duque Diego and his supporters over to Alejandro's side, it will vastly shorten the war. What more would you have me do?"

"It won't help as much as you think," Isabelle said. "Kantelvar has stirred up all the Risen Kingdoms. If Margareta finds her local support draining away she will turn to the troops waiting just across Aragoth's borders, Vecci and Oberholzers—"

"And Célestials," Julio added. "Let us not forget your people, either."

"My people." Isabelle stood up from the crate, her eyes round as an idea bloomed in her head. Kantelvar had been counting on a fight between two sides, neither of which could afford not to fight. Everything balanced on that assumption.

Sometimes the only way to win was to break the game.

She took a deep breath of humid air, met Julio's gaze, and said, "I'm going to give you an army."

He regarded her skeptically. "What?"

"Grand Leon appointed me his ambassador to Aragoth and granted me the power to declare which Aragothic faction l'Empire would support. I choose you, a third faction. Neither Alejandro nor Climacio will ally with each other for fear of betrayal, but neither one of them can afford to fight two opponents at once. You can force them to parley."

Julio looked stunned, but when the expression melted it was into a thoughtful, calculating look. Levelly he said, "You are assuming that Grand Leon has not reabsorbed that power or given it to another since your disappearance."

"Once he realizes I am alive, he will honor his word," she said, keeping the *Or this will all be for nothing* to herself. "He has no desire for this war, and I will make it plain to him that I have a plan to prevent it."

"You would make me a puppet of l'Empire Céleste, turn Aragoth into your satrapy."

"Of course not," Isabelle said.

"But that is not how my people will see it. There are still graybeards alive who remember the Skaladin occupation. Nobody wants another boot on our necks."

"Which is exactly what they will get if Kantelvar's plan plays out. Even with his death the war goes on, everybody gets drawn in, everybody loses.

I don't imagine you want Célestial barons rampaging through your lands any more than I do, but Alejandro and Clìmacio don't know that."

Julio's brows pinched in thought. "It won't be Clìmacio though, will it? It will be Margareta, and I cannot imagine her agreeing to any terms that do not involve keeping a large portion of what she has stolen."

Isabelle's pulse thrummed with the excitement of her speculation. "Not if you can steal Clìmacio's loyalty."

Julio bristled. "What makes you think that wretch has any loyalty to give?"

"Appeal to his self-interest. He didn't choose his path. He has had no choice but to pretend to be you or die, and indeed death is all he expects. You can give him a better option, convince him to sue for peace and pull him out from under Margareta's heel. She has no power except through him."

Julio shifted his weight from foot to foot as if in some wrestling match with himself. "Out of morbid curiosity, assuming we can dissolve Margareta's power base, what do you suggest we do with her?"

Isabelle stared at her reflection in the pool. She wore no crown. She had no authority to hand down judgment. "Are you asking me to pass judgment on your mother?"

Julio joined her in staring at their reflections. "She never had any affection for me, much less love. I eventually stopped trying to figure out what I had done to displease her, but I never stopped hurting. Now I know why she hated me, feared me, and it doesn't help."

Isabelle retreated from pain into the safety of logic. "If you're asking my advice, I would say Margareta should be judged by the Sacred Hundred, in public and with all due ceremony."

"Such would be a trial of politics rather than evidence," Julio pointed out.

"Yes," Isabelle said glumly. "But at least it would force everyone to bob their heads at the rule of law. It will help everyone get back to pretending the government into existence."

"You make it sound like some sort of dream."

"The most important things we have are dreams," Isabelle said. "Without them we cannot conjure new truths or better worlds. Where we get into trouble is when we tell ourselves dreams don't matter, or we let other people tell us our dreams are silly or stupid. I dream of peace, and I won't give it up."

Julio paced a few restless steps around the circumference of the pool and back again, like a bear in a cage. Isabelle sat calm and still, trying to be like water, reminding herself of Jean-Claude's maxim "Never interrupt someone who disagrees with you when they are in the process of changing their mind."

Gretl returned with an armload of cloth that shook out into a long, fur-lined cloak. Isabelle wrapped herself in it gladly. Maybe now she'd have enough body heat to send some down to her frozen toes.

At last, Julio stopped pacing. "I will accept l'Empire's aid and make a third faction, but be aware that what you ask may be as irretrievable as yesterday. We have no way of knowing what has transpired in San Augustus since the night you were kidnapped. The factions may have been at each other's throats for a week already. If it comes to that, I will do whatever it takes to ensure Alejandro emerges victorious. Carlemmo is my father whether he sired me or no, and I will not repay him by betraying his true heir. Nor will I allow his kingdom to be destroyed if it is within my power to prevent it."

Isabelle nodded. "We should get going. We should go first to the Céles-tial embassy and inform Hugo du Blain I am alive." Hopefully someone as urbane as du Blain would be able to defer judgment on her noncanonical sorcery.

"No." Julio stared grimly at the water. "I won't chance taking you with me. It's too much of a risk. Breaching through water is like . . . it's like melting, dissolving. It takes everything I have to hold myself together. After your bodyguard stabbed me, I couldn't even gather my sorcery; my espejismo was diluted. I was lost in the Argentwash for days and very nearly starved to death before Kantelvar returned, pulled me out, and locked me in that cell."

Julio flexed his right arm, the one Jean-Claude had stabbed. "I honestly don't know if I'll be able to make the passage now, but I do know it would be harder to take a passenger with me. I won't risk losing my grip on you and dissolving you through the Argentwash."

"But I have to be there," Isabelle protested. Then suspicion bloomed in Isabelle's mind. "Unless you plan to keep me isolated from my allies."

He gave her an offended look. "I cannot very well use you as a hostage given that my departure necessitates giving you care and control of my helpless body. The first thing I will do upon arrival in San Augustus is send a ship to pick both of us up and return us to civilization. In the meantime, how may I prove myself to your people?"

Isabelle reined in her distrust. She was the one who had made the overture of Célestial aid to him, after all. She had little choice but to rely on him.

She said, "Contact my musketeer; his name is Jean-Claude. I'm afraid he's the one who stabbed you. Tell him what I told you. He will relay it to du Blain." Kantelvar said he'd had Jean-Claude killed. *Not dead,* she prayed. *Please.* Kantelvar had underestimated Jean-Claude before; he could have done it again.

Julio said, "Given his proven animosity toward me, how should I recommend myself to him?"

"Tell him . . . I am safe, sound, secure, and several synonyms starting with 'S.'"

Julio's eyebrows quirked up. "That's a very long password."

"More like a private language, but he will understand it." *Please let him be alive.* "And someone has to find Marie, my handmaid—"

Julio looked exasperated. "I will not have time to locate everyone of your household. Approaching the Célestial embassy makes sense but—"

"Marie is my family," Isabelle snapped, "and Kantelvar damned her worse than anyone. She's spent twelve years as a bloodhollow, and now she's been left to rot in a cellar beneath the old Temple in the citadel with no one to look after her."

Julio backed away from her as if she were spitting fire. "I'll inform your ambassador; he should be able to send someone to fetch her."

"Thank you," Isabelle said. "May the saints smile upon your venture."

Julio crooked the unscarred corner of his mouth. The left side on his true form. "I am only doing the duty that was given to me, perhaps salvaging my honor. You are the one who serves a greater vision."

"Peace only seems like a great vision because the prizes of war are so small."

Julio nodded and held his hand out, palm up. "Builder keep you."

She floated her spark-hand over his, palm down. "Until the Savior comes."

Julio sat down with his legs folded under him on the lip of the pool. He bent and reached for the surface of the pool. The very tip of one finger brushed the surface of the water, bending it without causing so much as a ripple. At first, nothing seemed to be happening, but after perhaps a hundred heartbeats, the air grew tight and the glimmers of light on the pool warped and stretched toward Julio's reflection. Isabelle felt herself being pulled in that direction as well. Loose wisps of her hair and folds of cloth yearned toward Julio as if the direction of "down" had subtly altered and Julio were literally the center of the world.

Something snapped, the world rocked back into its ordinary shape, and the tension in the air disappeared. Isabelle wobbled, but recovered her balance in time to see Julio's reflection stand up in the pool. He bowed to her, and she curtsied to him. Then, with a fishlike flicker, his espejismo vanished into the deep. His physical body slumped backward and sprawled on the floor.

Julio's sudden absence seemed to suck the air from Isabelle's lungs. Had she done the right thing? There was no use for such a doubt. It was hard to admit it, but her part in this mad improvisation was done. The final act must be completed by others. As much as she hated conflict, she ought to be thankful. So why did she feel so empty?

The royal carriage rattled down the cobbled streets of San Augustus toward the Naval Orrery, wherein lay records of every ship that entered or departed the sky harbor, including, Jean-Claude fervently prayed, the one that had stolen Isabelle away. *I will find you,* he swore, *even if I have to storm the Halls of Torment.*

With only four people in its cabin, the carriage should have been quite spacious, but the guards at Jean-Claude's sides pressed him close and kept his arms pinned even though his hands were tied behind his back. Across from him, Felix's anger had grown so massive that it practically needed its own seat. In a way this was good, because angry people did not think clearly.

"It's not your fault you didn't know about Thornscar," Jean-Claude said by way of keeping the fire stoked. "I'm sure you were doing the best you could, but you had so many other things to worry about. Missing that little detail hardly matters."

"Silence," Felix snapped, "or I will have you gagged."

Jean-Claude stared out the coach's windows. The city's normal bustle was all but gone. The rivers of people who normally flooded the streets had dwindled to a mere trickle. City guards, soldiers, and mercenaries in every type of uniform hurried toward fortified rallying points, hauling loads of supplies. A few units had formed up in swift columns, making some pre-emptive tactical moves, seizing high ground, and setting up ambush points. It wouldn't be long until two such groups found each other and decided to dispute some advantageous position. Sooner or later, some nervous soldier was going to decide to shoot first. *And then we will find out if it's possible to set off just one keg of powder in a magazine.*

The people had not been told the king's death was imminent, but they knew. They knew the instant all military leaves had been canceled and all storehouses had been shuttered. The city held its breath as if, by some sympathetic magic, it might delay Carlemmo's last exhalation.

"Have they closed the gates?" Jean-Claude asked.

"Shut up," Felix said.

"If the gates are shut, all these people will be trapped in here when the fighting starts."

"There will be no fighting. Príncipe Julio's claim to the throne is irrefutable."

"That's Margareta talking. You've been fighting your whole life, and you know Alejandro's supporters will never give in without bloodshed."

Felix's eyes narrowed. "You know nothing of me."

Jean-Claude considered the man's odd appearance. "One of your parents was Skaladin. Your mother, I imagine. That makes you a mixed-blood sorcerer. By Temple law, you should have been given to the sky when you were born, but you were your father's only son."

Felix's dagger moved so quickly that Jean-Claude barely had time to flinch before the blade scored a bloody line along his left cheek just under his eye.

"You will be silent!"

Jean-Claude's pulse raced with anger born of pain. He wanted to take that dagger away from the little bush tit and carve his initials on his liver, but he had no right to take such a risk, not while Isabelle was still in peril. He hadn't any right to turn away from her, even for a second. That was the responsibility he'd taken when he had given Isabelle her name. He needed to unbalance Felix, not unhinge him.

He shrugged, inspiring the guards to tighten their grips. Good. Let them tire their fingers. It would make their grip clumsy if he could arrange an opportunity for escape.

When the coach arrived at the Naval Orrery, it was met by a small squad of outriders who had forged ahead to scout the place and make sure Jean-Claude had not somehow arranged an ambush to receive them. Only when Felix was satisfied that no enemies lurked in the wainscoting did he allow Jean-Claude to debark.

With his hands bound behind him, a poniard aimed at his ribs, and a smear of blood down his left cheek, Jean-Claude suffered himself to be led, limping theatrically, up the steps to the orrery building. It was an enormous, six-sided structure, four stories tall, faced with marble, and adorned with double-sized statues of famous admirals, explorers, philosophers, and, of course, kings. What else was nobility for, if not to provide fodder for artists?

The building's tall ironbound doors were propped open, revealing a broad barrel-vaulted corridor paved with glossy, caramel-colored stone and decorated top to bottom with intricate mosaics depicting famous voyages both recent and ancient.

Toward Jean-Claude's expeditionary party strode a tall, thin man in a frock coat. "Greetings, señors. I am given to understand you are on the queen's business. I am Don Amerigo, the Naval Orrery's curator."

The don's wiry frame seemed to be under siege by a small army of eyepieces. A pair of half-moon spectacles bestrode his nose while another set of glasses with thick dark lenses surmounted his forehead, two pairs of square-rimmed glasses hung from the pockets of his coat, and another set hung from a cord about his neck. A monocle bravely clung to its fob chain like a soldier scaling a wall on a grappling line, and Amerigo waved a jeweler's loupe in one hand. His expression was pleasantly bland, except for his eyes—clayborn brown, not Glasswalker silver—which were creased with the sort of nervous exasperation typical of a man who had been dragged away from doing something important to deal with someone important.

"We are," Felix said. "We require you to find for us a ship."

"Of course," Amerigo said. "Which ship?"

Felix glowered at Jean-Claude.

Jean-Claude made a respectful bow to Amerigo, a gesture that surely emphasized the fact that his arms were tied behind his back. "We are looking for a smuggler."

Amerigo looked Jean-Claude up and down, apparently unsure what to make of him. "Can you be more specific?"

Jean-Claude prevaricated. "Yes, we are looking for the smuggler with the queen's personal enemies on it. I understand that the Naval Orrery keeps records of every ship with an Aragothic flag. Does that include accounts of their movement through your aerial domain?"

"Oh, yes. It's one of our most important tasks. It keeps an entire regiment of clerks occupied around the clock."

"What exactly do you track? Just the ships that come into port?"

"Oh, no. We would miss too much that way. We have divided our aerial demesnes into precincts. Whenever a ship enters a precinct or leaves it, its passage is noted in the daily list and subsequently entered in the weekly ledger, which is then compiled in the monthly codex for long-term storage."

Builder bless the detail obsessive. "I need a map of these precincts. And I'll need to look at the lists going back five days." That would encompass the day Kantelvar had kidnapped Isabelle.

"All of the records?" Amerigo asked. "There will be thousands of listings."

"In that case, I will also need someone who knows how to read them."

"Ah." Amerigo looked to Felix for confirmation.

"Get him what he asks for," Felix said gruffly.

"It would be easier to bring him to the records than to bring the records to him."

"We will all go," Felix said.

Two guards frog-marched Jean-Claude along behind Felix and Amerigo. "No need to be so rough, lads," he said, being as cooperative as their rude handling allowed. They couldn't have detached him from this opportunity with block and tackle.

The Naval Orrery was said to be a miracle of modern philosophical engineering. It was an enormously sophisticated aetheric mechanism that kept track of every skyship with an Aragothic chartstone, anywhere in the great sky. It was to the average ship's orrery what the Solar was to a candle. As such, it was a point of pilgrimage for empirical philosophers, cartographers, merchants, ship captains, and anyone else who made their living from the deep sky. To Jean-Claude it was a hope. Here there might be—*had to be*—a thread that led to Isabelle, if only he could find it before a twitchy guard jabbed something pointy into his vital bits.

From the end of the hallway came a glow that limned the people in front of Jean-Claude with a green-bluish light, as if from an alchemical lamp burning underwater, and he became aware of a noise. It was not precisely a sound, but a vibration picked up by the hairs on the nape of his neck that settled into his mind as high-pitched humming.

Up ahead, Don Amerigo was providing commentary. "This is the Observatory." And the way he said it, Jean-Claude could hear the capital "O."

The curator turned aside, guiding Felix with him, and Jean-Claude stepped into the place of the curator's reverence. Only fierce national pride kept Jean-Claude from gawping like a stunned bullfrog; l'Empire Céleste had nothing like this.

He walked onto a balcony that girded a spherical room at least twenty meters across. The floor, if there was a floor down there, was obscured by swirling black clouds shot through with snaps of lightning, just like the Galvanosphere. The ceiling was a sprawling dome made up of hundreds of huge glass panes in a metal lattice that spiraled in, like the armor of some reef-dwelling mollusk, toward its apex. The light streaming in through those windows seemed to slick and slither through air, giving the whole space a glister of wetness.

But the most amazing thing was the shoal of skyships plying the air. There were hundreds of them, maybe thousands, but these were not the ghostly cloud pictures produced by simulacrascopes; they were tiny models made of wood, brass, cloth, and paint, all exquisitely detailed. The smallest was the size of his pinky knuckle, the largest the length of his forefinger with a sail span as big as his hand. They wheeled in vast slow schools, tacking and running, swooping and climbing around a perfect scale model of San Augustus and its harbor. The whole city was there, modeled with an obsessive attention to minutiae that was half art, half madness.

Jean-Claude walked slowly along the gallery. He caught up to and passed a tall ship just making a turn off the coast of a barrier skyland. He almost imagined he could see tiny sailors aboard, trimming the sails.

Isabelle would love this.

The thought of her stabbed him and snapped his attention back to the task at hand. He had to find out where Kantelvar's ship had gone and then find a way to get there without giving it away to the Aragoths.

Amerigo led Felix, Jean-Claude, and half a dozen inconvenient guards through several unadorned corridors to a long room, really nothing more than a wide stretch of the hallway with rows and rows of desks on either wall and a long line of simulacrascopes down the center. The place bubbled with babble as maybe a hundred clerks exchanged a rapid patter of fore-shortened Aragothic, mostly numbers and initials. Amerigo guided Jean-Claude to a long table upon which was spread a three-meter-long map of the Aragothic coast. The sky just off the continental cliff was divided up unto initialed boxes.

"These are the precincts," Amerigo said. "Each precinct is watched over by a simulacrascope. You will note that near San Augustus, the precincts are smaller and more densely packed because that is where we have our heaviest traffic. The farther you get from a harbor into the deep sky, the bigger the space one simulacrascope can effectively track."

"Impressive," Jean-Claude said, but it didn't tell him where Kantelvar had taken Isabelle. Damn it, with all this information wafting around, there had to be something he could use. "What do you use all this information for? It wouldn't help you detect a lurking enemy because you wouldn't have a shard of their chartstone."

"Correct. We use it for taxes, mostly. Any ship that passes through Aragothic sky is obliged to pay a fee for the protection afforded by the Aragothic fleet."

Of course. Only for money would people go to this much trouble.

"This is not relevant," Felix said. "Do what you came here to do."

We want miracles and we want them now. Jean-Claude examined the map. He doubted Kantelvar had docked his ship in the main harbor; it would be too obvious. More likely it had been stashed in a cove somewhere under the rim of the Craton Massif, away from the harbor, but not too far away. "I'll need the lists for precincts eleven, twelve, and thirteen starting five days ago." While he was waiting for that to happen, he asked, "And what happens if a ship just putters around in one precinct without crossing a boundary?"

"The presence of every ship in a precinct is noted at the beginning of every shift, so it would still be noted . . . unless—and I bring this up only because you are looking for smugglers—the ship's navigator removed the ship's chartstone from its matrix, say, while it was hidden in some cove. He'd only have to put it in when he wanted to feign legitimacy in order to pass through without being confronted by picket ships."

Jean-Claude grunted, for that was likely exactly what Kantelvar had done. Otherwise, a ship clinging like a barnacle to the bottom of the city would attract attention.

A clerk arrived with a tight stack of papers that he spread on the map table before Jean-Claude. They were covered in dense writing, mostly in an obscure condensed shorthand of letters and numbers that were too busy to speak in complete words, much less sentences. The clerk said, "This first code is the identification code of the ship, the second is its time of appearance or disappearance, the third is its coordinates in space." The clerk pointed at the first set of numbers. "This is a merchant ship. You can tell by the 'MC' prefix. It entered precinct ten from the harbor at five minutes after seventh bell and"—he ran his finger down the column until he found a similar entry—"left the precinct at the number eleven boundary two hours later."

Jean-Claude stared at the number blocks in dismay, for nowhere did they seem to correlate to a list of ships' names. "You wouldn't happen to have a registry, would you?"

Amerigo brightened. "Of course, we have dozens of them. What ship do you need to look up?"

The last thing Jean-Claude wanted to do was spit out the name in front of Felix.

"Yes, musketeer," Felix whispered, leaning in close. "What is the name of this ship? Tell me or I start cutting off fingers." The edge of a razor-sharp blade creased the knuckle of Jean-Claude's least left-hand finger.

"Señor, no," Amerigo said. "This is a sanctified building."

Felix glared at Amerigo. "Then summon an artifex and tell him he'll need to start over, unless this fat fool tells me the name of that ship right now."

"The *Fisherman's Dream*," Jean-Claude said, recalling the name of a wharf-side inn. Fortunately, the people who named taverns had the same sort of wit as those who named boats.

"Very good," said Amerigo, obviously relieved not to have blood on his floors.

"Or maybe it was the *Wandering Goose*," Jean-Claude said. It was a small tavern on the road outside Rocher Royale. "Or maybe it was the *Bosun's Ballast*." Demoiselle Planchette would get a good cackle out of that, if ever he survived to tell her about it. "My memory gets a bit slippery when I'm in pain."

Felix growled, "If I say you were killed trying to escape, no one will doubt me."

"But if you do that, you'll miss your one chance to catch your assassin. He's not a man you want to stay loose very long, or by the time you catch up with his tail, his serpent's head will have got round behind you."

"Assassin?" Amerigo asked. "I thought you said you were after a smuggler."

"The two categories are not mutually exclusive," Jean-Claude said.

Felix wrenched Jean-Claude's arm up even higher behind his back, sending stabs of pain through his shoulder. "Be quiet."

Jean-Claude grimaced. "You cannot expect me to talk and be quiet simultaneously."

"Which registry do you want?" Amerigo asked. "I'll bring it here."

That was a damned good question. "How are they organized?" Jean-Claude asked through gritted teeth. Finally, the guard got tired of holding Jean-Claude's arm twisted up and relaxed enough so that his shoulder stopped screaming at him.

"Chronologically."

"And how long has this project been going on?"

"Twenty-three years. Of course we've made some modifications to the accounting since then."

Jean-Claude didn't give a damn about accounting. The question was, for how long had Kantelvar stowed the *Voto Solemne*? And had he done it under that name? "Bring me the one from five years ago," he said. That was when Kantelvar had supposedly come to San Augustus from the hinterlands.

Amerigo dispatched one of his clerks at a gallop. To fill in the silence, and to stall Felix from trying anything else, Jean-Claude pointed with his nose at the day's ledger of ships. "So what do all these code things mean?"

Jean-Claude couldn't have found a better delaying tactic if he'd had a month of planning. This clerk was one of those people who loved details. They didn't have to do anything so long as he could keep himself occupied just knowing them. And he was more than happy to recite them. Jean-Claude let his ears listen to the man ramble on about how vessels were classed by function, type, and tonnage while his mind chipped away at the problem of what he really needed to know. It was like trying to pick a lock with a spoon.

Even if he found the ship in the registry, it wasn't along the coast anymore. It wouldn't be on the scopes, and all Kantelvar had to do was get out of the local area of interest, then remove the chartstone shard from the orrery to make it disappear from all scopes. Of course, if he did that, his own orrery wouldn't work anymore, either. The simulacrascopes worked on the principle of sympathy. The orrery on a ship had to have a chartstone matching the one in the ground beacon for them to be able to see each other. There was, however, nothing stopping a ship's captain from having two chartstone flags, one for common spaces and another for secret destinations.

Don't burn that bridge until you've crossed it. The best thing he could do was wait for the registry. The fetch-and-carry clerk returned at a stagger, the weight of the huge book bending him like a sapling. He aimed at an empty table and dropped the tome onto it with a resounding thud.

Jean-Claude stared at the volume in dismay. "Just how many ships are there in this harbor?" Certainly not enough to fill up a book that could double as a footstool.

"That's a yearly archive," Amerigo said. "Only part of it is the ship's registry. The rest is manifests, shipyard fees, and so on. Now, what ship are you looking for?"

Jean-Claude glowered at the intimidating book; this was going to take longer than he'd hoped, if it was even the right track. "Open it up and I'll let you know when I see it."

The whole book might not have been filled with ships' names, but it was still enough to make Jean-Claude's eyes cross. It was alphabetized by ship type and then name; he might as well have set the damned thing on fire and tried to read an answer in the rising entrails of smoke like some ancient haruspex. Still, he plodded on page after page, "Next" after "Next," until even the detail-oriented clerk got bored with it. Every now and again Jean-Claude startled when he saw a name similar to the one he sought; other times he twitched when he just wanted to set Felix on edge. So it was that nobody took notice when his gaze caught on the *Voto Solemne*. It was a spicer, a ship designed for long voyages with small but expensive cargoes. It was registered not to an individual but to the Temple, and it was berthed amongst the prison hulks at the lowest level of the harbor. Jean-Claude committed the numerical code to memory and then had the clerk advance a few more pages before saying, "Bring me the harbor records from five days ago."

"You have it?" asked Amerigo

"I'm on the scent," Jean-Claude said; he wanted to make sure the ship's number he'd just memorized matched an actual ship that had actually left.

Jean-Claude returned to the maps and charts, scanning column after column. It took going over several dozen pages before he found what was he was looking for. The *Voto Solemne* launched before daybreak the night after the fire, heading generally northwestward through several zones, and never returned. He cross-checked all five days' worth of records before he was sure.

"Got you, you bastard," he growled. Of course the ship could have swapped chartstones and changed directions as soon as it was out of range of the coastal scopes, but that was a problem for later. He'd learned as much as he could without surrendering a point to Felix.

"Where?" Felix asked, glancing at the chart without any comprehension.

Jean-Claude turned to Don Amerigo, who had been watching him with a wary curiosity. "Thank you, señor, you have been most helpful. Felix, if you don't mind taking us back to the palace, I have an answer for the queen."

Felix's eyes bulged. "What answer? All you've done is lead us on a wild-goose chase."

"I have done what I said I would do," Jean-Claude said. "I found the name of the ship on which the assassin escaped. I must bring her that information . . . or did you think I was going to hand it over to you so you could stab me like a dog in the street?"

Felix's glare promised Jean-Claude a slow, painful death, but Amerigo hastily interjected, "Gentlemen, this way, if you please." He captured Jean-Claude's arm and tugged him away from the spot where he'd been rooted.

Felix followed, cursing not quite under his breath. Amerigo led the not-so-merry band out the door opposite the one they'd come in. Now that Jean-Claude had gotten over being awed by the Naval Orrery, he considered the backstage architecture of the building. Most of it was laid out in concentric circles joined by a few radial hallways leading out from the spectacular central venue. There weren't many doors, and those few that did exist didn't seem to have bolts that a man with bound hands could easily close. It was not a good place for an old man with a game leg to escape a bunch of young, fit soldiers. His best bet would be to ride Felix like a rented mule all the way back to Margareta, to flatter her for influence.

From a great and muffled distance came the tolling of a bell. Amerigo stopped in his tracks and lifted his head like a deer sensing danger. Everyone else in the small parade piled up behind him. The bell tolled again, and was joined by another one, deep throated and slow, and another. The sound grew closer and louder until Jean-Claude guessed that every bell in the city must be booming.

Amerigo sagged. "Padre de Santos."

The soldiers shuffled nervously. Felix gave the first smile Jean-Claude had ever seen him generate. It was even less pleasant than his scowl. "The king is dead."

Did that mean Alejandro was a murderer? If so, Jean-Claude could not blame him.

"This way," Amerigo said. He took Jean-Claude by the elbow and guided him through a door. It took Jean-Claude one heartbeat to realize which door. Amerigo had been leading them toward the edge of the building. He propelled Jean-Claude through into the park outside the orrery. Amerigo stepped out after him and slammed the door shut in Felix's face, setting the lock before anyone inside had realized what happened. There was an outraged scream and several heavy bodies hit the door at once. It bowed outward, creaking.

"Run!" Amerigo shouted, and pelted along the side of the building, heading for a corner. Jean-Claude lurched after him as fast as he was able, his game leg straining. *Why? Who?* He had no time or breath for the questions. He had almost reached the corner when a coach came around it, heading in the opposite direction. It carried Duque Diego's banner. The doors swung open and the footmen riding outside boosted Amerigo in without slowing down. Jean-Claude lunged after him, slipped, and nearly got pulled under the wheels before strong hands grabbed his belt and hauled him in. He landed in a graceless heap on the floor.

"Would somebody mind untying me?" he muttered into the cabin's carpet.

Somebody sliced the thongs on his wrists, then Don Amerigo and Diego himself helped Jean-Claude into a seat. Diego was dressed in impeccable court garb, all in mourning black.

Jean-Claude said, "I thank you for the rescue. I'm guessing you two know each other." He gestured to the winded academic. "I hope I have not put you out too much."

"Not at all," Diego said. "When my eyes in the citadel told me that you were being sent to the Naval Orrery, I sent a fast messenger to warn Don Amerigo, who is my cousin."

"That doesn't explain why you bothered exposing yourself on my behalf."

"Because my informants tell me you were there when Príncipe Alejandro was apprehended. I want your account."

"How much do you already know?" Jean-Claude asked.

Diego made a balancing gesture. "I wish to compare it with what you can tell me. From the beginning, if you please."

Jean-Claude rubbed his rope-bitten wrists while he considered his options. Fortunately, Diego's interests seemed mostly to square with his own, at least insofar as rescuing Kantelvar's captives was concerned.

"To be fair, I didn't actually figure out that Lord DuJournal was Príncipe Alejandro until after he met me in the citadel . . ." He gave most of the story to Diego, omitting only the hellish bargain Margareta had tried to make with Alejandro. If the accusation of regicide was to be laid, let it be from other lips. "But the main point is that Kantelvar took ship on the *Voto Solemne,* and I believe he carried Isabelle and Julio into the upper sky somewhere spinward of here."

By the time he finished, Diego's coach had returned to his town home, and they all made their way inside. Jean-Claude acquired another cane and barely resisted a cup of wine.

"I will send a ship for them," Diego said. "Amerigo, if you will assist."

"I need soldiers. I imagine that Captain Felix has interdicted the Naval Orrery by now."

"Take what men you need."

"Kantelvar may have switched out the chartstone on his ship," Jean-Claude said.

Don Amerigo frowned but said, "We won't know until we look. And even if he has . . . well, we shall see."

"What is that supposed to mean?"

"It means I will explain on the way. Come."

Never had Jean-Claude wanted so much to pounce on an offer, not even when he had been admitted by the musketeer academy, but could he serve Isabelle by rushing forth to meet her, or by making sure she had a place to land?

"As much as my soul yearns to accompany you, if you can fetch Isabelle, then I am afraid I have work to do here." He had to contact Grand Leon and let him know Isabelle was still alive. That would be the greatest protection he could afford her. To Diego he said, "If I might prevail upon your guesthold for a change of clothes, a weapon to protect myself in these dangerous streets, and someone to go attend poor Marie . . ."

"Of course." Diego snapped his fingers and summoned a minion to fulfill Jean-Claude's needs. For once, Jean-Claude was more grateful than annoyed with this brusque efficiency. Barely had he shrugged into a new set of clothes, fine but not fancy, when another servant came in and summoned him to Diego's side. He found the duque in the entry hall.

Diego said, "Margareta has summoned all of her faithful servants to witness the king's passing and attend Alejandro's trial for regicide."

"That didn't take long," Jean-Claude said dryly. "You'd almost think she was expecting this turn of events."

"The trial is a sham, and everyone knows it. What will matter is whether his conviction and execution will enrage or dishearten his supporters, and that will depend on his behavior during the trial. If he is vigorous in his own defense, then his death will inflame his faction against the queen. If he is passive, it will dishearten them. As long as Margareta holds Xaviera in the Hellshard, he is likely to be passive."

"And you want him to be active. Why?"

"Because then, after he has been executed, Julio will return. Margareta's pretender will be exposed as a fraud and all the factions will unite behind Julio."

"Even l'Empire," Jean-Claude surmised, "because he will have Isabelle at his side."

"Precisely," Diego said, and Jean-Claude judged him sincere.

"And that is why you are going to ask me to rescue Xaviera, to put fire in Alejandro's heart, so that he will provide a more inspirational death."

Duque Diego was solemn. "You know as well as I that this can only end with the triumph of one prince and the death of the other. So has it always been, and your Isabelle is to be wedded to our faction. Will you not serve her now as you have so faithfully throughout?"

"Of course I will," Jean-Claude grunted. Nor would he so quickly turn his back on Alejandro, who had saved his life twice.

Duque Diego said, "Your master, as well as other heads of state, has been invited to attend in person or by proxy, to ensure that the event is as broadly and irrefutably witnessed as possible. At last report I heard Leon had arrived in the vessel of his emissary."

"I will convey your intent to him," Jean-Claude said.

They mounted the coach and spent much of the drive through the tense and empty streets discussing Jean-Claude's insertion into the castle. There was a cook who would open a door for a man with the right passphrase. Felix would almost certainly be at the queen's side, with the key to the Hellshard in his belt pouch.

"Just what is the Hellshard anyway?" Jean-Claude asked.

"It is a spike, a spire of quondam stone, six feet high and shaped like an obelisk, that hovers about a foot off the ground. Nobody knows how. Likely they will bring it out for the trial, just to remind Alejandro what is at stake. Nobody knows what its original purpose was, or if it even had one, but now it is a special kind of torture. The ring that Felix holds is like a door. Anything that passes through is drawn out, almost like a wire, and spooled into the Hellshard."

"Would that not be fatal?"

"One would think, but the transference itself is not damaging. I am informed, by a man who has been through it, that it was like having his identity torn apart, memory from memory. The man in question was only in there for a few minutes, but he was never quite the same again afterward."

"Xaviera has been in there for hours," Jean-Claude said, feeling sick.

"Then I fear for her sanity. The only way to get something out of the Hellshard is to run the shard itself through the ring. At that point, the Hellshard unspools and releases its captive."

The carriage entered the palace grounds and merged with a train of similar conveyances, all under heavy guard. The field in front of the royal residence was crowded with onlookers on foot, and thousands more streamed in through the outer gates. Apparently, no one had thought to keep them out. The changeless present in which the masses lived had just become a formless future, and so they milled together like cattle before an oncoming storm.

Progress slowed to a crawl as Diego's carriage pressed through the mob. It was all the outriders could do to keep a path clear.

Jean-Claude said, "I shall make better progress on foot." He pushed open the door and set off toward the side entrance of the palace, slithering through the crowd as easily as a snake through tall grass. Even so, it was a long way around the building for a man with a limp, and he had plenty of time to curse the Aragoths' love of oversized architecture.

He had just reached a corner that would take him out of sight of the main entrance when a great blast cracked the air. Bomb! He whirled to see a cloud of wooden splinters raining down from a rising cloud of black smoke. Diego's carriage. The duque's pennon fluttered and flapped like a wounded vulture, and in the space cleared by the blast, Jean-Claude viewed the shattered corpse of a man in mourning black. Diego.

"Breaker's hells!"

Terrified people and horses shrieked. The injured wailed. The crowd surged away from the point of detonation, thousands of people all trying to escape the same space at the same time. A wave of panic rippled outward, uniting the crowd in the purpose of flight.

Jean-Claude lurched toward the side of the palace. He rounded the corner just in time to take shelter from a wave of people crashing against the wall in their haste to escape, crushing and trampling one another in their fear.

Only then did he have time to wonder what had happened, or rather how it had been done. Had someone used the crowd for cover and just lobbed a bomb in the coach window? An anonymous face throwing an anonymous grenade . . . except that explosion was too big to be an ordinary hand bomb.

Even more important than how was why. What did Margareta know about Diego that he hadn't known she knew? Was Margareta even behind this? Builder only knew how many other factions there were in play.

So forget causes; what were the consequences? As far as Jean-Claude knew, everybody else in the court thought Diego was Margareta's staunchest ally. His death would therefore be blamed on her enemies, increasing the outrage against Alejandro and his faction. Worse, Jean-Claude knew of no one in Margareta's faction except Amerigo who knew enough to level a charge of treachery against Margareta, and by the time Amerigo returned from sending a ship for Julio and Isabelle, the trial would be over. When she did return, Isabelle would sail straight into a trap.

Jean-Claude had to find Grand Leon, let him know Isabelle was still alive, and warn him about Margareta's treachery. Then, with any luck, he would be ordered to make the way clear for Isabelle's return. Surely Grand Leon would not want Margareta or her puppet to be sitting on the throne when Isabelle returned, and here he was, with a way into her palace, where confusion was rampant and a lone assassin might find a way to improvise. He would never have a better chance at making sure her reign of terror never became official . . . but if he got caught, the entire blame would fall on l'Empire Céleste, and on Isabelle by proxy once she was brought back to San Augustus.

So don't get caught.

The palace's side entrances were all manned by guards who were demonstrating an annoying level of discipline by staying on post despite the commotion around the front of the building. Jean-Claude was supposed to meet his contact at the third door along. Could this be a trap as well? Jean-Claude checked the sword at his hip.

He raised his hands up away from the weapon as he approached the wary-looking guard at the door. "Excuse me."

"What's going on out there?" the guard asked. People were still streaming by behind Jean-Claude, but the force of the stampede had been absorbed by the size of the grounds.

"Fireworks," Jean-Claude said. "A very inappropriate display. It caused a panic. Look, I'm here to see Javier, it's about his mother." This was not exactly the script he was supposed to be using, but it hit on the key elements.

The guard looked momentarily nonplussed, then he knocked on the door. When a cook's helper stuck his head out the guard said, "Tell Javier there's a man here about his mother."

The assistant disappeared and was replaced a moment later by a swarthy man in a cook's apron. He gave Jean-Claude a look that said quite plainly that he was not the man Javier expected. "My mother?"

"She has a message for you concerning your wedding."

"Ah. Well, come in then." Javier looked at the guard for confirmation of permission and then drew Jean-Claude inside.

Jean-Claude stepped in warily, but the pastry kitchen was notably devoid of ambushers. No sooner had the door closed behind him than Javier whispered, "Did Diego send you? What's going on out there?"

"Yes, and somebody set off a bomb in the courtyard."

"What!" The cook's yelp got the attention of all the other kitchen workers. "Has the fighting started?"

Jean-Claude made a shushing motion and spoke through his teeth. "Don't panic. No, it has not, and with any luck it won't. You just go about your business, don't listen to any rumors, and if anyone asks, I was never here. Understand?"

Javier nodded, and Jean-Claude clapped him on the shoulder. "Good. Now point me in the direction of the royal wing."

On the way out of the kitchen, Jean-Claude absconded with a double handful of raspberry tarts; it had been ages since he'd had a decent meal. Amongst the many pieces of advice he was sure his mother would have given him if she'd ever thought about it was "Never set out to murder a monarch on an empty stomach."

The royal palace was so vast and convoluted that it seemed to Jean-Claude that it took him roughly two-thirds of forever to locate the royal wing, and he had yet to find a way in to get to Grand Leon. All the doors were guarded, the guests escorted, and the servants identified.

He could only imagine what was going on in the Hall of Mirrors: King Carlemmo's corpse laid out, the queen and her fake príncipe in mourning garb, the foreign dignitaries offering condolences of various levels of sincerity, the noble guests agitated by the king's demise and Duque Diego's murder, Alejandro in chains and surrounded by guards, his bloody knife on the table as evidence of his misdeed.

Jean-Claude made another slow orbit of the guarded perimeter, moving through secondary hallways, passageways, and the occasional drawing room while keeping far enough away from the guarded entrances to avoid earning any soldierly attention. Every now and then the floor vibrated with the reports of cannons. The shelling had started an hour ago, and Builder only knew how much of the city had already been engulfed in fighting. He was just debating whether it would be better to climb up on the roof and try to get in through one of the clerestory windows or sneak down into the basement to look for unguarded passages, when a familiar accent tugged his attention. Someone was speaking la Langue.

Jean-Claude hurried toward the sound, hoping to catch some diplomat or a member of Isabelle's Célestial entourage. Instead, he turned into a sitting room and all but barreled into Hugo du Blain coming the other direction. The ambassador was dressed all in traditional Célestial white with a bloodred shadow fanned out on the floor behind him, as gaudy as a peacock's tail.

Jean-Claude made a hasty bow. "Your Excellency," he said with all the humility his sweeping hat brim could scrape up off the carpet.

The man backed up a step in surprise, and his bloodshadow rippled.

A small crowd of finely dressed people in the room beyond all paused their conversations to watch this encounter.

"Monsieur musketeer," du Blain said in a sour tone. "I am surprised to see you here."

"Did you think me dead or fled?" Jean-Claude said. "No, just give me the odds and tell me where I can place a wager. Better yet, come with me, and I will give you such news as flummoxes all expectations."

As Jean-Claude swept his hat up to replace it on his head, he curled his pinky under the brim, exposing his three other fingers like the tines of the crown, the court sign for royal business.

The ambassador stepped from the room and allowed Jean-Claude to shut the door before speaking in a low tone. "And what makes you think His Most Royal Majesty wants to hear anything you have to say, after the bungle you have made of your duties?"

Jean-Claude had to take that one on the chin; he had no doubt le roi was furious with him. Indeed, Jean-Claude would be lucky to escape a royal audience with his life, his shadow, or his soul. Yet no matter his own future, the fate of kingdoms weighed in the balance, and Isabelle's future with it.

"Do not mistake the messenger for the message," Jean-Claude said. "Grand Leon will want to hear what I have to say."

"Certainly, but it will have to wait until after Príncipe Alejandro's trial. Not that it will be an extended affair. He was caught bloody-handed after murdering his father. I imagine the Sacred Hundred will find him guilty in short order."

Jean-Claude's pulse galloped. "This cannot wait. Besides which, Alejandro is innocent."

Du Blain shook his head. "But this is the outcome His Majesty wants."

"No, this is the best outcome His Majesty thinks he can get," Jean-Claude said. "I can offer him a better one, but only if we act quickly."

Du Blain asked, "What is this news, then?"

For this Jean-Claude was prepared. "I report to him, from my lips to his ears. Whether he wants to hear what I have to say is for him to decide."

Reluctantly, du Blain conceded this. He led Jean-Claude to a waiting room and then shoved off to inform His Imperial Majesty of his petitioner.

Jean-Claude reflexively straightened his borrowed tunic. Dread churned his gut. Would Grand Leon even come? Surely he would want to hear what

Jean-Claude had to say, unless he felt that the report of one who had bungled so badly was not worth hearing.

A reddening of the ambient light drew Jean-Claude's attention. The room's ordinary shadows rippled and parted as a great crimson shadow spilled through the doorway, spreading along the walls, ceiling, and floor, oozing into recesses and flowing over furniture, tinting everything the color of fresh blood.

The crimson stain brushed up against Jean-Claude's shadow. It tugged at his outline on the floor, pulling it into new shape. Like a marionette guided by some godlike puppeteer, Jean-Claude's body twitched to attention and stuck there despite the pain it caused in his thigh.

Grand Leon's sorcerous puissance was undiminished even when he was inhabiting several different vessels at once. *And this one's not even in the room yet. He can't even see me.*

For a dozen heartbeats, Jean-Claude contemplated his helplessness and how far Grand Leon's anger must have extended that he had seen fit to drive this point home. Would he even give Jean-Claude a chance to explain about Isabelle's survival, to make his case for thwarting Margareta, or would this shadow simply rip his mind and soul to pieces? It would be Grand Leon's style to turn Jean-Claude into a bloodhollow as a warning to other privileged servants who might fail him.

Grand Leon's emissary strolled into the room, his skinny frame and wraithlike flesh swollen with Grand Leon's unmistakable presence. The crimson shadows grew heavier and thicker as he approached, taking on an oily sheen that obscured the distinctive shapes of the furniture and gave the whole room the aspect of a great mouth wherein the emissary was a pale, white tongue.

Jean-Claude needed to get his main point out before Grand Leon started harrowing his soul, so he blurted, "Princess Isabelle is alive, and I have located her."

Grand Leon did not appear to hear Jean-Claude's announcement. He walked almost past Jean-Claude, so that, with his head clamped in a forward-facing position, he could only glimpse the side of the king's face, enough to know that Grand Leon was not looking at him.

Grand Leon's voice was casual but cold. "Those are good tidings, but how, pray tell, did you lose her to begin with?"

Jean-Claude had been kicking himself with that very question for the last several days, always without an answer to satisfy his heart. Somehow, it was easier to defend himself to le roi. "By treachery and betrayal. Kantelvar assassinated Vincent, tried to murder me, and stole her away."

Grand Leon walked to a point directly behind Jean-Claude. The blood-shadow deadened his footfalls to mere ghostly whispers. He stopped and held his silence for long enough that Jean-Claude's shoulder blades started twitching with anticipation of a knife . . . not that Grand Leon would ever resort to such crude murder. Clearly this display was meant to frighten Jean-Claude and put him in his place. It was working.

If anyone else had done this to him, he would have been furious, but Grand Leon had made him, had given him everything, including his duty to Isabelle. If anyone had the right to judge him . . . "Kantelvar arranged this marriage," Grand Leon said. "Why would he sabotage it?"

Why indeed? Jean-Claude still didn't know why the damned artifex had set up this game of knives and shadows.

Jean-Claude said, "His plans were deeply laid, Your Majesty. They began at least twenty-four years ago, because they were already in motion at the hour of Princess Isabelle's birth . . ."

Jean-Claude told him everything he knew or suspected of Kantelvar's plan, Vincent's killing, Margareta's plot, Príncipe Julio's and DuJournal's identities, Don Amerigo's assistance, and Duque Diego's murder. Grand Leon interrupted only to ask for clarification of key points.

"And that is how I came to be here," Jean-Claude concluded.

"Interesting," Grand Leon said, and, to Jean-Claude's surprise, the red shadow withdrew. It shrank to a small puddle around le roi's feet. "You have been a very busy man indeed. You have learned more about Aragothic intrigue in a week than my most diligent ambassador has told me in a year. Face me."

Jean-Claude turned in place. His leg pained him and he was still woozy from his encounter with the bloodshadow, but he managed not to fall flat on his face when he made a leg and swept his hat for his master.

"Majesty."

The king's presence, pressing through the emissary's glassy face, was thoughtful. "You failed to protect Princess Isabelle, as was your sworn duty."

Every time someone reminded him of that, it was like having a knife twisted in his ribs. "Yes, Majesty."

Grand Leon said, "But your remarkable persistence in trying to rectify your error has extracted an ember of opportunity from the ashes of catastrophe. The only question is whether I dare trust you to fetch that spark without snuffing it."

Jean-Claude heard the question in that statement and rose to answer it. "That depends on whether Your Majesty questions my competence or my loyalty."

Le roi nodded gravely. "No disloyal man would have dared face us, and we deem that your skills are merely tarnished, not rusted through. A good polish should have them sparkling like new again."

In other words, if he got this right, he would be forgiven. "Shall I carry on then, Majesty?"

Le roi nodded gravely. "Get yourself to the dockyard. When the ship bearing Isabelle and the real Príncipe Julio returns, take them to our embassy and to no other place. Make sure they are not seen."

"Of course," Jean-Claude said, his mind bolting to the mission before considering all the ramifications. "But what about Margareta and Príncipe Alejandro?"

"Alejandro was found standing over King Carlemmo's body. He appears guilty, or at least blamable. He will be found guilty regardless of the truth. Fortunately, this injustice may be put to good use. His legal assassination at Margareta's hand clears the way for Isabelle to be the next queen of Aragoth."

The sickness of betrayal settled in Jean-Claude's heart. Alejandro had saved Jean-Claude's life at least twice. To abandon him without a fight was poor recompense, but Jean-Claude could not force the Grand Leon to act on Alejandro's behalf, and he was in no position to ask for a favor, especially when the fate of empires was on the line.

A distant mortar boomed. Plaster dust from the ceiling drifted down.

Jean-Claude bowed, took three steps back, but couldn't bring himself to leave just yet. "Majesty, in the interest of clarity, Isabelle told me you wanted her to prevent a war."

"Alejandro's death should prevent the outbreak of a general war. Who, after all, would his supporters put on the throne? Isabelle's marriage to the heir will help secure that peace."

"And how do you intend to circumvent Margareta?" Surely Grand Leon wanted Isabelle to be the primary woman behind the throne.

The king's phantom brows drew down very slightly. "If she becomes a threat, surely Princess Isabelle's most loyal guardian can remove her."

"Of course, Majesty." Jean-Claude made a humble obeisance in self-defense and took himself out of the drawing room–cum–audience hall before Grand Leon's infamous temper roiled up. His mind buzzed with the implications of Grand Leon's plan. Alejandro would have to die. Climacio would have to be exposed and Julio put in his place . . . wouldn't he?

Jean-Claude stopped, as stunned as if he'd been shot, as the king's plan unfolded itself in his mind. *Merde!* Grand Leon intended to *keep* Climacio on the throne. He would kidnap the real Julio and use the threat of revealing him as leverage against the false king. In one swift move he would make himself the power behind the throne in Aragoth.

Jean-Claude would have laughed out loud. He would have marveled at the sinister beauty of it . . . except that le roi clearly meant to use Isabelle as the public face of his private conquest, the linchpin for his ambition. The stage on which her life played out would literally be wiped clean of every decent soul, of anyone Isabelle might befriend or trust. Her marriage would be based on blackmail. Her decisions would all be hostage to the necessity of maintaining her grip on people who would stop at nothing to turn the tables on her.

Jean-Claude resumed his march, falling into the familiar rhythm of the mission even as his mind boiled with dread. Did Grand Leon actually imagine he could control Margareta's power lust? The blackmail le roi proposed, or rather that Jean-Claude deduced, would drive her frothing mad, and the easiest way for her to strike back would be through Isabelle.

Jean-Claude's heart felt as if it were being torn in two. He could not let this pass, and yet he could not betray his master, either. Le roi had lifted him up from peasant stock and given him such authority and status as to confound the high and mighty. True, authority had turned out to be more of a mixed blessing than he'd anticipated, but he had ever been proud to don his blue-and-whites and thwart threats to l'Empire in Grand Leon's name.

So would he fail his princess or his king? Did he have a choice? It wasn't as if he would refuse to fetch Isabelle from the docks. Perhaps Julio could be killed while attempting to escape, but that would still leave Isabelle marrying Climacio.

"Señor musketeer," came a voice from behind him.

Jean-Claude turned. There in the servants' corridor stood Thornscar, Príncipe Julio marked by a long scar that ran from brow to cheek. Even without the scar there would have been no way to mistake this man for the cringing creature that clung like a stain to Margareta's skirt. His erect posture and squared shoulders made a kingly tabard of his ripped and bloody monk's habit, and his silver eyes gleamed like the edge of a blade.

"Príncipe Julio, I deduce," Jean-Claude said, even as his mind lifted into a gallop. If Julio was here . . . "Where is Princess Isabelle?"

"Safe for now, on a reef in the upper sky four days' sail from here. She bids me give a message to her faithful musketeer, Jean-Claude. She says she is safe, sound, secure, and several synonyms starting with 'S.'"

"What?" Jean-Claude stiffened to hear Isabelle's private speech uttered from Julio's lips.

Julio said, "She's also fine, feisty, fabulous, and fierce if that helps."

Jean-Claude's heart lifted like a balloon; that was Isabelle, no doubt. "She told you to tell me that?"

"She suggested it might stop you from killing me and wasting all the hard work she did rescuing me and saving my life."

"She rescued you?" Jean-Claude asked, cackling gleefully in his heart. *Yes. Yes. Yes.* That was his Isabelle.

"Yes, and she has charged me with putting an end to Kantelvar's war."

Questions piled up faster that Jean-Claude could voice them. "Did she have a plan for this? And where is Kantelvar?"

"He is dead, or at least incapacitated. It's hard to tell. But the plan was for her to give me control of l'Empire's armies and with it force Alejandro . . . my brothers to parley."

Jean-Claude nodded. Yes, that's the way Isabelle would think. "That's not going to work now. Carlemmo is dead; Margareta has captured Alejandro and accused him of regicide. I'd wager my balls he'll be convicted within the hour."

Julio took a step back, his regal expression warped in dismay. "Padre de Santos."

"It gets worse. Grand Leon plans to let Alejandro be killed so that Climacio can take over without shedding any additional blood." Time to leave out the bit about holding the real Julio hostage.

"Is he mad? Alejandro's supporters know they will get no mercy from Margareta. If he dies, they fight to the death."

"What if Alejandro orders them not to fight?"

"Why would he do that?"

"Because Margareta put Xaviera in the Hellshard."

Julio turned green. "That would do it. Alejandro would do anything for her."

"It will be for nothing, though. Margareta will kill them both."

Julio's hand balled into a fist. "I must get in there. Members of the Sacred Hundred can only be charged with a crime by someone of equal or greater rank. That means Alejandro could only have been charged by Clìmacio, who everyone thinks is me, or Margareta. If I can present myself as an alternative to Clìmacio, the Hundred may doubt the legitimacy of the charges and nullify the trials."

"You're assuming anyone in that room gives a fig about what's true." In Jean-Claude's experience men seeking power only acknowledged fact insofar as it supported their ambitions.

"Alejandro is the rightful heir and the best man for the job. If he dies Aragoth will shatter and we won't see peace for a century." In a voice of resolute conviction he added, "He's also my brother. I have to try."

"Pardon the obvious question, but it's called the Hall of Mirrors and you are a Glasswalker—"

Julio shook his head. "The speculis loci in the Hall of Mirrors are all warded. Any Glasswalker can use them for egress, but only those who are keyed to them can use them for ingress, and Margareta has interdicted me. I could likely break her wards, but it would attract attention and I'd be mobbed by her guards before I ever breached that side of the mirror."

"So all I have to do is get you into the Hall of Mirrors, and Alejandro's trial is off?" Jean-Claude's pulse quickened at the ever-so-quaint sensation of having a fixed and solid target.

"Perhaps, perhaps not, but it is the only chance we have."

Jean-Claude grinned as an idea bloomed. "Can you fetch Isabelle's espejismo here? Meanwhile, I will make my way into the Hall of Mirrors to announce her arrival. Grand Leon will send out an honor guard to bring her in, and you will enter under her aegis."

Julio blanched. "Señor, I cannot bring her. I used water as a mirror. I have only ever done that twice and never as a mirror guide—"

"Is there any danger in trying?" Jean-Claude asked. He could not endanger Isabelle, not for the sake of all kingdoms. "What would happen if you failed?"

"It would . . ." Julio caught himself and took a moment to answer. "When a mirror passage fails, the glass may shatter; sometimes it destroys the reflection. Water would splash; the ripples might tear her apart."

Jean-Claude's heart twisted at the thought of risking Isabelle, but abandoning her to the scheme he suspected le roi of harboring was even more unthinkable. "Do you have a better plan?"

Julio shook his head. "My not having a better plan does not make this one viable. Isabelle saved my life. I would not repay her by scattering her espejismo through the Argentwash."

Jean-Claude regarded him seriously. "Do you imagine she would be unwilling to take that risk? Trust to her competence and courage. Whether it be attacking an entrenched position or trusting a stranger's word, whether it be taking up the sword or setting it aside, a man's battle is fought when he does the thing he most fears to do."

Julio's visage was somber, his silver eyes dark. "Or putting the fate of his whole kingdom in the hands of a foreign power's most devious operative?"

"Or trusting a foreign sorcerer he has traded blows with to conduct his beloved princess across a dangerous threshold into a potential bloodbath," Jean-Claude said.

Julio raised two fingers to his temple in acknowledgment of the point.

Jean-Claude said, "Go then, and make it quick. Make it fifteen minutes."

"That's extremely tight timing. Traversing the Argentwash is not instantaneous."

"As fast as you can, then."

Julio said, "We will arrive at the mirrors in the Spindle. It's an old ceremonial tower just outside the palace grounds." He turned and loped into the dusty dark, leaving Jean-Claude to hustle toward the Hall of Mirrors. When Grand Leon had chased him out of the audience chamber earlier, he'd at least had the wit to exit through the royal wing, so he was in the right neighborhood. Now there was no more time for subtlety. He had to go in by the most direct route, before Julio returned, before Margareta killed Alejandro.

He still needed a ploy. There was no way even the most slack-witted guard would let Jean-Claude the musketeer anywhere near that room, so he would have to be someone else. Fortunately, he was already out of uniform. He sliced his left hand with his knife, smeared fresh blood on his face, rubbed some on his clothes, and shredded any cloth that wasn't already stained. Reluctantly, he discarded his weapons as inappropriate baggage for the role he was about to play.

There were only two manners by which to enter a noble's court if one wanted a sympathetic audience. The first was to be immaculate, polished, groomed up like a show horse, and dressed in clothes that were good for nothing but standing around. Then one could spend hours making small talk, gently stirring the simmering cauldron of noble favor, hoping for a sip . . . Or one could barge in looking like a messenger from the front, the sort of man who would have nothing less important to say than "The barbarians are at the gate!"

It was traditional for the grubby messenger to die after delivering his message, and Jean-Claude reasoned he was not likely to disappoint on that score. Grand Leon would be furious with him. After what he planned, Jean-Claude would be lucky indeed merely to end up a bloodhollow, but if that was what it took to give Isabelle a chance at a world worth living in . . . certainly men had suffered more for less.

He wondered if the shackle-rattling torturers of the damned would, upon admitting his soul to the Halls of Torment, at least give him points for style.

Jean-Claude hobbled into a corridor adjacent to the Hall of Mirrors. Five guards barred his way. They wore the royal family's crimson-and-black livery. No doubt they had orders to kill Jean-Claude on sight, albeit with the significant disadvantage that they didn't know what he looked like, especially not out of uniform and covered in blood and muck.

The guards caught sight of him and hefted their weapons.

Smiling inside, Jean-Claude staggered toward his audience, waving his hands frantically. "Señors, help! Help, someone is trying to kill Queen Margareta!"

CHAPTER

Twenty-two

Isabelle sent Gretl to fetch food and find out what the other denizens of this aerie were up to. Gretl did not seem to think that any of them would be disappointed by their master's defeat, but it would be foolish not to inquire.

Alone, Isabelle limped around the circumference of the cistern-room pool to keep her bruised and battered body from seizing up. Her mind insisted on parading for her every foolish thing she'd done since meeting Kantelvar. She revisited every missed clue, every double meaning and disconnected reference, every way she could have averted this predicament if only she hadn't been blinded by her desire to help Marie and her hope to please her ersatz in-laws. If only she had been paying closer attention. "If only" was the worst phrase in any language.

It was all out of her hands now, the fate of her chosen family, the peace of the world.

She nearly jumped out of her skin when Julio twitched and sat up with a gasp.

"Isabelle," he said.

She hurried toward him, thankful he was alive. "What news? Are you hurt? What's going on in San Augustus? Did you bring a ship?" Surely he hadn't had time to fetch a ship, but then again, her personal sense of time was all out of joint. It might have been but an instant since he left her, or it might have been a century.

"There is a ship on the way, but we have no time for it. Your musketeer tells me Margareta has put Alejandro on trial for murdering Father."

"Jean-Claude! He's alive! Is he whole?" Thank the Builder and all the saints. Excitement brought energy to her limbs, and drove her aches and pains behind the curtain.

"He was when I left, but listen, the . . . things are even worse than I . . . than we feared. Fighting has already broken out in San Augustus. The city is on fire and Alejandro may be slain within the hour."

Isabelle's hand flew to her throat. Only too well could she imagine that magnificent city in flames, and what had become of Marie? "Wait. How is Alejandro to be slain? He wasn't even in the city."

"Apparently he was. How I don't know, but Margareta has him and she claims he was caught bloody-handed murdering the king in his sleep. She has put him on trial for regicide."

Isabelle knew almost nothing of Alejandro. "Is that possible?"

"Never!" Julio said with such vehemence that Isabelle recoiled from him. "Alejandro worshipped Father."

"What about Xaviera?" The crown princesa had seemed competent and commanding, certainly not the type to sit idly by while her kingdom fell apart.

Julio's fists clenched in agitation. "Margareta captured her and put her into the Hellshard. It will tear her soul to shreds."

"How long can she last?" Were they already too late? She would not see that proud woman destroyed.

"It depends on the individual. Xaviera is strong but the Hellshard is old magic, quondam sorcery beyond our ken."

"Can we save her?" Isabelle asked. Not a fair question, since she was stuck here. He'd be doing all the work and taking all the risk.

"Possibly," he said, fixing her with his silver gaze. "I have a plan, but 'risky' is too kind a word for it, and I have to take you with me."

Isabelle's heart lurched. "You said you couldn't . . ."

Julio scratched his scar in nervous habit. "I said I wasn't willing to risk it, but now I have no choice. A charge against a high noble can only be adjudicated by a congress of the Sacred Hundred. Margareta has gathered all who would come in the Hall of Mirrors. It is likely that many of Alejandro's supporters refused the summons for fear of being trapped by Margareta's forces, so the jury will be heavily weighted in her favor. Even so, I don't think she intends to let the matter get to a vote. Using Xaviera as leverage, she'll force Alejandro to confess to murdering Father and then have him executed.

"This means that most of the Sacred Hundred will all be in one place. Margareta will be there and so will Climacio. I intend to present the Sacred Hundred with a choice of Julios. For once, Kantelvar may have done us a favor. There's no way of knowing which story he told to which noble about me and Climacio. Likely there are a dozen variations floating around by now. Even Climacio's supporters must balk at the possibility of supporting a changeling. If I can divide them enough we might be able to suggest Alejandro as an alternative."

"Even if he's accused of regicide?"

"Accused by Margareta, whose word will be suspect, especially if we can free Xaviera. Being put in the Hellshard is a punishment no noble is supposed to endure without trial."

Isabelle's mind whirled and she was acutely aware just how little she really understood of Aragoth's underlying politics, the inner patterns of its people's minds. "Will that work?"

"It's the best idea I have. There are too many players, too many moves to even think about controlling all outcomes. The only thing we can do is rip away as much of Margareta's support as possible and pounce on any opportunity that arises."

Isabelle's brows furrowed. "So how do I fit into this?"

"I need you to deliver me to the court. I met your musketeer in San Augustus. He plans to storm the Hall of Mirrors and make an opening for us. He intends to announce your arrival and send out an honor guard to escort you into the Hall of Mirrors and sneak me in as part of your retinue."

To her surprise, Isabelle felt as if a weight had been lifted from her chest. It had to be madness, but she preferred to risk all than be left behind, forced to wait and worry. She squared her shoulders and matched his gaze. "Then let us go."

"Are you sure? Once we step into that mirror there is no coming back.

If we do not defeat Margareta, we will die. If you stay, I imagine you will be spared. You are too valuable as a diplomatic—"

"No," Isabelle said, quietly but firmly. "I am no one's bargaining chip. No one's pawn. I will not stand idle while evil rises and corruption spreads. I will not retire to survive into a damnation that my effort and sacrifice might have prevented. If Jean-Claude is giving us a breach, we must charge into it, forlorn hope though it be, or do you think I will wilt in the heat of battle?"

Julio's mouth crooked up in a smile. "I may be a fool, Highness, but I am not blind. Still, I would not drag you into danger unawares."

"And would you think less of me if I stayed behind?"

The question caught Julio off guard. "Of course not."

Isabelle shook her head sadly. "Then you still think less of me than you should. When we walk into the Hall of Mirrors you must trust me as you would a battle brother."

Julio bristled but then let it go slowly. He extended a hand to her, his left hand. She extended her own and he clasped her around the forearm. "Trust."

"Trust," Isabelle said, and squeezed his arm firmly. "Your plan is as sound as it can be, I think, but we must not make Margareta fight to the death. As the *Codex Strategia* says, never put your enemies on deadly ground. We must give Margareta a line of retreat, an offer of mercy."

"After everything she has done?" Julio's outrage nearly cracked his voice.

"Yes," Isabelle said. "If she had not conspired with Kantelvar, you would never have been a príncipe, nor my betrothed, nor a hundred other good things sprinkled in amongst the bad. She must be cast out of power, surely, exiled somewhere she can do no harm, but it will do Aragoth no good if she burns it to the ground to save her skin. Just think of all the accusations she dare not lay if she still has something left to lose, all of those wrongdoings which ultimately implicate her."

Julio growled. "I concede your point, but what line of retreat can we give her?"

Isabelle gestured to Kantelvar's pickled head. "We make it all his fault. His idea, his manipulation, his machinations forcing her into sedition rather than her galloping there of her own free will."

After a moment's agonized calculation, Julio said, "That could work." He squeezed Isabelle's shoulders gently as if to reassure himself she was real, then released her and picked up the cask. "We'll take this as evidence, or rather as a trophy of your victory. It will be much more interesting than anything Margareta has to say, and while theater may not quite be everything in the high court, it can certainly shift the balance of opinion."

"Theater," Isabelle said, her mind churning. "Yes. There's one more actor here, Clìmacio, and we must assign him a part. He will be your long-lost twin brother."

"Have you lost your mind?" Julio asked.

"Is he not also Carlemmo's son?" Isabelle asked.

"He's been pretending to be me," Julio growled.

"He's had no more choice in his role than either you or I, and he's scared, which makes him dangerous. We need to offer him a way out that gives him hope, turns him against Margareta, and preserves both of your honor."

Julio's fists clenched and unclenched. "I don't like it, but I have nothing better and we have no time." He extended his free hand to Isabelle. "If your musketeer is as good as his word, there should be an honor guard awaiting us. If not, I imagine it will be a death squad."

"What the Builder omits, Jean-Claude provides," Isabelle said. "We could not be in better hands."

Julio huffed and said, "And when did you ever read the *Codex Strategia*?"

"I borrowed my brother's copy after he said girls couldn't understand such things."

Just then, Gretl returned with a heavy basket on one shoulder. Her eyes rounded when she saw Julio. She managed a curtsy and set the basket down on the crate holding the lamp hook. She gave Isabelle a quizzical look and made an eating gesture.

Isabelle's stomach growled at her, but she said, "I'm afraid not. We have to leave right now. What about the other servants?"

Gretl made a gesture as if to round everybody up followed by a gesture of thanks.

"Well that's a relief," Isabelle said. "Just keep them out of here until we get back. And if we don't come back tell them a ship is coming." It was the best hope she could offer.

Gretl looked worried, but her posture was resolute.

Isabelle and Julio lay down by the cistern, their heads sticking out far enough that they could see their reflections.

Julio squeezed her hand and spoke with an instructor's cadence. "This will be easier for you if you close your eyes. If you feel a tug like you're being peeled out of your skin, let go. Once you're on the other side, you can open your eyes, though there won't be much for you to see. Don't bother holding your breath because your lungs will still be here."

Isabelle dutifully closed her eyes and in a moment felt a tug on her mind, rather like a dream on the edge of drowsing. She let herself slide into it.

—

Jean-Claude allowed himself to be towed toward the Hall of Mirrors. His spirit sniggered with the glee of the moment. Not a man amongst the guards wanted the job of bursting into an assembly of the Sacred Hundred, but neither could they afford to delay lest Jean-Claude's warning of an imminent attack on the queen prove true. They therefore intended to throw him to the mercy of their betters.

The captain led him down a sumptuously decorated hallway, with cosmatesque floors, tapestried walls, portraits, and suits of outdated armor all lit by bright alchemical lanterns. Retainers in a stunning variety of liveries lined the walls waiting for their masters to emerge from council. Palace servants in soft slippers whisked about. Muffled voices drifted from an alcove. Jean-Claude exaggerated his limp, but he kept up his patter to distract his captors from too much thinking. "The conspirators said there would be blood on the walls."

"It will be yours if you don't be quiet," growled the captain.

At the end of the hallway, two tall white doors guarded the entrance to the Hall of Mirrors. The captain had just signaled to the guards standing at attention outside them when the doors swung open. Bright light and noise spilled out, as if from the gates of Paradise.

Felix emerged, looking as peeved as ever. Jean-Claude ducked his head and tried to maneuver so that the guard captain was between himself and the queen's champion.

Felix noted Jean-Claude's group approaching. "Captain Ortega, what are you doing away from your post?"

Ortega obligingly stepped to the side to gesture at Jean-Claude. "Lord DuJournal here claims there is an assassination plot—"

Felix's gaze fixed on Jean-Claude, and his eyes bulged with outrage. "You!"

Jean-Claude lunged, shedding his startled captors, and charged straight for Felix.

If only he'd been younger, he might have closed the gap in one swift lunge instead of three irregular lurches. If he had been faster, Felix wouldn't have had time to draw his sword. Jean-Claude bull-rushed him. Felix dropped his tip and thrust. The point bit through cotton, silk, and skin. Pain washed up Jean-Claude's arm as the blade ripped a gash. Blood spilled. Jean-Claude wrapped his arms around Felix and bore him through the doorway.

Steel rasped behind Jean-Claude, and somebody struck him square in the back. The blade that fetched up on his rib probably would have killed him instantly if he hadn't already been moving away from it. He gasped in pain and tripped over Felix's feet. Both of them went down in a heap.

They rolled over and over each other, seeking advantage. Felix wound up on top. His bony fist crashed into Jean-Claude's face. The back of Jean-Claude's skull bounced off the floor. His vision was nothing but blurry red, like blood smeared on glass.

Yet this was the Hall of Mirrors. Le roi must be here. "The princess!" Jean-Claude shouted as Felix hit him again and again. "Princess is alive! She is coming!"

"Stop!" roared Grand Leon, and a bloodshadow spilled across the floor. Jean-Claude recognized its icy touch lapping against his own shadow. Felix froze in mid-pummel, his eyes round and his mouth a silent scream as le roi's bloodshadow seized him and held him fast.

The beating stopped. In the sudden absence of fresh pain, Jean-Claude jerked his trapped hand free and relieved Felix's belt pouch of the Hellshard key in the process. The ring went up his sleeve like a rat into a rotten wall.

At the other end of the big blurry world, people were yelling.

"How dare you attack my captain—"

". . . my musketeer!"

". . . talking about the princess."

"She is dead . . ."

Not dead, and Jean-Claude wasn't finished yet. He had to make her safe. Slowly, achingly, he pulled himself from under Felix and to his feet. He found himself in a vast room lined with the largest mirrors he'd ever imagined, some of them twice as wide as his outstretched arms. On his left was a gathering of Glasswalkers, the Sacred Hundred, all of them on their feet.

Before him, Queen Margareta and the false Príncipe Julio, both in mourning black, stood atop a dais on which had been placed a casket, presumably containing King Carlemmo's body. Climacio leaned on a cane. His expression was grim and closed, his silver eyes wary. Margareta's whole posture was stiff and haughty. Behind them stood the throne, flanked by the floating spindle of the Hellshard. Black and oily, it repulsed sight, so that one could only look at it out of the corner of one's eye. It was solid and real, but also missing, like an absence in the world. If just looking at it bent the mind nearly in half, how much worse must it have been for Xaviera, trapped inside?

At the foot of the dais, chained by the neck and wearing the dirty gray cassock of the condemned, knelt Príncipe Alejandro. His expression was resigned and his broad shoulders drooped with the weight of defeat.

Margareta stood on the dais, her arm outthrust, pointing imperiously at Grand Leon, her voice ringing, "Leon, you were invited to witness these proceedings, not to interrupt them. You have defied custom and courtesy, and you have dared deploy your vile sorcery against a Glasswalker in my house. I should have you expelled."

The Sacred Hundred murmured in agreement. They might have loathed Felix to a man, but they rankled at any foreigner asserting himself in their hall.

All eyes turned to gaze upon Grand Leon in the form of his emissary, his great shadow billowing at his feet. He had stepped out from a gallery of witnesses, visiting nobles, and ambassadors and claimed center stage, as was his wont. Grand Leon's bloodshadow eased Felix away from Jean-Claude and let him go. "Is it a defiance of courtesy and custom to prevent a murder? My musketeer may be guilty of trespass, but allowing your man to beat him to death would serve no purpose except to extinguish his message before it could be delivered, and I do believe he mentioned Princess Isabelle, who was to be your boy's bride."

Climacio bristled at being called a boy, but then he seemed in no hurry to interrupt the adults.

Jean-Claude took a step forward. The wound in his back complained at every shift of his balance, but he bowed to Margareta and said, "Your Majesty. If I may."

"You may not," Margareta said. "You have no right to speak here, and by sacred law I should cut out your tongue."

"Let him speak," called another man, a hoary old gentleman from the ranks of the Sacred Hundred. His hair was more silver than his age-tarnished eyes, and his voice quavered, but his manner was shrewd. "Only a fool or a tyrant silences a messenger because his message is unwanted."

Margareta glared at him. "Order in the congress. You have not been called upon to speak, Duque Reyes."

"Since when has that ever stopped him," muttered one of the other Glasswalkers, by no means below his breath.

Jean-Claude didn't waste the cue. "I beg your forgiveness, but I would not have interrupted this solemn ceremony except that the future of your line is in immediate danger. Princess Isabelle is alive, a ship has been sent to retrieve her, and she will arrive in the city within the hour." That won a round of astonished whispers from the witnesses.

Jean-Claude continued, riding a glorious updraft of invention. "Unfortunately, there is a conspiracy afoot to assassinate her. A plot conceived and carried out by that man!" He jabbed a finger at Felix, no matter that the gesture sent spikes of agony up his arm. The wound was not deep, but it was long. "By murdering Princess Isabelle, he seeks to bring l'Empire Céleste into your war on the side of your enemies."

"Outrageous!" Felix shouted. "This man was in league with the traitor Alejandro. He and his king would like nothing better than to see Aragoth dissolve into chaos so they can seize our ancient lands for themselves."

That argument won a murmur of agreement from the Sacred Hundred. They were all too willing to pin the blame for their troubles on outsiders.

Jean-Claude turned his attention to the Sacred Hundred. They swam in his sight, but he refused to yield to his body's pain. Isabelle needed him. "If that were so, señors and señoras, then why would I be bringing Princess Isabelle here? Her supposed death was meant to give l'Empire ample pretext to invade. Her resurrection takes that cause away."

"Enough," Margareta snapped, but Jean-Claude could see the gears of political triangulation mesh behind her eyes. "Princess Isabelle will be heard, but this court and this trial are not the place for it."

Margareta turned her glower on Jean-Claude. She could hardly condemn him publicly for bringing her such a dreadful warning. "Your dedication to your princesa is laudable. Not so your discourtesy. Felix is an officer of this court and a member of the Sacred Hundred. No clayborn may challenge his word or besmirch his honor, much less lay a charge against him, no matter who that clayborn works for."

Grand Leon spoke, his voice pitched to carry without the impression of shouting. "Jean-Claude has embarrassed us as well. Rest assured, he shall be punished." He gestured at a seat in the gallery. "Jean-Claude, sit, stay, and be silent."

Jean-Claude resisted the temptation to woof at him. His vision was sloshing from side to side. Sitting might help. He stumbled through the small crowd of dignitaries—what a show they were getting; he should pass around his hat for coins—and collapsed in the indicated seat next to the bedazzlingly bedecked Ambassador du Blain. Jean-Claude's vision blurred and sound became like wind in his ears. He blinked a few times to clear his sight.

Margareta whispered in Felix's ear. Felix marched out of court, though not without a backward glare at Jean-Claude. The Sacred Hundred and the visiting dignitaries all muttered to one another in low voices.

Grand Leon returned to his seat, which managed to be slightly taller than everyone else's, and said to Jean-Claude sotto voce, "I distinctly recall giving you an order."

"Yes, Majesty," Jean-Claude said. "You gave me two orders. I was to go to the docks to await Isabelle's arrival, but she is not arriving by the docks, which makes that order moot. Also you told me that if Margareta became a threat to Isabelle, it was my job to dispose of her, which I am in the process of doing."

"How very much like a lawyer of you," Grand Leon said. "Is this ploy worth your life?"

Jean-Claude said, "I gave you my life long ago, sire. If all I have left to give is my death, so be it."

"I was not aware you had a poet in your soul," Grand Leon said. "To go along with the lawyer."

"The bastards have been squatting there for a while, mucking up the place," Jean-Claude replied. "I'm going to start charging them rent. In the meantime, Isabelle will be arriving at the Spindle very soon, and she relies upon Your Majesty for protection."

"I don't suppose I can blame her for your disobedience." Grand Leon made a subtle hand signal, and Ambassador du Blain took himself off.

Jean-Claude said, "I make no apologies, sire. To obey you would have been to betray you and bring your plan to ruin." After a moment he added, "Though if you do find it necessary to execute me, I request that my funeral include a tower of horse shit burned in my honor."

Grand Leon glanced at him from the corner of his eye. "In the tradition of a great hero being sent off with his preferred weapon?"

"Yes, sire."

—

Towed by Julio, Isabelle slithered through the Argentwash. It was as if she had plunged into thin cold mud, a wet chill that swallowed her from crown to toes. She opened her eyes with a start and found herself in the mirror realm, dissolved in and carried along by a river of quicksilver. There was nothing to see but eddies and whorls of silver, nothing to hear at all. How in the name of all the saints did Glasswalkers navigate this?

Even counting time by the number of thoughts flitting through her mind, she could not tell how long it was before a pane of glass resolved itself before her, and beyond it an unfamiliar room, a round chamber, clad in marble with stately pillars holding up a domed ceiling. Its walls were lined with mirrors. The space her awareness occupied, the speculum loci, was quite literally the mirror image of the physical world before her. To her left, which was ordinarily her right, was a marble pillar, except that the back portion of it, the bit the mirror could not see, merely faded away to nothing. She reached out to touch it, just to see if it had any substance at all, but her phantom arm was gone, and in its place her old familiar arm of flesh and blood, complete with wormfinger.

She had no time to absorb this new fact before Julio pulled her forward. She had seen curds strained from milk, the colloidal liquid becoming solid. Now she knew what those curds felt like as they congealed into firmer matter. It was rather squishy. She would have stumbled to the ground and possibly splattered like a butter sculpture had not Julio's arm snaked around her waist to hold her up.

A tepid breeze brought a whiff of brick dust and gun smoke. The distant blast of cannons rumbled like thunder across the city. Isabelle gasped and drew in a huge breath of air that didn't seem to touch her lungs.

"My arm," she said. "I got my old arm back."

Julio frowned and said, "That's still how you think of yourself, deep down."

It was profoundly strange to know that her body had been changed and yet be unable to feel that it was true. Even so, this was an unexpected blessing. People might have found her wormfinger revolting, but at least it was easy to conceal.

"Princess!" called a voice in la Langue.

She looked up to see the Hugo du Blain, all frills and lace and fancy embroidery, hurrying toward her. He looked oddly distorted, almost lopsided. So did everything in the room.

"Ambassador," she said. "I am pleased to see you."

The ambassador stopped short of her by a respectful distance and bowed, sweeping a gaudily magnificent hat that could have doubled as a prizewinning arrangement of exotic flowers. The ambassador said, "I am delighted that you are alive. And you . . . Príncipe Julio, I presume. This is a surprise."

"I am Julio," he said.

"The real Julio," Isabelle explained. "The one who resides under Margareta's thumb is a fraud." She needed to establish that fact early and often.

Du Blain nodded and continued, "And who is your other friend?"

Puzzled, Isabelle followed his gaze. Her face grew slack in astonishment, for where before had been Kantelvar's head in a jar was a young man dressed in yellow robes with a black mantle embroidered with gearwheels. His young face was lined with deep grooves of pain, and his glassy eyes stared into the middle distance. Hands with knobby knuckles folded and unfolded spasmodically.

"Kantelvar," she breathed. He was still alive in the jar when they brought his reflection through the mirror, but since he had no eyes to see himself with, his espejismo had emerged as he remembered himself, thanks to soul distortion. This must have been how his very first body had looked.

"Padre de Santos!" Julio said, his surprise at least equal to Isabelle's.

Kantelvar's glassy eyes fixed on Isabelle and he growled, in the Saints-tongue, "Traitress!"

Kantelvar's espejismo lurched toward Isabelle. "I rearranged the world for you! I overthrew kingdoms. I started wars, and this is how you repay me!"

Isabelle stepped out of his way. Julio recovered and grabbed Kantelvar's arms. After a brief struggle, the cleric sagged in Julio's grip like a sail on a becalmed sky.

"Is this the artifex?" du Blain asked.

"What's left of him," Isabelle said.

"Traitress," Kantelvar mumbled. "I gave you the world."

Julio asked, "Do you have any great suggestions for what to do with him? Or should I snap his neck and be done with it?"

"I thought we were going to use him as evidence," Isabelle said.

"As a pickled head," Julio said. "When he couldn't argue."

"You will burn for this," Kantelvar promised. "Both of you and all you hold dear. The prophecy was given to me—"

Julio gagged him with an expertly applied chokehold.

Isabelle's expression soured. "You have a point, but don't kill him yet." She turned to du Blain. "Please enlighten me as to the state of the court."

The ambassador coughed into his hand. "King Carlemmo is dead. Príncipe Julio"—he paused to give the real Julio a significant look—"and Queen Margareta have called the Sacred Hundred to put Príncipe Alejandro on trial. Alejandro was just about to admit to regicide when your musketeer burst into the room and announced that you were on your way and that there was a plot afoot to assassinate you. He did not mention your Príncipe Julio. Grand Leon dispatched me to welcome you and provide you safe escort."

Julio looked surprised. "Did Margareta send no one?"

"The musketeer sent them on a wild goose chase to the harbor."

"Bless Jean-Claude," Isabelle said. "How is he?"

Du Blain took a second to answer. "He still lives, but he had to fight his way into the hall, and he was sorely wounded. Worse, he embarrassed Grand Leon with his antics."

Isabelle's heart all but seized at the thought of Jean-Claude wounded on her behalf. Too brave he was.

Du Blain gestured to Julio. "Evidence suggests we do not want any forewarning of Your Highness's escort to reach the court before we do."

"That is correct," Isabelle said, relieved. "And might Príncipe Julio borrow your hat, er, minus the flora?" If Julio played the part of Isabelle's escort, hauling her captive, with the wide brim of his hat pulled far down, hopefully nobody would be able to see Julio's face to identify him until he chose to reveal himself.

"But of course," du Blain said, discarding the flowers and handing the much humbler brim to Julio.

Julio donned the hat, readjusted his grip on Kantelvar, and said, "This one will do everything he can to destroy us."

"Perhaps, but he's more of a threat to Margareta than to us. If only because she has farther to fall."

"Assuming she recognizes him."

"She will," Isabelle said. "I'll make sure of that. Just keep him quiet and your face covered until I give the word."

"Any word in particular, or am I supposed to guess?"

"I'll make it obvious," Isabelle said, hoping the dryness in her mouth translated to a dryness in her tone. She had foolishly imagined that merely delivering Julio, alive, to the court would be sufficient to disrupt Margareta's plans, that she could turn the hard work of dismantling the queen's conspiracy over to someone else, but if Alejandro had already confessed . . . The possibilities for disaster spun out too fast to be elaborated upon.

The strange little band set off from the Spindle. A long staircase wound completely around the outside of the building, providing a distressing view of the city. Plumes of smoke and tongues of fire already consumed whole neighborhoods. The air shook with the rattle of muskets and the bass hammering of cannons, and she was glad when they descended to street level, where at least the scope of the chaos was obscured.

They hurried through the empty streets and into the palace. The grounds were already crowded with refugees, seeking some sanctuary from the fighting. Du Blain flashed his credentials and rippled his bloodshadow at every guard or servant who sought to intercept them.

By the time she strode through the wide-flung doors of the Hall of Mirrors, Isabelle's heart had gone numb from hammering on her ribs. Fear ached like a bruise in her soul much worse than the ones blooming all over her body. So many people's lives depended on her: Julio, Alejandro, even Clímacio, and all those souls who would be lost if Kantelvar's civil war grew into the nightmare he had planned.

Trumpets announced her arrival, and a herald called out, "Her Highness Princess Isabelle des Zephyrs de l'Empire Céleste."

Everyone in the room stood. All gazes fell upon her as she limped down the center of the aisle toward the royal dais. The Sacred Hundred and their retainers stared at her with various levels of calculation, antagonism, and fear. Their situation was just as precarious as hers. If they should pick the loser in the succession debate, it could cost them everything from their titles to their heads. And there were the foreign dignitaries, Grand Leon chief amongst them, and—yes!—Jean-Claude stood by his side, though he was pale and his clothes were soaked with blood. He grinned and made a careful bow, sweeping his hat as if to clear all obstacles from her path.

She smiled at him, glad despite her dread. She wanted to rush over to him and touch him, to feel the warmth and the life of him.

Instead, she paused only long enough to dip a curtsy to Grand Leon. "Your Majesty. I have come to discharge the duty you laid upon me."

One corner of Grand Leon's mouth quirked up and he nodded ever so slightly, appreciating her double meaning and giving his blessing.

His approval gave Isabelle courage. She lifted her chin and marched toward the royal dais, where awaited Queen Margareta and Climacio.

Margareta remained in her seat, still playing the part of the widowed queen, but she followed Isabelle's progress with lupine intensity. Did she still dream of securing an alliance with l'Empire through Isabelle, or did she consider her victory over Alejandro absolute? Isabelle prayed that her presence was strong enough to draw attention away from her companions. Julio had his hat pulled down and this version of Kantelvar certainly looked nothing like the one Margareta was used to.

Climacio, wearing Julio's likeness, gazed down woodenly from his perch, his face no more animate than that of a puppet, which his mother wanted him to be. Half a dozen guards had been posted at the foot of the dais.

Margareta said, "Welcome, Princesa. We are glad to see that you are well, but this is hardly the moment for a wedding. Please be seated with Grand Leon. We are almost finished here, and we will be happy to celebrate your return more graciously once we have done with this dire business." She gestured to the foot of the dais, where Príncipe Alejandro knelt in bondage, his feet bare, his neck fastened to the floor by a short length of chain.

Before him stood a judge holding up a large scroll. "Príncipe Alejandro de Aragoth, by means of your confession, thrice freely given, this court has no choice but to find you guilty of regicide. From this moment forward you are stripped of all name and title. Your eyes shall be burned from your head with hot irons, you shall be castrated, drawn, and quartered . . ."

Isabelle surveyed the galley of Glasswalkers. From the number of seats that were filled, less than half were present, presumably Margareta's loyalists.

Assume I only get to say one thing. After that the axe would come down. Julio had said he would force the Sacred Hundred to choose between Julios, but that would only compound the problem of loyalty and treason. Once the príncipes started fighting and blood flowed, everybody would be a traitor in the eyes of his or her enemies. The only path to peace remained what it had always been, an accord between the brothers.

All *three* brothers.

Like a gladiator in the pits of ancient Om, Isabelle lengthened her stride and marched into the center of the floor, straight toward Alejandro.

"Mercy!" she cried, startling the judge to silence. She extended her hand toward Clìmacio in a gesture of supplication. "My betrothed, I beg you have mercy on Príncipe Alejandro."

Margareta came out of her chair. "Isabelle, be silent. Alejandro is condemned by his own admission."

"I beg your pardon, Majesty, but I do not answer to you. If your son is to be my husband, he and he alone is my lord and master. Only he can command my silence. Only he can order my punishment if I disobey, and I am sure he would think twice before having someone whipped."

Clìmacio twitched at the mention of whipping. Every abuse Margareta had inflicted upon him was a weapon in Isabelle's hand.

He cleared his throat and said, "Isabelle, this is a legal proceeding."

Isabelle declined to dispute the dubious jurisprudence on display. "That is beside the point. The point is, this is your choice. Today, in this place, you have the singular power to begin the world anew. The question is, what world will you create? Will you create a world of strife? Where brother slays brother, where your beautiful city burns, where old rivalries crush new hopes, a world without friends where every shadow holds an enemy? That is the world Kantelvar wanted for you."

Behind her, Kantelvar squirmed in Julio's grip. Isabelle gestured them forward and Julio forced Kantelvar to his knees beside Alejandro. Alejandro let one shoulder fall to the ground and twisted his head enough to get a look up under Julio's hat. His eyes grew wide.

Isabelle focused all her will on Clìmacio. "Here is the architect of all this misery. Here is Artifex Kantelvar, who had you tortured, who cut off your leg. By my hand, his power is broken. He cannot hurt you anymore."

Clìmacio stared, eyes riveted to Kantelvar. A susurration of disbelief rippled through the Sacred Hundred. No doubt most of them had received Kantelvar and sipped of his poison.

One of the Hundred called, "That looks nothing like him, not even before he was Exalted."

"This is his espejismo, the way he sees himself," Isabelle said. "Shall I let him speak and recite all the promises he made to each of you, and the price he extracted when he did?"

The speaker in the crowd recoiled and many of the Hundred exchanged worried, thoughtful, calculating glances. Margareta, who had the most to lose if Kantelvar spouted off, just about stepped off the dais as she shouted, "Enough of this. Julio, control your woman."

But Climacio's face was rapt, his breathing quick and shallow. "Let her speak."

Isabelle's pulse thrummed with terrified exhilaration as she prized Margareta's grip from Climacio's strings, one finger at a time. "You're not his slave anymore. You're not Margareta's puppet. You can be the man who undoes all their wickedness and overthrows all their designs. Make peace with your brothers. Forgive and be forgiven."

Climacio's fascinated expression twisted into a snarl. "And what have I done to be forgiven for?"

From his awkward crouch, Alejandro said, "You put Xaviera in the Hellshard."

"Lies," Margareta said, stepping between Isabelle and Climacio. "Heed not the traitor who murdered your father or the poison-tongued Célestial witch. She has been sent here to sicken your mind, to snatch victory from your very grasp."

To Isabelle's surprise, Jean-Claude stepped forward, brandishing what looked to be a ring of onyx. Grand Leon steepled his fingers but made no move to restrain him.

Jean-Claude said, "Not lies, a testable hypothesis, as a friend of mine would say. Shall we put the key to the lock and see what happens?"

Margareta's face grew pale at the sight of the ring, but she rounded on Jean-Claude like a bear in a trap. "That only proves that you are the villain here. If there is anyone in the Hellshard, it is you who put them there, not I."

Jean-Claude turned to the Sacred Hundred. "What say you all? Shall we pull Xaviera from the Hellshard and see whom she identifies as her gaoler?"

The rumbling from the Hundred grew louder, and most of them were on their feet.

"Silence!" Margareta shouted. "You have tested our patience for the last time."

Julio pulled off his hat. "And you have deceived the Sacred Hundred long enough, Mother." He faced the Hundred. "I am Príncipe Julio de Aragoth, and that man—" He gestured, open-handed, to Clïmacio— "is my twin brother, stolen away at birth and brought back by my enemies to take my place."

Clïmacio recoiled, exactly as if he'd seen a ghost. "I had no choice. I thought you were dead!"

The Sacred Hundred yammered with excitement, denial, outrage, and began emptying their roped-off jurors' box. Even the gallery of witnesses were on their feet now.

Julio squared his shoulders and met Clïmacio's gaze. "I know. And I forgive you. Can you do the same?"

Margareta's shock turned to fury. She jabbed a finger at Julio. "Guards, take that imposter! Take them all!"

The guards who'd been stationed at the dais charged, apparently translating "take" as "murder." Isabelle retreated. Grand Leon stepped forward. His crimson shadow flared like a cape and flowed over the ground to intercept the soldiers, but before it reached the first guard's shadow, the emissary rocked back, clutching a gash in his throat. Arterial blood sprayed.

Jean-Claude spun round in dismay. "Majesty!" Ambassador du Blain, apparently not one for the sight of blood, slumped over in a dead faint.

Julio looked around wildly and pointed to one of the many mirrors covering the walls. "Assassin!"

Isabelle espied the reflection of a man in a mirror who was not there in the real world: Felix. His espejismo had cut the emissary's throat in the mirror. Saints, he could murder anyone in the room. His espejismo shook reflected blood from his blade as Grand Leon's emissary crumpled to the ground. Felix in the mirror raised his blade to strike at Jean-Claude's reflection.

"Jean-Claude, duck!" Isabelle shouted.

Jean-Claude threw himself flat just as the assassin stabbed where his reflection had been.

The swiftest guard rushed Isabelle, sword drawn. She lurched to the side. Too slow, but Julio flew in, hammering the guard in the jaw with one hand even while relieving him of his sword with the other.

Then the mass of guards was upon them, and Julio all but disappeared under a wave of crimson-clad guardsmen.

"Julio!" Isabelle screamed, but he emerged from the crush, gained a step of separation, and proceeded to demonstrate just what "greatest swordsman in Aragoth" actually meant. Back in the aerie, he had been exhausted, half-starved, and wounded, but his espejismo knew no such pains. He was what he believed himself to be. He moved like an angry wasp, evading every blow until he could drive home his sting. He stabbed one guard through the belly, reaped the legs out from under another, and shattered the jaw of a third with a punch that would have broken his own knuckles had they been made of mere flesh and bone.

The remaining guards learned caution, circling him like hounds on a bear.

"Señors, to me!" Julio shouted to the Hundred. "If ever you were loyal to Carlemmo, to me!"

Most of the Hundred had already produced hidden weapons from the folds of their garments. A handful rushed toward Julio, though to reinforce or betray him Isabelle could not guess.

Margareta seized Clìmacio and dragged him from the dais. More guards rushed into the room from all sides, racing to her aid. Isabelle took one step toward the retreating queen—she was the key—then something slammed into her from the side and tackled her to the ground.

"Traitress!" Kantelvar howled. He belted her in the face and cracked her head off the marble floor. "You could have been a saint!"

Stars exploded in Isabelle's vision. Silvery mirrorblood ran from her nose, and her limbs were as saggy as old rope. A manifestation of will it might have been, but her espejismo could still be hurt or killed.

Kantelvar straddled her, grabbed her throat with one hand, and belted her with the other.

"Whore!" he screamed, giving her no chance to regroup. "I made you. I crafted you to be the mother of the Savior. You belong to me!"

Isabelle squirmed and fended off his blows with her crippled right hand, yanking at Kantelvar's grip on her throat with her left, but nothing about her espejismo made her stronger than him.

"Off, cur!" A bellow of rage and a heavy thump. Kantelvar's weight flipped from Isabelle's back as Jean-Claude put a thunderous boot in his side. The artifex's howls of outrage became a scream of pain.

Isabelle pushed to hands and knees and Jean-Claude scooped her the rest of the way up.

"Get you out of here," he gasped. His face was white as suet, his clothes sticky with fresh blood. Isabelle's heart wailed for him even as she forced her mind back to the fray, the guards, the dons. Julio and his loyal dons fended off a full dozen guards. Margareta retreated, towing Clìmacio.

"Get the queen!" Isabelle commanded. *Control the head, control the body.*

Jean-Claude changed direction with a lurch. Isabelle forced her wobbly legs to move.

Jean-Claude screamed and fell, a sudden gash appearing in his calf. A glance over her shoulder showed Felix in the mirror, his espejismo standing over Jean-Claude's reflection, lining up for the coup de grâce.

"No!" she shrieked. Time seemed to stretch and slow. Her espejismo had no reflection of its own, so she could not shield him in the mirror. She could do nothing but stand in horror as Felix snarled something wicked and—

There came a massive bang and the mirror shattered. Isabelle whirled to see a tall thin man bedecked with lenses striding out from a pall of gun smoke at the head of a squad of arquebusiers. A black sooty ribbon of smoke rose from the mouth of his long musket.

"Shoot any mirror with a sorcerer in it!" he bellowed.

"Go!" Jean-Claude moaned, clutching his bleeding leg.

Isabelle yanked herself from her paralysis and charged after Margareta. The queen was halfway to the back door, but she was dragging Clìmacio and Isabelle's legs were longer. *Reach and strike and push. Faster. Faster.*

Margareta saw her coming, shrieked, and let go of Clìmacio.

Isabelle crashed into Margareta from behind, looped her good arm around the stout queen's neck, and bore her to the ground. The woman thrashed like a stuck boar. Over and over they rolled until the queen ended up on top, her back to Isabelle. Her weight would have smashed the breath from Isabelle's lungs if her true lungs hadn't been elsewhere. She got hold of Isabelle's arm to pry it loose. Isabelle couldn't get a choking grip.

Isabelle reached for her maidenblade, but her right hand still ended in a wormfinger because the espejismo was a reflection of the soul, of who she believed she was, of who she accepted herself to be.

She'd reached for the knife, hadn't she, expecting her spark-hand to be there?

She closed her eyes and opened herself to the truth given to her by her enemy. *I am Isabelle. Greatest-granddaughter of Saint Céleste. I am a sorcerer. I am l'Étincelle!*

Isabelle's bones buzzed as if touched by lightning. Her crippled arm sloughed away like a snake shedding its skin and revealed her luminous spark-flesh beneath, pink and purple glimmers in the maroon clouds that expanded to fill the space she claimed for her limb.

She yanked her maidenblade from its sheath and brought the point up under the queen's throat. "Hold! Stop or the queen dies! All of you, stop!"

"Abomination!" Margareta said. "She's an abomination."

Fear churned Isabelle's belly, for that was an accusation that might actually stick. "I am St. Celeste's greatest granddaughter, now stop thrashing or my blade will bite deep."

"You wouldn't dare," Margareta said. "You need me—"

Isabelle whipped the maidenblade down and then jammed it up to its hilt in her rump. Margareta screamed.

"Tell them to stop," Isabelle snarled. "Or I carve you a new arse."

The queen howled, "Stop! Halt!" The nearest guards hesitated.

"Throw down your weapons!" Isabelle shouted. "Hold! The queen is mine!"

"Do what she says!" Margareta wailed.

Isabelle kept shouting, and slowly, the melee ground to a stop.

Isabelle's gaze fell on Jean-Claude, who lay but a few paces away, It might as well have been a kilometer.

His face was pale, but he grinned at her. "Well done."

Isabelle's heart swelled with relief to see him alive. "A surgeon!" she shouted. "Someone get this man a surgeon!"

Kantelvar had picked himself up from the ground and stood clutching his side. A silvery mist leaked from where Jean-Claude had kicked him.

He glared at Isabelle holding the queen. "Go ahead and kill her," he spat. Kantelvar reeled about and shouted at the Sacred Hundred, "Kill the traitorous queen. Kill the changeling príncipe. Kill the regicidal heir. Kill the wretched abomination. Kill that limping churl, shat from his mother's bowels."

The guards, the Sacred Hundred, and all the witness milled uncertainly. Many of the bystanders stared at Isabelle's spark arm. Several made signs against evil, and the whisper of "Abomination" reached her ears, but no one challenged her just now. That was a battle for later.

"Be quiet!" shouted Clìmacio. Rapier in hand, he stumped toward Kantelvar. "You filthy lying son of a goat."

Kantelvar sneered at him. "Down on your knees, whelp. You are nothing but a whipping boy, sired by a cur and farrowed by a sow. I made you and I will unmake you, but not before you feel my lash! Your father was nothing but a—"

Clìmacio wailed and thrust with all his might. The blade struck true. Kantelvar gasped and looked down at the hilt sticking out of his chest, and then up at Clìmacio, whose face was contorted in panic and anger.

"You," Kantelvar said. "You cannot. I made—"

Clìmacio twisted the blade and Kantelvar gasped. He sagged to his knees and began to melt. His body lost its color, becoming a grayish silver. Rivulets of his mirror-flesh ran away and turned to silver mist before vanishing completely. Within seconds, he evaporated, leaving Clìmacio in the center of the platform, shaking like the last leaf in a high breeze, his sword stuck in nothing.

Isabelle needed no air, but she blew out a long breath anyway. It was fitting that Kantelvar had been finally ended by one he had so cruelly debased. It was only ironic that Clìmacio thought he was defending a lie when in fact he was the true prince . . . or at least *a* true prince . . . to a certain value of true.

She said, "Well done, Your Highness. I am glad to see you have come back to yourself after all your mother and Kantelvar did to you. I have read Kantelvar's secret books, and I've seen the truth. How your mother bore twins, not identical, and gave you to Kantelvar in return for his help in bringing her to power."

Margareta heaved against Isabelle's grip. The strangled squawk of pain and outrage from her throat did nothing to diminish the verisimilitude of Isabelle's lie; quite the contrary. Every greater struggle made Margareta seem like a woman undone. Isabelle heaved her back down, drew out the knife, and put it to Margareta's throat hard enough that it drew a trickle of blood.

Clìmacio stared at Isabelle with the same starved look as a beggar at a king's feast. "You read that?"

"Oh yes," Isabelle said. "Little did Margareta know that Kantelvar was going to make you a slave in your own house. You grew up thinking you were a mere whipping boy. Your brother never knew the truth, but your mother did. She loathed you and she beat you, trying to scourge away the stain of her own betrayal. She didn't know that Kantelvar meant to give you your brother's face in the end, to put you on the throne. Kantelvar wanted you to believe you were a pretender, so that you would murder both your brothers, rebel against your mother, and tear all of Aragoth asunder.

"But now your true nature has shone through. Your inner nobility shines.

Now the balance of war and peace lies in your hands. You're not a pawn anymore. You have an open move." Isabelle's mouth was dry by the time she finished crafting this confection of wishful thinking. Could such a fabrication support the weight of a single moment, much less the whole future?

"Lies," Margareta whimpered, but so low and garbled that only Isabelle heard. "None of them are fit to rule. Julio is gutterborn, Clìmacio a fool, and Alejandro drove a knife through his own father's heart."

"Good lies," Isabelle corrected softly, squeezing Margareta's throat tighter. "Julio is a good prince, Clìmacio more perceptive than you think, and if Alejandro held the knife, it was you who thrust it in."

Clìmacio licked his lips and said. "Go on."

Isabelle said, "The question that faces you is, to which outcome will you lend your weight? Will you follow the path that Kantelvar and Margareta laid out for you, choosing war and death and destruction, or will you chose peace and prosperity? Will you release your brother, Príncipe Alejandro, from his shackles and repudiate the lies told against him?"

Clìmacio's eyes narrowed. "In other words, will I take the path you choose for me, exchanging one master for another."

"Say rather a fellow traveler on a common road." She took note of the sword hanging loose in his hand. "You've killed your first man today, a just killing, but a killing nonetheless. Do you like the taste of it? Because war will provide an endless feast." *Take the chance,* she willed him. *Bite!*

Clìmacio stared at the sword in his hand, and a look of dismay stole over his face. He turned to Príncipe Alejandro, still chained to the floor at the foot of the dais, and said, "And what does Alejandro say?"

Alejandro glared at Clìmacio. "Release my wife from the Hellshard."

"Here," Jean-Claude croaked, tugging the onyx ring from up what was left of his sleeve. "The key."

Julio took the ring from Jean-Claude and hurried to the tall, black, hard-to-look-at spindle that hovered at the flank of the throne. He passed the ring over the needle point and swept it downward.

It seemed to Isabelle that the space within the circle was stretched tight, like the surface of a drum, and when the needle passed through it, it bent and warped and strained and finally popped. When that skin broke, the space around the spindle seemed to unwind, spiraling outward like a whirlpool in reverse, distorting everything around it to make room for a rapidly unfolding shape, the dark and haggard and harrowed Princesa Xaviera.

She manifested several inches off the ground and literally fell into Julio's arms, where she hung trembling, a long, anguished moan escaping her. Her silver eyes, wide and staring, were tarnished almost black. Julio carried her to Alejandro. Clìmacio was releasing him from his chains with the same trepidation as a man setting loose an angry badger. The elder príncipe took his wife in his arms. She clung to his shoulders, sobbing uncontrollably.

Julio made his way to Isabelle, his face full of concern, and asked, "Are you well?"

"We still have this problem," Isabelle said, squeezing Margareta's neck for emphasis.

Julio held up the Hellshard key. "I think this is only fair."

"No!" Margareta bucked against Isabelle so hard that she lost her grip, and the maidenblade made a long, shallow gash in her neck. But Julio had seized the queen's foot and deftly thrust it through the circlet.

As her toes passed the circle's plane, her body stretched like pulled taffy. She screamed and grabbed the floor to gain some sort of purchase on the slick marble, but space twisted around her, folding her into a tighter and tighter spiral, like fibers being twisted into an infinitely thin thread. Her legs went first, then her torso, then her shoulders, her head, and her flailing, beating hands. Then she was gone. The last thing to die away was her scream.

Isabelle's eyes felt like they were about to pop out of her head. "Saints preserve."

"The saints preserve those who follow their guidance," Julio said, reaching out a hand to pull her up. "Margareta was not good at that."

Isabelle surveyed the scene. Príncipe Alejandro cradled Xaviera, a surgeon arrived for Jean-Claude, and the newly minted Príncipe Clìmacio stood looking somewhat alone and uncertain in the middle of the dais. The guards, the Sacred Hundred, and all the witnesses milled uncertainly.

"Then who shall be king?" shouted someone from the floor.

Julio drew himself up. "By right, the crown goes to Alejandro. I was pleased that he should be the heir before I was kidnapped, and I am still pleased that he should be."

"And what of him?" One of the dons pointed at Clìmacio.

Clìmacio looked to Isabelle; she gestured him toward Alejandro. Clìmacio swallowed and said. "Alejandro is king."

Alejandro looked up from comforting his stricken wife and glowered at Clìmacio. "I will leave it up to Xaviera whether or not to forgive you."

Climacio winced but said nothing, which was probably for the best.

Isabelle said, "I doubt Margareta consulted him before torturing Xaviera, nor provided him any chance to protest afterward." She took in the assemblage with her gaze. "Indeed, no one here is guiltless. If justice were something handed down from on high, then we should all be punished most heinously. But justice is not handed down from on high, it is a thing we mortals make for ourselves. It is therefore imperfect and flawed and it breaks from time to time and we must repair it, rebuild it, and improve it so that at least we will be forced to make new mistakes." She met Alejandro's gaze. "Have you no memory you wish you could change, no act to undo?"

A look of anguish crossed Alejandro's face, and he turned away from Isabelle. For a moment his body shook as if with grief. Yet when he looked up again, his mien was resolute. He turned to Climacio and said, "Much pain and suffering could have been averted if you had shown any courage at all. But if I were to condemn everyone who ever failed a test of courage, my kingdom would be a much emptier place."

With Xaviera in his arms, Alejandro turned to face the Sacred Hundred. "The last words my father spoke were these: 'I have three sons.' Go forth and let it be known that all who lay down their arms and swear to me will be forgiven."

CHAPTER
Twenty-three

Isabelle gasped and drew a huge breath of air as her espejismo returned to her body. How long had it been since she had actually been able to feel herself breathing? Ten hours? Twelve? She and Julio had stayed at the Hall of Mirrors as long as possible, hammering out the general shape of an agreement for the disposition and allotment of royal authority, pedigree, inheritance, and clemency. Both she and Julio had felt it urgent to finalize the major points of the agreement while everyone was still confused and distraught and willing to take direction.

To Isabelle, who had played the role of arbiter of truth, the ad hoc congress had been rather like watching ice crystals form on a windowpane, order appearing almost spontaneously from chaos. Eventually, however, the needs of the flesh overcame the program of the mind. She and Julio had been forced to retreat. Isabelle had left Jean-Claude, weak as a newly hatched chick but steadfast in his resolve, in charge of her personal negotiations.

Now she found herself curled on her side, her head braced by fat pillows and her body wrapped in a thick blanket, her flesh hand still clasped in Julio's. Between them lay a platter of bread and cheese and fresh fruit.

Isabelle shuddered with a wave of returning sensation, her whole body tingling and aching. Julio, similarly swaddled, smiled at her and sat up. She returned his admiration and allowed him to help her up. Gretl sat nearby, fast asleep in a wooden armchair.

"How do you feel?" Julio asked.

Isabelle took an inventory of sensations. "Tired, hungry, bladder sore. And you?"

His smile faded. "When Kantelvar originally approached my father with the idea of bringing in a foreign princess to marry, I objected. It was against all tradition and it reeked of intrigue. I . . . Since meeting you I have come to the conclusion that was a mistake, and I would like to withdraw my opposition."

Isabelle's pulse fluttered just a little at this very indirect proposal, and yet it also left a chill. She scuffed the ground with her toe.

"When Kantelvar first came to my father with this proposal, or at least when I first found out about it, I saw it as my escape, my one golden chance to get away from my father. He was the worst villain in the world, or at least my world. I could not have imagined what Kantelvar turned out to be, or what he had in mind for me, to bear the Savior. Even if not for the danger of mixing bloodlines as . . . complex as ours, I am reluctant to carry on his plan without him. I want to give birth to a child, not a god or an abomination."

Julio chuckled softly. "Judging by the ladies in court, you'd think all children were both saints and monsters."

"True," Isabelle said, momentarily distracted by visions of screaming, laughing squalling sub-adults. "Growing up seems a bit like taking an average of the extremes." And if she couched it in mathematical terms, so what? If Julio wanted to marry her, he was going to have to accept her philosophical pursuits.

Julio said, "Besides, now we know the purity doctrine is false. The saints mixed bloodlines all the time. And those crosses that created you brought back a sorcery long thought dead."

"A sorcery that many will feel marks me as the Breaker's get." She gave him a calculating look. "Or are you hoping that Kantelvar's prophecy really will come true, and you will be the father of the Savior?"

Julio recoiled. "Saints spare me, no."

Isabelle pulled a blanket around her shoulders as a shawl against the cold, damp cistern air. "Then why do you want to marry me? Aside from the fact that you no longer find me objectionable?"

"Because you are special. You saved a kingdom and stopped a war. You gave me my life back, and my brother. We make a good team."

"Tight allies in a narrow ditch, as Jean-Claude would say, but most of life isn't like that—at least I hope it isn't. Most of life is just getting through the day." She paused, changing her tack. "A month ago I would have married you sight unseen. Except it wouldn't have been you, just some vague dream of you; anything was better than what I had. Yet now that I've known you all of twelve hours, it seems I don't know you at all."

Julio pinched his chin in thought. He paced in a slow circle around the reflecting pool. When he reached his starting point he gazed into her eyes with such intensity that she felt suddenly naked before him. Her cheeks burned, and it was all she could do to keep her expression steady. No one had ever looked at her that way before.

"Yes?" she prompted, keeping the quaver out of her voice.

"One year," he said. "You want time and I will give it to you. Time to think about children, time to decide what you want, time to hear other offers. Not for one whole year will I ask you to marry me. I can't make the same promise for anyone else, of course, and I imagine that you will be besieged by suitors, but that is a risk I am willing to take if, at the end of one year, you will consent to hear my offer."

Isabelle's spirit lifted, ebullient, as the pressure of commitment withdrew.

"Thank you," she said, and wrapped her arms around him in a great hug, grabbing her stump with her good hand for a firmer grip even as her spark-hand passed through him. How lovely it would be to have time to think, to reason, to get to know someone, to be friends.

And when he brushed his lips across hers, it was but a question, ever so politely asked. And because this was her time to do as she desired rather than as she ought, she parted her mouth for him. His lips caressed hers and her whole skin seemed on the verge of melting. Oh saints. She'd never felt anything like that before. Her toes curled in delight and she twined his dark curls around her fingers, luxuriating in the springy silk of them.

"All those men you say will try to court me," she teased. "They'll say you're getting an unfair head start."

"They would be right," he said.

—

A thick, slow wind tugged at Jean-Claude's hat and hair as he escorted his most recent charge along the quay overlooking the endless drop beneath the harbor of San Augustus. The greenish fog of the Miasma veiled the thunder-shot layer of the Galvanosphere, and below that the Gloom. His leg ached, and his skin itched madly from all his recent scars, but he was finally done with the cursed crutches. Yes, he'd probably always have a bit of a limp, but he'd be damned if he'd carry a cane like some decrepit old man. *Elder. Graybeard.* No. Not yet.

"Mind the edge," he said to Marie, who had stopped to stare down at the catch boats on their daily drop into the cloudy shoals. She wasn't really close to the drop, but he was in a mind to be careful with the white girl.

Pure white. The process that had relieved Marie of the bloodhollow curse and given her back her mind and soul had also drained her entirely of color. She was white from the soles of her feet to the fringes of her hair. The irises of her eyes, her lips, and her tongue as well. She made new snow look grungy by comparison. What's more, she had no shadow at all. Darkness did not seem to stick to her unless she was completely immersed in it, so in all but the blackest night, she shone like the white moon, Kore.

It had been Isabelle's idea to put Jean-Claude in her dark room to give her company while they both convalesced, and he had spent many hours telling her stories of the years she'd missed, and of Isabelle's long hunt for a cure for her condition. She had proven to be a good audience, if a rather ghostly one. Her face never changed from its doll-like expression and her voice was a monotone. Yet she asked questions and drew his stories on. He kept having to remind himself that, mentally speaking, she was only twelve years old, though she was catching up quickly. She still had a perfect memory and could recall any conversation word for word.

"I've never seen so many boats," she said in her hollow ghostly whisper. "There was never such a fleet on l'Île des Zephyrs."

"This is one of the biggest harbors in the world," Jean-Claude said.

Marie watched the ships and gulls wheel for a few more moments. The shouts of men, the rustle of wind grappling with ropes and sails, and the cry of the birds echoed up and down the harbor's walls.

"How is your leg?" she asked in that same wispy voice.

"Subsiding nicely," he said stiffly. What was the world coming to when young women were stopping to let him catch his breath?

She resumed her stroll, falling in beside him as if he were leading, and

414 — CURTIS CRADDOCK

they progressed in companionable silence around the great curve of the harbor toward the dock where Princess Isabelle, newly minted special envoy of l'Empire Céleste in the matter of what was being dubbed the Grand Peace, made ready to set sail on her first diplomatic errand to sort out some disputes amongst border nobles.

Jean-Claude shuddered in his boots at the thought of another week aloft but dared not protest, lest Isabelle decide he was not required. With Príncipe Julio stuck like a barnacle to her hip, what need had she for poor old Jean-Claude? Once she got that idea in her head, who knew where it would lead?

About halfway around the long arc of the quay, they passed the gibbets. A long spar of rock extended out over the deeps. A row of cages hung beneath it, and in the farthest of these slumped the corpse of Margareta, the traitor queen. After her stint in the Hellshard, her trial had been little more than a recounting of the facts against her. By popular outcry, the newly crowned King Alejandro had been compelled to sentence her to death by exposure, rather than some cleaner, more humane execution.

Indeed, Julio's and Climacio's stated desire not to be forced to sentence their own mother to death was one of the official reasons Alejandro had been proclaimed king, and why his first act was to absolve them and the rest of their family of blame in the matter.

Jean-Claude had to admit that Isabelle was spinning a wonderful story to put the country back together, one where just about everyone could wash the blood from their hands and cleanse the stain from their reputations. He could not have done better. He could not have made the lies true. The student had surpassed the master. *She doesn't need me anymore.* But that was what was supposed to happen, wasn't it? Children were supposed to grow up. They were supposed to surpass their teachers. Otherwise, what was the point?

But then what happens to the master?

He and Marie reached the end of the quay, or rather the beginning of the maelstrom of activity surrounding Isabelle's ship. Longshoremen, porters, and sailors of all descriptions bustled about like so many oversized ants, but the crowd parted before him, and he led Marie toward Isabelle's coach.

"Monsieur musketeer!" called a fruity voice. Jean-Claude turned to greet Hugo du Blain, whose sense of fashion still made extravagant demands on the silkworms of the world while offering no concessions at all to practicality.

The ambassador had Felix in tow. The dead queen's ex-lieutenant stood at rigid attention, pinned in place by du Blain's bloodshadow, his face a mask of despair and desolation. For having killed Grand Leon's emissary, Felix had been condemned to replace him. Delivering him to Grand Leon would be du Blain's task.

And what fate awaited Jean-Claude when he stood before Grand Leon at the end of this voyage? The only certainty was that he had to present himself to his master of his own free will and on his own two feet, or else risk bringing shame on himself, on his fellow King's Own Musketeers, and on Isabelle.

Du Blain turned to Jean-Claude and said, "Jean-Claude, I began to despair of your arrival. His Imperial Majesty has a message for you."

Jean-Claude's stomach dropped and tried to hide behind his liver. Was Grand Leon going to condemn him at a distance without a further hearing? There was no reason not to. Why, after all, should he believe anything Jean-Claude had to say at this point?

Jean-Claude forced himself to smile and asked, "And what message would that be?"

Du Blain cocked a very odd smile at him. "He said, and I quote, 'We don't have that much horse shit.' I don't suppose that means anything to you?"

It took Jean-Claude several minutes to stop laughing. At last he wiped the tears from his eyes and said, "Tell him his command is my wish." After all, what choice did he have?

The ambassador chuckled. "I will give him your words exactly."

"Jean-Claude! Marie!" Isabelle hailed them, waving with her star-shot arm. One of Jean-Claude's prouder moments during the many diplomatic sessions it had taken to establish Aragoth's new government was convincing the Temple legate, the newly minted Aragothic artifex, that Isabelle's l'Étincelle sorcery was really nothing more than an unexpected by-product of the metal cap that sheathed her stump, a cap that had been bestowed on her by a Temple artifex. It certainly couldn't be a noncanonical sorcery; she had after all been declared unhallowed by a Temple hormougant. Isabelle had squealed with delight when Jean-Claude had presented her with an official document declaring her new arm theologically benign.

That wouldn't stop the fearful and the superstitious from condemning her, but it took away their official sanction to commit violence against her.

No doubt the next elected Omnifex would choke on that designation, but those were problems for the future.

Isabelle rushed up and gathered both Marie and Jean-Claude in with extremely improper but heartfelt hugs. "Great news. Xaviera is up and walking!"

Jean-Claude grinned, and Marie said tonelessly, "That is good news." The whole kingdom had been hanging on news of her recovery, as if her improvement were some sort of barometer for Aragoth as a whole. First she had followed her attendants around the room with her gaze, and then she had called for Alejandro. And then she had accepted a very small number of visitors, and now a month on she had finally left her bed. Nobody knew what she'd been through; even mentioning the Hellshard threw her into fits of hysterical shrieking. The first time that happened Alejandro had promptly thrown the horrid thing off the sky cliff and persuaded the Sacred Hundred to pass a law against torture in all its forms.

Isabelle went on to other news. "I've got an idea about how to approach that border dispute between Conde Sancho and le Baron de Soumans . . ."

Jean-Claude's smile kept growing as she gabbled. Isabelle was in her element here. She'd finally found room to grow and she was filling it as rapidly as possible. If she had less use for him than before, it was only because she had grown so much stronger.

"The ship is just about ready to get under way," Isabelle said. "Could you two help Gretl with my crates? There are volatiles in them, and I don't trust the longshoremen not to stack them upside down. One burning ship was enough."

Jean-Claude bowed and Marie curtsied, and they moved off through the press. Some of the workers were almost too eager to get out of the way. More than one of them made a sign against the evil eye at Marie.

Jean-Claude scowled; Marie was a fine young lady, but innocent in spite of her ordeal, and with an obvious link to Princess Isabelle. To a certain kind of mind, that would make her a target, and her strangeness would make superstitious fears easy to arouse into violence.

Jean-Claude rolled his shoulders to loosen them and checked his sword in its sheath. Anyone intending Marie harm would have to get through Jean-Claude first.